THE HUMANITY OF MONSTERS

THE HUMANITY OF MONSTERS

EDITED BY
MICHAEL MATHESON

FIRST EDITION

The Humanity of Monsters © ChiZine Publications
Interior design by Natasha Bozorgi
Cover layout design by Samantha Beiko
Cover design by Erik Mohr

Distributed in Canada by
Publishers Group Canada
76 Stafford Street, Unit 300
Toronto, Ontario, M6J 2S1
Toll Free: 800-747-8147
e-mail: info@pgcbooks.ca

Distributed in the U.S. by
Diamond Comic Distributors, Inc.
10150 York Road, Suite 300
Hunt Valley, MD 21030
Phone: (443) 318-8500
e-mail: books@diamondbookdistributors.com

Library and Archives Canada Cataloguing in Publication

Matheson, Michael, 1984-, editor

    The humanity of monsters / edited by Michael Matheson.

Short stories.

Includes bibliographical references and index.

Issued in print and electronic formats.

ISBN 978-1-77148-359-9 (paperback).--ISBN 978-1-77148-360-5 (pdf)

    I. Title.

PN6120.95.S9H86 2015   808.8'037   C2015-904985-7
                                      C2015-904986-5

bitlit

A free eBook edition is available
with the purchase of this print book.

CHIZINE PUBLICATIONS
Toronto, Canada
www.chizinepub.com
info@chizinepub.com

CLEARLY PRINT YOUR NAME ABOVE IN UPPER CASE

Instructions to claim your free eBook edition:
1. Download the BitLit app for Android or iOS
2. Write your name in **UPPER CASE** on the line
3. Use the BitLit app to submit a photo
4. Download your eBook to any device

Edited by Michael Matheson
Proofread by Dominik Parisien

Canada Council
for the Arts

Conseil des Arts
du Canada

We acknowledge the support of the Canada Council for the Arts which last year invested $20.1 million in writing and publishing throughout Canada.

ONTARIO ARTS COUNCIL
CONSEIL DES ARTS DE L'ONTARIO
an Ontario government agency
un organisme du gouvernement de l'Ontario

Published with the generous assistance of the Ontario Arts Council.

Printed in Canada

CONTENTS

INTRODUCTION 9

TASTING GOMOA 11
by Chinelo Onwualu

DEAD SEA FRUIT 19
by Kaaron Warren

THE BREAD WE EAT IN DREAMS 29
by Catherynne M. Valente

THE EMPEROR'S OLD BONES 45
by Gemma Files

THE THINGS 63
by Peter Watts

MUO-KA'S CHILD 80
by Indrapramit Das

SIX 89
by Leah Bobet

THE NAZIR 100
by Sofia Samatar

A HANDFUL OF EARTH 110
by Silvia Moreno-Garcia

IN WINTER 116
by Sonya Taaffe

GHOSTWEIGHT 119
by Yoon Ha Lee

HOW TO TALK TO GIRLS AT PARTIES 140
by Neil Gaiman

NIGHT THEY MISSED THE HORROR SHOW   152
by Joe R. Lansdale

IF YOU WERE A DINOSAUR, MY LOVE   168
by Rachel Swirsky

GIVE HER HONEY WHEN YOU HEAR HER SCREAM   171
by Maria Dahvana Headley

THE HORSE LATITUDES   183
by Sunny Moraine

BOYFRIEND AND SHARK   193
by Berit Ellingsen

NEVER THE SAME   196
by Polenth Blake

MANTIS WIVES   211
by Kij Johnson

PROBOSCIS   214
by Laird Barron

OUT THEY COME   236
by Alex Dally MacFarlane

AND LOVE SHALL HAVE NO DOMINION   242
by Livia Llewellyn

YOU GO WHERE IT TAKES YOU   252
by Nathan Ballingrud

DREAM OF THE FISHERMAN'S WIFE   265
by A.C. Wise

THEORIES OF PAIN   276
by Rose Lemberg

TERRIBLE LIZARDS   279
by Meghan McCarron

ACKNOWLEDGEMENTS   284

ABOUT THE AUTHORS   286

COPYRIGHT ACKNOWLEDGEMENTS   293

INTRODUCTION

I am extremely tempted to leave this book without an introduction and simply let the stories speak for themselves.

Now, I love reading anthology introductions. I was gleaning everything I could about publishing, process, and writing and editing as a whole from them years before I ever actually got into the industry. But I strongly considered skipping writing this one anyway.

Primarily because these stories speak for themselves quite ably, and in chorus, without any help from an introduction on my part. *The Humanity of Monsters* being a larger conversation than it would appear from its title alone, and the stories of course conversant not only with their immediate neighbours (welcome to Anthology Making 101), but also across the breadth of the book's larger narrative (that would be Anthology Making 201). This anthology's narrative is a somewhat pointed conversation, true. Though multi-faceted as well.

And, actually, it's a combination of that last function and the dangers of overly ready assumption that make an introduction necessary for this book. So grab a seat, we're going to have a (very) brief chat about interpretation and semiotics:

First, it's only fair to note that the anthology's title is a *little* misleading. The implication that the book is solely about the "humanity" of monsters (literal, figurative, or otherwise) is one thing the book is exploring, yes. The anthology is, however, also exploring the reverse: the "inhumanity" of the delusively non-monstrous. But approaching this book with only that base dichotomy in mind does the collected works within a disservice.

That's because the larger, and overarching, conversation at work in *The Humanity of Monsters* is rather more about the liminality of state.

INTRODUCTION

There are monsters in the book, certainly. Both literal and figurative. But there are far more stories here that explore monstrosity from a semantically exegetical approach. It would, in point of fact, be more appropriate to label what this book is doing an act of sociolinguistics. For what are the stories in this book doing but questioning nomenclature as a function of societal and cultural norms and expectations, context, and use of language and label as active choice?

Now, *why*, you may be asking, discuss that instead of simply letting the stories inform the reader of this directly?

Because the unannotated presentation of stories that discuss mental disability, trauma, social, racial, or economic marginalization, Othering, socially conscious narratives, and Queer subject matter without a note about the role of said stories as examinations of the deeply mutable definition of the term *Monster*—in a book ostensibly foregrounding "monsters" as the thing people expect to see—is not a responsible action. Especially if one's aim is to address the all too easy application of that term to anyone who is different from oneself, and how we apply it all too readily in shades of white and black (pointed commentary intended), and all too reticently when the situation is less easily defined or begs more complicated questions.

Monstrosity will always be a matter of degree and perspective. But one ought warn one's readers about the implications of taking things too literally, or with too little interrogation.

A warning perhaps decidedly appropriate given that the modern usage of "Monster" finds its root in the Latin *monere*, meaning "to warn."

In light of that, then, consider yourself warned:

There *be* monsters here. Though not always. And form and presentation are, as ever, hardly honest guides. No, in the end, it's the why and the who of it that's the devil of the thing.

Michael Matheson
Toronto, 2015

TASTING GOMOA
CHINELO ONWUALU

Today is the day the new wife arrives. I had long known they were going to take a second to me. Old and barren as I am, it was only a matter of time. As I circle the square hole that looks down into the main courtyard, I note their shoes at the doorway to the main room: Shigoram's heavy army-issue boots, black and shiny in the yellow noon sun. Amah's large misshapen slippers, stretched out by her girth, and a new pair, small and delicate, stitched with pink flowers and almost new. I reach the heavy front door of polished cedar and begin to descend the stone steps that wind through the dark tunnel to the main house.

At the doorway of the main room, I slip off my battered grey slippers and enter. It is dark and cool inside, a welcome relief from the heat. I feel the sweat between my breasts and thighs begin to dry. The room is only large enough for six or seven, though we rarely have so many visitors at a time. The stone floor is strewn with several colourful rugs, but the carpet that dominates the raised dais at the end of the room was part of my dowry. It is a magnificent thing of red wool covered with intricate Hespian designs picked in gold thread. The leather cushions were also mine and still have the crest of my father's house stitched upon them. They were a rare gift Amah had once admitted to me, in the days when she had more than curses and orders for me. The walls are decorated with porcelain plates, glazed vases of blue and red, and rich tapestries. Someone has lit sticks of incense and the sweet, spicy smell of myrrh envelopes the space.

Amah and Shigoram are facing the doorway. Amah has leaned her bulk into the pile of cushions, her legs stretched out before her. She has taken off her veil and her grey hair has been scraped back into a bun. Her face is turned towards me but for once her heavy-lidded eyes, which conceal a sharp gaze, are not trained on me. As usual, Shigoram sits straight-backed and uncomfortable, his legs tucked beneath him as if this is not his house. He too has eyes only for the woman in front of him.

As I hang my headscarf and veil on the hook by the entrance, I note the new bride. She is performing a tea ceremony for them, pouring the tea from one pot to another to cool it. I cannot see her face, but I note her back and shoulders. Her dark hair hangs down to her waist in a thousand intricate braids each topped by a tiny coloured glass bead. Her shoulders are as pale as milk and her hips flare wide from a slim waist— what my mother used to call a water jug figure, designed to bear. Her feet, which peek out from under her ample bottom are small and pink.

She finishes the ceremony just as I come to kneel beside her. I help her pass out the tiny cups of fragrant mint tea. Amah takes the cup I offer with a small, triumphant sneer. Perhaps she expects me to be upset that she has married her son a new wife? Ten years in her house and she still does not know me.

"Galim Che," Amah calls to me. She has not used my blood name in a long time. "Greet our new wife. This is Gomoa; I trust you will treat her as your sister and daughter."

I turn to the girl, expecting the look of controlled fear one usually sees in young brides. Her face is broad and flat with high cheekbones and large almond-shaped eyes; her small bow lips are curved into a broad grin. She bows formally, head touching the tips of her fingers. I return the bow.

I had vowed not to hate her, this child who had come to take my place, but I did not realise that I would come to love her as I did.

That night, I wake with a start. I sit up on the straw-stuffed pallet and look around. The room is pitch black, still and cold. Faint moonlight peeps in from under the door. Even through the thick stone walls I can hear Amah snoring softly in the room next to mine. I am the only one in the room, yet I could have sworn I had felt someone tug at my leg. Shivering, I ball myself up into a foetal position and burrow deeper under my wool quilt.

I fall immediately into the dream, as if it has been waiting for me.

I am lying on my back, naked. The lamp at the foot of the bed casts a soft golden glow and I can feel its faint warmth at the soles of my feet. Shigoram kneels above me, hands on either side of my head, naked as well. His long wavy hair is unbound and falls about his shoulders. His face has the same look I remember from our wedding night: Hungry and apprehensive. I reach up and stroke his beard, something I have never done in life, feeling the coarse hair underneath my hands. He closes his eyes as if savouring my touch. I run my hands along his body, skimming the soft down on his chest and stomach until I grasp his penis. He dips his head down to kiss my neck and a jolt runs through me. His kisses fall soft across my throat and down, down until he reaches my breasts. He takes my right nipple in his mouth, sucking and teasing with his wet tongue until the pleasure is too much to bear. As I reach down to bury my hands in his hair, I take a moment to note that this body is not my own. My own breasts have never been so small, so pert. But then he is sliding himself into me and I part, wet and yielding to allow him entrance. He is filling me, his breath a warm moan against my ear. Together, we move in rhythm; I thrusting up to meet him, him plunging down into me . . .

I awake trembling with pleasure, my sex slick. It has been many years since Shigoram called me to his bed. I had forgotten what desire felt like and in forgetting I was able to endure. I fear this spark now ignited will grow to a conflagration. A true wife would turn away; gird herself for the sake of the family. But I am weak and it has been so long. . . . Blinking back tears of shame, I shove my hand down between my legs and, knowing the dream still waits for me, I will myself to fall asleep again.

The next day I am awake before dawn, as is my custom. I begin my chores by sweeping the fallen leaves under the ancient olive trees at each corner of the round courtyard with a broom of soft straw bound to a short handle. The sound echoes against the rock walls and I imagine that it floats up out of the depression and into the desert above. The house was once home to ten families, generations of Shigoram's people who occupied each of the rooms. Now it is only us. Though it allows us many rooms for storage and gives each of us our own bedroom, I often find it lonely.

As I sweep past the door to Shigoram's room, I pause to listen. They already consummated the marriage at the wedding ceremony at her father's home—which I was not invited to—but I am sure he must have called his new bride to him last night. Imagining them together, I am taken back to my dream and my heart begins to race, a rhythmic pounding matched in my temples and between my legs.

The door to the room opens suddenly and I almost stumble into Shigoram's arms. He closes the door swiftly, but not before I catch a glimpse of her, naked and sated, lying on her stomach with one leg dangling off the bed. He is wearing his faded purple morning robe cinched at the waist with a fraying belt. His dark hooded eyes are red and puffy from fatigue but he has taken the time to brush his dark hair back and braid it into its long queue.

"Good morning, husband," I greet him. I bow quickly to hide my embarrassment. He nods at me, but he does not answer. Shigoram has never been a man of many words at the best of times but since his deployment to the front lines, he has had even less to say. He hurries to the toilet and bath rooms on the other side of the courtyard. I watch his long legs flash from beneath the robe as he moves, all golden skin and taut muscle. My sex clenches. I redouble my sweeping.

By the time I return with the extra firewood, the new bride, Gomoa, is with Amah in the kitchen. I can hear Amah's voice as I drop the bundle of wood by the kitchen door. She is showing Gomoa how to prepare Shigoram's breakfast the way he likes it. He has only been given leave from the army for a moon—and only so long because he was getting married. He will be returning to the battlefield this afternoon and Amah is determined that her only son be well-fed before then. It does not matter that I know all his tastes and preferences, my time has passed and it is the new bride's turn to care for him.

I am fetching water from the well in the centre of the courtyard when the new bride passes by with a covered tray carrying Shigoram's breakfast. Dressed in a loose blouse of blue and white stripes with a full matching skirt knotted under her breasts, her hair is uncovered and she is lovely in the dappled morning light. She greets me cheerfully and I see that she is not much older than I was when I married—fourteen at the most. Slipping her feet out of her tiny slippers, she pushes in the door with one hand and disappears into Shigoram's room.

She does not emerge until it is time for Shigoram to leave us once again.

Standing at the door to the main entrance we bid him goodbye. Amah is tearful as she performs the prayers for his safe journey and return. This time, it is the new bride, Gomoa, who holds the small gold tray with the sacred flame burning in its tiny brass brazier. As she paints his forehead with ash and red ochre, chanting softly, my mind goes to the last night Shigoram and I shared together.

I had come to him unbidden that night. It was his first deployment and he had been gone nearly a year; I had no patience to wait for his summons. I had spent the day before preparing myself—I had gone all the way to my cousin in Aqor town to have my body plucked of all hair and my tresses coiffed high and held in place with ivory combs and pins. I had spent the last of my dowry gold on costly bath oils and perfumes. That night, when the last of the candles had been blown out, I crept into his room. Naked, I slid into his bed. I should have known the night was not with me when he first recoiled at my touch. But I was blind with desire and I pressed on. He lay on his back staring up at the blank stone ceiling, silently enduring my caresses. But no matter what I did, where I kissed, what I stroked or sucked or nuzzled, he did not stir. Finally, in a quiet voice he had asked me to leave. Burning with shame, I slipped on my robe and crept out of the room.

Only then did I allow myself to cry.

The mumbling has stopped and I jolt out of my reverie in time to see the new bride, Gomoa, bowing to Shigoram. I catch the ghost of a smile on his face as he inclines his head in return. He catches sight of me as he turns away and his thick black brows knot in confusion. He starts towards me, then thinks better of it. In the end, he makes do with a nod. Then he turns and walks off towards the road where a neighbour waits in an ox-drawn cart to take him to the city.

Amah begins to wail as soon as he is out of sight and it is Gomoa who comforts her. She looks at me over the old woman's head and gives me a wry smile. I do my best to return it. I imagine Shigoram kissing those full rosebud lips and I wonder what she tastes like.

I have to find a way to get her alone, but it is impossible. After Shigoram leaves, Gomoa becomes Amah's pet—as I had been when I first came to the house. She insists on taking the girl everywhere with her. Gomoa accompanies her to the market where she is widely introduced; she acts as Amah's escort to weddings and is shown off at visits with neighbours. During the day, Amah continues to give her cooking lessons and in the evenings she has Gomoa massage her feet and trim her toenails. I remember how much I had hated this task, but the new bride does it without complaint, joking as she rubs fragrant eucalyptus oil between Amah's gnarled toes.

In the end, it is she who comes to me.

They had gone out to visit relatives and I had found myself between chores. I pulled out one of my books—I had brought a whole library with me when I married—and settled beneath one of the olive trees to read. I was so engrossed that I did not hear them return.

"Woman!" Amah's voice was like a whip. "I see you have nothing better to do than idle away with dry paper. If you wish to keep occupied, then give me a grandchild. Otherwise, find something more useful to do with those empty hands of yours."

But her words lack the sting they once had. She has a new bride now, and the hope of grandchildren blooms in her once more.

I slip the book under my cushion and I rise to relieve her of the goods she has brought from the market. I catch Gomoa's eye, still fixed on the book's hiding place.

"Do you know how to read?" I ask her.

"A little," she says shyly.

"Would you like to learn more? I can teach you."

"Really?" Gomoa asks breathlessly. Her face lights up with joy.

"Come to my room this night, after Amah sleeps," I tell her.

She is so happy that she insists on carrying my bags as well as her own. For the rest of the day her steps are lighter and that evening, as she massages Amah's feet, her laughter is sweet.

She comes to my room after dark, knocking softly on my door. She is dressed like me, in a long tunic with bell sleeves and a low scoop neck. To keep out the cold, she is wrapped in an old quilt—the one thing she could afford to bring from her father's house. I let her in and allow her to take in my room.

My father had made sure I came to my husband's house with everything I would ever need for my comfort. Once, thick rugs of the finest make piled my floor from one end of the room to another, now I have a single strip of knitted wool carpet that runs from the foot of my dais to the door. My walls, which were once lined with colourful brocades and silks, boast colourful straw mats instead. Gone also are the brass and copper trays I had once hung above the cloths. And the two cedar boxes against either wall, which once contained the best of my elaborate robes and gold jewellery, are empty. They were sold item by item during those dark times when Shigoram's army stipend did not arrive in time.

All I have left are my books. It is difficult to build shelves on curved walls, but I managed it. The whole back wall above the raised dais of my bed is filled with books—volumes on history, medicine, folklore and religion. I even have a number of long poems like the Song of Muster and a romance about the doomed lovers Aki and Melota.

I choose the romance for its easy language. It is also beautifully illustrated, which I know she will appreciate. She sits on the edge of the dais, the book in her hands. Though the lantern hangs just above us, she has to bring the volume up to her face to read. I sit behind her, towering over her small frame, to read over her shoulder. We go through her letters. Someone had taught her the basics, but she has had little practice. So I have her read aloud, sounding out the words as she goes along.

"'Is it in the-thy poh-wer to make me ree-al?'" She reads slowly. Her voice is sweet and musical.

Straddled behind her, I slip a hand down the front of her tunic. Her voice falters.

"Keep reading," I whisper gently. She starts up again, her voice quavering with uncertainty. I correct her when she stumbles over the longer words.

Her breasts are just as I dreamed them: small and smooth and pert with large rough nipples. I run a thumb across them and feel them harden against my touch. I press my face into her hair, breathing in the clean, fresh smell of her. I cup her left breast and heft it, lightly twirling a thumb and forefinger over the nipple.

She gasps and almost drops the book.

"Continue," I whisper. She tries to keep reading, but her voice is a low moan as I run my lips over the delicate skin of her neck sucking in small nips. She leans into me and I take the opportunity to hike up her tunic, pulling it up to her thighs, and slip a hand in between her legs.

I find her warm and moist. I part the folds of her and slide a finger against the hard nub there. She shudders and lets out a soft choking sound. Then, I am plunging my fingers into the soft flesh—deeper and deeper—my hand now slick with her wetness. Her breaths grow shallow, become hard pants, and she is sucking at the air as if she cannot draw in enough. Until finally, I feel her quiver, her sex twitching between my fingers, and she lets out a final breath like a long low moan.

I take my hand away and I allow her to stand. She flings the book aside and gathers up her quilt. She is gone almost before I realise it.

Alone, I examine my hand. It is still wet. I put it into my mouth and suck. She tastes like salt, like tears.

Gomoa avoids me after that. Her greetings are perfunctory and there are no more secret smiles between us. Amah notes the change but she believes there is another cause. Her hopes are confirmed when, at month's end, there is no sign of Gomoa's moon blood. But it is still another month before Amah pulls me aside.

She is reasonable, almost kind, when she asks me to leave the house. She explains that her sister will be coming to help with the chores while Gomoa's belly grows and there will be nowhere for me stay. She shows me the letter Shigoram sent after she had sent word to him of Gomoa's baby. In it, he grants me an honourable divorce; it leaves me without shame and free to marry again—if I can manage it. At four and twenty years old, I am far past my prime.

The day I leave, there is no sign of Gomoa. My cousins from Aqor come to help me move my belongings; I will be living with them until I can either find a trade or a husband. My own possessions fit in a single chest, the rest are books.

Still, I make sure to leave Gomoa the romance. I know she will appreciate it.

DEAD SEA FRUIT

KAARON WARREN

I have a collection of baby teeth, sent to me by recovered anorexics from the ward. Their children's teeth, proof that their bodies are working.

One sent me a letter. "Dear Tooth Fairy, you saved me and my womb. My son is now six, here are his baby teeth."

They call the ward Pretty Girl Street. I don't know if the cruelty is intentional; these girls are far from pretty. Skeletal, balding, their breath reeking of hard cheese, they languish on their beds and terrify each other, when they have the strength, with tales of the Ash Mouth Man.

I did not believe the Pretty Girls. The Ash Mouth Man was just a myth to scare each other into being thin. A moral tale against promiscuity. It wouldn't surprise me to hear that the story originated with a group of protective parents, wanting to shelter their children from the disease of kissing.

"He only likes fat girls," Abby said. Her teeth were yellow when she smiled, though she rarely smiled. Abby lay in the bed next to Lori; they compared wrist thickness by stretching their fingers to measure.

"And he watches you for a long time to make sure you're the one," Lori said.

"And only girls who could be beautiful are picked," Melanie said. Her blonde hair fell out in clumps and she kept it in a little bird's nest beside her bed. "He watches you to see if you could be beautiful enough if you were thinner then he saunters over to you."

The girls laughed. "He saunters. Yes," they agreed. They trusted me; I listened to them and fixed their teeth for free.

"He didn't saunter," Jane said. I sat on her bed and leaned close to hear. "He beckoned. He did this," and she tilted back her head, miming a glass being poured into her mouth. "I nodded. I love vodka," she said. "Vodka's made of potatoes, so it's like eating."

The girls all laughed. I hate it when they laugh. I have to maintain my smile. I can't flinch in disgust at those bony girls, mouths open, shoulders shaking. All of them exhausted with the effort.

"I've got a friend in New Zealand and she's seen him," Jane said. "He kissed a friend of hers and the weight just dropped off her."

"I know someone in England who kissed him," Lori said.

"He certainly gets around," I said. They looked at each other.

"I was frightened at the thought of him at first," Abby said. "'Cos he's like a drug. One kiss and you're hooked. Once he's stuck in the tongue, you're done. You can't turn back."

They'd all heard of him before they kissed him. In their circles, even the dangerous methods of weight loss are worth considering.

I heard the rattle of the dinner trolley riding the corridor to Pretty Girl Street. They fell silent.

Lori whispered, "Kissing him fills your mouth with ash. Like you pick up a beautiful piece of fruit and bite into it. You expect the juice to drip down your chin but you bite into ashes. That's what it's like to kiss him."

Lori closed her eyes. Her dry little tongue snaked out to the corners of her mouth, looking, I guessed, for that imagined juice. I leaned over and dripped a little water on her tongue.

She screwed up her mouth.

"It's only water," I said. "It tastes of nothing."

"It tastes of ashes," she said.

"They were hoping you'd try a bite to eat today, Lori," I said. She shook her head.

"You don't understand," she said. "I can't eat. Everything tastes like ashes. Everything."

The nurse came in with the dinner trolley and fixed all the Pretty Girls' IV feeds. The girls liked to twist the tube, bend it, press an elbow or a bony buttock into it to stop the flow.

"You don't understand," Abby said. "It's like having ashes pumped directly into your blood."

They all started to moan and scream with what energy they could muster. Doctors came in, and other nurses. I didn't like this part, the physicality of the feedings, so I walked away.

I meet many Pretty Girls. Pretty Girls are the ones who will never recover, who still see themselves as ugly and fat even when they don't have the strength to defecate. These ones the doctors try to fatten up so they don't scare people when laid in their coffins.

The recovering ones never spoke of the Ash Mouth Man. And I did not believe, until Dan entered my surgery, complaining he was unable to kiss women because of the taste of his mouth. I bent close to him and smelt nothing. I found no decay, no gum disease. He turned his face away.

"What is it women say you taste like?" I said.

"They say I taste of ashes."

I blinked at him, thinking of Pretty Girl Street.

"Not cigarette smoke," the girls had all told me. "Ashes."

"I can see no decay or internal reason for any odour," I told Dan.

After work that day I found him waiting for me in his car outside the surgery.

"I'm sorry," he said. "This is ridiculous. But I wondered if you'd like to eat with me." He gestured, lifting food to his mouth. The movement shocked me. It reminded me of what Jane had said, the Ash Mouth Man gesturing a drink to her. It was nonsense and I knew it. Fairytales, any sort of fiction, annoy me. It's all so very convenient, loose ends tucked in and no mystery left unsolved. Life isn't like that. People die unable to lift an arm to wave and there is no reason for it.

I was too tired to say yes. I said, "Could we meet for dinner tomorrow?"

He nodded. "You like food?"

It was a strange question. Who didn't like food? Then the answer came to me. Someone for whom every mouthful tasted of ash.

"Yes, I like food," I said.

"Then I'll cook for you," he said.

He cooked an almost perfect meal, without fuss or mess. He arrived at the table smooth and brown. I wanted to sweep the food off and make love to him right there. "You actually like cooking," I said. "It's nothing but a chore for me. I had to feed myself from early on and I hate it."

"You don't want the responsibility," he said. "Don't worry. I'll look after you."

The vegetables were overcooked, I thought. The softness of them felt like rot.

He took a bite and rolled the food around in his mouth.

"You have a very dexterous tongue," I said. He smiled, cheeks full of food, then closed his eyes and went on chewing.

When he swallowed, over a minute later, he took a sip of water then said, "Taste has many layers. You need to work your way through each to get to the base line. Sensational."

I tried keeping food in my mouth but it turned to sludge and slipped down my throat. It was fascinating to watch him eat. Mesmerising. We talked at the table for two hours, then I started to shake.

"I'm tired," I said. "I tend to shake when I'm tired."

"Then you should go home to sleep." He packed a container of food for me to take. His domesticity surprised me; on entering his home, I laughed at the sheer seductiveness of it. Self-help books on the shelf, their spines unbent. Vases full of plastic flowers with a fake perfume.

He walked me to my car and shook my hand, his mouth pinched shut to clearly indicate there would be no kiss.

Weeks passed. We saw each other twice more, chaste, public events that always ended abruptly. Then one Wednesday, I opened the door to my next client and there was Dan.

"It's only me," he said.

My assistant giggled. "I'll go and check the books, shall I?" she said. I nodded. Dan locked the door after her.

"I can't stop thinking about you," he said. "It's all I think about. I can't get any work done."

He stepped towards me and grabbed my shoulders. I tilted my head back to be kissed. He bent to my neck and snuffled. I pulled away.

"What are you doing?" I said. He put his finger on my mouth to shush me. I tried to kiss him but he turned away. I tried again and he twisted his body from me.

"I'm scared of what you'll taste," he said.

"Nothing. I'll taste nothing."

"I don't want to kiss you," he said softly.

Then he pushed me gently onto my dentist's chair. And he stripped me naked and touched every piece of skin, caressed, squeezed, stroked until I called out.

He climbed onto the chair astride me, and keeping his mouth well away, he unzipped his pants. He felt very good. We made too much noise. I hoped my assistant wasn't listening.

Afterwards, he said, "It'll be like that every time. I just know it."

And it was. Even massaging my shoulders, he could make me turn to jelly.

I had never cared so much about kissing outside of my job before but now I needed it. It would prove Dan loved me, that I loved him. It would prove he was not the Ash Mouth Man because his mouth would taste of plums or toothpaste, or of my perfume if he had been kissing my neck.

"You know we get pleasure from kissing because our bodies think we are eating," I said, kissing his fingers.

"Trickery. It's all about trickery," he said.

"Maybe if I smoke a cigarette first. Then my breath will be ashy anyway and I won't be able to taste you."

"Just leave it." He went out, came back the next morning with his lips all bruised and swollen. I did not ask him where he'd been. I watched him outside on the balcony, his mouth open like a dog tasting the air, and I didn't want to know. I had a busy day ahead, clients all through and no time to think. My schizophrenic client tasted yeasty; they always did if they were medicated.

Then I kissed a murderer; he tasted like vegetable waste. Like the crisper in my fridge smells when I've been too busy to empty it. They used to say people who suffered from tuberculosis smelled like wet leaves; his breath was like that but rotten. He had a tooth he wanted me to fix; he'd cracked it on a walnut shell.

"My wife never shelled things properly. Lazy. She didn't care what she ate. Egg shells, olive pits, seafood when she knew I'm allergic. She'd eat anything."

He smiled at me. His teeth were white. Perfect. "And I mean anything." He paused, wanting a reaction from me. I wasn't interested in his sexual activities. I would never discuss what Dan and I did. It was private, and while it remained that way I could be wanton, abandoned.

"She used to get up at night and raid the fridge," the murderer said after he rinsed. I filled his mouth with instruments again. He didn't close his eyes. Most people do. They like to take themselves elsewhere, away from me. No matter how gentle a dentist is, the experience is not pleasant.

My assistant and I glanced at each other.

"Rinse," I said. He did, three times, then sat back. A line of saliva stretched from the bowl to his mouth.

"She was fat. Really fat. But she was always on a diet. I accused her of secretly bingeing and then I caught her at it."

I turned to place the instruments in my autoclave.

"Sleepwalking. She did it in her sleep. She'd eat anything. Raw bacon. Raw mince. Whole slabs of cheese."

People come to me because I remove the nasty taste from their mouths. I'm good at identifying the source. I can tell by the taste of them and what I see in their eyes.

He glanced at my assistant, wanting to talk but under privilege. I said to her, "Could you check our next appointment, please?" and she nodded, understanding.

I picked up a scalpel and held it close to his eye. "You see how sharp it is? So sharp you won't feel it as the blade gently separates the molecules. Sometimes a small slit in the gums releases toxins or tension. You didn't like your wife getting fat?"

"She was disgusting. You should have seen some of the crap she ate."

I looked at him, squinting a little.

"You watched her. You didn't stop her."

"I could've taken a football team in to watch her and she wouldn't have woken up."

I felt I needed a witness to his words and, knowing Dan was in the office above, I pushed the speaker phone extension to connect me to him.

"She ate cat shit. I swear. She picked it off the plate and ate it," the murderer said. I bent over to check the back of his tongue. The smell of vegetable waste turned my stomach.

"What was cat shit doing on a plate?" I asked.

He reddened a little. When I took my fingers out of his mouth he said, "I just wanted to see if she'd eat it. And she did."

"Is she seeking help?" I asked. I wondered what the breath of someone with a sleep disorder would smell like.

"She's being helped by Jesus now," he said. He lowered his eyes. "She ate a bowlful of dishwashing powder with milk. She was still holding the spoon when I found her in the morning."

There was a noise behind me as Dan came into the room. I turned to see he was wearing a white coat. His hands were thrust into the pockets.

"You didn't think to put poisons out of reach?" Dan said. The murderer looked up.

"Sometimes the taste of the mouth, the smell of it, comes from deep within," I said to the murderer. I flicked his solar plexus with my forefinger and he flinched. His smile faltered. I felt courageous.

As he left, I kissed him. I kiss all of my clients, to learn their nature from the taste of their mouths. Virgins are salty, alcoholics sweet. Addicts taste like fake orange juice, the stuff you spoon into a glass then add water.

Dan would not let me kiss him to find out if he tasted of ash.

"Now me," Dan said. He stretched over and kissed the man on the mouth, holding him by the shoulders so he couldn't get away.

The murderer recoiled. I smiled. He wiped his mouth. Scraped his teeth over his tongue.

"See you in six months' time," I said.

I had appointments with the Pretty Girls, and Dan wanted to come with me. He stopped at the ward doorway, staring in. He seemed to fill the space, a door himself.

"It's okay," I said. "You wait there."

Inside, I thought at first Jane was smiling. Her cheeks lifted and her eyes squinted closed. But there was no smile; she scraped her tongue with her teeth. It was an action I knew quite well. Clients trying to scrape the bad taste out of their mouths. They didn't spit or rinse, though, so the action made me feel queasy. I imagined all that buildup behind their teeth. All the scrapings off their tongue.

The girls were in a frenzy. Jane said, "We saw the Ash Mouth Man." But they see so few men in the ward I thought, "Any man could be the Ash Mouth Man to these girls." I tended their mouths, tried to clear away the bad taste. They didn't want me to go. They were jealous of me, thinking I was going to kiss the Ash Mouth Man. Jane kept talking to make me stay longer, though it took her strength away. "My grandmother was kissed by him. She always said to watch out for handsome men, 'cos their kiss could be a danger. Then she kissed him and wasted away in about five days."

The girls murmured to each other. *Five days! That's a record! No one ever goes down in five days.*

In the next ward there are Pretty Boys, but not so many of them. They are much quieter than the girls. They sit in their beds and close their eyes most of the day. The ward is thick, hushed. They don't get many visitors and they don't want me as their dentist. They didn't like me to attend them. They bite at me as if I was trying to thrust my fingers down their throats to choke them.

Outside, Dan waited, staring in.

"Do you find those girls attractive?" I said.

"Of course not. They're too skinny. They're sick. I like healthy women. Strong women. That's why I like you so much. You have the self-esteem to let me care for you. Not many women have that."

"Is that true?"

"No. I really like helpless women," he said. But he smiled.

He smelt good to me, clean, with a light flowery aftershave which could seem feminine on another man. He was tall and broad; strong. I watched him lift a car to retrieve a paper I'd rolled onto while parking.

"I could have moved the car," I said, laughing at him.

"No fun in that," he said. He picked me up and carried me indoors.

I quite enjoyed the sense of subjugation. I'd been strong all my life, sorting myself to school when my parents were too busy to care. I could not remember being carried by anyone, and the sensation was a comfort.

Dan introduced me to life outside. Before I met him, I rarely saw daylight; too busy for a frivolous thing like the sun. Home, transport, work, transport, home, all before dawn and after dusk. Dan forced me to go out into the open. He said, "Your skin glows outdoors. Your hair moves in the breeze. You couldn't be more beautiful." So we walked. I really didn't like being out. It seemed like time wasting.

He picked me up from the surgery one sunny Friday and took my hand. "Come for a picnic," he said. "It's a beautiful day."

In my doorway, a stick man was slumped.

"It's the man who killed his wife," I whispered.

The man raised his arm weakly. "Dentist," he rattled. "Dentist, wait!"

"What happened to you? Are you sleepwalking now?" I asked.

"I can't eat. Everything I bite into tastes of ash. I can't eat. I'm starving." He lisped, and I could see that many of his white teeth had fallen out.

"What did you do to me?" he whispered. He fell to his knees. Dan and I stepped around him and walked on. Dan took my hand, carrying a basket full of food between us. It banged against my legs, bruising my shins. We walked to a park and everywhere we went girls jumped at him. He kissed back, shrugging at me as if to say, "Who cares?" I watched them.

"Why do it? Just tell them to go away," I said. They annoyed me, those silly little girls.

"I can't help it. I try not to kiss them but the temptation is too strong. They're always coming after me."

I had seen this.

"Why? I know you're a beautiful looking man, but why do they forget any manners or pride to kiss you?"

I knew this was one of his secrets. One of the things he'd rather I didn't know.

"I don't know, my love. The way I smell? They like my smell."

I looked at him sidelong. "Why did you kiss him? That murderer. Why?"

Dan said nothing. I thought about how well he understood me. The meals he cooked, the massages he gave. The way he didn't flinch from the job I did.

So I didn't confront him. I let his silence sit. But I knew his face at the Pretty Girls ward. I could still feel him fucking me in the car, pulling over into a car park and taking me, after we left the Pretty Girls.

"God, I want to kiss you," he said.

I could smell him, the ash fire warmth of him and I could feel my stomach shrinking. I thought of my favourite cake, its colour leached out and its flavour making my eyes water.

"Kissing isn't everything. We can live without kissing," I said.

"Maybe you can," he said, and he leant forward, his eyes wide, the white parts smudgy, grey. He grabbed my shoulders. I usually loved his strength, the size of him, but I pulled away.

"I don't want to kiss you," I said. I tucked my head under his arm and buried my face into his side. The warm fluffy wool of his jumper tickled my nose and I smothered a sneeze.

"Bless you," he said. He held my chin and lifted my face up. He leant towards me.

He was insistent.

It was a shock, even though I'd expected it. His tongue was fat and seemed to fill my cheeks, the roof of my mouth. My stomach roiled and I tried to pull away but his strong hands held my shoulders 'til he was done with his kiss.

Then he let me go.

I fell backward, one step, my heels wobbling but keeping me standing. I wiped my mouth. He winked at me and leant forward. His breath smelt sweet, like pineapple juice. His eyes were blue, clear and honest. You'd trust him if you didn't know.

The taste of ash filled my mouth.

Nothing else happened, though. I took a sip of water and it tasted fresh, clean. A look of disappointment flickered on his face before he concealed it. I thought, *You like it. You like turning women that way*.

I said, "Have you heard of the myth the Pretty Girls have? About the Ash Mouth Man?"

I could see him visibly lifting, growing. Feeling legendary. His cheeks reddened. His face was so expressive I knew what he meant without hearing a word. I couldn't bear to lose him but I could not allow him to make any more Pretty Girls.

I waited 'til he was fast asleep that night, lying back, mouth open. I sat him forward so he wouldn't choke, took up my scalpel, and with one perfect move I lifted his tongue and cut it out of his mouth.

THE BREAD WE EAT IN DREAMS

CATHERYNNE M. VALENTE

In a sea of long grass and tiny yellow blueberry flowers some ways off of Route 1, just about halfway between Cobscook Bay and Passamaquoddy Bay, the town of Sauve-Majeure puts up its back against the Bald Moose Mountains. It's not a big place—looks a little like some big, old cannon shot a load of houses and half-finished streets at the foothills and left them where they fell. The sun gets here first out of just about anywhere in the country, turning all the windows bloody-orange and filling up a thousand lobster cages with shadows.

Further up into the hills, outside the village but not so far that the post doesn't come regular as rain, you'll find a house all by itself in the middle of a tangly field of good red potatoes and green oats. The house is a snug little hall-and-parlor number with a moss-clotted roof and a couple of hundred years of whitewash on the stones. Sweet William and vervain and crimson beebalm wend out of the window-jambs, the door-hinges, the chimney blocks. There's carrots in the kitchen garden, some onions, a basil plant that may or may not come back next year.

You wouldn't know it to look at the place, but a demon lives here.

The rusted-out mailbox hangs on a couple of splinters and a single valiant, ancient bolt, its red flag at perpetual half-mast. Maybe there's mail to go out, and maybe there isn't. The demon's name is Gemegishkirihallat, but the mailbox reads: Agnes G. and that seems respectable enough to the mailman, who always has to check to see if that red flag means business, even though in all his considerable experience working for the postal service, it never has. The demon is neither male nor female—that's not how things work where it came from. But when it passed through the black door it came out Agnes on the other side. She's stuck with she now, and after five hundred years, give or take, she's just about used to it.

The demon arrived before the town. She fell out of a red oak in the primeval forest that would eventually turn into Schism Street and Memorial Square into a white howl of snow and frozen sea-spray. She was naked, her body branded with four-spoked seals, wheels of banishment, and the seven psalms of hell. Her hair burnt off and she had no fingernails or toenails. The hair grew back—black, naturally— and the 16th century offered a range of options for completely covering female skin from chin to heel, black-burnt with the diamond trident-brand of Amdusias or not.

The fingernails never came in. It's not something many people ever had occasion to notice.

The ice and lightning lasted for a month after she came; the moon got big and small again while the demon walked around the coves. Her footsteps marked the boundaries of the town to come, her heels boiling the snow, her breath full of thunder. When she hungered, which she did, often, for her appetites had never been small, she put her head back in the frigid, whipping storm and howled the primordial syllable that signified stag. Even through the squall and scream of the white air, one would always come, his delicate legs picking through the drifts, his antlers dripping icicles.

She ate her stags whole in the dark, crunching the antlers in her teeth.

Once, she called a pod of seals up out of the sea and slept on the frozen beach, their grey mottled bodies all around her. The heat of her warmed them, and they warmed her. In the morning the sand beneath them ran liquid and hot, the seals cooked and smoking.

The demon built that house with her own hands. Still naked come spring, as she saw no particular reason not to be, she put her ear to the mud and listened for echoes. The sizzling blood of the earth moved beneath her in crosshatch patterns, and on her hands and knees she followed them until she found what she wanted. Hell is a lot like a bad neighbor: it occupies the space just next to earth, not quite on top of it or underneath it, just to the side, on the margins. And Hell drops its chestnuts over the fence with relish. Agnes was looking for the place on earth that shared a cherry tree and a water line with the house of Gemegishkirihallat in Hell. When she found it, she spoke to the trees in proto-Akkadian and they understood her; they fell and sheared themselves of needles and branches. Grasses dried in a moment and thatched themselves, eager to please her. With the heat of her hands she blanched sand into glass for her windows; she demanded the hills give her iron and clay for her oven, she growled at the ground to give her snap peas and onions.

Some years later, a little Penobscot girl got lost in the woods while her tribe was making their long return from the warmer south. She did not know how to tell her father what she'd seen when she found him again, having never seen a house like the place the demon had built, with a patch of absurd English garden and a stone well and roses coming in bloody and thick. She only knew it was wrong somehow, that it belonged to someone, that it made her feel like digging a hole in the dirt and hiding in it forever.

The demon looked out of the window when the child came. Her hair had grown so long by then it brushed her ankles. She put out a lump of raw, red, bleeding meat for the girl. Gemegishkirihallat had always been an excellent host. Before he marked her flesh with his trident, Amdusias had loved to eat her salted bread, dipping his great long unicorn's horn into her black honey to drink.

The child didn't want it, but that didn't bother Agnes. Everybody has a choice. That's the whole point.

Sauve-Majeure belongs to its demon. She called the town to herself, on account of being a creature of profound order. A demon cannot function alone. If they could, banishment would be no hurt. A demon craves company, their own peculiar camaraderie. Agnes was a wolf abandoned by her pack. She could not help how she sniffed and howled for her litter-mates, nor how that howl became a magnetic pull for the sort of human who also loves order, everything in its place, all souls accounted for, everyone blessed and punished according to strict and immutable laws.

The first settlers were mostly French, banded together with whatever stray Puritans they'd picked up along the way north. Those Puritans would spice the Gallic stew of upper Maine for years, causing no end of trouble to Agnes, who, to be fair, was a witch and a succubus and everything else they ever called her, but that's no excuse for being such poor neighbors, when you think about it.

The demon waited. She waited for Martin le Clerq and Melchior Pelerin to raise their barns and houses, for Remy Mommacque to breed his dainty little cow to William Chudderley's barrel of a bull, for John Cabot to hear disputes in his rough parlor. She waited for Hubert Sazarin to send for both money and a pair of smooth brown stones from Sauve-Majeure Abbey back home in Gironde, and use them to lay out the foundations of what he dreamed would be the Cathedral of St. Geraud and St. Adelard, the grandest edifice north of Boston. She waited for Thomas Dryland to get drunk on Magdeleine Loliot's first and darkest beer, then march over to the Sazarin manse and knock him round the ears for flaunting his Papist devilry in the face of good honest folk. She waited for Dryland to take up a collection amongst the Protestant minority and, along with John Cabot and Quentin Pole, raised the frame of the Free Meeting House just across what would eventually be called Schism Street, glaring down the infant Cathedral, and pressed Quentin's serious young son Lamentation into service as pastor. She waited, most importantly, for little Crespine Moutonnet to be born, the first child of Sauve-Majeure. (Named by Sazarin, stubbornly called Help-on-High by the congregation at the Free Meeting House up until Renewal Pole was shot over the whole business by Henri Sazarin in 1890, at which point it was generally agreed to let the matter drop and the county take the naming of the place—which they did, once Sazarin had quietly and handsomely paid the registrar the weight of his eldest daughter in coin, wool, beef, and blueberries.) She waited for the Dryland twins, Reformation and Revelation, for Madame le Clerq to bear her five boys, for Goodwife Wadham to deliver her redoubtable seven daughters and single stillborn son. She waited for Mathelin Minouflet to bring his gentle wife over the sea from Cluny—she arrived already, and embarrassingly, pregnant, since she had by then been separated from her good husband for five years. Mathelin would have beaten her soundly, but upon discovering that his brother had the fault of it, having assumed Mathelin dead and the responsibility of poor Charlotte his own, tightened his belt and hoped it would be a son. The demon waited for enough children to be born and grow up, for enough village to spring up, for enough order to assert itself that she could walk among them and be merely one of the growing, noisy lot of new young folk fighting over Schism Street and trading grey, damp wool for hard, new potatoes.

The demon appeared in Adelard-in-the-Garden Square, the general marketplace ruled wholly by an elderly, hunched Hubert Sazarin and his son Augustine. Adjoining it, Faith-My-Joy Square hosted the Protestant market, but as one could not get decent wine nor good Virginia pipe tobacco in Faith-My-Joy nor Margery Cabot's sweet butter and linen cloth in Adelard, a great deal of furtive passage went on between the two. The demon chose Adelard, and laid out her wares among the tallow candles and roasting fowl and pale bluish honey sold by the other men. A woman selling in the market caused a certain amount of consternation among the husbands of Sauve-Majeure. Young Wrestling Dryland, though recently bereaved of his father Thomas, whose heart had quite simply burst with rage when Father Simon Charpentier arrived from France to give Mass and govern the souls of St. Geraud and Adelard, had no business at all sneaking across the divide to snatch up a flask of Sazarin's Spanish Madeira. Wrestling worked himself up into a positively Thomas-like fury over the tall figure in a black bonnet, and screwed in his courage to confront the devil-woman. He took in her severe dress, her covered hair, her table groaning with breads he had only heard of from his father's tales of a boyhood in London—braided rounds and glossy cross-buns studded with raisins (where had she got raisins in this forsaken land?), sweet French egg bread and cakes dusted with sugar, (what act of God or His Opposite granted this brazen even the smallest measure of sugar?), dark jams and butter-plaits stuffed with cream. He fixed to shame the slattern of Adelard, as he already thought of her, his gaze meant to cut down—but when he looked into the pits of her eyes he quieted, and said nothing at all, but meekly purchased a round of her bread even though his mother Anne made a perfectly fine loaf of her own.

Gemegishkirihallat had been the baker of Hell.

It had been her peculiar position, her speciality among all the diverse amusements and professions of Hades, which performs as perfectly and smoothly in its industries as the best human city can imagine, but never accomplish. Everything in its place, all souls accounted for, everyone blessed and punished according to strict and immutable laws. She baked bread to be seen but ultimately withheld, sweetcakes to be devoured until the skin split and the stomach protruded like the head of a child through the flesh, black pastry to haunt the starved mind. The ovens of Gemegishkirihallat were cathedral towers of fire and onyx, her under-bakers Akalamdug and Ekur pulling out soft and perfect loaves with bone paddles. But also she baked for her own table, where her comrades Amdusias, King of Thunder and Trumpets, Agares, Duke of Runaways and his loyal pet crocodile, Samagina, Marquis of the Drowned, Countess Gremory Who-Rides-Upon-a-Camel, and the

Magician-King Barbatos gathered to drink the wines crushed beneath the toes of rich and heartless men and share between them the bread of Gemegishkirihallat. She prepared the bloodloaf of the great Emperor's own infinite table, where, on occasion, she was permitted to sit and keep Count Andromalius from stealing the slabs of meat beloved of Celestial Marquis Oryax.

And in her long nights, in her long house of smoke and miller's stones, she baked the bread we eat in dreams, strangest loaves, her pies full of anguish and days long dead, her fairy-haunted gingerbread, her cakes wet with tears. The Great Duke Gusion, the Baboon-Lord of Nightmares, came to her each eve and took up her goods into his hairy arms and bore them off to the Pool of Sleep.

Those were the days the demon longed for in her lonely house with only one miserable oven that did not even come up to her waist, with her empty table and not even Shagshag, the weaver of Hell, to make her the Tea of Separation-from-God and ravage her in the dark like a good neighbor should. Those were the days she longed for in her awful heart—for a demon has no heart as we do, a little red fist in our chest. A demon's body is nothing but heart, its whole interior beating and pulsing and thundering in time to the clocks of Pandemonium.

Those were the days that floated in the demon's vast and lightless mind when she brought, at long last, her most perfect breads to Adelard-in-the-Garden. She would have her pack again, here between the mountains and the fish-clotted bay. She would build her ovens high and feed them all, feed them all and their children until no other bread would sate them. They would love her abjectly, for no other manner of loving had worth.

They burned her as a witch some forty years later.

As you might expect, it was a Dryland's hand at work in it, though the fingers of Sébastienne Sazarin as well as Father Simon's successor, Father Audrien, made their places in the pyre.

The demon felt it best, when asked, to claim membership in a convent on the other side of Bald Moose Mountain, traveling down into the bay-country to sell the sisters' productions of bread. She herself was a hermit, of course, consecrated to the wilderness in the manner of St. Viridiana or St. Julian, two venerated ladies of whom the poor country priest Father Simon had never heard. This relieved everyone a great deal, since a woman alone is a kind of unpredictable inferno that might at any moment light the hems of the innocent young. Sister Agnes had such a fine hand at pies and preserves, it couldn't hurt to let little Piety and Thankful go and learn a bit from her—even if she was a Papist demoness, her shortbread would make you take Communion just to get a piece. She's a right modest handmaiden, let Marie and Heloise and Isabelle learn their letters from her. She sings so beautifully at Christmas Mass, poor Christophe Minouflet fell into a swoon when she sang the Ave—why not let our girl Beatrice learn her scales and her octaves at her side?

And then there was the matter of Sister Agnes's garden. Not a soul in Sauve-Majeure did not burn to know the secret of the seemingly inexhaustible earth upon which their local hermit made her little house. How she made her pumpkins swell and her potatoes glow with red health, how her peas came up almost before the snow could melt, how her blueberry bushes groaned by June with the weight of their dark fruit. Let Annabelle and Elisabeth and Jeanne and Martha go straight away and study her methods, and if a seed or two of those hardy crops should find its way into the pockets of the girls' aprons, well, such was God's Will.

Thus did the demon find herself with a little coven of village girls, all bright and skinny and eager to grow up, more eager still to learn everything Sister Agnes could teach. The demon might have wept with relief and the peculiar joy of devils. She took them in, poor and rich, Papist and Puritan, gathered them round her black hearth like a wreath of still-closed flowers—and she opened them up. The clever girls spun wool that became silk in their hands. They baked bread so sweet the body lost all taste for humble mother's loaf. They read their Scriptures, though Sister Agnes's Bible seemed rather larger and heavier than either Father Audrien's or Pastor Pole's, full of books the girls had never heard of—the Gospel of St. Thomas, of Mary Magdalen, the Apocryphon of James, the Pistis Sophia, the Trimortic Protennoia, the Descent of Mary, and stranger ones still: the Book of the Two Thieves, the Book of Glass, the Book of the Evening Star. When they had tired of these, they read decadent and thrilling novels that Sister Agnes just happened to have on hand.

You might say the demon got careless. You could say that—but a demon has no large measure of care to begin with. The girls seated around her table like Grand Dukes, like seals on a frozen beach, made her feel like her old self again, and who among us can resist a feeling like that? Not many, and a demon hasn't even got a human's meager talent for resisting temptation.

Sébastienne Sazarin did not like Sister Agnes one bit. Oh, she sent her daughter Basile to learn lace from her, because she'd be damned if Marguerite le Clerq's brats would outshine a Sazarin at anything, and if Reformation Dryland's plain, sow-faced grand-daughter made a better marriage than her own girl, she'd just have to lie down dead in the street from the shame of it. But she didn't like it. Basile came home smiling in a secretive sort of way, her cheeks flushed, her breath quick and delighted. She did her work so quickly and well that there was hardly anything left of the household industries for Sébastienne to do. She conceived her fourth child, she would always say, out of sheer boredom.

"Well, isn't that what you sent her for?" her husband Hierosme said. "Be glad for ease, for it comes but seldom."

"It's unwholesome, a woman living alone out there. I wish Father Audrien would put a stop to it."

But Father Simon had confided to his successor before he passed into a peaceful death that he felt Sauve-Majeure harbored a saint. When she died, and the inevitable writ of veneration arrived from Rome, the Cathedral of St. Geraud and Adelard might finally have the funds it needed—and if perhaps St. Geraud, who didn't have much to recommend him and wasn't patron of anything in particular, had to be replaced with St. Agnes in order to secure financing from Paris, such was the Will of God. Hubert Sazarin's long dream would come to pass, and Sauve-Majeure would become the Avignon of the New World. A cathedral required more in the way of coin and time than even the Sazarins could manage on their own, and charged with this celestial municipal destiny, Father Audrien could not bring himself to censure the hermit woman on which it all depended.

Pastor Pole had no such hesitation. Though the left side of Schism Street thought it unsavory to hold the pastorship in one family, Lamentation Pole had raised his only son Troth to know only discipline and abstinence, and no other boy could begin to compete with him in devotion or self-denial. Pastor Pole's sermons in the Free Meeting House (which he would rename the Free Gathered Church) bore such force down on his congregation that certain young girls had been known to faint away at his roaring words. He condemned with equal fervor harvest feasting, sexual congress outside the bonds of marriage, woman's essential nature, and the ridiculous names the Sazarins and other Papist decadents saddled themselves with as they were certainly not fooling God with that nonsense.

Yet, still, the grumbling might have stayed just that, if not for the sopping-wet summer of '09 and the endless, bestial winter that followed. If it had not been bad enough that the crops rotted on the vine and sagged on the stalk, cows and sheep froze where they stood come December, and in February, Martha Chedderley discovered frantic mice invading her thin, precious stores of flour.

Yet the demon's garden thrived. In May her tomatoes were already showing bright green in the rain, in June she had bushels of rhubarb and knuckle-sized cherries, and in that miserable, grey August she sent each of her students home with a sack of onions, cabbages, apples, squash, and beans. When Basile Sazarin showed her mother her treasure, her mother's gaze could have set fire to a block of ice. When Weep-Not Dryland showed her father, Wrestling's eldest and meanest child, Elected Dryland, her winter's store, his bile could have soured a barrel of honey.

Schism Street was broached. Sébastienne Sazarin, prodding her husband and her priest before her, walked out halfway across the muddy, contested earth. Pastor Pole met her, joined by Elected Dryland and his mother, Martha and Makepeace Chedderley, and James Cabot, grandson of the great judge John Cabot may God rest his soul. On the one side of them stood the perpetually unfinished Cathedral of St. Geraud and St. Adelard, its ancient clerestory, window pane, and foundation stones standing lonely beside the humble chapel that everyone called the Cathedral anyhow. On the other, the clean steeple and whitewash of the Free Gathered Church.

She's a witch. She's a succubus. Why should we starve when she has the devil's own plenty?

You know this song. It's a classic, with an old workhorse of a chorus.

My girl Basile says she waters her oats with menstrual blood and reads over them from some Gospel I've never heard of. My maid Weep-Not says her cows give milk three times a day. Our Lizzie says she hasn't got any fingernails. She holds Sabbats up there and the girls all dance naked in a circle of pine. My Bess says on the full moon they're to fornicate with a stag up on the mountain while Sister Agnes sings the Black Vespers. If I ask my poor child, what will I hear then?

The demon heard them down in the valley. She heard the heat of their whispers, and knew they would come for her. She waited, as she had always waited. It wasn't long. James Cabot made out a writ of arrest and Makepeace Chedderley got burly young Robert Mommacque and Charles Loliot to come with him up the hill to drag the witch out of her house and install her in the new jail, which was the Dryland barn, quite recently outfitted with chains forged in Denis Minouflet's shop and a stout hickory chair donated out of the Sazarin parlor.

The demon didn't fight when they bound her and gagged her mouth—to keep her from bewitching them with her devil's psalms. It did not actually occur to her to use her devil's psalms. She was curious. She did not yet know if she could die. The men of Sauve-Majeure carried Gemegishkirihallat in their wagon down through the slushy March snow to stand trial. She only looked at them, her gaze mild and interested. Their guts twisted under those hollow eyes, and this was further proof.

It took much longer than anticipated. The two Sauve-Majeures had never agreed on much, and they sure as spring couldn't agree on the proper execution of a witch's trial. Hanging, said Dryland and Pole. Burning, insisted Sazarin and le Clerq. One judge or a whole bench, testimony from the children or just a simple quiet judgment once the charges were read? A water test or a needle test? Who would question her and what questions would they ask? Would Dr. Pelerin examine her, who had been sent down for schooling in Massachusetts, where they knew about such dark medicine, or the midwife Sarah Wadham? Who would have the credit of ferreting out the devil in their midst, the Church in Rome or their own stalwart Pastor Pole? What name would the town bear on the warrants, Sauve-Majeure (nest of snakes and Papistry) or Help-on-High (den of jackals and schismatics)? Most importantly, who would have the caring of her garden now and when she was gone? Who would have her house?

The demon waited. She waited for her girls to come to her—and they did. First the slower students who craved her approval, then finally Basile and Weep-Not and Lizzie Wadham and Bess Chedderley and the other names listed on the writ though no one had asked them much about it. The demon slipped her chains easily and put her hands to their little heads.

"Go and do as I have done," Sister Agnes said. "Go and make your gardens grow, make your men double over with desire, go and dance until you are full up of the moon."

"Are you really a witch?" ventured Basile Sazarin, who would be the most beautiful woman Sauve-Majeure would ever reap, all the way up 'til now and further still.

"No," said the demon. "A witch is just a girl who knows her mind. I am better than a witch. But look at the great orgy coming up like a rose around me. No night in Hell could be as bright."

And Sister Agnes took off her black wool gown before the young maids. They saw her four-spoked seals and her wheels of banishment and the seven burnt psalms on her skin. They saw that she had no sex. They saw her long name writ upon her thighs. They knew awe in that barn, and they danced with their teacher in the starlight sifting through the moldering hay.

A certain minister came to visit the demon while she waited for her trial. Pastor Pole managed not to wholly prostrate himself before the famous man, but took him immediately to speak with the condemned woman, whom that illustrious soul had heard of all the way down in Salem: a confirmed demoness, beyond any doubt.

Pastor Pole's own wife Mary-in-the-Manger brought a chair to seat the honored minister upon, and what cider and cheese they had to spare (in truth the Poles had used up the demon's apples to make it, and the demon's milk besides). The great man looked upon the black-clad woman chained in her barn-prison. Her gaze sounded upon his soul and boomed there, deafening.

"Art thee a witch, then?" he whispered.

"No," said the demon.

"But not a Christian lady, either," said he.

"No," said the demon.

"How came you to grow such bounty on your land without the help of God?"

The demon closed her hands in her lap. Her long hair hung around her like an animal's skin.

"My dear Goodman Mather, there is not a demon in Hell who was not once something quite other, and more interesting. In the land where the Euphrates runs green and sweet, I was a grain-god with the head of a bull. In the rough valley of the Tyne I was a god of fertility and war, with the head of a crow. I was a fish-headed lord of plenty in the depths of the Tigris. Before language I was she-who-makes-the-harvest-come, and I rode a red boar. The earth answers when I call it by name. I know its name because we are family."

"You admit your demonic nature?"

"I would have admitted it before now if anyone had asked. They ask only if I am a witch, and a witch is small pennies to me. I am what I am, as you are what you are. I want to live, as all creatures do. I cannot sin, so I have done no wrong."

The minister wet his throat with the demon's cider. His hand shook upon the tankard. When he had mastered himself he spoke quickly and softly, in the most wretched tones. He poured out onto the ground between him all his doubt and misery, all his grief and guilt. He gave her those things because she proved his whole heart, his invisible world, she proved him a good man, despite the hanging hill in his heart.

"Tell me," he rasped finally, as the dawn came on white and pitiless, "tell me that I will know the Kingdom of God in my lifetime. Tell me the end of days is near—for you must be the harbinger of it, you must be its messenger and its handmaiden. Tell me the dead will rise and we will shed our bodies like the shells of beautiful snails, that I will leave behind this horror that is flesh and become as light. Tell me I need never again be a man, that I need never err more, nor dwell in the curse of this life. Tell me you have come to murder this world, so that the new one might swallow us all."

The demon looked on him with infernal pity, which is, in the end, not worth the tears it sheds. Demons may pity men every hour of the day, but that pity never moves.

"No," the demon said.

And, slipping her chains, Gemegishkirihallat shed her gown once more before the famous man, showing the black obliteration of her skin. She folded her arms around him like wings and brought down the scythe of her mouth on his. Straddling his doubt, the demon made plain the reality of his flesh, and the arrow of his need.

They burned her at sunrise, before the Free Gathered Church could say anything about it. Bad enough they had brought that man to their town, the better people of Sauve-Majeure would not stand to let a Protestant nobody pass judgment on her. There were few witnesses: Father Audrien, who made his apologies to Father Simon in Heaven, Sébastienne and Hierosme Sazarin with young Basile clutched between them, Marguerite le Clerq and her husband Isaac. The Church would handle their witch, and the schismatics, to be bold, could lump it. They had all those girls down south—Rome had to have its due in the virtuous north.

Father Audrien tied the demon to a pine trunk and read her the last rites. She did not spit or howl, but only stared down the priest with a gaze like dying. She said one word before the end, and no one understood it. Each of the witnesses lit the flames so that none alone would have to bear the weight of the sin. A year later, Sébastienne Sazarin would insist, drunk and half-toothless, hiding sores on her breast and losing her voice, would rasp to her daughter, insisting that as Sister Agnes burned she saw a bull's head glowing through the pyre, its horns molten gold, and garlanded in black wheat. Marguerite le Clerq, half-mad with syphilis her husband brought home from Virginia, would weep to her priest that she had seen a red boar in the flames, its tusks made of diamond, its head crowned with millet and barley. Hierosme Sazarin, shipwrecked three years hence in Nova Scotia, his cargo of Madeira spilling out into the icy sea, would tell his blue-mouthed, doomed sailors that once he had seen a saint burn, and in the conflagration a white crow, its beak wet with blood, had flown up to Heaven, its wings seared black.

Father Audrien dreamed of the demon's burning body every night until he died, and the moment her bones shattered into a thousand fiery fish, he woke up reaching for his Bible and finding nothing in the dark.

The demon's house stood empty for a long while. Daisies grew in her stove. Moss thickened her great Bible. The girls she had drawn close around her grew up—Basile Sazarin so lovely men winced to look at her, so lovely she married a Parisian banker and never returned to Sauve-Majeure. Weep-Not Dryland bore eight daughters without pain or even much blood, and every autumn took them up to the top of the Bald Moose while her husband slept in his comfort. Lizzie Wadham's cloth wove so fine she could sell it in Boston and even New York for enough money to build a school, where she insisted on teaching the young ladies' lessons, the content of which no male was ever able to spy out.

And whenever Basile and Weep-Not went up to Sister Agnes's house to shoo out the foxes and raccoons and keep the garden weeded, they saw a crow perched on the chimney or pecking at an old apple, or a boney old cow peering at them with a rheumy eye, or a fat piglet with black spots scampering off into the forest as soon as they called after it.

The cod went scarce in the bays. The textile men came up from Portland and Augusta, with bolts of linen and money to build a mill on the river, finding ready buyers in Remembrance Dryland and Walter Chedderley. The few Penobscot and Passamaquoddy left found themselves corralled into bare land not far from where a little girl had once run crying from a strange doorstep in the snow. The Free Gathered

Church declined into Presbyterianism and the Cathedral of St. Geraud and St. Adelard remained a chapel, despite obtaining a door and its own relic—the kneecap of St. Geraud himself—before the Sazarin fortune wrecked on the New York market and scattered like so much seafoam. And the demon waited.

She had found burning to be much less painful than expulsion from Hell, and somewhat fortifying, given the sudden warmth in the March chill. When they buried the charred stumps of her bones, she was grateful, to be in the earth, to be closed up and safe. She thought of Prince Sitri, Lord of Naked Need, and how his leopard-skin and griffin-wings had burnt up every night, leaving his bare black bones to dance before the supper table of the upper Kings. His flesh always returned, so that it could burn again. When she thought about it, he looked a little like Thomas Dryland, with his stern golden face. And Countess Gremory—she'd had a body like Basile Sazarin had hid under those dingy aprons—riding her camel naked through the boiling fields to her door, when she'd had a door. When the shards of the demon dreamed, she dreamed of them all eating her bread together, in one house or another, Agares and Lamentation Pole and Amdusias and Sébastienne Sazarin and lovely old Akalamdug and Ekur serving them.

Gemegishkirihallat slowly fell apart into the dirt of Sauve-Majeure.

Sometimes a crow or a dog would dig up a bone and dash off with it, or a cow would drag a knuckle up with her cud. They would slip their pens or wing north suddenly, as if possessed, and before being coaxed home, would drop their prize in a certain garden, near a certain dark, empty house.

The lobster trade picked up, and every household had their pots. Schism Street got its first cobblestones, and cherry trees planted along its route. Something rumbled down south and the Minouflet boys were all killed in some lonely field in Pennsylvania, ending their name. In the name of the war dead, Pastor Veritas Pole and Father Jude dug up the strip of grass and holly hedges between Faith-My-Joy Square and Adelard-in-the-Garden Square and joined them into Memorial Square. The Dryland girls married French boys and buried whatever hatchet they still had biting at the tree. Raulguin Sazarin and his Bangor business partner Lucas Battersby found tourmaline up in Bald Moose, brilliant pink and green and for a moment it seemed Sauve-Majeure really would be something, would present a pretty little ring to the state of Maine and become its best bride, hoping for better days, for bigger stones sometime down the way—but no. The seam was shallow, the mine closed down as quickly as it had sprung up, and that was all the town would ever have of boom and bustle.

One day Constance Chedderley and Catherine le Clerq came home from gathering blackberries in the hills and told their mother that they'd seen chimney smoke up there. Wasn't that funny? Deliverance Dryland and Restitue Sazarin, best friends from the moment one had stolen a black-gowned, black-haired doll from the other, started sneaking up past the town line, coming home with muffins and shortbread in their school satchels. When questioned, they said they'd found a nunnery in the mountains, and one of the sisters had given them the treats as presents, admonishing them not to tell.

The mill went bust before most of the others, a canary singing in the textile mine of New England. The fisherman trade picked up, though, and soon enough even Peter Mommacque had a scallop boat going, despite having the work ethic of a fat housecat. A statue of Minerva made an honest woman of Memorial Square, with a single bright tourmaline set into her shield, which was promptly stolen by Bernard and Richie Loliot. First Presbyterian Church crumpled up into Second Methodist, and the first Pastor not named Pole, though rather predictably called Dryland instead, spoke on Sundays about the dangers of drink. And you know, old Agnes has just always lived up there, making her pies and candies and muffins. A nicer old lady you couldn't hope to meet. Right modest, always wearing her buttoned-up old-fashioned frocks even in summer. Why, Marie Pelerin spends every Sunday up there digging in the potatoes and learning to spin wool like the wives in Sauve-Majeure did before the mill. Janette Loliot got her cider recipe but she won't share it round. We're thinking of sending Maude and Harriet along as well. Young ladies these days can never learn too much when it comes to the quiet industries of home.

Far up into the hills above the stretch of land between Cobscook and Passamaquoddy Bay, if you go looking for it, you'll find a house all by itself in the middle of a brambly field of good straight corn and green garlic. It's an old place, but kept up, the whitewash fresh and the windows clean. The roof needs mending, it groans under the weight of hensbane and mustard and rue. There's tomatoes coming in under the kitchen sill in the kitchen, a basil plant that may or may not come back next year.

Jenny Sazarin comes by Sunday afternoons for Latin lessons and to trade a basket of cranberries from her uncle's bog down in Lincolnville for a loaf of bread with a sugar-crust that makes her heart beat faster when she eats it. She looks forward to it all week. It's quiet up there. You can hear the potatoes growing down in the dark earth. When October acorns drop down into the old lady's soot-colored wheelbarrow, they make a sound like guns firing. Agnes starts the preserves right away, boiling the bright, sour berries in her great huge pot until they pop.

"D'you know they used to burn witches here? I read about it last week," she says while she munches on a trifle piled up with cream.

"No," the demon says. "I've never heard that."

"They did. It must have been awful. I wonder if there really are witches? Pastor Dryland says there's demons, but that seems wrong to me. Demons live in Hell. Why would they leave and come here? Surely there's work enough for them to do with all the damned souls and pagans and gluttons and such."

"Perhaps they get punished, from time to time, and have to come into this world," the demon says, and stirs the wrinkling cranberries. The house smells of red fruit.

"What would a demon have to do to get kicked out of Hell?" wonders little Jenny, her schoolbooks at her feet, the warm autumn sun lighting up her face so that she looks so much like Hubert Sazarin and Thomas Dryland, both of whom can claim a fair portion of this bookish, gentle girl, that Gemegishkirihallat tightens her grip on her wooden spoon, stained crimson by the bloody sugar it tends.

The demon shuts her eyes. The orange coal of the sun lights up the skin and the bones of her skull show through. "Perhaps, for one moment, only one, so quick it might pass between two beats of a sparrow's wings, she had all her folk around her, and they ate of her table, and called her by her own name, and did not vie against the other, and for that one moment, she was joyful, and did not mourn her separation from a God she had never seen."

Cranberries pop and steam in the iron pot; Jenny swallows her achingly sweet bread. The sun goes down over Bald Moose mountain, and the lights come on down in the soft black valley of Sauve-Majeure.

THE EMPEROR'S OLD BONES
GEMMA FILES

"Oh, buying and selling . . . you know . . . life."
—Tom Stoppard, after J.G. Ballard

One day in 1941, not long after the fall of Shanghai, my *amah* (our live-in Chinese maid of all work, who often doubled as my nurse) left me sleeping alone in the abandoned hulk of what had once been my family's home, went out, and never came back . . . a turn of events which didn't actually surprise me all that much, since my parents had done something rather similar only a few brief weeks before. I woke up without light or food, surrounded by useless luxury—the discarded detritus of Empire and family alike. And fifteen more days of boredom and starvation were to pass before I saw another living soul.

I was ten years old.

After the war was over, I learned that my parents had managed to bribe their way as far as the harbor, where they became separated in the crush while trying to board a ship back "Home." My mother died of dysentery in a camp outside of Hangkow; the ship went down halfway to Hong Kong, taking my father with it. What happened to my amah, I honestly don't know—though I do feel it only fair to mention that I never really tried to find out, either.

The house and I, meanwhile, stayed right where we were—uncared for, unclaimed—until Ellis Iseland broke in, and took everything she could carry.

Including me.

"So what's your handle, *tai pan*?" she asked, back at the dockside garage she'd been squatting in, as she went through the pockets of my school uniform.

(It would be twenty more years before I realized that her own endlessly evocative name was just another bad joke—one some immigration official had played on her family, perhaps.)

"Timothy Darbersmere," I replied, weakly. Over her shoulder, I could see the frying pan still sitting on the table, steaming slightly, clogged with burnt rice. At that moment in time, I would have gladly drunk my own urine in order to be allowed to lick it out, no matter how badly I might hurt my tongue and fingers in doing so.

Her eyes followed mine—a calm flick of a glance, contemptuously knowing, arched eyebrows barely sketched in cinnamon.

"Not yet, kid," she said.

"I'm really very hungry, Ellis."

"I really believe you, Tim. But not yet."

She took a pack of cigarettes from her sleeve, tapped one out, lit it. Sat back. Looked at me again, eyes narrowing contemplatively. The plume of smoke she blew was exactly the same non-color as her slant, level, heavy-lidded gaze.

"Just to save time, by the way, here're the house rules," she said. "Long as you're with me, I eat first. Always."

"That's not fair."

"Probably not. But that's the way it's gonna be, 'cause I'm thinking for two, and I can't afford to be listening to my stomach instead of my gut." She took another drag. "Besides which, I'm bigger than you."

"My father says adults who threaten children are bullies."

"Yeah, well, that's some pretty impressive moralizing, coming from a mook who dumped his own kid to get out of Shanghai alive."

I couldn't say she wasn't right, and she knew it, so I just stared at her. She was exoticism personified—the first full-blown Yank I'd ever met, the first adult (Caucasian) woman I'd ever seen wearing trousers. Her flat, Midwestern accent lent a certain fascination to everything she said, however repulsive.

"People will do exactly whatever they think they can get away with, Tim," she told me, "for as long as they think they can get away with it. That's human nature. So don't get all high-hat about it, use it. Everything's got its uses—everything, and everybody."

"Even you, Ellis?"

"Especially me, Tim. As you will see."

It was Ellis, my diffident ally—the only person I have ever met who seemed capable of flourishing in any given situation—who taught me the basic rules of commerce: To always first assess things at their true value, then gauge exactly how much extra a person in desperate circumstances would be willing to pay for them.

And her lessons have stood me in good stead, during all these intervening years. At the age of sixty-six, I remain not only still alive, but a rather rich man, to boot—import/export, antiques, some minor drug-smuggling intermittently punctuated (on the more creative side) by the publication of a string of slim, speculative novels. These last items have apparently garnered me some kind of cult following amongst fans of such fiction, most specifically—ironically enough—in the United States of America.

But time is an onion, as my third wife used to say: The more of it you peel away, searching for the hidden connections between action and reaction, the more it gives you something to cry over.

So now, thanks to the established temporal conventions of literature, we will slip fluidly from 1941 to 1999—to St. Louis, Missouri, and the middle leg of my first-ever Stateside visit, as part of a tour in support of my recently-published childhood memoirs.

The last book signing was at four. Three hours later, I was already firmly ensconced in my comfortable suite at the downtown Four Seasons Hotel. Huang came by around eight, along with my room service trolley. He had a briefcase full of files and a sly, shy grin, which lit up his usually impassive face from somewhere deep inside.

"Racked up a lotta time on this one, Mr. Darbersmere," he said, in his second-generation Cockney growl. "Spent a lotta your money, too."

"Mmm." I uncapped the tray. "Good thing my publisher gave me that advance, then, isn't it?"

"Yeah, good fing. But it don't matter much now."

He threw the files down on the table between us. I opened the top one and leafed delicately through, between mouthfuls. There were schedules, marriage and citizenship certificates, medical records. Police records, going back to 1953, with charges ranging from fraud to trafficking in stolen goods, and listed under several different aliases. Plus a sheaf of photos, all taken from a safe distance.

I tapped one. "Is this her?"

Huang shrugged. "You tell me—you're the one 'oo knew 'er."

I took another bite, nodding absently. Thinking: *Did I? Really? Ever?*

As much as anyone, I suppose.

To get us out of Shanghai, Ellis traded a can of petrol for a spot on a farmer's truck coming back from the market—then cut our unlucky savior's throat with her straight razor outside the city limits, and sold his truck for a load of cigarettes, lipstick and nylons. This got us shelter on a floating whorehouse off the banks of the Yangtze, where she eventually hooked us up with a pirate trawler full of U.S. deserters and other assorted scum, whose captain proved to be some slippery variety of old friend.

The trawler took us up- and down-river, dodging the Japanese and preying on the weak, then trading the resultant loot to anyone else we came in contact with. We sold opium and penicillin to the warlords, maps and passports to the D.P.s, motor oil and dynamite to the Kuomintang, Allied and Japanese spies to each other. But our most profitable commodity, as ever, remained people—mainly because those we dealt with were always so endlessly eager to help set their own price.

I look at myself in the bathroom mirror now, tall and silver-haired—features still cleanly cut, yet somehow fragile, like Sir Laurence Olivier after the medical bills set in. At this morning's signing, a pale young woman with a bolt through her septum told me: "No offense, Mr. Darbersmere, but you're—like—a real babe. For an old guy."

I smiled, gently. And told her: "You should have seen me when I was twelve, my dear."

That was back in 1943, the year that Ellis sold me for the first time—or rented me out, rather, to the mayor of some tiny port village, who threatened to keep us docked until the next Japanese inspection. Ellis had done her best to convince him that we were just another boatload of Brits fleeing internment, even shucking her habitual male drag to reveal a surprisingly lush female figure and donning one of my mother's old dresses instead, much as it obviously disgusted her to do so. But all to no avail.

"You know I'd do it, Tim," she told me, impatiently pacing the trawler's deck, as a passing group of her crewmates whistled appreciatively from shore. "Christ knows I've tried. But the fact is, he doesn't want me. He wants you."

I frowned. "Wants me?"

"To go with him, Tim. You know—grown-up stuff."

"Like you and Ho Tseng, last week, after the dance at Sister Chin's?"

"Yeah, sorta like that."

She plumped herself down on a tarpaulined crate full of dynamite—

clearly labeled, in Cantonese, as "dried fruit"—and kicked off one of her borrowed high-heeled shoes, rubbing her foot morosely. Her cinnamon hair hung loose in the stinking wind, back-lit to a fine fever.

I felt her appraising stare play up and down me like a fine grey mist, and shivered.

"If I do this, will you owe me, Ellis?"

"You bet I will, kid."

"Always take me with you?"

There had been some brief talk of replacing me with Brian Thompson-Greenaway, another refugee, after I had mishandled a particularly choice assignment—protecting Ellis's private stash of American currency from fellow scavengers while she recuperated from a beating inflicted by an irate Japanese officer, into whom she'd accidentally bumped while ashore. Though she wisely put up no resistance—one of Ellis's more admirable skills involved her always knowing when it was in her best interest *not* to defend herself—the damage left her pissing blood for a week, and she had not been happy to discover her money gone once she was recovered enough to look for it.

She lit a new cigarette, shading her eyes against the flame of her Ronson. "'Course," she said, sucking in smoke.

"Never leave me?"

"Sure, kid. Why not?"

From Ellis, I learned to love duplicity, to distrust everyone except those who have no loyalty and play no favorites. Lie to me, however badly, and you are virtually guaranteed my fullest attention.

I don't remember if I really believed her promises, even then. But I did what she asked anyway, without qualm or regret. She must have understood that I would do anything for her, no matter how morally suspect, if she only asked me politely enough.

In this one way, at least, I was still definitively British.

Afterward, I was ill for a long time—some sort of psychosomatic reaction to the visceral shock of my deflowering, I suppose. I lay in a bath of sweat on Ellis's hammock, under the trawler's one intact mosquito net. Sometimes I felt her sponge me with a rag dipped in rice wine, while singing to me—softly, along with the radio:

A faded postcard from exotic places . . . a cigarette that's marked with lipstick traces . . . oh, how the ghost of you clings . . .

And did I merely dream that once, at the very height of my sickness, she held me on her hip and hugged me close? That she actually slipped her jacket open and offered me her breast, so paradoxically soft and firm, its nipple almost as pale as the rest of her night-dweller's flesh?

That sweet swoon of ecstasy. That first hot stab of infantile desire. That unwitting link between recent childish violation and a desperate longing for adult consummation. I was far too young to know what I was doing, but she did. She had to. And since it served her purposes, she simply chose not to care.

Such complete amorality: It fascinates me. Looking back, I see it always has—like everything else about her, fetishized over the years into an inescapable pattern of hopeless attraction and inevitable abandonment.

My first wife's family fled the former Yugoslavia shortly before the end of the war; she had high cheekbones and pale eyes, set at a Baltic slant. My second wife had a wealth of long, slightly coarse hair, the color of unground cloves. My third wife told stories—ineptly, compulsively. All of them were, on average, at least five years my elder.

And sooner or later, all of them left me.

Oh, Ellis, I sometimes wonder whether anyone else alive remembers you as I do—or remembers you at all, given your well-cultivated talent for blending in, for getting by, for rendering yourself unremarkable. And I really don't know what I'll do if this woman Huang has found for me turns out not to be you. There's not much time left in which to start over, after all.

For either of us.

Last night, I called the number Huang's father gave me before I left London. The man on the other end of the line identified himself as the master chef of the Precious Dragon Shrine restaurant.

"Oh yes, *tai pan* Darbersmere," he said, when I mentioned my name. "I was indeed informed, by that respected personage who we both know, that you might honor my unworthiest of businesses with the request for some small service."

"One such as only your estimable self could provide."

"The *tai pan* flatters, as is his right. Which is the dish he wishes to order?"

"The Emperor's Old Bones."

A pause ensued—fairly long, as such things go. I could hear a Cantopop ballad filtering in, perhaps from somewhere in the kitchen, duelling for precedence with the more classical strains of a wailing erhu. The Precious Dragon Shrine's master chef drew a single long, low breath.

"*Tai pan*," he said, finally, "for such a meal . . . one must provide the meat oneself."

"Believe me, Grandfather, I am well aware of such considerations. You may be assured that the meat will be available, whenever you are ready to begin its cooking."

Another breath—shorter, this time. Calmer.

"Realizing that it has probably been a long time since anyone has requested this dish," I continued, "I am, of course, more than willing to raise the price our mutual friend has already set."

"Oh, no, *tai pan*."

"For your trouble."

"*Tai pan*, please. It is not necessary to insult me."

"I must assure you, Grandfather, that no such insult was intended."

A burst of scolding rose from the kitchen, silencing the ballad in mid-ecstatic lament. The master chef paused again. Then said: "I will need at least three days' notice to prepare my staff."

I smiled. Replying, with a confidence which—I hoped—at least sounded genuine:

"Three days should be more than sufficient."

The very old woman (eighty-nine, at least) who may or may not have once called herself Ellis Iseland now lives quietly in a genteelly shabby area of St. Louis, officially registered under the far less interesting name of Mrs. Munro. Huang's pictures show a figure held carefully erect, yet helplessly shrunken in on itself—its once-straight spine softened by the onslaught of osteoporosis. Her face has gone loose around the jawline, skin powdery, hair a short, stiff grey crown of marcelled waves.

She dresses drably. Shapeless feminine weeds, widow-black. Her arthritic feet are wedged into Chinese slippers—a small touch of nostalgic irony? Both her snubbed cat's nose and the half-sneering set of her wrinkled mouth seem familiar, but her slanted eyes—the most important giveaway, their original non-color perhaps dimmed even further with age, from light smoke-grey to bone, ecru, white—are kept hidden beneath a thick-lensed pair of bifocal sunglasses, essential protection for someone whose sight may not last the rest of the year.

And though her medical files indicate that she is in the preliminary stages of lung and throat cancer, her trip a day to the local corner store always includes the purchase of at least one pack of cigarettes, the brand apparently unimportant, as long as it contains a sufficient portion of nicotine. She lights one right outside the front door, and has almost finished it by the time she rounds the corner of her block.

Her neighbors seem to think well of her. Their children wave as she goes by, cane in one hand, cigarette in the other. She nods acknowledgement, but does not wave back.

This familiar arrogance, seeping up unchecked through her last, most perfect disguise: the mask of age, which bestows a kind of retroactive innocence on even its most experienced victims. I have recently begun to take advantage of its charms myself, whenever it suits my fancy to do so.

I look at these pictures, again and again. I study her face, searching in vain for even the ruin of that cool, smooth, inventively untrustworthy operator who once held both my fortune and my heart in the palm of her mannishly large hand.

It was Ellis who first told me about The Emperor's Old Bones—and she is still the only person in the world with whom I would ever care to share that terrible meal, no matter what doing so might cost me.

If, indeed, I ever end up eating it at all.

"Yeah, I saw it done down in Hong Kong," Ellis told us, gesturing with her chopsticks. We sat behind a lacquered screen at the back of Sister Chin's, two nights before our scheduled rendezvous with the warlord Wao Ruyen, from whom Ellis had already accepted some mysteriously unspecified commission. I watched her eat—waiting my turn, as ever—while Brian Thompson-Greenaway (also present, much to my annoyance) sat in the corner and watched us both, openly ravenous.

"They take a carp, right—you know, those big fish some rich Chinks keep in fancy pools, out in the garden? Supposed to live hundreds of years, you believe all that 'Confucius says' hooey. So they take this carp and they fillet it, all over, so the flesh is hanging off it in strips. But they do it so well, so carefully, they keep the carp alive through the whole thing. It's sittin' there on a plate, twitching, eyes rollin' around. Get close enough, you can look right in through the ribcage and see the heart still beating."

She popped another piece of Mu Shu pork in her mouth, and smiled down at Brian, who gulped—apparently suddenly too queasy to either resent or envy her proximity to the food.

"Then they bring out this big pot full of boiling oil," she continued, "and they run hooks through the fish's gills and tail, so they can pick it up at both ends. And while it's floppin' around, tryin' to get free, they dip all those hangin' pieces of flesh in the oil—one side first, then the other, all nice and neat. Fish is probably in so much pain already it doesn't even notice. So it's still alive when they put it back down . . . alive, and cooked, and ready to eat."

And then—they eat it."

"Sure do, Tim."

"Alive, I mean."

Brian now looked distinctly green. Ellis shot him another glance, openly amused by his lack of stamina, then turned back to me.

"Well yeah, that's kinda the whole point of the exercise. You keep the carp alive until you've eaten it, and all that long life just sorta transfers over to you."

"Like magic," I said. She nodded.

"Exactly. 'Cause that's exactly what it is."

I considered her statement for a moment.

"My father," I commented, at last, "always told us that magic was a load of bunk."

Ellis snorted. "And why does this not surprise me?" She asked, of nobody in particular. Then: "Fine, I'll bite. What do you think?"

"I think . . ." I said, slowly, ". . . that if it works . . . then who cares?"

She looked at me. Snorted again. And then—she actually laughed, an infectious, unmalicious laugh that seemed to belong to someone far younger, far less complicated. It made me gape to hear it. Using her chopsticks, she plucked the last piece of pork deftly from her plate, and popped it into my open mouth.

"Tim," she said, "for a spoiled Limey brat, sometimes you're okay."

I swallowed the pork, without really tasting it. Before I could stop myself, I had already blurted out: "I wish we were the same age, Ellis."

This time she stared. I felt a sudden blush turn my whole face crimson. Now it was Brian's turn to gape, amazed by my idiotic effrontery.

"Yeah, well, not me," she said. "I like it just fine with you bein' the kid, and me not."

"Why?"

She looked at me again. I blushed even more deeply, heat prickling at my hairline. Amazingly, however, no explosion followed. Ellis simply took another sip of her tea, and replied—

"'Cause the fact is, Tim, if you were my age—good-lookin' like you are, smart like you're gonna be—I could probably do some pretty stupid things over you."

Magic. Some might say it's become my stock in trade—as a writer, at least. Though the humble craft of buying and selling also involves a kind of legerdemain, as Ellis knew so well; sleight of hand, or price, depending on your product . . . and your clientele.

But true magic? Here, now, at the end of the twentieth century, in this brave new world of 100-slot CD players and incessant afternoon talk shows?

I have seen so many things in my long life, most of which I would have thought impossible, had they not taken place right in front of me. From the bank of the Yangtze river, I saw the bright white smoke of an atomic bomb go up over Nagasaki, like a tear in the fabric of the horizon. In Chungking harbor, I saw two grown men stab each other to death over the corpse of a dog because one wanted to bury it, while the other wanted to eat it. And just beyond the Shanghai city limits, I saw Ellis cut that farmer's throat with one quick twist of her wrist, so close to me that the spurt of his severed jugular misted my cheek with red.

But as I grow ever closer to my own personal twilight, the thing I remember most vividly is watching—through the window of a Franco-Vietnamese arms-dealer's car, on my way to a cool white house in Saigon, where I would wait out the final days of the war in relative comfort and safety—as a pair of barefoot coolies pulled the denuded skeleton of Brian Thompson-Greenaway from a culvert full of malaria-laden water. I knew it was him, because even after Wao Ruyen's court had consumed the rest of his pathetic little body, they had left his face nearly untouched—there not being quite enough flesh on a child's skull, apparently, to be worth the extra effort of filleting . . . let alone of cooking.

And I remember, with almost comparable vividness, when—just a year ago—I saw the former warlord Wao, Huang's most respected father, sitting in a Limehouse nightclub with his Number One and Number Two wife at either elbow. Looking half the age he did when I first met him, in that endless last July of 1945, before black science altered our world forever. Before Ellis sold him Brian instead of me, and then fled for the Manchurian border, leaving me to fend for myself in the wake of her departure.

After all this, should the idea of true magic seem so very difficult to swallow? I think not.

No stranger than the empty shell of Hiroshima, cupped around Ground Zero, its citizenry reduced to shadows in the wake of the blast's last terrible glare. And certainly no stranger than the fact that I should think a woman so palpably incapable of loving anyone might nevertheless be capable of loving me, simply because— at the last moment—she suddenly decided not to let a rich criminal regain his youth and prolong his days by eating me alive, in accordance with the ancient and terrible ritual of the Emperor's Old Bones.

This morning, I told my publicist that I was far too ill to sign any books today—a particularly swift and virulent touch of the twenty-four-hour flu, no doubt. She said she understood completely. An hour later, I sat in Huang's car across the street from the corner store, watching "Mrs. Munro" make her slow way down the street to pick up her daily dose of slow, coughing death.

On her way back, I rolled down the car window and yelled: "*Lai gen wo ma, wai guai!*"

(*Come with me, white ghost!* An insulting little Mandarin phrase, occasionally used by passing Kuomintang jeep drivers to alert certain long-nosed Barbarian smugglers to the possibility that their dealings might soon be interrupted by an approaching group of Japanese soldiers.)

Huang glanced up from his copy of *Rolling Stone*'s Hot List, impressed. "Pretty good accent," he commented.

But my eyes were on "Mrs. Munro," who had also heard—and stopped in mid-step, swinging her half-blind grey head toward the sound, more as though scenting than scanning. I saw my own face leering back at me in miniature from the lenses of her prescription sunglasses, doubled and distorted by the distance between us. I saw her raise one palm to shade her eyes even further against the sun, the wrinkles across her nose contracting as she squinted her hidden eyes.

And then I saw her slip her glasses off to reveal those eyes: Still slant, still grey. Still empty.

"It's her," I told him.

Huang nodded. "Fought so. When you want me to do it?"

"Tonight?"

"Whatever y'say, Mr. D."

Very early on the morning before Ellis left me behind, I woke to find her sitting next to me in the red half-darkness of the ship's hold.

"Kid," she said, "I got a little job lined up for you today."

I felt myself go cold. "What kind of job, Ellis?" I asked, faintly—though I already had a fairly good idea. Quietly, she replied: "The grown-up kind."

"Who?"

"French guy, up from Saigon, with enough jade and rifles to buy us over the border. He's rich, educated; not bad company, either. For a fruit."

"That's reassuring," I muttered, and turned on my side, studying the wall. Behind me, I heard her lighter click open, then catch and spark—felt the faint lick of her breath as she exhaled, transmuting nicotine into smoke and ash. The steady pressure of her attention itched like an insect crawling on my skin: Fiercely concentrated, alien almost to the point of vague disgust, infinitely patient.

"War's on its last legs," she told me. "That's what I keep hearing. You got the Communists comin' up on one side, with maybe the Russians slipping in behind 'em, and the good old U.S. of A. everywhere else. Philippines are already down for the count, now Tokyo's in bombing range. Pretty soon, our little outfit is gonna be so long gone, we won't even remember what it looked like. My educated opinion? It's sink or swim, and we need all the life-jackets that money can buy." She paused. "You listening to me? Kid?"

I shut my eyes again, marshalling my heart-rate.

"Kid?" Ellis repeated.

Still without answering—or opening my eyes—I pulled the mosquito net aside, and let gravity roll me free of the hammock's sweaty clasp. I was fourteen years old now, white-blonde and deeply tanned from the river-reflected sun; almost her height, even in my permanently bare feet. Looking up, I found I could finally meet her grey gaze head-on.

"'Us,'" I said. "'We.' As in you and I?"

"Yeah, sure. You and me."

I nodded at Brian, who lay nearby, deep asleep and snoring. "And what about him?"

Ellis shrugged.

"I don't know, Tim," she said. "What about him?"

I looked back down at Brian, who hadn't shifted position, not even when my shadow fell over his face. Idly, I inquired—

"You'll still be there when I get back, won't you, Ellis?"

Outside, through the porthole, I could see that the rising sun had just cracked the horizon; she turned, haloed against it. Blew some more smoke. Asking:

"Why the hell wouldn't I be?"

"I don't know. But you wouldn't use my being away on this job as a good excuse to leave me behind, though—would you?"

She looked at me. Exhaled again. And said, evenly: "You know, Tim, I'm getting' pretty goddamn sick of you asking me that question. So gimme one good reason not to, or let it lie."

Lightly, quickly—too quickly even for my own well-honed sense of self-preservation to prevent me—I laid my hands on either side of her face and pulled her to me, hard. Our breath met, mingled, in sudden intimacy; hers tasted of equal parts tobacco and surprise. My daring had brought me just close enough to smell her own personal scent, under the shell of everyday decay we all stank of: A cool, intoxicating rush of non-fragrance, firm and acrid as an unearthed tuber. It burned my nose.

"We should always stay together," I said, "because I *love* you, Ellis."

I crushed my mouth down on hers, forcing it open. I stuck my tongue inside her mouth as far as it would go and ran it around, just like the mayor of that first tiny port village had once done with me. I fastened my teeth deep into the inner flesh of her lower lip, and bit down until I felt her knees give way with the shock of it. Felt myself rear up, hard and jerking, against her soft underbelly. Felt *her* feel it.

It was the first and only time I ever saw her eyes widen in anything but anger.

With barely a moment's pause, she punched me right in the face, so hard I felt jaw crack. I fell at her feet, coughing blood.

"Eh—!" I began, amazed. But her eyes froze me in mid-syllable—so grey, so cold.

"Get it straight, *tai pan*," she said, "'cause I'm only gonna say it once. I don't *buy*. I *sell*."

Then she kicked me in the stomach with one steel-toed army boot, and leant over me as I lay there, gasping and hugging myself tight—my chest contracting, eyes dimming. Her eyes pouring over me like liquid ice. Like sleet. Swelling her voice like some great Arctic river, as she spoke the last words I ever heard her say—

"So don't you even *try* to play me like a trick, and think I'll let you get away with it."

Was Ellis evil? Am I? I've never thought so, though earlier this week I did give one of those legendary American Welfare mothers $25,000 in cash to sell me her least-loved child. He's in the next room right now, playing Nintendo. Huang is watching him. I think he likes Huang. He probably likes me, for that matter. We are the first English people he has ever met, and our accents fascinate him. Last night, we ordered in pizza; he ate until he was sick, then ate more, and fell asleep in front of an HBO basketball game. If I let him stay with me another week, he might become sated enough to convince himself he loves me.

The master chef at the Precious Dragon Shrine tells me that the Emperor's Old Bones bestows upon its consumer as much life-force as the consumed would have eventually gone through, had he or she been permitted to live out the rest of their days unchecked—and since the child I bought claims to be roughly ten years old (a highly significant age, in retrospect), this translates to perhaps an additional sixty years of life for every person who participates, whether the dish is eaten alone or shared. Which only makes sense, really: It's magic, after all.

And this is good news for me, since the relative experiential gap between a man in his upper twenties and a woman in her upper thirties—especially compared to that between a boy of fourteen and a woman of twenty-eight—is almost insignificant.

Looking back, I don't know if I've ever loved anyone but Ellis—if I'm even capable of loving anyone else. But finally, after all these wasted years, I do know what I want. And who.

And how to get them both.

It's a terrible thing I'm doing, and an even worse thing I'm going to do. But when it's done, I'll have what I want, and everything else—all doubts, all fears, all piddling, queasy little notions of goodness, and decency, and basic human kinship—all that useless lot can just go hang, and twist and rot in the wind while they're at it. I've lived much too long with my own unsatisfied desire to simply hold my aching parts— whatever best applies, be it stomach or otherwise—and congratulate myself on my forbearance anymore. I'm not mad, or sick, or even yearning after a long-lost love that I can never regain, and never really had in the first place. I'm just hungry, and I want to *eat*.

And morality . . . has nothing to do with it.

Because if there's one single thing you taught me, Ellis—one lesson I've retained throughout every twist and turn of this snaky thing I call my life—it's that hunger has no moral structure.

Huang came back late this morning, limping and cursing, after a brief detour to the office of an understanding doctor who his father keeps on international retainer. I am obscurely pleased to discover that Ellis can still defend herself; even after Huang's first roundhouse put her on the pavement, she still somehow managed to slip her razor open without him noticing, then slide it shallowly across the back of his Achilles tendon. More painful than debilitating, but rather well done nevertheless, for a woman who can no longer wear shoes which require her to tie her own laces.

I am almost as pleased, however, to hear that nothing Ellis may have done actually succeeded in preventing Huang from completing his mission—and beating her, with methodical skill, to within an inch of her corrupt and dreadful old life.

I have already told my publicist that I witnessed the whole awful scene, and asked her to find out which hospital poor Mrs. Munro has been taken to. I myself, meanwhile, will drive the boy to the kitchen of the Precious Dragon Shrine restaurant, where I am sure the master chef and his staff will do their best to keep him entertained until later tonight. Huang has lent him his pocket Gameboy, which should help.

Ah. That must be the phone now, ringing.

The woman in bed 37 of the Morleigh Memorial Hospital's charity wing, one of the few left operating in St. Louis—in America, possibly—opens her swollen left eye a crack, just far enough to reveal a slit of red-tinged white and a wandering, dilated pupil, barely rimmed in grey.

"Hello, Ellis," I say.

I sit by her bedside, as I have done for the last six hours. The screens enshrouding us from the rest of the ward, with its rustlings and moans, reduce all movement outside this tiny area to a play of flickering shadows—much like the visions one might glimpse in passing through a double haze of fever and mosquito net, after suffering a violent shock to one's fragile sense of physical and moral integrity.

... and oh, how the ghost of you clings ...

She clears her throat, wetly. Tells me, without even a flicker of hesitation:

"Nuh ... Ellis. Muh num iss ... Munro."

But: She peers up at me, straining to lift her bruise-stung lids. I wait, patiently.

"Tuh—"

"That's a good start."

I see her bare broken teeth at my patronizing tone, perhaps reflexively. Pause. And then, after a long moment: "*Tim.*"

"Good show, Ellis. Got it in one."

Movement at the bottom of the bed: Huang, stepping through the gap between the screens. Ellis sees him, and stiffens. I nod in his direction, without turning.

"I believe you and Huang have already met," I say. "Mr. Wao Huang, that is; you'll remember his father, the former warlord Wao Ruyen. He certainly remembers you—and with some gratitude, or so he told me."

Huang takes his customary place at my elbow. Ellis's eyes move with him, helplessly—and I recall how my own eyes used to follow her about in a similarly fascinated manner, breathless and attentive on her briefest word, her smallest motion.

"I see you can still take quite a beating, Ellis," I observe, lightly. "Unfortunately for you, however, it's not going to be quite so easy to recover from this particular melee as it once was, is it? Old age, and all that." To Hunag: "Have the doctors reached any conclusion yet? Regarding Mrs. Munro's long-term prognosis?"

"Wouldn't say as 'ow there was one, *tai pan*."

"Well, yes. Quite."

I glance back, only to find that Ellis's eyes have turned to me at last. And I can read them so clearly, now—like clean, black text through grey rice-paper, lit from behind by a cold and colorless flame. No distance. No mystery at all.

When her mouth opens again, I know exactly what word she's struggling to shape.

"Duh . . . deal?"

Oh, yes.

I rise, slowly, as Huang pulls the chair back for me. Some statements, I find, need room in which to be delivered properly—or perhaps I'm simply being facetious. My writer's over-developed sense of the dramatic, working double-time.

I wrote this speech out last night, and rehearsed it several times in front of the bathroom mirror. I wonder if it sounds rehearsed. Does calculated artifice fall into the same general category as outright deception? If so, Ellis ought to be able to hear it in my voice. But I don't suppose she's really apt to be listening for such fine distinctions, given the stress of this mutually culminative moment.

"I won't say you've nothing I want, Ellis, even now. But what I really want—what I've always wanted—is to be the seller, for once, and not the sold. To be the only one who has what you want desperately, and to set my price wherever I think it fair."

Adding, with the arch of a significant brow: "—or *know* it to be *un*fair."

I study her battered face. The bruises form a new mask, impenetrable as any of the others she's worn. The irony is palpable: Just as Ellis's nature abhors emotional accessibility, so nature—seemingly—reshapes itself at will to keep her motivations securely hidden.

"I've arranged for a meal," I tell her. "The menu consists of a single dish, one with which I believe we're both equally familiar. The name of that dish is the Emperor's Old Bones, and my staff will begin to cook it whenever I give the word. Now, you and I may share this meal, or we may not. We may regain our youth, and double our lives, and be together for at least as long as we've been apart—or we may not. But I promise you this, Ellis: No matter what I eventually end up doing, the extent of your participation in the matter will be exactly defined by how much you are willing to pay me for the privilege."

I gesture to Huang, who slips a pack of cigarettes from his coat pocket. I tap one out. I light it, take a drag. Savor the sensation.

Ellis just watches.

"So here's the deal, then: If you promise to be very, very nice to me—and never, ever leave me again—for the rest of our extremely long partnership—"

I pause. Blow out the smoke. Wait. And conclude, finally:

"—then you can eat first."

I offer Ellis the cigarette, slowly. Slowly, she takes it from me, holding it delicately between two splinted fingers. She raises it to her torn and grimacing mouth. Inhales. Exhales those familiar twin plumes of smoke, expertly, through her crushed and broken nose. Is that a tear at the corner of her eye, or just an upwelling of rheum? Or neither?

"Juss like . . . ahways," she says.

And gives me an awful parody of my own smile. Which I—return.

With interest.

Later, as Huang helps Ellis out of bed and into the hospital's service elevator, I sit in the car, waiting. I take out my cellular phone. The master chef of the Precious Dragon Shrine restaurant answers on the first ring.

"How is . . . the boy?" I ask him.

"Fine, *tai pan.*"

There is a pause, during which I once more hear music filtering in from the other end of the line—the tinny little song of a video game in progress, intermittently punctuated by the clatter of kitchen implements. Laughter, both adult and child.

"Do you wish to cancel your order, *tai pan* Darbersmere?" the master chef asks me, delicately.

Through the hospital's back doors, I can see the service elevator's lights crawling steadily downward—the floors reeling themselves off, numeral by numeral. Fifth. Fourth. Third.

"*Tai pan?*"

Second. First.

"No. I do not."

The elevator doors are opening. I can see Huang guiding Ellis out, puppeting her deftly along with her own crutches. Those miraculously-trained hands of his, able to open or salve wounds with equal expertise.

"Then I may begin cooking," the master chef says. Not really meaning it as a question.

Huang holds the door open. Ellis steps through. I listen to the Gameboy's idiot song, and know that I have spent every minute of every day of my life preparing to make this decision, ever since that last morning on the Yangtze. That I have made it so many times already, in fact, that nothing I do or say now can ever stop it from being made. Any more than I can bring back the child Brian Thompson-Greenaway was, before he went up the hill to Wao Ruyen's fortress, hand in stupidly trusting hand with Ellis—or the child I was, before Ellis broke into my parents' house and saved me from one particular fate worse than death, only to show me how many, many others there were to choose from.

Or the child that Ellis must have been, once upon a very distant time, before whatever happened to make her as she now is—then set her loose to move at will through an unsuspecting world, preying on other lost children.

. . . *these foolish things . . . remind me of you.*

"Yes," I say. "You may."

THE THINGS

PETER WATTS

I am being Blair. I escape out the back as the world comes in through the front.

I am being Copper. I am rising from the dead.

I am being Childs. I am guarding the main entrance.

The names don't matter. They are placeholders, nothing more; all biomass is interchangeable. What matters is that these are all that is left of me. The world has burned everything else.

I see myself through the window, loping through the storm, wearing Blair. MacReady has told me to burn Blair if he comes back alone, but MacReady still thinks I am one of him. I am not: I am being Blair, and I am at the door. I am being Childs, and I let myself in. I take brief communion, tendrils writhing forth from my faces, intertwining: I am BlairChilds, exchanging news of the world.

The world has found me out. It has discovered my burrow beneath the tool shed, the half-finished lifeboat cannibalized from the viscera of dead helicopters. The world is busy destroying my means of escape. Then it will come back for me.

There is only one option left. I disintegrate. Being Blair, I go to share the plan with Copper and to feed on the rotting biomass once called *Clarke*; so many changes in so short a time have dangerously depleted my reserves. Being Childs, I have already consumed what was left of Fuchs and am replenished for the next phase. I sling the flamethrower onto my back and head outside, into the long Antarctic night.

I will go into the storm, and never come back.

I was so much more, before the crash. I was an explorer, an ambassador, a missionary. I spread across the cosmos, met countless worlds, took communion: the fit reshaped the unfit and the whole universe bootstrapped upwards in joyful, infinitesimal increments. I was a soldier, at war with entropy itself. I was the very hand by which Creation perfects itself.

So much wisdom I had. So much experience. Now I cannot remember all the things I knew. I can only remember that I once knew them.

I remember the crash, though. It killed most of this offshoot outright, but a little crawled from the wreckage: a few trillion cells, a soul too weak to keep them in check. Mutinous biomass sloughed off despite my most desperate attempts to hold myself together: panic-stricken little clots of meat, instinctively growing whatever limbs they could remember and fleeing across the burning ice. By the time I'd regained control of what was left the fires had died and the cold was closing back in. I barely managed to grow enough antifreeze to keep my cells from bursting before the ice took me.

I remember my reawakening, too: dull stirrings of sensation in real time, the first embers of cognition, the slow blooming warmth of awareness as body and soul embraced after their long sleep. I remember the biped offshoots surrounding me, the strange chittering sounds they made, the odd *uniformity* of their body plans. How ill-adapted they looked! How *inefficient* their morphology! Even disabled, I could see so many things to fix. So I reached out. I took communion. I tasted the flesh of the world—

—and the world attacked me. It *attacked* me.

I left that place in ruins. It was on the other side of the mountains— the *Norwegian camp*, it is called here—and I could never have crossed that distance in a biped skin. Fortunately there was another shape to choose from, smaller than the biped but better adapted to the local climate. I hid within it while the rest of me fought off the attack. I fled into the night on four legs, and let the rising flames cover my escape.

I did not stop running until I arrived here. I walked among these new offshoots wearing the skin of a quadruped; and because they had not seen me take any other shape, they did not attack.

And when I assimilated them in turn—when my biomass changed and flowed into shapes unfamiliar to local eyes—I took that communion in solitude, having learned that the world does not like what it doesn't know.

I am alone in the storm. I am a bottom-dweller on the floor of some murky alien sea. The snow blows past in horizontal streaks; caught against gullies or outcroppings, it spins into blinding little whirlwinds. But I am not nearly far enough, not yet. Looking back I still see the camp crouched brightly in the gloom, a squat angular jumble of light and shadow, a bubble of warmth in the howling abyss.

It plunges into darkness as I watch. I've blown the generator. Now there's no light but for the beacons along the guide ropes: strings of dim blue stars whipping back and forth in the wind, emergency constellations to guide lost biomass back home.

I am not going home. I am not lost enough. I forge on into darkness until even the stars disappear. The faint shouts of angry frightened men carry behind me on the wind.

Somewhere behind me my disconnected biomass regroups into vaster, more powerful shapes for the final confrontation. I could have joined myself, all in one: chosen unity over fragmentation, resorbed and taken comfort in the greater whole. I could have added my strength to the coming battle. But I have chosen a different path. I am saving Child's reserves for the future. The present holds nothing but annihilation.

Best not to think on the past.

I've spent so very long in the ice already. I didn't know how long until the world put the clues together, deciphered the notes and the tapes from the Norwegian camp, pinpointed the crash site. I was being Palmer, then; unsuspected, I went along for the ride.

I even allowed myself the smallest ration of hope.

But it wasn't a ship any more. It wasn't even a derelict. It was a fossil, embedded in the floor of a great pit blown from the glacier. Twenty of these skins could have stood one atop another, and barely reached the lip of that crater. The timescale settled down on me like the weight of a world: how long for all that ice to accumulate? How many eons had the universe iterated on without me?

And in all that time, a million years perhaps, there'd been no rescue. I never found myself. I wonder what that means. I wonder if I even exist any more, anywhere but here.

Back at camp I will erase the trail. I will give them their final battle, their monster to vanquish. Let them win. Let them stop looking.

Here in the storm, I will return to the ice. I've barely even been away, after all; alive for only a few days out of all these endless ages. But I've learned enough in that time. I learned from the wreck that there will be no repairs. I learned from the ice that there will be no rescue. And I learned from the world that there will be no reconciliation. The only hope of escape, now, is into the future; to outlast all this hostile, twisted biomass, to let time and the cosmos change the rules. Perhaps the next time I awaken, this will be a different world.

It will be aeons before I see another sunrise.

This is what the world taught me: that adaptation is provocation. Adaptation is incitement to violence.

It feels almost obscene—an offense against Creation itself—to stay stuck in this skin. It's so ill-suited to its environment that it needs to be wrapped in multiple layers of fabric just to stay warm. There are a myriad ways I could optimize it: shorter limbs, better insulation, a lower surface:volume ratio. All these shapes I still have within me, and I dare not use any of them even to keep out the cold. I dare not adapt; in this place, I can only *hide*.

What kind of a world rejects *communion*?

It's the simplest, most irreducible insight that biomass can have. The more you can change, the more you can adapt. Adaptation is fitness, adaptation is *survival*. It's deeper than intelligence, deeper than tissue; it is *cellular*, it is axiomatic. And more, it is *pleasurable*. To take communion is to experience the sheer sensual delight of bettering the cosmos.

And yet, even trapped in these maladapted skins, this world doesn't *want* to change.

At first I thought it might simply be starving, that these icy wastes didn't provide enough energy for routine shapeshifting. Or perhaps this was some kind of laboratory: an anomalous corner of the world, pinched off and frozen into these freakish shapes as part of some arcane experiment on monomorphism in extreme environments. After the autopsy I wondered if the world had simply *forgotten* how to change: unable to touch the tissues the soul could not sculpt them, and time and stress and sheer chronic starvation had erased the memory that it ever could.

But there were too many mysteries, too many contradictions. Why these *particular* shapes, so badly suited to their environment? If the soul was cut off from the flesh, what held the flesh together?

And how could these skins be so *empty* when I moved in?

I'm used to finding intelligence everywhere, winding through every part of every offshoot. But there was nothing to grab onto in the mindless biomass of this world: just conduits, carrying orders and input. I took communion, when it wasn't offered; the skins I chose struggled and succumbed; my fibrils infiltrated the wet electricity of organic systems everywhere. I saw through eyes that weren't yet quite mine, commandeered motor nerves to move limbs still built of alien protein. I wore these skins as I've worn countless others, took the controls and left the assimilation of individual cells to follow at its own pace.

But I could only wear the body. I could find no memories to absorb, no experiences, no comprehension. Survival depended on blending in, and it was not enough to merely *look* like this world. I had to *act* like it— and for the first time in living memory I did not know how.

Even more frighteningly, I didn't have to. The skins I assimilated continued to move, *all by themselves*. They conversed and went about their appointed rounds. I could not understand it. I threaded further into limbs and viscera with each passing moment, alert for signs of the original owner. I could find no networks but mine.

Of course, it could have been much worse. I could have lost it all, been reduced to a few cells with nothing but instinct and their own plasticity to guide them. I would have grown back eventually—reattained sentience, taken communion and regenerated an intellect vast as a world—but I would have been an orphan, amnesiac, with no sense of who I was. At least I've been spared that: I emerged from the crash with my identity intact, the templates of a thousand worlds still resonant in my flesh. I've retained not just the brute desire to survive, but the conviction that survival is *meaningful*. I can still feel joy, should there be sufficient cause.

And yet, how much more there used to be.

The wisdom of so many other worlds, lost. All that remains are fuzzy abstracts, half-memories of theorems and philosophies far too vast to fit into such an impoverished network. I could assimilate all the biomass of this place, rebuild body and soul to a million times the capacity of what crashed here—but as long as I am trapped at the bottom of this well, denied communion with my greater self, I will never recover that knowledge.

I'm such a pitiful fragment of what I was. Each lost cell takes a little of my intellect with it, and I have grown so very small. Where once I thought, now I merely *react*. How much of this could have been avoided, if I had only salvaged a little more biomass from the wreckage? How many options am I not seeing because my soul simply isn't big enough to contain them?

The world spoke to itself, in the same way I do when my communications are simple enough to convey without somatic fusion. Even as *dog* I could pick up the basic signature morphemes—this offshoot was *Windows*, that one was *Bennings*, the two who'd left in their flying machine for parts unknown were *Copper* and *MacReady*—and I marveled that these bits and pieces stayed isolated one from another, held the same shapes for so long, that the labeling of individual aliquots of biomass actually served a useful purpose.

Later I hid within the bipeds themselves, and whatever else lurked in those haunted skins began to talk to me. It said that bipeds were called *guys*, or *men*, or *assholes*. It said that *MacReady* was sometimes called *Mac*. It said that this collection of structures was a *camp*.

It said that it was afraid, but maybe that was just me.

Empathy's inevitable, of course. One can't mimic the sparks and chemicals that motivate the flesh without also *feeling* them to some extent. But this was different. These intuitions flickered within me yet somehow hovered beyond reach. My skins wandered the halls and the cryptic symbols on every surface—*Laundry Sched*, *Welcome to the Clubhouse*, *This Side Up*—almost made a kind of sense. That circular artefact hanging on the wall was a *clock*; it measured the passage of time. The world's eyes flitted here and there, and I skimmed piecemeal nomenclature from its—from *his*—mind.

But I was only riding a searchlight. I saw what it illuminated but I couldn't point it in any direction of my own choosing. I could eavesdrop, but I could only eavesdrop; never interrogate.

If only one of those searchlights had paused to dwell on its own evolution, on the trajectory that had brought it to this place. How differently things might have ended, had I only *known*. But instead it rested on a whole new word:

Autopsy.

MacReady and Copper had found part of me at the Norwegian camp: a rearguard offshoot, burned in the wake of my escape. They'd brought it back—charred, twisted, frozen in mid-transformation—and did not seem to know what it was.

I was being Palmer then, and Norris, and dog. I gathered around with the other biomass and watched as Copper cut me open and pulled out my insides. I watched as he dislodged something from behind my eyes: an *organ* of some kind.

It was malformed and incomplete, but its essentials were clear enough. It looked like a great wrinkled tumor, like cellular competition gone wild—as though the very processes that defined life had somehow turned against it instead. It was obscenely vascularised; it must have consumed oxygen and nutrients far out of proportion to its mass. I could not see how anything like that could even exist, how it could have reached that size without being outcompeted by more efficient morphologies.

Nor could I imagine what it did. But then I began to look with new eyes at these offshoots, these biped shapes my own cells had so scrupulously and unthinkingly copied when they reshaped me for this world. Unused to inventory—why catalog body parts that only turn into other things at the slightest provocation?—I really *saw*, for the first time, that swollen structure atop each body. So much larger than it should be: a bony hemisphere into which a million ganglionic interfaces could fit with room to spare. Every offshoot had one. Each piece of biomass carried one of these huge twisted clots of tissue.

I realized something else, too: the eyes, the ears of my dead skin had fed into this thing before Copper pulled it free. A massive bundle of fibers ran along the skin's longitudinal axis, right up the middle of the endoskeleton, directly into the dark sticky cavity where the growth had rested. That misshapen structure had been wired into the whole skin, like some kind of somatocognitive interface but vastly more massive. It was almost as if . . .

No.

That was how it worked. That was how these empty skins moved of their own volition, why I'd found no other network to integrate. *There* it was: not distributed throughout the body but balled up into itself, dark and dense and encysted. I had found the ghost in these machines.

I felt sick.

I shared my flesh with thinking cancer.

Sometimes, even hiding is not enough.

I remember seeing myself splayed across the floor of the kennel, a chimera split along a hundred seams, taking communion with a handful of *dogs*. Crimson tendrils writhed on the floor. Half-formed iterations sprouted from my flanks, the shapes of dogs and things not seen before on this world, haphazard morphologies half-remembered by parts of a part.

I remember Childs before I was Childs, burning me alive. I remember cowering inside Palmer, terrified that those flames might turn on the rest of me, that this world had somehow learned to shoot on sight.

I remember seeing myself stagger through the snow, raw instinct, wearing Bennings. Gnarled undifferentiated clumps clung to his hands like crude parasites, more outside than in; a few surviving fragments of some previous massacre, crippled, mindless, taking what they could and breaking cover. Men swarmed about him in the night: red flares in hand, blue lights at their backs, their faces bichromatic and beautiful. I remember Bennings, awash in flames, howling like an animal beneath the sky.

I remember Norris, betrayed by his own perfectly-copied, defective heart. Palmer, dying that the rest of me might live. Windows, still human, burned preemptively.

The names don't matter. The biomass does: so much of it, lost. So much new experience, so much fresh wisdom annihilated by this world of thinking tumors.

Why even dig me up? Why carve me from the ice, carry me all that way across the wastes, bring me back to life only to attack me the moment I awoke?

If eradication was the goal, why not just kill me where I lay?

Those encysted souls. Those tumors. Hiding away in their bony caverns, folded in on themselves.

I knew they couldn't hide forever; this monstrous anatomy had only slowed communion, not stopped it. Every moment I grew a little. I could feel myself twining around Palmer's motor wiring, sniffing upstream along a million tiny currents. I could sense my infiltration of that dark thinking mass behind Blair's eyes.

Imagination, of course. It's all reflex that far down, unconscious and immune to micromanagement. And yet, a part of me wanted to stop while there was still time. I'm used to incorporating souls, not rooming with them. This, this *compartmentalization* was unprecedented. I've assimilated a thousand worlds stronger than this, but never one so strange. What would happen when I met the spark in the tumor? Who would assimilate who?

I was being three men by now. The world was growing wary, but it hadn't noticed yet. Even the tumors in the skins I'd taken didn't know how close I was. For that, I could only be grateful—that Creation has *rules*, that some things don't change no matter what shape you take. It doesn't matter whether a soul spreads throughout the skin or festers in grotesque isolation; it still runs on electricity. The memories of men still took time to gel, to pass through whatever gatekeepers filtered noise from signal—and a judicious burst of static, however indiscriminate, still cleared those caches before their contents could be stored permanently. Clear enough, at least, to let these tumors simply forget that something else moved their arms and legs on occasion.

At first I only took control when the skins closed their eyes and their searchlights flickered disconcertingly across unreal imagery, patterns that flowed senselessly into one another like hyperactive biomass unable to settle on a single shape. (*Dreams*, one searchlight told me, and a little later, *Nightmares*.) During those mysterious periods of dormancy, when the men lay inert and isolated, it was safe to come out.

Soon, though, the dreams dried up. All eyes stayed open all the time, fixed on shadows and each other. Offshoots once dispersed throughout the camp began to draw together, to give up their solitary pursuits in favor of company. At first I thought they might be finding common ground in a common fear. I even hoped that finally, they might shake off their mysterious fossilization and take communion.

But no. They'd just stopped trusting anything they couldn't see.

They were merely turning against each other.

My extremities are beginning to numb; my thoughts slow as the distal reaches of my soul succumb to the chill. The weight of the flamethrower pulls at its harness, forever tugs me just a little off-balance. I have not been Childs for very long; almost half this tissue remains unassimilated. I have an hour, maybe two, before I have to start melting my grave into the ice. By that time I need to have converted enough cells to keep this whole skin from crystallizing. I focus on antifreeze production.

It's almost peaceful out here. There's been so much to take in, so little time to process it. Hiding in these skins takes such concentration, and under all those watchful eyes I was lucky if communion lasted long enough to exchange memories: compounding my soul would have been out of the question. Now, though, there's nothing to do but prepare for oblivion. Nothing to occupy my thoughts but all these lessons left unlearned.

MacReady's blood test, for example. His *thing detector*, to expose imposters posing as men. It does not work nearly as well as the world thinks; but the fact that it works at *all* violates the most basic rules of biology. It's the center of the puzzle. It's the answer to all the mysteries. I might have already figured it out if I had been just a little larger. I might already know the world, if the world wasn't trying so hard to kill me.

MacReady's test.

Either it is impossible, or I have been wrong about everything.

They did not change shape. They did not take communion. Their fear and mutual mistrust was growing, but they would not join souls; they would only look for the enemy *outside* themselves.

So I gave them something to find.

I left false clues in the camp's rudimentary computer: simpleminded icons and animations, misleading numbers and projections seasoned with just enough truth to convince the world of their veracity. It didn't matter that the machine was far too simple to perform such calculations, or that there were no data to base them on anyway; Blair was the only biomass likely to know that, and he was already mine.

I left false leads, destroyed real ones, and then—alibi in place—I released Blair to run amok. I let him steal into the night and smash the vehicles as they slept, tugging ever-so-slightly at his reins to ensure that certain vital components were spared. I set him loose in the radio room, watched through his eyes and others as he rampaged and destroyed. I listened as he ranted about a world in danger, the need for containment, the conviction that *most of you don't know what's going on around here*—but I *damn well know that* some *of you do....*

He meant every word. I saw it in his searchlight. The best forgeries are the ones who've forgotten they aren't real.

When the necessary damage was done I let Blair fall to MacReady's counterassault. As Norris I suggested the tool shed as a holding cell. As Palmer I boarded up the windows, helped with the flimsy fortifications expected to keep me contained. I watched while the world locked me away *for your own protection, Blair*, and left me to my own devices. When no one was looking I would change and slip outside, salvage the parts I needed from all that bruised machinery. I would take them back to my burrow beneath the shed and build my escape piece by piece. I volunteered to feed the prisoner and came to myself when the world wasn't watching, laden with supplies enough to keep me going through all those necessary metamorphoses. I went through a third of the camp's food stores in three days, and—still trapped by my own preconceptions—marveled at the starvation diet that kept these offshoots chained to a single skin.

Another piece of luck: the world was too preoccupied to worry about kitchen inventory.

There is something on the wind, a whisper threading its way above the raging of the storm. I grow my ears, extend cups of near-frozen tissue from the sides of my head, turn like a living antennae in search of the best reception.

There, to my left: the abyss *glows* a little, silhouettes black swirling snow against a subtle lessening of the darkness. I hear the sounds of carnage. I hear myself. I do not know what shape I have taken, what sort of anatomy might be emitting those sounds. But I've worn enough skins on enough worlds to know pain when I hear it.

The battle is not going well. The battle is going as planned. Now it is time to turn away, to go to sleep. It is time to wait out the ages.

I lean into the wind. I move toward the light.

This is not the plan. But I think I have an answer, now: I think I may have had it even before I sent myself back into exile. It's not an easy thing to admit. Even now I don't fully understand. How long have I been out here, retelling the tale to myself, setting clues in order while my skin dies by low degrees? How long have I been circling this obvious, impossible truth?

I move towards the faint crackling of flames, the dull concussion of exploding ordnance more felt than heard. The void lightens before me: gray segues into yellow, yellow into orange. One diffuse brightness resolves into many: a lone burning wall, miraculously standing. The smoking skeleton of MacReady's shack on the hill. A cracked smoldering hemisphere reflecting pale yellow in the flickering light: Child's searchlight calls it a *radio dome*.

The whole camp is gone. There's nothing left but flames and rubble.

They can't survive without shelter. Not for long. Not in those skins.

In destroying me, they've destroyed themselves.

Things could have turned out so much differently if I'd never been Norris.

Norris was the weak node: biomass not only ill-adapted but *defective*, an offshoot with an off switch. The world knew, had known so long it never even thought about it anymore. It wasn't until Norris collapsed that *heart condition* floated to the surface of Copper's mind where I could see it. It wasn't until Copper was astride Norris's chest, trying to pound him back to life, that I knew how it would end. And by then it was too late; Norris had stopped being Norris. He had even stopped being me.

I had so many roles to play, so little choice in any of them. The part being Copper brought down the paddles on the part that had been Norris, such a faithful Norris, every cell so scrupulously assimilated, every part of that faulty valve reconstructed unto perfection. I hadn't *known*. How was I to know? These shapes within me, the worlds and morphologies I've assimilated over the aeons—I've only ever used them to adapt before, never to hide. This desperate mimicry was an improvised thing, a last resort in the face of a world that attacked anything unfamiliar. My cells read the signs and my cells conformed, mindless as prions.

So I became Norris, and Norris self-destructed.

I remember losing myself after the crash. I know how it feels to *degrade*, tissues in revolt, the desperate efforts to reassert control as static from some misfiring organ jams the signal. To be a network seceding from itself, to know that each moment I am less than I was the moment before. To become nothing. To become legion.

Being Copper, I could see it. I still don't know why the world didn't; its parts had long since turned against each other by then, every offshoot suspected every other. Surely they were alert for signs of *infection*. Surely *some* of that biomass would have noticed the subtle twitch and ripple of Norris changing below the surface, the last instinctive resort of wild tissues abandoned to their own devices.

But I was the only one who saw. Being Childs, I could only stand and watch. Being Copper, I could only make it worse; if I'd taken direct control, forced that skin to drop the paddles, I would have given myself away. And so I played my parts to the end. I slammed those resurrection paddles down as Norris's chest split open beneath them. I screamed on cue as serrated teeth from a hundred stars away snapped shut. I toppled backwards, arms bitten off above the wrist. Men swarmed, agitation bootstrapping to panic. MacReady aimed his weapon; flames leaped across the enclosure. Meat and machinery screamed in the heat.

Copper's tumor winked out beside me. The world would never have let it live anyway, not after such obvious contamination. I let our skin play dead on the floor while overhead, something that had once been me shattered and writhed and iterated through a myriad random templates, searching desperately for something fireproof.

They have destroyed themselves. They.

Such an insane word to apply to a world.

Something crawls towards me through the wreckage: a jagged oozing jigsaw of blackened meat and shattered, half-resorbed bone. Embers stick to its sides like bright searing eyes; it doesn't have strength enough to scrape them free. It contains barely half the mass of this Childs' skin; much of it, burnt to raw carbon, is already dead.

What's left of Childs, almost asleep, thinks *motherfucker*, but I am being him now. I can carry that tune myself.

The mass extends a pseudopod to me, a final act of communion. I feel my pain:

I was Blair, I was Copper, I was even a scrap of dog that survived that first fiery massacre and holed up in the walls, with no food and no strength to regenerate. Then I gorged on unassimilated flesh, consumed instead of communed; revived and replenished, I drew together as one.

And yet, not quite. I can barely remember—so much was destroyed, so much memory lost—but I think the networks recovered from my different skins stayed just a little out of synch, even reunited in the same soma. I glimpse a half-corrupted memory of dog erupting from the greater self, ravenous and traumatized and determined to retain its *individuality*. I remember rage and frustration, that this world had so corrupted me that I could barely fit together again. But it didn't matter. I was more than Blair and Copper and Dog, now. I was a giant with the shapes of worlds to choose from, more than a match for the last lone man who stood against me.

No match, though, for the dynamite in his hand.

Now I'm little more than pain and fear and charred stinking flesh. What sentience I have is awash in confusion. I am stray and disconnected thoughts, doubts and the ghosts of theories. I am realizations, too late in coming and already forgotten.

But I am also Childs, and as the wind eases at last I remember wondering *Who assimilates who?* The snow tapers off and I remember an impossible test that stripped me naked.

The tumor inside me remembers it, too. I can see it in the last rays of its fading searchlight—and finally, at long last, that beam is pointed *inwards*.

Pointed at me.

I can barely see what it illuminates: *Parasite. Monster. Disease. Thing.*

How little it knows. It knows even less than I do.

I know enough, you motherfucker. You soul-stealing, shit-eating rapist.

I don't know what that means. There is violence in those thoughts, and the forcible penetration of flesh, but underneath it all is something else I can't quite understand. I almost ask—but Childs's searchlight has finally gone out. Now there is nothing in here but me, nothing outside but fire and ice and darkness.

I am being Childs, and the storm is over.

In a world that gave meaningless names to interchangeable bits of biomass, one name truly mattered: MacReady.

MacReady was always the one in charge. The very concept still seems absurd: *in charge*. How can this world not see the folly of hierarchies? One bullet in a vital spot and the Norwegian *dies*, forever. One blow to the head and Blair is unconscious. Centralization is vulnerability—and yet the world is not content to build its biomass on such a fragile template, it forces the same model onto its metasystems as well. MacReady talks; the others obey. It is a system with a built-in kill spot.

And yet somehow, MacReady stayed *in charge*. Even after the world discovered the evidence I'd planted; even after it decided that MacReady was *one of those things*, locked him out to die in the storm, attacked him with fire and axes when he fought his way back inside. Somehow MacReady always had the gun, always had the flamethrower, always had the dynamite and the willingness to take out the whole damn camp if need be. Clarke was the last to try and stop him; MacReady shot him through the tumor.

Kill spot.

But when Norris split into pieces, each scuttling instinctively for its own life, MacReady was the one to put them back together.

I was so sure of myself when he talked about his *test*. He tied up all the biomass—tied *me* up, more times than he knew—and I almost felt a kind of pity as he spoke. He forced Windows to cut us all, to take a little blood from each. He heated the tip of a metal wire until it glowed and he spoke of pieces small enough to give themselves away, pieces that embodied instinct but no intelligence, no self-control. MacReady had watched Norris in dissolution, and he had decided: men's blood would not react to the application of heat. Mine would break ranks when provoked.

Of course he thought that. These offshoots had forgotten that *they* could change.

I wondered how the world would react when every piece of biomass in the room was revealed as a shapeshifter, when MacReady's small experiment ripped the façade from the greater one and forced these twisted fragments to confront the truth. Would the world awaken from its long amnesia, finally remember that it lived and breathed and changed like everything else? Or was it too far gone—would MacReady simply burn each protesting offshoot in turn as its blood turned traitor?

I couldn't believe it when MacReady plunged the hot wire into Windows's blood and *nothing happened*. Some kind of trick, I thought. And then *MacReady's* blood passed the test, and Clarke's.

Copper's didn't. The needle went in and Copper's blood *shivered* just a little in its dish. I barely saw it myself; the men didn't react at all. If they even noticed, they must have attributed it to the trembling of MacReady's own hand. They thought the test was a crock of shit anyway. Being Childs, I even said as much.

Because it was too astonishing, too terrifying, to admit that it wasn't.

Being Childs, I knew there was hope. Blood is not soul: I may control the motor systems but assimilation takes time. If Copper's blood was raw enough to pass muster than it would be hours before I had anything to fear from this test; I'd been Childs for even less time.

But I was also Palmer, I'd been Palmer for days. Every last cell of that biomass had been assimilated; there was nothing of the original left.

When Palmer's blood screamed and leapt away from MacReady's needle, there was nothing I could do but blend in.

I have been wrong about everything.

Starvation. Experiment. Illness. All my speculation, all the theories I invoked to explain this place—top-down constraint, all of it. Underneath, I always knew the ability to change—to *assimilate*—had to remain the universal constant. No world evolves if its cells don't evolve; no cell evolves if it can't change. It's the nature of life everywhere.

Everywhere but here.

This world did not forget how to change. It was not manipulated into rejecting change. These were not the stunted offshoots of any greater self, twisted to the needs of some experiment; they were not conserving energy, waiting out some temporary shortage.

This is the option my shriveled soul could not encompass until now: out of all the worlds of my experience, this is the only one whose biomass *can't* change. It *never could*.

It's the only way MacReady's test makes any sense.

I say goodbye to Blair, to Copper, to myself. I reset my morphology to its local defaults. I am Childs, come back from the storm to finally make the pieces fit. Something moves up ahead: a dark blot shuffling against the flames, some weary animal looking for a place to bed down. It looks up as I approach.

MacReady.

We eye each other, and keep our distance. Colonies of cells shift uneasily inside me. I can feel my tissues redefining themselves.

"You the only one that made it?"

"Not the only one . . ."

I have the flamethrower. I have the upper hand. MacReady doesn't seem to care.

But he does care. He *must*. Because here, tissues and organs are not temporary battlefield alliances; they are *permanent*, predestined. Macrostructures do not emerge when the benefits of cooperation exceed its costs, or dissolve when that balance shifts the other way; here, each cell has but one immutable function. There's no plasticity, no way to adapt; every structure is frozen in place. This is not a single great world, but many small ones. Not parts of a greater thing; these are *things*. They are *plural*.

And that means—I think—that they *stop*. They just, just *wear out* over time.

"Where *were* you, Childs?"

I remember words in dead searchlights: "Thought I saw Blair. Went out after him. Got lost in the storm."

I've worn these bodies, felt them from the inside. Copper's sore joints. Blair's curved spine. Norris and his bad heart. They are not built to last. No somatic evolution to shape them, no communion to restore the biomass and stave off entropy. They should not even exist; existing, they should not survive.

They try, though. How they try. Every thing here is walking dead and yet it all fights so hard to keep going just a little longer. Each skin fights as desperately as I might, if one was all I could ever have.

MacReady tries.

"If you're worried about me—" I begin.

MacReady shakes his head, manages a weary smile. "If we've got any surprises for each other, I don't think we're in much shape to do anything about it . . ."

But we are. I am.

A whole planet of worlds, and not one of them—not *one*—has a soul. They wander through their lives separate and alone, unable even to communicate except through grunts and tokens: as if the essence of a sunset or a supernova could ever be contained in some string of phonemes, a few linear scratches of black on white. They've never known communion, can aspire to nothing but dissolution. The paradox of their biology is astonishing, yes; but the scale of their loneliness, the futility of these lives, overwhelms me.

I was so blind, so quick to blame. But the violence I've suffered at the hands of these things reflects no great evil. They're simply so used to pain, so blinded by disability, that they literally can't conceive of any other existence. When every nerve is whipped raw, you lash out at even the lightest touch.

"What should we do?" I wonder. I cannot escape into the future, not knowing what I know now. How could I leave them like this?

"Why don't we just—wait here awhile," MacReady suggests. "See what happens."

I can do so much more than that.

It won't be easy. They won't understand. Tortured, incomplete, they're not *able* to understand. Offered the greater whole, they see the loss of the lesser. Offered communion, they see only extinction. I must be careful. I must use this newfound ability to hide. Other things will come here eventually, and it doesn't matter whether they find the living or the dead; what matters is that they find something like themselves, to take back home. So I will keep up appearances. I will work behind the scenes. I will save them from the *inside*, or their unimaginable loneliness will never end.

These poor savage things will never embrace salvation.

I will have to rape it into them.

MUO-KA'S CHILD

INDRAPRAMIT DAS

Ziara watched her parent, muo-ka, curl up and die, like an insect might on Earth.

muo-ka was a giant of a thing, no insect. Ziara was the one who'd always felt like an insect around it. Its curled body pushed against the death shroud it had excreted in its dying hours, the membrane stretched taut against rigid limbs. She touched the shroud. It felt smooth but sticky. Her fingertips stuck lightly to it, leaving prints. It felt different from her clothes. muo-ka had excreted the ones she wore a month ago. They smelled softer than the death shroud, flowers from Earth on a distant, cosmic breeze. She raised her fingers to her face, touching them with her tongue. So salty and pungent it burned. She gagged instantly, coughing to stop herself retching.

"muo-ka" she said, throat thick. "You are my life." Ziara thought about this. "You *are* my life, here." She meant these words, but felt a hollow, aching relief that muo-ka's presence was gone.

She closed her eyes to remember the blue rind of Earth, furred with clouds, receding behind the glass as she drifted into amniotic sleep. Orphan. Volunteer. Voyager. A mere twenty years on that planet. When she had opened her eyes after the primordial dream of that year of folding space, the first thing she saw and felt was muo-ka pulling her from the coma, breaking open the steaming pod with predatory lurches. Its threaded knot of limbs rippling like a shredded banner in the sweltering light, stuck on the leviathan swell of its dark shape. She had opened her mouth, spraying vomit into the air, lazy spurts that moved differently than on Earth. muo-ka had pulled her out of the pod and towards it, its limbs sometimes whiplashes, sometimes articulated arms, flickering between stiffness and liquid softness so quickly it hurt her eyes to see that tangled embrace. Stray barbed limbs tugged and snapped at the rubbery coil of her umbilicus, ripping it off so pale shreds clung to the valve above her navel.

muo-ka had grasped at Ziara's strange, small, alien body, making her float in the singing air as she tried and tried to scream.

Ziara watched the shroud settle over muo-ka. Already the corpse had shrunk considerably as air and water left it. Its body whistled softly. A quiet song for coming evening. With a bone knife, she cut small slits into the shroud to let the gas escape more freely, even though the membrane was porous. The little rents fluttered. A breeze ruffled the flat waters of the eya-rith basin into undulations that lapped across muo-ka's islet, washing Ziara's bare feet and wetting the weedy edges of the stone deathbed. The water sloshed in the ruined shell of the pod at the edge of the islet, its sleek surfaces cracked and scabbed with mossy growth. Inside was a small surveying and recording kit. She had discovered the kit, sprung free of its wall compartment, shattered and drowned from the rough landing. Even if it had worked, it seemed a useless thing to her now.

When the pod had once threatened to float away, Ziara had clung to it, trying to pull it back with her tiny human arms, heaving with frantic effort. muo-ka had lunged, sealed the wreck to the islet with secretions. Now it stood in a grassy thatch of fungal filaments, a relic from another planet.

muo-ka had no spoken words. Yet, its islet felt quieter than it had ever been. Ziara had learned its name, and some of its words, by becoming its mouth, speaking aloud the language that hummed in a part of its body that she had to touch. It had been shockingly easy to do this. What secret part of her had muo-ka unlocked, or taught to wake? muo-ka's skin had always felt febrile when she touched it, and when it spoke through her she felt hot as well.

The first thing it had said through her mouth was "muo-ka," and she had known that was its name. "Ziara," she had said, still touching it. "Jih-ara," it had said in her mouth, exuding a humid heat, a taste of blood and berries in her head. Ziara had disengaged her palm with a smack, making it shiver violently. Clammy with panic, she had walked away. It had felt too strange, too much like becoming a part of muo-ka, becoming an organ of its own.

Ziara rarely spoke to muo-ka in the time that followed. When she got an urge to communicate, she'd often stifle it. And she did get the urge, again and again. In those moments she'd hide in the broken pod on the islet's shore. She'd curl into its clammy, broken womb and think of the grassy earth of the hostel playground, of playing catch with her friends until the trees darkened, of being reprimanded by the wardens, and smoking cigarettes by the barred moonlight of the cavernous bathrooms, stifling coughs into silent giggles when patrols came by. Daydreams of their passing footsteps would become apocalyptic with the siren wail of muo-ka's cries. It never could smell or detect her in the strange machinery of the wrecked pod. She assumed the screams were ones of alarm.

"You've fed me," Ziara said to the corpse. "And clothed me. And taught me to leap across the sky." Those stiffened limbs that its shroud now clung to had snatched her from the air if she leaped too high, almost twisting her shoulders out of their sockets once. She'd landed on the mud of the islet safe, alive. In the shadow of muo-ka she'd whispered "Fuck you. Just, fuck you. Fuck you, muo-ka."

She had tasted the sourness of boiled fruit at the back of her throat. muo-ka covered the sky above her, and offered one of its orifices. Gushing with the steam of regurgitate cooked inside it. She'd reached inside and took the scorching gumbo in her hands. The protein from dredged sea and air animals tasted like spongy fish. It was spiced with what might have been fear.

Ziara didn't have an exact idea of how long it had been since muo-ka had pulled her into the air of this world from the pod. She had marked weeks, months and years on a rock slick with colonies of luminescent bacteria. Left a calendar of glowing fingerprints that she had smeared clean and then restarted at the end of every twelve months, marking the passing years with long lines at the top. She had three lines now. They glowed strongest at dusk. If they were right, they told her she was twenty-four years old now. muo-ka had been her parent for three years.

Not that the number mattered. Days and years were shorter here. muo-ka had always lingered by that rocky calendar of fingerprints, hovering over it in quiet observation when it thought she wasn't looking, when she was off swimming in the shallows. Watching from afar in the water, she could always taste an ethanol bitterness at the back of her throat and sinuses. A taste she came to associate with sadness, or whatever muo-ka would call sadness.

muo-ka had never washed the calendar clean. It had never touched it. It had only ever looked at that glimmering imprint of time mapped according to a distant world invisible in the night sky. The dancing fingertips of its incredible child.

The evening began to cast shadows across the shallow seas. Across the horizon, uong-i was setting into mountains taller than Everest and Olympus Mons. uong-i at this time was the blue of a gas flame on a stove, though hot and bright. Sometimes the atmosphere would tint it green at dawn and dusk, and during the day it was the white of daylit snow. But now it was blue.

Ziara touched muo-ka's shroud again. It was drier, slightly more tough as it wrapped around the contours of the moaning, rattling body. She lit the flares by scratching them on the mossed rocks. The two stalks arced hot across the water, sparks dancing across her skin. She plunged them into the soil by the deathbed.

Her eyes ached with the new light. Again, she remembered her first moment with muo-ka, remembered her panic at the thing ensnaring her in blinding daylight. The savagery with which it severed her umbilicus, the painful spasming of its limbs around her. She remembered these things, and knew muo-ka had been in as much panic as she had. She had long since realized this, even if she hadn't let it sink in.

From her first moment here, muo-ka remained a giant, terrifying thing. The days of recovery in the chrysalid blanket it wove around her. She'd been trapped while it smothered her with boiling food from its belly, trying and failing to be gentle. Fevers raging from nanite vaccines recalibrating her system, to digest what her parent was feeding her and breathe the different air, the new soup of microbes. "Stop," she would tell muo-ka. "Please stop. I can't eat your food. I'm dying." But it would only clutch her cocooned body and tilt her so she could vomit, the ends of its limbs sharp against her back. It would continue feeding her, keep letting her shit and piss and vomit in that cocoon, which only digested it all, preventing any infections.

Sure enough, the fevers faded away and one day the cocoon came off in gummy strips. Ziara could move again, could move like she had on Earth. At first it was an aching crawl, leaving troughs in the rich mud of the islet. But she'd balled that mud in her fists and growled, standing on shaking legs. She watched her human shadow unfurl long across the silty islet, right under the eclipsing shape of muo-ka above her, its limbs whipping around her, supporting her until she shrugged them off.

Ziara had laughed and laughed, to be able to stand again, until phlegm had gathered in her throat and she had to spit in joy. So she walked, walked over this human stain she had left on the ground, walked over the wet warmth of muo-ka's land. She walked until she could run. She was so euphoric that she could only dance and leap across the basin, flexing her muscles, testing her augmented metal bones in this low gravity. Sick with adrenalin, she soared through the air, watching the horizon expand and expand, bounding from rock to rock, whipping past exoskeletal flying creatures that flashed in the sun. muo-ka watched, its leviathan darkness suddenly iridescent. Then Ziara stood in one place panting, and she screamed, emptied her lungs of that year of deep sleep through a pierced universe. She screamed goodbye to the planet of her first birth. As this unknown sound swept across the basin, muo-ka's limbs glittered with barbs that it flung into itself.

Ziara nodded at this memory. "muo-ka. Leaping? You taught me to walk," she said with a smile.

She had avoided muo-ka's oppressive presence by hiding in the pod. She would shit and piss, too, under the shade of the tilted wreck, in its rain of re-leaked tidal water. When she didn't want the smallness of the pod, she slipped into the basin's seas, walked across the landbridges and glittering sandbars to swirling landscapes of rock and mud fronded with life-colonies that clung like oversized froth. But always her parent would be looming on the horizon, its hovering shape bobbing over the water, limbs alternating in a flicker over the surface as it dredged for food. Sometimes it would soar over her in the evening, its blinking night eyes flickering lights, stars or aircraft from the striated skies of Earthly dusks. With those guiding lights it would lead her back to the islet. Her throat would throb in anger and frustration, at the miles of watery, rocky, mountainous horizon she couldn't escape, but she'd know that straying far would likely mean she'd be killed by something on land or sea that was deadlier than her.

It took her a while to have her first period on the planet, because of the nanite vaccine calibrations and the shock of acclimatisation. All things considered, it hadn't been her worst. But she had recognized the leaden pain of cramps immediately, swallowed the salty spit of nausea and gone to the pod again. She'd squatted under it and bled into the unearthly sea.

Looking at that, she'd wondered what she was doing. Whether she was seeding something, whether she was changing the ecosystem. She'd felt like an irresponsible teenager. But looking at those crimson blossoms in the waves, she'd also felt a sudden, overwhelming longing. She'd become breathless at the thought that there was nobody else in the world. Not a single human beyond that horizon of seas and mountains and mudflats. Only the unbelievably remote promise that the mission would continue if the unmanned ship that had ejected her pod managed to return to Earth, with the news that the visitation had been successful. Another human might be sent, years later, maybe two if they could manage, hurtling down somewhere on the world with no means of communicating with her. Or a robot probe sent to scour the planet until it found and recorded her impact, just like the first probes that had seeded messages and artifacts to indicate Ziara's arrival.

But at that moment, she was as alone as any human could be. It was conceivable that she might never see a human again. Her eyelids had swollen with tears, and she'd watched her blood fall into the sea. She hadn't been able to see muo-ka from under the pod then. But she'd heard it secreting something, with loud rattling coughs. She'd sat and waited until her legs ached, until the rising tide lapped at her thighs.

Later she'd found fresh, coarse membranes strewn across the ground next to her rock calendar. They were waterproof.

New clothes.

Ziara had wrapped the membranes around herself like a saree, not knowing how else to wear them. She became light-headed when she caught the scent of flowers in them. It was a shocking sensation, a smell she'd never encountered on this world before.

muo-ka had been absent that whole day. When it returned, lights flickering in sunset, she held out her hand. It lurched gracelessly through the air as if caught in turbulence, before hovering down to her, curtaining her in softened limbs. Her palm fell against the familiar spot behind the limbs. She flinched at the heat.

"Thank you," Ziara said.

It said nothing through her, only unfurling, drowning the back of her throat in bloody sweetness.

muo-ka had been dying for months. It had told Ziara, in its sparse way, a cloying thick taste of both sweet berried blood and bitterness in her head.

"Sick?" she had asked.

"Sh-ikh," it had said in her mouth. "Ii-sey-na," it said, and when the word formed in her throat she knew it meant "death."

"Sorry," she had whispered.

"Euh-i," it had said. No. Not sorry.

Ziara had let it talk for longer than ever before. For hours, her hand flushed red from its heat. It had told her several words, sentences, that made up an idea of what to do with its dead body. Then it went on, forming concepts, ideas, lengthier than ever before. muo-ka told her many things.

Ziara thought about her relief, now, looking at dead muo-ka. It disturbed her, but it was the truth. There was a clarity to her world now. To this world. She would move along the mudflats and sandbridges and mountains. She would make blades of her parent's bones, as it had told her, and explore the world. She would finally go beyond that horizon, which now flared and dimmed with the setting of uong-i.

She was an alien, and the world would kill her, sooner rather than later. Even if by some miracle the second human arrived in the coming months, he'd be too weak to help. If one of the leviathans adopted him— and it would be a man that fell this time—it might even violently keep Ziara away from him as its own child, and she had no chance of fighting that. She knew nothing about the dynamics of this adoption. She was the first, after all. They had come into this without much knowledge, except their curiosity and gentle handling of the initial probes.

Until and unless Earth sent an actual colonization team that could touch down a vessel with equipment and tools on the surface, humans wouldn't be able to survive here without the help of muo-ka's kind. As muo-ka's child, she wondered if she might be able to befriend one of them, or whether she'd be killed in an instant.

Ziara shook her head. It was no point overthinking. She would walk this world, and see what came. She had chosen this, after all. She hadn't chosen her parent, but there it was, in front of her, dead as she was alive. And she was alive because of it.

The blue dome of the gas giant appeared over the horizon, filling the seas with reflections. In the sparking light of the flares, Ziara waited. The shroud had fossilized into a flexible papyrus, with an organic pattern that looked like writing, symbols. The shrunken behemoth finally vented its innards as the stars and far moons appeared in the night sky, behind streaks of radiant aurora. Ziara clenched her jaw and began to scoop the entrails up to give to the sea, as was dignified. For a moment, she wondered what the deaths of these solitary creatures were normally like. She had seen others on the horizons, but always so far they seemed mirages. They lived their lives alone on this world, severed from each other. It had to be the child that conducted the death rites, once it was ready to move on. Perhaps they induced death in themselves once their child was mature enough.

She stopped, recoiling from the mess.

In the reeking slop of its guts, she saw muo-ka replicated. A small muo-ka. But not muo-ka. A nameless one, budded in its leviathan body. It was dead. The child's limbs were tangled in the oily foam of its parent's death. The body was crushed. Her hands slid over its cold, broken form.

muo-ka had budded a child. A child that would have done muo-ka's death rites once it had matured, ready to go on its own.

"Oh," she said, fingers squelching in the translucent mud seeping out of muo-ka's child. "Oh, no. My muo-ka. My dear muo-ka," she whispered, to both corpses.

muo-ka had budded a child, and finding a mature child already ready to venture out into the world, it had crushed the one growing inside it. Only ziara was muo-ka's child.

"You brought me to life," ziara said, leaning in her parent's guts, holding her dead sibling, wrapped in clothes her parent had made. Her face crumpled as she buried it in the remains of muo-ka's life, her body shaking.

ziara left her sibling in the sea with muo-ka's guts. Using the bone-knife, she cut away the death shroud carefully and wore it around her shoulders. One day, ziara swore to herself, she would translate the symbols it had excreted on it. Her parent's death letter. She sliced off a part of the deflated hide, scrubbed it in the sea, and wore it as a cowl to keep her head warm during nights. The flares had smoked out. She looked at muo-ka curled dead. It had told her the creatures of the air would come and consume it, slowly, as it should be. She felt bad leaving it there on that stony deathbed, but that was what it had told her to do. She wiped her eyes and face. A bone knife and a whole world she didn't belong in, except right here on this islet.

A fiery line streaked across the sky. A human vessel. Or a shooting star. ziara gazed at its afterimage for a moment, and walked off the islet and across the shallows and mudflats of the basin. She had named that basin once, or muo-ka had, with her mouth.

eya-rith. Earth, so she would not be homesick.

SIX

LEAH BOBET

Six and Joe bunk together nights in the smallest north-side billet on the twentieth floor. "Take care of your brother," Mama said when she gave them the key to the rooms. They shut the door behind them on their brand new domain: polished parquet floors and a fresh-netted balcony, a mattress in the corner and walls white as white, ready to be decorated with scribbles or artwork or sun, moon, and stars. And Joe pulled a face.

"She meant it to me," he said, with a flip of his curly girl's hair, and strutted into the tiled bathroom to wash.

That's not when Six started hating him, but it's when he knew it to the bone.

Six's name is really Charlie, but he's the devil's boy right through, and they've been calling him by the devil's number since he was old enough to walk. Sixth son of a seventh son: "You're bad news," the brothers' wives tell him afternoons between rows of peas trained up to the ceiling on the seventeenth floor. A couple of them ruffle his hair after they say it, fix him with a crooked, between-you-and-me smile. A couple of 'em don't.

Nobody ever tells Joe he's bad news.

Six locked him out twice when he pulled faces behind Six's back, and he wailed in the halls 'til Mama gave him his own key at seven, and *no* Higgins ever got their own key at seven. Six hid Joe's stuffy toy next and Mama strapped him for the first time ever over that, and now Six is Bad News. Six won't punch Joe in the nose for that insult 'cause Joe's still the baby, and it's his job to take care of the baby no matter what Joe thinks Mama said to who.

But Joe gets away with murder, gets the steals of pastry and half-days off that Six never got even before he was Bad News. Joe's seventh, Sunday-born seventh, and he's had a destiny since he was yea high.

It drives Six clean nuts.

"I'll die," Six whispers, late at night, curled up in his bedroll on the edge of the fat mattress that the littlest Higgins boys share. "I'll throw myself off the tall pasture and then you won't be seventh no more."

This used to freeze Joe mid-breath. He's nine years old now and got himself wise to it. "You're fulla shit," he says proudly—nobody ever boxed his ears none for saying *shit* like a street-picker's boy—and puts a pillow over his ear.

"I will," Six breathes. Imagines leaping, the tug of wind, falling, falling. "I will and you'll go to the devil."

Of course, Joe squeals in the morning.

Six gets hauled into Father's office after breakfast with last year's blackberry jam still on his mouth. "What're you telling your brother?" Father says, back to his desk and leaning heavy in his big black leather-backed chair. There are papers scattered on his desk, Market language that Six can't yet read. Interrupting Father's work used to be worth a spanking too, when more of the brothers and sisters were young. Father is a busy man. Except when it comes to Joe.

"Nothin'," Six mutters, knowing there's no good answer to give.

Father clucks his tongue, and Six bounces back and forth from foot to foot, rearing, raring to go. The air in Father's office smells dry and sweet like paper. All the other air in the clan building smells like dirt and green.

"Saturday's child has far to go," Six's father sighs under his fat moustache, and Six hates him. Father is the agribaron of the whole central district. Everyone in central knows him; he has three whole cars on the Moving Market staffed by Six and Joe's big sisters, and on Sunday market the papermen and water-sellers and the three rich owners of Hydro tip their hats at his clan through the windows.

Six isn't allowed to work the Market cars. Six makes trouble. The last time, he threw fresh tomatoes at the tailor's little boy, and Mama went white with rage and sentenced him to garden work until he knew the value of good food.

So now Six works in the gardens, underfoot between his big sister Lucinda and stupid little Joe, who's small enough and spoiled to only do half-chores in the kitchen and be a pain in the ass the rest of the day.

SIX

All the Higgins children know their sums and their letters, but Joe's gonna go to the alchemists when he's ten. Seventh son of a seventh son's strong magic by them, so he doesn't do full-chores and hasn't learned the garden. There's no use in it if you're going away.

Six weeds tomato beds all afternoon in whispery silent disgrace, stared at crinkle-eyed by sisters and brothers and their wives, but he doesn't throw them at no one. He goes up to the tall pasture, spread over the soaring rooftop, and feeds the ducks that lay in the pond that used to be a tiled swimming pool. And Joe follows him everywhere, kicking and pinching and chattering so loud the mama ducks flutter their wings and stick their necks out in case Joe's starting something with their brats.

Sunshine comes through the windows around the pond, through the thick glass door that goes out to the pasture and the wall that keeps the goats and sheep from the thirty-floor drop below. Six goes to the rail and looks down, way down: the cracked pavement streets and rubbled-out buildings stretch all the way to the lakeshore, empty of people, of ships. He turns around, fingers tight on the rail, tries to glance casual over the backs of the Uncles' prize flock of sheep.

Joe watches him. He don't even flinch.

It's halfway down to dinnertime before Six finally loses Joe, trailing him into the kitchens Mama keeps on floor twenty-six and making a run for it when Joe's eyes stray to the fat raisin cake for dessert time. He runs pounding down the stairs down to floor number six, still uncleared, full of pigeon shit where the screen doors came open once upon a time.

When Father and his brothers claimed the clan building for their own they started cleaning from the top: the work hasn't gone down past nine these days, not with all hands busy with the milking and shearing and growing and weeding and tending to the biggest clan farm in all of central district—and with the cousins clearing their own buildings, taking up their trades and moving out. The twenty-second floor was once Uncle Elmer's yarnshop. The twenty-first, Uncle Ignatz's dairy. The nineteenth was Uncle Eddie's garden, but Uncle Eddie grew devil's weed and the rest of them kicked him out.

Uncle Eddie was a sixth son. He smoked little brown cigarettes that smelled like cinnamon toast and talked with his hands open like he was bringing fire into the universe. Six was too young to remember much more when they threw out Uncle Eddie and burned his crop on the wasteheap, but Mama called Uncle Eddie a bad seed. Bad seeds don't grow when you put them in the dirt, but Six doesn't know why that meant burning. Bad seeds don't hurt anyone else.

They cleaned out Uncle Eddie's garden when they booted him out, but Six snagged a lamp and hid it real good from Father. Over the years he's got himself a bunch of Uncle Elmer's spare string, old herb stakes, cracked pots, odds and ends and unwanted things too busted to recycle. It all gets smuggled down to the sixth floor, through the peeling walls and dust-stink carpets, where Six has set up his workshop.

The workshop's behind a broken-locked door, or never locked by whoever lived there once when the world fell one night between evening and dawn. Six cleared it all by himself, broken machines and moldering paper snuck out to the waste on odd, switched-up days. The water's dirty here, but the water runs. It keeps Six's little garden.

Six plants the flawed seeds. He plants the bad seeds, the ones that don't grow when you lay 'em down, or grow crooked, or bear limp and yearning fruit. He sneaks down and waters them every other day, shoos flies away from the opening leaves and nibbles the produce at night when the whole clan's down asleep.

"I'll take care of you," he tells the bum seeds. They make spindly, delicate, blight-prone plants. Half of them die before they can strengthen out. Six has to tie them to popsicle sticks with Uncle Elmer's old grey string, and they lean like addled sheep against the snap-end, dirty wood.

Six don't think they're beautiful. He knows the difference between strong and busted, good and no-good.

He and his plants, they stick together. They're bad news.

The alchemists run their long black train only at full midnight. Market girls tell stories about it, rushing through the platforms like a ghost of what the city used to be, rustling the flyers and wrappers and dust into a hiss against black book-magic.

People talk 'bout the alchemists only in whispers. They bring the good weather. They bring the out-of-district news and keep books, mounds of books written in faded-out scripts that no-one can read since the world fell two generations past. Nobody ever sees their faces, knows their names.

They give out magic, and they take sons.

They take sons to their Destinies.

Father throws a feast for Joe's tenth birthday. He gets paper from the papermen and the sisters take a whole day off to pen the invitations, and come the afternoon of Joe's nativity the whole clan gathers in, cousins and uncles and aunts and brothers, and holds a festival day in the downstairs meeting-hall.

Six helps set the buffet table. The sisters and brothers'-wives boss him around, dump basket or plate in his arms to ferry one to the other, every single one of them sharp-voiced and mad. None of the brothers'-wives ruffle his hair today. Everyone's edgy. Everyone's bad.

The clan puts on its best Sunday clothes and Father holds up his glass, handed down from before the world fell and full of out-district oaked white wine.

"To our son," Father says, and the whole clan roars.

To our son!

Six slides out of his chair between the stamping and cheering and weeping. He boots it around the cousins and the table with the soup tureen down the rattletrap metal-gray stairs to the sixth floor.

His workshop's quiet. Six floors above, he can't hear the cheering and congratulations and condolences, the aunts touching shoulders and saying how brave one is to give up a loved little brother for the good of the district, the world. "They didn't have a party for you," Six tells the empty air, the bent-stemmed plants and his green and growing bastard-born potatoes.

The absence of Uncle Eddie says no, they did not.

The air ducts whisper and clank, and go silent.

Someone's watching.

Six feels the gaze like spider legs on his neck, somewhere behind him where he can't see, in the dark. But there's no-one on the balcony, no one in the closets, no one in the bedroom of the billet he's made his own. He peeks careful careful out the never-locked broken-locked door, but nobody's picking their way through the sixth floor, through the piles of debris that only little kids can get around.

"Uncle Eddie?" Six whispers, skin prickling, belly aching, but there ain't nobody there but the ghosts.

He hides from the dead men. From the dead Uncles haunting through the uncleared halls and the live ones drinking up Father's wine and laughing up their sleeves at his first, his one misfortune, this demand of a seventh son by the alchemists in their black train. He hides upstairs in the clan quarters, in the billet he'll share for one more night with goddamn Joe the special kid, Joe who'll be gone from the sheep-fold and the dirt.

When the party breaks up goddamn special blond-curls smartmouth Joe comes up full of sweet cream and holiday raisin cake. Six stares up at him with his empty mad eyes.

"I'll jump," Six whispers, holding his pillow against the length of his body. His tummy feels hot and terrible, like the fall of the whole big world. "I'll die, and they won't want you anymore, and they'll send you back tomorrow night and that'll show you."

"*So do it*," Joe screams clean as torchlight, and leaps.

Joe punches like a girl. Six's never been punched by a girl, but Joe sure's hell don't punch like a boy, and half the hits don't even hurt. Six just holds him off, catching his fists with his own hands or the soft bits along his belly, until Joe lands him one right in the nose and the night goes bright with sparkles.

"God*damn!*" Six roars and throws Joe off him, throws him clear across the mattress and into the wad of baby blanket that he sleeps with every night. He rears back to go after him, to beat the sense right good into his special stupid skull, and his breath comes hot and bitter, liquidy. Wrong.

Six wipes his nose. There's blood stinking up his mouth and something else: hot and wet and bitter.

It's crying. Not his. The baby's crying.

Six feels the red from his face to his elbows, hot right down to his toes. "Hey," he says, then softer: "Hey. Cut it out."

But Joe doesn't cut it out, he just hugs himself down in his padded corner and cries without making one sound, cries like the sisters getting ready to throw another nephew, in the worst part where Six gets sent out for water so he can't hear them stop pushing and make a sound that's all the lost hope in the world.

Six scrubs at the blood on his right hand with the sheet and it don't come off.

He goes running down the hall for Mama.

There's fighting behind the door where Mama and Father make their billet. They always fight in low polite voices, more polite than anyone ever speaks in the clan farm where usually it's yelling across whole rooms and floors. Six presses his ear to the old brass mailslot in the brown wood door, heart running up against the inside of his chest like it might run right out. *Please be done with it*, he thinks, the first time he's thought please to his parents since Joe got himself a key at seven years old. Maybe when they're done with it he can knock, pretend he don't know nothing about it. Get one of them to make that soundless crying stop.

But "They never come back," Mama's saying, far and near and far and near. Six pushes up the mailslot, slow and careful hands, and she's rocking on the long black couch that Father bought her for a bearing-gift after she had Marabel. Her Sunday dress is all wrinkled. Her face is puffed-up crying.

"They'll raise him up right," Father rumbles. He's standing behind her, both hands on her shoulders, resting heavier than they should to hold her back straight. "There's good education there. Book-smarts. He'll learn things to help us all build back up."

"How d'you know that's what they do?" Mama asks, her voice going high and thin as the fingers she's got clenched in her lap. "Maybe they kill them. Maybe they use them. *Nobody comes back.*"

The blood smears down Six's lip and drips onto his chin. He has never heard his Mama scared, not in his life.

"Talk sense," says Father, the agribaron of the central district. The most respected man from the north stations to the lakeside where the sugar factory churns. "They're learned. And they're the only men in this district or the next who seem to care about—about *why*, about more than eating and shitting and dying."

"Nobody comes back," Mama repeats, and shakes off Father's hands, paces back and forth across their soft-carpeted floor. "I've tried to let the boy have fun. I've tried to make his life here good—"

"It's done."

"He's only a baby—"

"Martha—"

"I wish you'd never let them in," Mama says, and slaps Father's face so hard the silence echoes for a three-count after. And soft, polite and very very soft: "I wish I'd not given you enough children that you can spend them so very cheap."

Father doesn't move. He stands still as a pigeon scarecrow, hands straight at his sides and not one single feeling on his face.

Six backs up. He shuffles back on the carpet, eyes big as the bright blue sky.

The mailslot clangs, and the silence spreads out like a strapping.

Six runs.

He scrambles up and runs hard down the hallway, back to the billet and inside and locks the door fast behind him. "Pretend you're sleeping," he pants to Joe, and Joe, red-faced and still dripping baby snot, doesn't say one word against him.

They lie together silent, eyes pressed shut and gulping down their breathing for five minutes, ten, until there's no steps down the hallway and there isn't gonna be. Six sits up, lets himself cough. He's tacky with sweat.

"Is it safe?" Joe asks, curled up in the blankets, one eye open as if the other can keep the nightmares out.

"Yeah," Six whispers, pats his little fist. Taking care of the baby. "C'mon. I'll show you a special thing."

The sixth floor is scary at night. Lucinda's new beau hasn't drawn down the power to the uncleared floors, and the emergency lights are long burned out, dead as dead for twenty-five years.

Six's workshop runs on filched batteries, a beat-up old charger he hides under the laundry pile in their billet on the twentieth floor. He hits one of the old slap-lights and it clicks into glowing, casts shadows across the dusty floor. There's no feeling like ghosts. Joe holds his hand tight, and it keeps the ghosts away.

"You got a garden," he says, just as breathless in wonder as he was in fear, and Six feels something he hasn't in a long time, not since Father let them all know about Joe and his destiny. He feels things going right.

"Yeah. It's a secret," he says, and brushes a curled-up leaf with his free right hand.

"What'd you make?" Joe whispers, hugging himself in outlines, in the dark.

"Mint plant," Six says, and his head comes up a little, his eyes go bright with pride. "Strawberries. The little potatoes Mama didn't want last year. Spinach."

"The old seeds."

"I saved them."

Six and Joe sit on Six's old emergency blanket and share out the crop on a beat-up kitchen plate. Their fingers poke each other on the way to strawberries and light-washed spinach. It washes the taste of blood away.

"Thanks," Joe says sleepy when the harvest's all done. "S'good."

Joe's not a little kid anymore. He's not half as light as a chicken or a goat. But Six carries him up fourteen floors of stairway to their billet, mouth smeared with strawberries, fast asleep.

The alchemists' train is the black train that comes down the tracks come midnight. Six has never seen it up close: by midnight every good kid and even the bad ones have locked the doors of their billets and are fast asleep, full knowing they've got a six A.M. wakeup.

The turnstile men don't guard the station gates when the alchemists' train comes in. They unlatch the metal bars that're for strollers and wheelchairs and market-buggies, and everyone walks free to the platform, free out again until the sunlight spills sickly down the stairs and announces it Market time.

The boy who comes through the gate, hooded, face covered 'gainst public eyes is too big for a ten-year-old if you look hard, or look twice. His arms are too thick, his legs too thin and gangling. He doesn't say goodbye to his father, who stands at the stairway under his best Sunday hat, mouth a tight line under his bushy moustache.

But midnight's so that nobody notices: the too-long cloak, the shaky step. The blond-haired brother smuggled down early evening to a broken-backed sixth floor garden, holding himself in outlines, in the dark, with the taste of secret strawberries on his tongue. Midnight's the alchemists' hour, and in their hands things go strange.

The wind rises from the tunnel, from the dark. The train comes in.

The midnight train is dark as stars. The midnight train's painted up with planets, each car banded with the swoop of a heavenly body ringed or striped or pitted. It moves like a snake along the tracks every child in central's seen so many times on Market days, cheering as the rumble gets loud and the Moving Market comes in.

The doors all open. Nobody cheers the midnight train.

At the staircase, somebody sobs.

The boy in the black rough cloak looks into the dark of the lead car. There's no lights at midnight on the platform, in the train. He steps from dark to darker; he steps inside.

"Greetings," say the alchemists, and their voices are sharp like devil weed, bad seed, breaking the rules. The alchemists in their black train, learned men, terror-men, are hard to see for a boy who grew up billeting in a place where it's never full dark. They're flashes of patched knees and sunless skin. They're eyes that reflect metal and never close.

The train doors shut behind him with a hiss of dead men watching. The sobbing's sliced clean from his ears with metal and rubber seal, and then the only sound's one he hasn't heard since he was littler: the train, whish-whisper, the moving of wheels on track.

It's too much to close his eyes, hands up and ready to fight. But he counts three, counts the deepening of the shadow that's tunnel-not-station before the boy lets down his cloak.

"I'm not the seventh son," Six says, and his voice is all squeaky like a kids. "I'm bad news. Bad seed. You won't have him," he says, and waits to be struck down.

It won't keep secret more than a day. They'll open the billet door for breakfast and it'll be the wrong baby boy lying curled up in the blankets, arm around his stuffy, ruined from Great Destiny by complicity with his bad boy, bad seed big brother. They'll be so mad. They'll be furious.

They'll hug little Joe to their chests and cry happy for his keeping and teach him the garden and the chicken-feed times.

"You must love your brother very much," the alchemists say, circled, leaning close and closer. Their train smells like paper and dry sweet. No, their breaths. Their breaths are hot and paper. They eat tales. They eat children.

"No," Six chokes out, and lifts his chin up high even though deep inside he's crying, crying right to his belly now that there's no chance of scaring the baby. Pictures himself falling, falling. The tug of the wind. "I hate him."

There's a silence.

Then: "Good," one of the alchemists laughs, crackling, crumple-paged. "I like bad sixth sons."

His eyes are working again, in the dark; his eyes work enough to see the turn of a chin, the half-light of eyelids drooped low. "We didn't agree—"

"I *like* bad sixth sons," the alchemist repeats sharp as a papercut to the tongue, and breaks the hovering circle, steps in close.

His robes rustle like pigeon wings, like the wind going through the tall pasture, and his hands are clean-nailed but rough as any farmsman's. The walls are covered, lined, padded with books and books and books. His eyes are dark. His eyes are dark as stars, and the smell of his hands and books and eyes is burnt cinnamon toast and the devil.

I'm a brave boy, Six tells himself, breathing shallow so's to not get the smoke and devil in. *I grew right. I saved things. I didn't hurt no one else.*

He takes him by the hands. He leads him into the black, black car as the train pulls free through the tunnels to travel the nighttime tracks.

"Come along, bad seed," he says, in a voice that echoes like a child's tunnel scream, a voice that might be kind or hard or mocking. "There's much to do before morning."

THE NAZIR

SOFIA SAMATAR

Before that stifling evening in 1924 the children had always thought it impossible for grownups to see the Nazir and live.

Cynthia's elder brother Roddy was the authority in this matter, as in all others. A tall, sullenly handsome fourteen-year-old, who would later drink himself to death with majestic nonchalance among the hollyhocks of a house in Dorset inherited from their uncle, Roddy had first seen the Nazir at the age of eight. He was out in his little boat, *Ward el-Sham*, with Mansour the gardener at the helm, when the surface of the river had suddenly gone dark and a wind rattled wildly in the fig trees. A terrible odor had rained from the sky with a delicate pattering sound, along with a number of little bright objects he thought at first were pearls. When they dropped in the water he saw they were maggots. The Nazir passed over him, crooning. Its voice resembled that of the Italian head matron at the Anglo-American Hospital. He couldn't tell what it said, or even whether it spoke English or Arabic or its own strange tongue. It turned its head and winged southward along the river.

"It had talons like this," said Roddy, making a great C with his arms. "There were shreds of something hanging from them. Like cloth."

"Did the gardener see it?" asked Hugh, wiping his nose on his wrist.

"Of course not," said Roddy. "He's a grownup. He'd be dead."

Hugh had never seen the Nazir himself. Cynthia had never seen it either, but she thought she had caught a glimpse of its shadow once, soon after her nurse Félicité had gone back to Lausanne. Félicité, rosy, cheerful and short of breath, helmeted in a brilliant topee, fond of Offenbach and jam, had drunk rat poison. She had floated for a week between life and death, laid out like a stout white pillow on the bed in her little room, and when she was well she was sent away. She left

Cynthia her button collection, a postcard of the Rhine and the lumpy armchair in the nursery where she used to do the mending.

The first night Félicité was away—not ill upstairs, but really gone—Cynthia curled up in bed clutching a rag doll and the postcard. She ran the edge of the card along her teeth and took a few experimental, consoling bites of the worn paper. Félicité's chair was in darkness, but the lamp with the colored beads on the table beside it gave back a ghost of garden moonlight. Downstairs the servants were laughing, and there was a splash as someone tossed out a basin of water. Then a low rumble, a pressure, a killing fear. The Nazir.

"I didn't really see it," she explained some years later to a group of girls at her aunt's home in London, at a time when she had a respect for accuracy. "It was more of a feeling—like a weight pressing me down. All I saw was a shadow drifting by. The shadow of a huge wing."

Her audience gave a gratifying shiver, a chorus of mews. And Cynthia, bobbed and self-assured, clad in a tasteful blue wool jersey, recalled the specific terror of that Cairo night, the wind, the conviction that life, like a row of candles, was going out.

The grownup who saw the Nazir and lived was Hugh's mother, Mrs. Ashgrove.

The Ashgroves lived in a villa on Kasr el-Nil. Mr. Ashgrove, weedy and dyspeptic, was in the Civil Service. Mrs. Ashgrove rode, favored trousers and scarves, and smoked a hookah. Cynthia had once heard her father describe Mrs. Ashgrove as "a real blonde, of a type more common in Germany than in England." She remembered the words for their tone rather than their meaning: it was rare for her father to speak so mellowly and appreciatively of anyone. It made her shy every time her mother took her to call on the Ashgroves. "Careful," her mother warned her as they went up the ill-kept little path, picking their way among the discarded fruit-skins. They both jumped when the monkey, Marco Polo, threw himself the length of his rope, screeching a welcome. The hair on his neck was quite rubbed away. "Dreadful creature," cried Cynthia's mother, trotting a few steps, for Marco Polo had been known to hurl feces at guests. The doors of the villa stood open, and in the parlor Mrs. Ashgrove perched on a ladder, blurred by the sunlight, hanging curtains.

"Minna, dear," gasped Cynthia's mother. "What are you doing?"

"Lovely, aren't they?" Mrs. Ashgrove called down. "So much more cheerful!"

"Look out," Cynthia advised her mother, who was about to stumble over the suffragi, Sherif, who sat on the floor grinding coffee in a mortar.

Cynthia's mother recoiled. She picked up her skirts, sailed round the suffragi and approached the ladder. "Minna, my dear, come down. It isn't safe."

"Oh, I've a head for heights."

"But why not let the servants take care of it?"

"No need. I'll be through in a moment. Hello, Cynthia."

"Hello," said Cynthia, lingering in the doorway.

Her mother turned round a few times. There were books and unfinished bits of embroidery scattered on the couches. Most of the squares of embroidery had needles in them. A cut-glass bowl occupied an armchair, glittering like a tiara.

Cynthia's mother moved the bowl to the table, pushing aside a plate of fish-bones and an illustrated magazine. "Really, Minna," she said, looking about her despairingly. Sherif thumped his mortar, scattering coffee-grounds.

"There," said Mrs. Ashgrove. She climbed down the ladder, smacked her palms together and greeted Cynthia and her mother with kisses. Her thick hair was tied on her neck with a ribbon. Up close she was less beautiful, but more disturbing. Her white shirt smelled of cucumbers freshly sliced.

"Hugh's in the garden," she said, "plotting mischief."

Cynthia trailed outside. She knew that Hugh was not plotting anything interesting. He hadn't the brain. He shared with his mother only his shock of golden hair and the appearance of impregnable good health. Crossing the veranda she passed a window and saw her mother leaning toward Mrs. Ashgrove, murmuring urgently, and she knew that in an hour, seated at Groppi's with Mrs. Bourne-Hopewell, her mother would sigh over dear Minna, her inexperience, her disorder. "Trousers!" she would say. "Absolutely alone with the suffragi!" And Mrs. Bourne-Hopewell would shake her military jowls. But Cynthia would be happy. She was going to have lemon ice, the kind that came with a little rosewater sprinkled on top.

THE NAZIR
By Roderick Rutherford

The sages say the Nazir lives in the moon. It prefers the half-moon, and lies on top of it with its huge tail hanging down. This is why the period of the half-moon is best for traveling by night. Full-moon nights are risky, and the dark of the moon even worse.

The Nazir is in decay. Nearly all who have seen it mention its stench. It likes grownups to eat, but only children can see it.

It eats very slowly, lying in its lair. Sometimes you can see the bones it tosses down. We call them falling stars.

Cynthia, who had a stubborn streak and was careless with breakable objects, was never whipped. Roddy, organized and withdrawn, was whipped rather often. He was whipped for laziness at lessons, for eating the nasty messes the servants cooked for themselves, and for what their father called his "crooked eye." "Don't look at me with your crooked eye," their father would shout, and if Roddy did not look down in time he was certain to be whipped. Strangely, it was their father who had something wrong with his eyes: one was of glass, the original having been mislaid at Ladysmith.

Roddy was beaten a few days before they learned that Mrs. Ashgrove had seen the Nazir.

Cynthia was skating through the drawing room in her stockings. The vast room, with its floor of reddish marble, was perfect for this exercise, although of course you had to avoid the carpets. She was humming, skating closer with each pass to the carved sideboard, tasting the danger of banging into it and shattering a decanter, when her father's dragoman Ahmed passed through the room on his way to the library, buttoned tightly into the Circassian costume he used as livery. The skin between his brows was dusted with dandruff, a sign of November. He nodded to Cynthia, said "Good afternoon, Miss," and went into the library. He left the door open and Cynthia heard his murmur and then her father's voice. "If you will excuse me for a moment, gentlemen."

She skated into the corner and crouched in the shadow of a cabinet. Her father strode through the drawing room, purposeful, his head thrust forward. Through the open door she could see part of the library: there was a map on the wall, stuck all over with colored pins. Ahmed, bowing, led two men out into the drawing room: Mr. Ashgrove and Robertson Bey. They sank in the cushioned chairs. "Whiskey, Ahmed," said Mr. Ashgrove. He scratched nervously underneath his stubbly chin. Robertson Bey sat frowning, his coat pulled tight across his shoulders, his big hands on his knees.

A moment later her father returned. He moved at the same determined pace. One of his hands gripped the collar of Roddy's jacket. Roddy, inside the jacket, skipped along beside him, trying to keep his footing. He wore only one shoe.

They went into the library and her father slammed the door.

Ahmed brought the whiskey on a tray.

Robertson Bey swallowed his and gestured for more, and Ahmed poured. Cynthia's father could be heard in the library, shouting.

"*Endanger yourself . . . Disgrace . . . The native quarter . . .*"

"Bloody mess," said Mr. Ashgrove.

"Started two years ago," grunted Robertson Bey.

"Started in 1919," said Mr. Ashgrove. He covered his eyes as if he were suffering from a headache. "I don't know. . . . Sometimes I think . . ."

"Think what?" Robertson Bey inquired sharply.

"Nothing," said Mr. Ashgrove, lowering his hand. When he picked up his glass the ice rattled.

"Don't want to lose your nerve."

"Oh, it's nothing like that. It's Minna. She's upset about things. Brooding. It makes the house—well, it's a strain."

"Only to be expected," said Robertson Bey, losing interest at once, gazing at the picture above the sideboard, camels in an oasis. He took another swallow of whiskey. His scalp had begun to sweat. "Damned hot for November," he remarked. "Could be the cause of all the trouble."

Mr. Ashgrove laughed weakly. Cynthia shifted her weight with care, trying to ease the cramp in her legs. It will be over soon, she thought. Surely the sun was advancing across the carpet.

In the silence the strokes of the belt came faint and rhythmic like the ticking of a watch.

THE TALE OF ABU WALEED AND ABU SAMEER
By Roderick the Younger

A tale is told of Abu Waleed, a holy man of the desert. On a time a man called Abu Sameer went to visit him in his cave. "How can a man see the Nazir?" he asked.

"He cannot," replied Abu Waleed. "It is a grace given only to children."

"But I desire to see the Nazir," said Abu Sameer.

Then the sage smiled and said: "Very well. You will see the Nazir when you walk east and west at the same time, when you are able to lick your palm without either bowing or raising your hand, and when you look through the back of your head."

Then Abu Sameer went away disappointed, not knowing how to achieve these things. Some years later he was captured at Constantinople. His enemies tied each of his legs to a horse, and drove one horse east and the other west, so that his legs were torn from his body. Then they pulled out his tongue and made him hold it in his hand. Lastly they flayed his head, starting at the nape, and brought the skin down over his face, leaving him in darkness.

It is believed that in his last moments he saw the Nazir.

They went to the Ashgroves' for dinner in their father's big motorcar. The unseasonable heat continued; Cynthia's white piqué stockings prickled. The streets were empty except for policemen, standing on the corners, who saluted smartly as the car went past.

Someone had begun clearing the path at the Ashgroves', but stopped halfway through. Marco Polo was nowhere to be seen. As they neared the house a white shape coalesced in the evening grey and glided toward them: Mrs. Ashgrove in her evening gown.

"Hello," she said. She kissed their parents as if everything were quite normal, as if she'd come down the steps of the house and not through the dry, exhausted garden. Her hair was plaited and circled her head like a crown.

"Minna, darling," their mother stammered, "what have you done with your shoes?"

Mrs. Ashgrove glanced down at her feet, pale and bare on the banana-skins of the path. "Left them somewhere. Please go in, don't wait for me. Evan's in the library, I think." She looked up, and Cynthia realized it was her eyes that made one uncomfortable: so bright and so direct.

"But," said Cynthia's mother, gesturing helplessly at the garden, a wilderness of thorns and fallen eucalyptus leaves.

"Come on, Addie," their father muttered. Their mother took his arm.

"He'll tell you I've been seeing dragons," Mrs. Ashgrove called after them.

She glanced at the children. Her arms were crossed, as if she had a chill. Sequins glittered in the deep V of her gown. "True, you know. At least, it wasn't a dragon. More like an enormous bat. Horrible." She looked away then, at the guardhouse, the iron gate. And Roddy, who had barely spoken to Cynthia since his last beating, who for the first time had refused to allow her into his room afterward, although she had brought a cloth and a bowl of water to cool his head because he said the headache afterward was the worst thing about being caned—Roddy clasped Cynthia's hand.

"What did you say, Mrs. Ashgrove?"

Again her flashing gaze. "Something awful flew over the house. But no one else saw it."

"Roddy's seen it," Cynthia cried.

"Hush!" Roddy glanced at the house, then grasped Mrs. Ashgrove's hand and pulled them both away from the path, through the trees.

Dry leaves crackled beneath them, releasing fragrance. They paused among the slender shadows. "You've seen the Nazir, Mrs. Ashgrove," Roddy said.

Her eyes widened. "You've really seen it, then. You're not joking."

"No."

"Oh God," she whispered. "You've told the Colonel? Your father, I mean?"

"No good. Look, you can't stay here."

"I know." The brightness in her eyes grew sharper, more concentrated, and became tears. "I know. I've got to get away. But I don't know how."

"Roddy could talk to the guard," said Cynthia, knowing he could persuade anyone.

Roddy shook his head. "No, he'd be sacked, maybe put in prison."

"I've thought about going over the wall."

"But why not?" said Roddy, excited. He crunched through the leaves and looked up at the wall. "You could do it. We'd help you get up."

"There's broken glass," Mrs. Ashgrove said. Her voice trembled, and she was not, suddenly, distant and invincible, armored in her golden laugh, fearless with horses and ladders, but one of them.

"Cynthia," Roddy said. "Get a blanket from the house. And shoes."

Cynthia ran to the house. The door was open, the drawing room empty. They must be in the music room, where it was cooler. She ran up the staircase, past the bust of Kitchener. In the hall she met Hugh.

"Where are you going?" he asked.

"We're playing hide and seek," she said.

He frowned.

"Quick," she told him, "Roddy's coming," and he ran to his room to hide, and years later, when they met in London at a dance, she still felt guilty enough to dance with him and to agree to a drive in the countryside the following afternoon.

She ran downstairs, a blanket over her shoulder, Mrs. Ashgrove's riding boots under her arm. In the garden Mrs. Ashgrove pulled on the boots, and when she lost her balance she put her hand on Cynthia's shoulder for a moment, her touch as chilly and pure as moonlight.

When Cynthia thinks of Cairo now she remembers a garden party. She and Roddy stood at the window in their nightclothes, looking down. The garden sparkled with fairy lights and everyone looked lovely and somehow distant, the dancers turning slow to the music of the band. They wore transparent wings and garlands of flowers, and laughed as they leaned together, streaks of glitter shining on their cheeks. Her mother held a wand and was tall and beautiful, like a stranger; and the sad donkey's head with gilt ears was her father. The whole scene often comes back to her in dreams, silent, mysterious. Sometimes it speeds up suddenly, like a film being played too fast. Then it slows down, so that she can read every gesture, every smile. And then it speeds up. And then it slows down. And then it stops.

Cynthia has never seen the Nazir. Not once.

She's tried everything. At first she thought the key was running away. After she was sent to school in England she ran away twice: once as far as Chiddingly on the train, and once into the woods. After the second time she was sent to London to stay with her aunt. She let a boy take down her knickers in the airing cupboard. Soon afterward her mother arrived from Cairo, dabbing tears of rage with a crumpled glove, and decided that Cynthia had better go to France.

She never saw the Nazir in France, or Italy, or Greece.

She has drunk ouzo and water. She has planted a bomb in a public garden. She has bathed nude in the Arno. She has marched and shouted. She has been jailed. She has never been married. What does the Nazir want?

Sometimes she tells herself that the Nazir cannot leave Egypt. She knows it isn't true.

Sometimes she tells herself that the Nazir has passed away, that it faded and fell with the old Cairo life, a life crammed into suitcases now, imprisoned in attics.

She knows it isn't true.

THE SONG OF THE NAZIR
By Saif Al-Atfal

One and two and one and two
Carry me off to the moon with you!
No, my child, my chick, my crow,
You're far too small to the moon to go.
Teeth you have, but they are thin,
Buds to keep the summer in;
Claws you lack and gizzard too
To crack the skull and grind the stew.
You must stay a little while,
And paint the mirror with a smile,
And hope I do not find you lone
And weak at night, when you are grown.
Hope I never find you slack,
Bearing a rifle on your back,
Riding a camel, tally-ho,
Into a desert white as snow.
If I do, I'll drink your wails,
And comb your flesh out with my nails;
Your brains I'll suck, your marrow tap;
I'll wear your stomach like a cap.
And bits of bone I'll sprinkle down
In every street, in every town,
While the little ones cry, "Oh Nazir, do
Eat our wicked parents too!"

Sometimes she tells herself that she's too old. If she sees the Nazir now it will kill her.

She knows that this isn't true either, because of Mrs. Ashgrove. Mrs. Ashgrove saw the Nazir when she was already grown up, though she was younger then than Cynthia is now. Sometimes when her lover is sleeping Cynthia goes to the window, cups her hands at either side of her face and whispers: "Come." The glass is so cold, like the ice-cream freezer at Groppi's. She wants to look into the Nazir's eyes just once and say: "Do you forgive me?"

"Come," she whispers. A fragile print of steam on the dark glass. "Come. If you don't forgive me, then you can take me, I don't care." She strikes the glass with her fist, but softly, so as not to wake the man in the bed. She closes her eyes and imagines a claw breaking through from outside.

Cynthia heard of Mrs. Ashgrove only once after the war. It was springtime and freezing in Paris, where Cynthia was waiting for the baby to be born. Her mother wrote, with barely concealed triumph, that Mrs. Ashgrove had been recognized by Robertson Bey on one of his trips to Cairo. She was seated in a cart, being pulled through the streets by a little Arab girl. Her legs were horribly deformed, as if they had both been broken. She wore a dirty black abaya, but when it slipped back Robertson knew her profile at once, although it appeared she had cut off all her hair. He spoke to her, but she refused to speak English and shouted in Arabic for the girl to pull her away, and of course people gathered to see what was going on, and there was nothing poor Robertson Bey could do, being English in Cairo these days. *Mad*, her mother wrote. *Quite mad. She'll never come home again either, poor girl.*

Cynthia laid the letter on the bed. She drew her shawl about her and huddled closer to the heat of the gas ring. Downstairs the drunken newspaper vendor was coming in; the floors were so thin she could hear the landlady snapping at him to close the door. Thank God, she thought with tears in her eyes. She wished Roddy were still alive so that she could tell him. She knew, of course, what had happened to Mrs. Ashgrove's legs. The Nazir had caught her after all, but then, before it could bear her away, before she was lost forever, it had dropped her.

A HANDFUL OF EARTH

SILVIA MORENO-GARCIA

He left, crates filled with earth, bound for England. Left us behind, promising to send for us. We believed him. But as the days went by, I realized he'd lied.

Live forever. Love forever.

Anca and Ioana looked to me for guidance, as they always did. Technically, they were older than me. I was the last one to be brought to the castle. Mentally, they were younger. Frozen in their teenage years, letting me mother them and lead. I'd had five sisters and watched over them. Authority came naturally.

My sisters and I had shared a single, cramped room. Some days, when I was tired of doing the washing and watching over the others— our mother died birthing the youngest child, our father was a strict man who filled my days with endless household tasks—I'd look out the window, towards the distant silhouette of the castle. It had no name. We simply called it "the castle." High upon a cliff, edging towards the sky, while we lived beneath its shadow. I pictured myself going up its hundreds of steps, rushing through the hallways and dancing in rooms decorated with rich tapestries.

When he swooped from the towers, a piece of night detaching from the sky, why would I resist?

I had five sisters, but disease took them from us. Tiny little graves marked their passing, though I did not recall their precise location afterwards.

My father and I sat alone at the table. He was quiet, staring at a distant point.

We were already half-dead. The air stank, everyone rotting and melting away. So why not live forever?

I stood in the highest tower of the castle and tried to pierce the night with my eyes, to see beyond the mountains and the forests and gaze upon the distant shores he'd escaped to. I wondered if he thought of us or if the memory had been ripped apart.

Anca and Ioana were not twins. But they might have been. So close in looks and mannerisms, with the same glossy black hair and knowing eyes. Something about them always made me think of birds of prey. They flew easily, bodies light and bone-thin, their laughter streaming from the rafters.

Flight did not come naturally to me. My other shape was of a massive white wolf. Smaller than his own wolf body had been, but still a sight to see.

Anca and Ioana feared the outside; they spoke of arrows raining over a castle. There had been a great battle, though they could not recall if it had taken place in this fortress or another one. Either way, they would not venture with me.

I rushed through the forest, seeing all manner of things in the dark as I hunted for us.

He had kept us in our rooms, like the women in a Turkish harem I spied in the etchings of books, before the books were ravaged by moths and time. There we were to patiently wait for him, never stepping outside the walls of the castle.

There is death outside, he'd warned us.

Yet he'd gone out, beyond the safe limits of our home and aboard a ship.

I'd been right. He had never loved. He never loves.

Not that it mattered now.

There were Anca and Ioana to look after.

I ran through the forest, sometimes naked in my woman-shape, sometimes in the wolf's pelt. I chanced upon a traveler or sneaked into a small house, creeping through the windows. Then I'd drink upon a sleeper, compel him to follow me through the night, and back to the castle. I'd let him ride upon my back, my wolf legs taking us swiftly through the darkness. Up, up. Towards Anca and Ioana.

In the daytime we slept in the old chapel, inside carved sarcophagi much more ornate than the graves my sisters had been given. Ioana once told me the castle was built upon an older castle and I thought this might be true, for the sarcophagi seemed of a style that did not entirely correspond to the ruined chapel, images of women holding garlands of flowers upon the lids. But even Ioana could not say how long ago the previous castle had stood, or who had been its master.

Not that it mattered. Now we were its mistresses, laughing as we swirled inside the empty chambers, decked in clothes of ladies who had long turned to dust, ravaged by worms.

He had not liked our liquid laughter, the way it bounced against the ancient walls. Hating it as though it might peel the bricks away revealing an older layer of stones. He was gone, and we laughed.

I braided tiny flowers into Anca's hair while Ioana told us fairy tales from her childhood. Sometimes, she forgot the endings and we invented our own.

I was careful with my looks and attire. I'd compel Anca and Ioana to bathe with me under the cold rain. Or to pull water from an old well and fill a great copper tub. Anca always said I was the vainest of us all. Ioana said I was the fairest.

I knew I'd been his favourite and the constant ablutions, the ribbons in the hair and the heavy, old pieces of gold against my skin had been meant all for him. His absence had not altered my routine. I was still prim and careful with my clothes, my hair. Through the years, I had noticed that Anca and Ioana sometimes ignored such niceties, nails caked with dirt and blood. As though they had forgotten, or did not care, to keep any semblance of life.

When they were in this state—and they sank into this miasma, deeply upon his departure—they might remain still for several days. Not a muscle twitching. Nothing. Just a deep silence interrupted by bouts of terrible ferocity. They sometimes gnawed at each other, not a pup's nipping, but a full-blown attack.

In those moments I did not know them and I wondered if this was a sign of their true age. Or simply the vast melancholy that clothed them.

Either way, I reeled them out of this state. Reeled them into little dances and the clapping of hands. The castle vibrated with our voices.

And whenever I'd catch myself thinking of him again, my hands running over the maps he had left behind, I'd seek their comfort and their smiles.

It happened as it was meant to happen. The spell shattering abruptly, as it must.

Ioana dreamt the castle crashed into the river far below. I held her in my arms as she wept, speaking of a terrible omen. I convinced Ioana and Anca to play hide-and-seek with me, like I'd done with my sisters when we were little. We rushed through long corridors, sneaking beneath archways and laying still, as lizards and slugs crawled beside us. Night creatures, the lot of us, out to play.

The wind and rain whipped the castle, lightning striking nearby, and we giggled.

I raced up to the tallest tower of the castle, wolves howling, wind screeching, and stopped in my tracks feeling a tug and a pull inside my skull.

I knew he was returning home.

Emboldened by his nearness, Ioana and Anca agreed to step out of the fortress some nights later. We looked for him in the coldness, in the dark, hoping we might encounter his carriage. Instead, we found the woman and the strange man. The woman bore his mark upon her, glowing like an ember. Another sister for our tribe.

The man was untainted. Strongly-built and blue-eyed. He reminded me vaguely of my stern and resolute father and I stared at him for a long time. I thought of the night I slipped out of my house, headed up to the old castle, and the distant cry of surprise I must have imagined—I must have—springing from my father's lips, escaping the desolate, little white house.

We can never look back or we will be turned into pillars of salt. I suppose that is why Anca and Ioana remembered very little of their youth. Perhaps that is why they forgot themselves some days, growing fierce and empty.

I stared at the man and he stared back at me while Anca and Ioana laughed.

I think my silence, my eyes upon him, were my salvation.

I do not know why he did not kill me. Though he tried. He did try. But the stake did not lodge firm against the heart. Distraction? Weariness? Perhaps my own power over mortal minds, woven in that long look, shielded me. Perhaps he felt pity.

Whatever it was, I woke to the icy knowledge of Anca and Ioana's death. I did not even have to look at their sarcophagi to know. But I did look. Empty. Not a bit of hair, not a speck of bone. Nothing but dust.

I knew he was dead too. I felt his absence. I had not been this alone in years upon years. Centuries even. The loneliness reverberated through my body.

My shift was stained with my own blood upon the breast, where a stake or a knife bit the flesh before he pulled away. I let my usual sense of cleanliness escape me and did not change my dress, eating millipedes and insects for three whole days.

I feared leaving the chapel. I thought his enemies might return. On the third day there was a great murmur through the fortress, a rumble that startled me and had me pressed against the wall in terror. When I ventured out of the chapel I realized a section of the castle had collapsed. The old bricks had finally given away, groaning and plunging into the river below.

The sight roused me. I no longer felt safe in the chapel.

I turned into a wolf and leapt beyond the castle walls, not knowing where I'd go. The icy night air cut my hands, my feet.

It was easy to find my sisters' graves. I had not forgotten the location. I had merely buried it away, and now dug through layers of memory until I arrived at the plot of earth that kept their bones. My father's remains might be there too, though I did not know for sure.

I curled upon the ground and crossed my arms upon my chest.

He had never loved. But I had. I'd loved Anca and Ioana. Their little smiles and their games. Their sweetness and their cruelty, and the way their black eyes shone in the darkness, as if burnished. It was all gone and I couldn't even muster the energy to crave revenge.

My fingers dug into the earth and I thought I might bury myself with my sisters. Rest my bones against their own. Cradle them once more. I would not be alone then, for their ghosts would keep me company.

I lay like this for a very long time and then, finally, I stood up and ripped my shift off. I fashioned a simple pouch out of it, scooping earth into it and tying it close. I thought of returning to the castle for some of the valuables there. Perhaps one of the maps. I discarded the idea.

Years later, I wonder if I shouldn't have returned and scooped a trinket, a map, after all. My memories of those days have grown dimmer and dimmer. I sometimes wake up with a vision of two dark-haired women, but their names escape me. I wonder if a memento might help pin the thoughts in place. Or perhaps it would not make a difference. Perhaps we are all meant to wander with nothing but a handful of earth in our hands, never looking over our shoulders.

IN WINTER

SONYA TAAFFE

They call her the robber girl because she takes whatever she wants, and what she wants to take most are lives. She does it best with her Mosin-Nagant, iron-sighted like all sensible snipers; she has done it with flare matches and bottles of sticky petrol, with a borrowed rifle when her own jammed in a fog of snow and cordite and once, the time she remembers because she wore it back to camp like a uniform, with a knife and the freezing bark of pine branches, smashed like red windows in the snow. Glass is the enemy of secrecy: it glints, it clouds, it splinters. The robber girl's breath dances reflections on her lashes and she blinks them clear, looking for Soviet coats and caps, summer-khaki against the winter's white eye. There is snow in everyone's hearts these days.

She sleeps with her arm around the neck of the boy called Reindeer, for his dark, delicate eyes and his long-legged stride over the wind-crusted drifts. He makes a poor soldier, but she swore to herself when she was eight that she would keep him safe and she has kept that promise through the Mannerheim Line and Taipale and Tolvajärvi, showing him how to stuff his boots and sling his rifle and stitch bedsheets into snow-smocks, the little blue-and-white badge he pinned to his student's cap almost the same color as the forget-me-nots he picked once for her. She has never wanted to kiss him, with his face all wind-skinned angles and his soft lank hair as buttery as cloudberries; she never had a brother to love him like and when she dreams with her fellow-soldiers of clean deep-pillowed beds and warm stoves and nothing itching anywhere, it is not a body like his, broad-shouldered and bony, that entangles her. But she will set herself against all odds between him and the snow that wraps itself around the bodies of dying men, whispers itself into their mouths, leaves their eyes open so that they stare, dazzled, forever into its heart; he is the last companion of her childhood and so she understands the girl who comes from the south with not even a pistol in her hand, looking for a boy lost, like so many before him, to the winter and the war.

She brought her name with her, but the robber girl thinks of her as the rose girl—she looks like a schoolgirl with her long, fair plait and her blouse that comes untucked at the back when she bends, her cheeks as flushed as if they were newly scrubbed, but her nails are bitten short and broken, so that sometimes, passing a plate or a cartridge, she scratches, and the green of her eyes is pricked around the edges with something that will smart if touched; the robber girl is careful not to. Her pockets are full of bark bread and salmiakki, the dried skin of a stockfish like a letter from which the writing has been scraped clean; she came on foot over birch forests and spruce bogs, behind the lines of battle, asking at every camp she found. She was lucky, river-led, charmed as a mad thing. An officer by the sedge-lashed shores of Ladoga gave her a coat of furs sent by his fiancée, a scout with crow-black hair warned her away from the trails frozen hard enough for tanks not to mire down in. Her boots were stitched with red once, but the snow broke every thread until she turned north. Cross-legged by the stove at night as it spits over ice-grained knots of pine, she shows the robber girl her only token of a boy who loved mathematics and puzzles and strode off into the cold sunshine of a recruiting day as if he could see the snow calling, hollowing itself a place to fit his limbs when he threw his arms open for the bullet and fell: the burnt red petals of a rose, dried and crushed close as a heart. It fits in her palm, when she curls up to sleep. She smells like moss and the sweat of a long road, dusty crescents behind her ears like a child that needs washing. With one arm around her neck, one hand on her knife as she has slept since she left home to learn to kill, the robber girl does not sleep.

She gives the rose girl a knife, because she cannot fight Russians with salt candy and summer flowers; she gives her a kiss on the mouth, because she cannot fight snow with steel. When their hair curls together, she cuts the bright and dark strands and twines them like a compass, though she knows it will not lead the rose girl back to her. The robber girl has deaths to steal and Reindeer to look after, the war to fight until she falls like a broken window in the snow or walks home to a quiet house she can hardly remember, with forget-me-nots in the meadow and rye bread rising on the stove; the rose girl has a boy in steel-rimmed spectacles to find, if they have not shattered like cat-ice, blinded him, deceived him, given him away. He wore a soldier's new boots and loved the taste of licorice, black as biting frost. It burned the robber girl's lips, strong as tears in a kiss. When he asks, she gives her Reindeer, just as far as the forest's edge, his light-footed swiftness to lead her over the treacherous rime, the branch-tangles that lie under the breaking crusts of snow, and she lies with her arm around no one's neck that night. She dreams of running with them, over endless snowfields without ski-tracks or the treads of stopped tanks; she dreams of summer, as distant and strange as home. She dreams of her finger on the trigger, the sun on the shine of glass. She dreams of blood, blooming like roses in the snow.

GHOSTWEIGHT

YOON HA LEE

It is not true that the dead cannot be folded. Square becomes kite becomes swan; history becomes rumor becomes song. Even the act of remembrance creases the truth.

What the paper-folding diagrams fail to mention is that each fold enacts itself upon the secret marrow of your ethics, the axioms of your thoughts.

Whether this is the most important thing the diagrams fail to mention is a matter of opinion.

"There's time for one more hand," Lisse's ghost said. It was composed of cinders of color, a cipher of blurred features, and it had a voice like entropy and smoke and sudden death. Quite possibly it was the last ghost on all of ruined Rhaion, conquered Rhaion, Rhaion with its devastated, shadowless cities and dead moons and dimming sun. Sometimes Lisse wondered if the ghost had a scar to match her own, a long, livid line down her arm. But she felt it was impolite to ask.

Around them, in a command spindle sized for fifty, the walls of the war-kite were hung with tatters of black and faded green, even now in the process of reknitting themselves into tapestry displays. Tangled reeds changed into ravens. One perched on a lightning-cloven tree. Another, taking shape amid twisted threads, peered out from a skull's eye socket.

Lisse didn't need any deep familiarity with mercenary symbology to understand the warning. Lisse's people had adopted a saying from the Imperium's mercenaries: *In raven arithmetic, no death is enough.*

Lisse had expected pursuit. She had deserted from Base 87 soon after hearing that scouts had found a mercenary war-kite in the ruins of a sacred maze, six years after all the mercenaries vanished: suspicious timing on her part, but she would have no better opportunity for revenge. The ghost had not tried too hard to dissuade her. It had always understood her ambitions.

For a hundred years, despite being frequently outnumbered, the mercenaries in their starfaring kites had cindered cities, destroyed flights of rebel starflyers, shattered stations in the void's hungry depths. What better weapon than one of their own kites?

What troubled her was how lightly the war-kite had been defended. It had made a strange, thorny silhouette against the lavender sky even from a long way off, like briars gone wild, and with the ghost as scout she had slipped past the few mechanized sentries. The kite's shadow had been human. She was not sure what to make of that.

The kite had opened to her like a flower. The card game had been the ghost's idea, a way to reassure the kite that she was its ally: Scorch had been invented by the mercenaries.

Lisse leaned forward and started to scoop the nearest column, the Candle Column, from the black-and-green gameplay rug. The ghost forestalled her with a hand that felt like the dregs of autumn, decay from the inside out. In spite of herself, she flinched from the ghostweight, which had troubled her all her life. Her hand jerked sideways; her fingers spasmed.

"Look," the ghost said.

Few cadets had played Scorch with Lisse even in the barracks. The ghost left its combinatorial fingerprints in the cards. People drew the unlucky Fallen General's Hand over and over again, or doubled on nothing but negative values, or inverted the Crown Flower at odds of thousands to one. So Lisse had learned to play the solitaire variant, with jerengjen as counters. *You must learn your enemy's weapons*, the ghost had told her, and so, even as a child in the reeducation facility, she had saved her chits for paper to practice folding into cranes, lilies, leaf-shaped boats.

Next to the Candle Column she had folded stormbird, greatfrog, lantern, drake. Where the ghost had interrupted her attempt to clear the pieces, they had landed amid the Sojourner and Mirror Columns, forming a skewed late-game configuration: a minor variant of the Needle Stratagem, missing only its pivot.

"Consider it an omen," the ghost said. "Even the smallest sliver can kill, as they say."

There were six ravens on the tapestries now. The latest one had outspread wings, as though it planned to blot out the shrouded sun. She wondered what it said about the mercenaries, that they couched their warnings in pictures rather than drums or gongs.

Lisse rose from her couch. "So they're coming for us. Where are they?"

She had spoken in the Imperium's administrative tongue, not one of the mercenaries' own languages. Nevertheless, a raven flew from one tapestry to join its fellows in the next. The vacant tapestry grayed, then displayed a new scene: a squad of six tanks caparisoned in Imperial blue and bronze, paced by two personnel carriers sheathed in metal mined from withered stars. They advanced upslope, pebbles skittering in their wake.

In the old days, the ghost had told her, no one would have advanced through a sacred maze by straight lines. But the ancient walls, curved and interlocking, were gone now. The ghost had drawn the old designs on her palm with its insubstantial fingers, and she had learned not to shudder at the untouch, had learned to thread the maze in her mind's eye: one more map to the things she must not forget.

"I'd rather avoid fighting them," Lisse said. She was looking at the command spindle's controls. Standard Imperial layout, all of them—it did not occur to her to wonder why the kite had configured itself thus— but she found nothing for the weapons.

"People don't bring tanks when they want to negotiate," the ghost said dryly. "And they'll have alerted their flyers for intercept. You have something they want badly."

"Then why didn't they guard it better?" she demanded.

Despite the tanks' approach, the ghost fell silent. After a while, it said, "Perhaps they didn't think anyone but a mercenary could fly a kite."

"They might be right," Lisse said darkly. She strapped herself into the commander's seat, then pressed three fingers against the controls and traced the commands she had been taught as a cadet. The kite shuddered, as though caught in a hell-wind from the sky's fissures. But it did not unfurl itself to fly.

She tried the command gestures again, forcing herself to slow down. A cold keening vibrated through the walls. The kite remained stubbornly landfast.

The squad rounded the bend in the road. All the ravens had gathered in a single tapestry, decorating a half-leafed tree like dire jewels. The rest of the tapestries displayed the squad from different angles: two aerial views and four from the ground.

Lisse studied one of the aerial views and caught sight of two scuttling figures, lean angles and glittering eyes and a balancing tail in black metal. She stiffened. They had the shadows of hounds, all graceful hunting curves. Two jerengjen, true ones, unlike the lifeless shapes that she folded out of paper. The kite must have deployed them when it sensed the tanks' approach.

Sweating now, despite the autumn temperature inside, she methodically tried every command she had ever learned. The kite remained obdurate. The tapestries' green threads faded until the ravens and their tree were bleak black splashes against a background of wintry gray.

It was a message. Perhaps a demand. But she did not understand.

The first two tanks slowed into view. Roses, blue with bronze hearts, were engraved to either side of the main guns. The lead tank's roses flared briefly.

The kite whispered to itself in a language that Lisse did not recognize. Then the largest tapestry cleared of trees and swirling leaves and rubble, and presented her with a commander's emblem, a pale blue rose pierced by three claws. A man's voice issued from the tapestry: "Cadet Fai Guen." This was her registry name. They had not reckoned that she would keep her true name alive in her heart like an ember. "You are in violation of Imperial interdict. Surrender the kite at once."

He did not offer mercy. The Imperium never did.

Lisse resisted the urge to pound her fists against the interface. She had not survived this long by being impatient. "That's it, then," she said to the ghost in defeat.

"Cadet Fai Guen," the voice said again, after another burst of light, "you have one minute to surrender the kite before we open fire."

"Lisse," the ghost said, "the kite's awake."

She bit back a retort and looked down. Where the control panel had once been featureless gray, it was now crisp white interrupted by five glyphs, perfectly spaced for her outspread fingers. She resisted the urge to snatch her hand away. "Very well," she said. "If we can't fly, at least we can fight."

She didn't know the kite's specific control codes. Triggering the wrong sequence might activate the kite's internal defenses. But taking tank fire at point-blank range would get her killed, too. She couldn't imagine that the kite's armor had improved in the years of its neglect.

On the other hand, it had jerengjen scouts, and the jerengjen looked perfectly functional.

She pressed her thumb to the first glyph. A shadow unfurled briefly but was gone before she could identify it. The second attempt revealed a two-headed dragon's twisting coils. Long-range missiles, then: thunder in the sky. Working quickly, she ran through the options. It would be ironic if she got the weapons systems to work only to incinerate herself.

"You have ten seconds, Cadet Fai Guen," said the voice with no particular emotion.

"Lisse," the ghost said, betraying impatience.

One of the glyphs had shown a wolf running. She remembered that at one point the wolf had been the mercenaries' emblem. Nevertheless, she felt a dangerous affinity to it. As she hesitated over it, the kite said, in a parched voice, "Soul strike."

She tapped the glyph, then pressed her palm flat to activate the weapon. The panel felt briefly hot, then cold.

For a second she thought that nothing had happened, that the kite had malfunctioned. The kite was eerily still.

The tanks and personnel carriers were still visible as gray outlines against darker gray, as were the nearby trees and their stifled fruits. She wasn't sure whether that was an effect of the unnamed weapons or a problem with the tapestries. Had ten seconds passed yet? She couldn't tell, and the clock of her pulse was unreliable.

Desperate to escape before the tanks spat forth the killing rounds, Lisse raked her hand sideways to dismiss the glyphs. They dispersed in unsettling fragmented shapes resembling half-chewed leaves and corroded handprints. She repeated the gesture for *fly*.

Lisse choked back a cry as the kite lofted. The tapestry views changed to sky on all sides except the ravens on their tree—birds no longer, but skeletons, price paid in coin of bone.

Only once they had gained some altitude did she instruct the kite to show her what had befallen her hunters. It responded by continuing to accelerate.

The problem was not the tapestries. Rather, the kite's wolf-strike had ripped all the shadows free of their owners, killing them. Below, across a great swathe of the continent once called Ishuel's Bridge, was a devastation of light, a hard, glittering splash against the surrounding snow-capped mountains and forests and winding rivers.

Lisse had been an excellent student, not out of academic conscientiousness but because it gave her an opportunity to study her enemy. One of her best subjects had been geography. She and the ghost had spent hours drawing maps in the air or shaping topographies in her blankets; paper would betray them, it had said. As she memorized the streets of the City of Fountains, it had sung her the ballads of its founding. It had told her about the feuding poets and philosophers that the thoroughfares of the City of Prisms had been named after. She knew which mines supplied which bases and how the roads spidered across Ishuel's Bridge. While the population figures of the bases and settlement camps weren't exactly announced to cadets, especially those recruited from the reeducation facilities, it didn't take much to make an educated guess.

The imperium had built 114 bases on Ishuel's Bridge. Base complements averaged 20,000 people. Even allowing for the imprecision of her eye, the wolf-strike had taken out—

She shivered as she listed the affected bases, approximately sixty of them.

The settlement camps' populations were more difficult. The Imperium did not like to release those figures. Imperfectly, she based her estimate on the zone around Base 87, remembering the rows of identical shelters. The only reason they did not outnumber the bases' personnel was that the mercenaries had been coldly efficient on Jerengjen Day.

Needle Stratagem, Lisse thought blankly. The smallest sliver. She hadn't expected its manifestation to be quite so literal.

The ghost was looking at her, its dark eyes unusually distinct. "There's nothing to be done for it now," it said at last. "Tell the kite where to go before it decides for itself."

"Ashway 514," Lisse said, as they had decided before she fled base: scenario after scenario whispered to each other like bedtime stories. She was shaking. The straps did nothing to steady her.

She had one last glimpse of the dead region before they curved into the void: her handprint upon her own birthworld. She had only meant to destroy her hunters.

In her dreams, later, the blast pattern took on the outline of a running wolf.

In the mercenaries' dominant language, jerengjen originally referred to the art of folding paper. For her part, when Lisse first saw it, she thought of it as snow. She was four years old. It was a fair spring afternoon in the City of Tapestries, slightly humid. She was watching a bird try to catch a bright butterfly when improbable paper shapes began drifting from the sky, foxes and snakes and stormbirds.

Lisse called to her parents, laughing. Her parents knew better. Over her shrieks, they dragged her into the basement and switched off the lights. She tried to bite one of her fathers when he clamped his hand over her mouth. Jerengjen tracked primarily by shadows, not by sound, but you couldn't be too careful where the mercenaries' weapons were concerned.

In the streets, jerengjen unfolded prettily, expanding into artillery with dragon-shaped shadows and sleek four-legged assault robots with wolf-shaped shadows. In the skies, jerengjen unfolded into bombers with kestrel-shaped shadows.

This was not the only Rhaioni city where this happened. People crumpled like paper cutouts once their shadows were cut away by the onslaught. Approximately one-third of the world's population perished in the weeks that followed.

Of the casualty figures, the Imperium said, *It is regrettable*. And later, *The stalled negotiations made the consolidation necessary*.

Lisse carried a map of the voidways with her at all times, half in her head and half in the Scorch deck. The ghost had once been a traveler. It had shown her mnemonics for the dark passages and the deep perils that lay between stars. Growing up, she had laid out endless tableaux between her lessons, memorizing travel times and vortices and twists.

Ashway 514 lay in the interstices between two unstable stars and their cacophonous necklace of planets, comets, and asteroids. Lisse felt the kite tilting this way and that as it balanced itself against the stormy voidcurrent. The tapestries shone from one side with ruddy light from the nearer star, 514 Tsi. On the other side, a pale violet-blue planet with a serenade of rings occluded the view.

514 was a useful hiding place. It was off the major tradeways, and since the Battle of Fallen Sun—named after the rebel general's emblem, a white sun outlined in red, rather than the nearby stars—it had been designated an ashway, where permanent habitation was forbidden.

More important to Lisse, however, was the fact that 514 was the ashway nearest the last mercenary sighting, some five years ago. As a student, she had learned the names and silhouettes of the most prominent war-kites, and set verses of praise in their honor to Imperial anthems. She had written essays on their tactics and memorized the names of their most famous commanders, although there were no statues or portraits, only the occasional unsmiling photograph. The Imperium was fond of statues and portraits.

For a hundred years (administrative calendar), the mercenaries had served their masters unflinchingly and unfailingly. Lisse had assumed that she would have as much time as she needed to plot against them. Instead, they had broken their service, for reasons the Imperium had never released—perhaps they didn't know, either—and none had been seen since.

"I'm not sure there's anything to find here," Lisse said. Surely the Imperium would have scoured the region for clues. The tapestries were empty of ravens. Instead, they diagrammed shifting voidcurrent flows. The approach of enemy starflyers would perturb the current and allow Lisse and the ghost to estimate their intent. Not trusting the kite's systems—although there was only so far that she could take her distrust, given the circumstances—she had been watching the tapestries for the past several hours. She had, after a brief argument with the ghost, switched on haptics so that the air currents would, however imperfectly, reflect the status of the void around them. Sometimes it was easier to feel a problem through your skin.

"There's no indication of derelict kites here," she added. "Or even kites in use, other than this one."

"It's a starting place, that's all," the ghost said.

"We're going to have to risk a station eventually. You might not need to eat, but I do." She had only been able to sneak a few rations out of base. It was tempting to nibble at one now.

"Perhaps there are stores on the kite."

"I can't help but think this place is a trap."

"You have to eat sooner or later," the ghost said reasonably. "It's worth a look, and I don't want to see you go hungry." At her hesitation, it added, "I'll stand watch here. I'm only a breath away."

This didn't reassure her as much as it should have, but she was no longer a child in a bunk precisely aligned with the walls, clutching the covers while the ghost told her her people's stories. She reminded herself of her favorite story, in which a single sentinel kept away the world's last morning by burning out her eyes, and set out.

Lisse felt the ghostweight's pull the farther away she walked, but that was old pain, and easily endured. Lights flicked on to accompany her, diffuse despite her unnaturally sharp shadow, then started illuminating passages ahead of her, guiding her footsteps. She wondered what the kite didn't want her to see.

Rations were in an unmarked storage room. She wouldn't have been certain about the rations, except that they were, if the packaging was to be believed, field category 72: better than what she had eaten on training exercises, but not by much. No surprise, now that she thought about it: from all accounts, the mercenaries had relied on their masters' production capacity.

Feeling ridiculous, she grabbed two rations and retraced her steps. The fact that the kite lit her exact path only made her more nervous.

"Anything new?" she asked the ghost. She tapped the ration. "It's a pity that you can't taste poison."

The ghost laughed dryly. "If the kite were going to kill you, it wouldn't be that subtle. Food is food, Lisse."

The food was as exactingly mediocre as she had come to expect from military food. At least it was not any worse. She found a receptacle for disposal afterward, then laid out a Scorch tableau, Candle column to Bone, right to left. Cards rather than jerengjen, because she remembered the scuttling hound-jerengjen with creeping distaste.

From the moment she left Base 87, one timer had started running down. The devastation of Ishuel's Bridge had begun another, the important one. She wasn't gambling her survival; she had already sold it. The question was, how many Imperial bases could she extinguish on her way out? And could she hunt down any of the mercenaries that had been the Imperium's killing sword?

Lisse sorted rapidly through possible targets. For instance, Base 226 Mheng, the Petaled Fortress. She would certainly perish in the attempt, but the only way she could better that accomplishment would be to raze the Imperial firstworld, and she wasn't that ambitious. There was Bridgepoint 663 Tsi-Kes, with its celebrated Pallid Sentinels, or Aerie 8 Yeneq, which built the Imperium's greatest flyers, or—

She set the cards down, closed her eyes, pressed her palms against her face. She was no tactician supreme. Would it make much difference if she picked a card at random?

But of course nothing was truly random in the ghost's presence.

She laid out the Candle Column again. "Not 8 Yeneq," she said. "Let's start with a softer target. Aerie 586 Chiu."

Lisse looked at the ghost: the habit of seeking its approval had not left her. It nodded. "The safest approach is via the Capillary Ashways. It will test your piloting skills."

Privately, Lisse thought that the kite would be happy to guide itself. They didn't dare allow it to, however.

The Capillaries were among the worst of the ashways. Even starlight moved in unnerving ways when faced with ancient networks of voidcurrent gates, unmaintained for generations, or vortices whose behavior changed day by day.

They were fortunate with the first several capillaries. Under other circumstances, Lisse would have gawked at the splendor of lensed galaxies and the jewel-fire of distant clusters. She was starting to manipulate the control interface without hesitating, or flinching as though a wolf's shadow might cross hers.

At the ninth—

"Patrol," the ghost said, leaning close.

She nodded jerkily, trying not to show that its proximity pained her. Its mouth crimped in apology.

"It would have been worse if we'd made it all the way to 586 Chiu without a run-in," Lisse said. That kind of luck always had a price. If she was unready, best to find out now, while there was a chance of fleeing to prepare for a later strike.

The patrol consisted of sixteen flyers: eight Lance 82s and eight Scout 73s. She had flown similar Scouts in simulation.

The flyers did not hesitate. A spread of missiles streaked toward her. Lisse launched antimissile fire.

It was impossible to tell whether they had gone on the attack because the Imperium and the mercenaries had parted on bad terms, or because the authorities had already learned of what had befallen Rhaion. She was certain couriers had gone out within moments of the devastation of Ishuel's Bridge.

As the missiles exploded, Lisse wrenched the kite toward the nearest vortex. The kite was a larger and sturdier craft. It would be better able to survive the voidcurrent stresses. The tapestries dimmed as they approached. She shut off haptics as wind eddied and swirled in the command spindle. It would only get worse.

One missile barely missed her. She would have to do better. And the vortex was a temporary terrain advantage; she could not lurk there forever.

The second barrage came. Lisse veered deeper into the current. The stars took on peculiar roseate shapes.

"They know the kite's capabilities," the ghost reminded her. "Use them. If they're smart, they'll already have sent a courier burst to local command."

The kite suggested jerengjen flyers, harrier class. Lisse conceded its expertise.

The harriers unfolded as they launched, sleek and savage. They maneuvered remarkably well in the turbulence. But there were only ten of them.

"If I fire into that, I'll hit them," Lisse said. Her reflexes were good, but not that good, and the harriers apparently liked to soar near their targets.

"You won't need to fire," the ghost said.

She glanced at him, disbelieving. Her hand hovered over the controls, playing through possibilities and finding them wanting. For instance, she wasn't certain that the firebird (explosives) didn't entail self-immolation, and she was baffled by the stag.

The patrol's pilots were not incapable. They scorched three of the harriers. They probably realized at the same time that Lisse did that the three had been sacrifices. The other seven flensed them silent.

Lisse edged the kite out of the vortex. She felt an uncomfortable sense of duty to the surviving harriers, but she knew they were one-use, crumpled paper, like all jerengjen. Indeed, they folded themselves flat as she passed them, reducing themselves to battledrift.

"I can't see how this is an efficient use of resources," Lisse told the ghost.

"It's an artifact of the mercenaries' methods," it said. "It works. Perhaps that's all that matters."

Lisse wanted to ask for details, but her attention was diverted by a crescendo of turbulence. By the time they reached gentler currents, she was too tired to bring it up.

They altered their approach to 586 Chiu twice, favoring stealth over confrontation. If she wanted to char every patrol in the Imperium by herself, she could live a thousand sleepless years and never be done.

For six days they lurked near 586 Chiu, developing a sense for local traffic and likely defenses. Terrain would not be much difficulty. Aeries were built near calm, steady currents.

"It would be easiest if you were willing to take out the associated city," the ghost said in a neutral voice. They had been discussing whether making a bombing pass on the aerie posed too much of a risk. Lisse had balked at the fact that 586 Chiu Second City was well within blast radius. The people who had furnished the kite's armaments seemed to have believed in surfeit. "They'd only have a moment to know what was happening."

"No."

"Lisse—"

She looked at it mutely, obdurate, although she hated to disappoint it. It hesitated, but did not press its case further.

"This, then," it said in defeat. "Next best odds: aim the voidcurrent disrupter at the manufactory's core while jerengjen occupy the defenses." Aeries held the surrounding current constant to facilitate the calibration of newly built flyers. Under ordinary circumstances, the counterbalancing vortex was leashed at the core. If they could disrupt the core, the vortex would tear at its surroundings.

"That's what we'll do, then," Lisse said. The disrupter had a short range. She did not like the idea of flying in close. But she had objected to the safer alternative.

Aerie 586 Chiu reminded Lisse not of a nest but of a pyre. Flyers and transports were always coming and going, like sparks. The kite swooped in sharp and fast. Falcon-jerengjen raced ahead of them, holding lattice formation for two seconds before scattering toward their chosen marks.

The aerie's commanders responded commendably. They knew the kite was by far the greater threat. But Lisse met the first flight they threw at her with missiles keen and terrible. The void lit up in a clamor of brilliant colors.

The kite screamed when a flyer salvo hit one of its secondary wings. It bucked briefly while the other wings changed their geometry to compensate. Lisse could not help but think that the scream had not sounded like pain. It had sounded like exultation.

The real test was the gauntlet of Banner 142 artillery emplacements. They were silver-bright and terrible. It seemed wrong that they did not roar like tigers. Lisse bit the inside of her mouth and concentrated on narrowing the parameters for the voidcurrent disrupter. Her hand was a fist on the control panel.

One tapestry depicted the currents: striations within striations of pale blue against black. Despite its shielding, the core was visible as a knot tangled out of all proportion to its size.

"Now," the ghost said, with inhuman timing.

She didn't wait to be told twice. She unfisted her hand.

Unlike the wolf-strike, the disrupter made the kite scream again.

It lurched and twisted. Lisse wanted to clap her hands over her ears, but there was more incoming fire, and she was occupied with evasive maneuvers. The kite folded in on itself, minimizing its profile. It dizzied her to view it on the secondary tapestry. For a panicked moment, she thought the kite would close itself around her, press her like petals in a book. Then she remembered to breathe.

The disrupter was not visible to human sight, but the kite could read its effect on the current. Like lightning, the disrupter's blast forked and forked again, zigzagging inexorably toward the minute variations in flux that would lead it toward the core.

She was too busy whipping the kite around to an escape vector to see the moment of convergence between disrupter and core. But she felt the first lashing surge as the vortex spun free of its shielding, expanding into available space. Then she was too busy steadying the kite through the triggered subvortices to pay attention to anything but keeping them alive.

Only later did she remember how much debris there had been, flung in newly unpredictable ways: wings torn from flyers, struts, bulkheads, even an improbable crate with small reddish fruit tumbling from the hole in its side.

Later, too, it would trouble her that she had not been able to keep count of the people in the tumult. Most were dead already: sliced slantwise, bone and viscera exposed, trailing banners of blood; others twisted and torn, faces ripped off and cast aside like unwanted masks, fingers uselessly clutching the wrack of chairs, tables, door frames. A fracture in one wall revealed three people in dark green jackets. They turned their faces toward the widening crack, then clasped hands before a subvortex hurled them apart. The last Lisse saw of them was two hands, still clasped together and severed at the wrist.

Lisse found an escape. Took it.

She didn't know until later that she had destroyed 40% of the aerie's structure. Some people survived. They knew how to rebuild.

What she never found out was that the disrupter's effect was sufficiently long-lasting that some of the survivors died of thirst before supplies could safely be brought in.

In the old days, Lisse's people took on the ghostweight to comfort the dead and be comforted in return. After a year and a day, the dead unstitched themselves and accepted their rest.

After Jerengjen Day, Lisse's people struggled to share the sudden increase in ghostweight, to alleviate the flickering terror of the massacred.

Lisse's parents, unlike the others, stitched a ghost onto a child.

"They saw no choice," the ghost told her again and again. "You mustn't blame them."

The ghost had listened uncomplainingly to her troubles and taught her how to cry quietly so the teachers wouldn't hear her. It had soothed her to sleep with her people's legends and histories, described the gardens and promenades so vividly she imagined she could remember them herself. Some nights were more difficult than others, trying to sleep with that strange, stabbing, heartpulse ache. But blame was not what she felt, not usually.

The second target was Base 454 Qo, whose elite flyers were painted with elaborate knotwork, green with bronze-tipped thorns. For reasons that Lisse did not try to understand, the jerengjen disremembered the defensive flight but left the painted panels completely intact.

The third, the fourth, the fifth—she started using Scorch card values to tabulate the reported deaths, however unreliable the figures were in any unencrypted sources. For all its talents, the kite could not pierce military-grade encryption. She spent two days fidgeting over this inconvenience so she wouldn't have to think about the numbers.

When she did think about the numbers, she refused to round up. She refused to round down.

The nightmares started after the sixth, Bridgepoint 977 Ja-Esh. The station commander had kept silence, as she had come to expect. However, a merchant coalition had broken the interdict to plead for mercy in fourteen languages. She hadn't destroyed the coalition's outpost. The station had, in reprimand.

She reminded herself that the merchant would have perished anyway. She had learned to use the firebird to scathing effect. And she was under no illusions that she was only destroying Imperial soldiers and bureaucrats.

In her dreams she heard their pleas in her birth tongue, which the ghost had taught her. The ghost, for its part, started singing her to sleep, as it had when she was little.

The numbers marched higher. When they broke ten million, she plunged out of the command spindle and into the room she had claimed for her own. She pounded the wall until her fists bled. Triumph tasted like salt and venom. It wasn't supposed to be so *easy*. In the worst dreams, a wolf roved the tapestries, eating shadows—eating souls. And the void with its tinsel of worlds was nothing but one vast shadow.

Stores began running low after the seventeenth. Lisse and the ghost argued over whether it was worth attempting to resupply through black market traders. Lisse said they didn't have time to spare, and won. Besides, she had little appetite.

Intercepted communications suggested that someone was hunting them. Rumors and whispers. They kept Lisse awake when she was so tired she wanted to slam the world shut and hide. The Imperium certainly planned reprisal. Maybe others did, too.

If anyone else took advantage of the disruption to move against the Imperium for their own reasons, she didn't hear about it.

The names of the war-kites, recorded in the Imperium's administrative language, are varied: *Fire Burns the Spider Black. The Siege of the City with Seventeen Faces. Sovereign Geometry. The Glove with Three Fingers.*

The names are not, strictly speaking, Imperial. Rather, they are plundered from the greatest accomplishments of the cultures that the mercenaries have defeated on the Imperium's behalf. *Fire Burns the Spider Black* was a silk tapestry housed in the dark hall of Meu Danh, ancient of years. *The Siege of the City with Seventeen Faces* was a saga chanted by the historians of Kwaire. *Sovereign Geometry* discussed the varying nature of parallel lines. And more: plays, statues, games.

The Imperium's scholars and artists take great pleasure in reinterpreting these works. Such achievements are meant to be disseminated, they say.

They were three days' flight from the next target, Base 894 Sao, when the shadow winged across all the tapestries. The void was dark, pricked by starfire and the occasional searing burst of particles. The shadow singed everything darker as it soared to intercept them, as single-minded in its purpose as a bullet. For a second she almost thought it was a collage of wrecked flyers and rusty shrapnel.

The ghost cursed. Lisse startled, but when she looked at it, its face was composed again.

As Lisse pulled back the displays' focus to get a better sense of the scale, she thought of snowbirds and stormbirds, winter winds and cutting beaks. "I don't know what that is," she said, "but it can't be natural." None of the Imperial defenses had manifested in such a fashion.

"It's not," the ghost said. "That's another war-kite."

Lisse cleared the control panel. She veered them into a chancy voidcurrent eddy.

The ghost said, "Wait. You won't outrun it. As we see its shadow, it sees ours."

"How does a kite have a shadow in the void in the first place?" she asked. "And why haven't we ever seen our own shadow?"

"Who can see their own soul?" the ghost said. But it would not meet her eyes.

Lisse would have pressed for more, but the shadow overtook them. It folded itself back like a plumage of knives. She brought the kite about. The control panel suggested possibilities: a two-headed dragon, a falcon, a coiled snake. Next a wolf reared up, but she quickly pulled her hand back.

"Visual contact," the kite said crisply.

The stranger-kite was the color of a tarnished star. It had tucked all its projections away to present a minimal surface for targeting, but Lisse had no doubt that it could unfold itself faster than she could draw breath. The kite flew a widening helix, beautifully precise.

"A mercenary salute, equal to equal," the ghost said.

"Are we expected to return it?"

"Are you a mercenary?" the ghost countered.

"Communications incoming," the kite said before Lisse could make a retort.

"I'll hear it," Lisse said over the ghost's objection. It was the least courtesy she could offer, even to a mercenary.

To Lisse's surprise, the tapestry's raven vanished to reveal a woman's visage, not an emblem. The woman had brown skin, a scar trailing from one temple down to her cheekbone, and dark hair cropped short. She wore gray on gray, in no uniform that Lisse recognized, sharply tailored. Lisse had expected a killer's eyes, a hunter's eyes. Instead, the woman merely looked tired.

"Commander Kiriet Dzan of—" She had been speaking in administrative, but the last word was unfamiliar. "You would say *Candle*."

"Lisse of Rhaion," she said. There was no sense in hiding her name.

But the woman wasn't looking at her. She was looking at the ghost.

She said something sharply in that unfamiliar language.

The ghost pressed its hand against Lisse's. She shuddered, not understanding. "Be strong," it murmured.

"I see," Kiriet said, once more speaking in administrative. Her mouth was unsmiling. "Lisse, do you know who you're traveling with?"

"I don't believe we're acquainted," the ghost said, coldly formal.

"Of course not," Kiriet said. "But I was the logistical coordinator for the scouring of Rhaion." She did not say *consolidation*. "I knew why we were there. Lisse, your ghost's name is Vron Arien."

Lisse said, after several seconds, "That's a mercenary name."

The ghost said, "So it is. Lisse—" Its hand fell away.

"Tell me what's going on."

Its mouth was taut. Then: "Lisse, I—"

"Tell me."

"He was a deserter, Lisse," the woman said, carefully, as if she thought the information might fracture her. "For years he eluded Wolf Command. Then we discovered he had gone to ground on Rhaion. Wolf Command determined that, for sheltering him, Rhaion must be brought to heel. The Imperium assented."

Throughout this Lisse looked at the ghost, silently begging it to deny any of it, all of it. But the ghost said nothing.

Lisse thought of long nights with the ghost leaning by her bedside, reminding her of the dancers, the tame birds, the tangle of frostfruit trees in the city square; things she did not remember herself because she had been too young when the jerengjen came. Even her parents only came to her in snatches: curling up in a mother's lap, helping a father peel plantains. Had any of the ghost's stories been real?

She thought, too, of the way the ghost had helped her plan her escape from Base 87, how it had led her cunningly through the maze and to the kite. At the time, it had not occurred to her to wonder at its confidence.

Lisse said, "Then the kite is yours."

"After a fashion, yes." The ghost's eyes were precisely the color of ash after the last embers death.

"But my parents—"

Enunciating the words as if they cut it, the ghost said, "We made a bargain, your parents and I."

She could not help it; she made a stricken sound.

"I offered you my protection," the ghost said. "After years serving the Imperium, I knew its workings. And I offered your parents vengeance.

Don't think that Rhaion wasn't my home, too."

Lisse was wrackingly aware of Kiriet's regard. "Did my parents truly die in the consolidation?" The euphemism was easier to use.

She could have asked whether Lisse was her real name. She had to assume that it wasn't.

"I don't know," it said. "After you were separated from them, I had no way of finding out. Lisse, I think you had better find out what Kiriet wants. She is not your friend."

I was the logistical coordinator, Kiriet had said. And her surprise at seeing the ghost—*It has a name*, Lisse reminded herself—struck Lisse as genuine. Which meant Kiriet had not come here in pursuit of Vron Arien. "Why are you here?" Lisse asked.

"You're not going to like it. I'm here to destroy your kite, whatever you've named it."

"It doesn't have a name." She had been unable to face the act of naming, of claiming ownership.

Kiriet looked at her sideways. "I see."

"Surely you could have accomplished your goal," Lisse said, "without talking to me first. I am inexperienced in the ways of kites. You are not." In truth, she should already have been running. But Kiriet's revelation meant that Lisse's purpose, once so clear, was no longer to be relied upon.

"I may not be your friend, but I am not your enemy, either," Kiriet said. "I have no common purpose with the Imperium, not anymore. But you cannot continue to use the kite."

Lisse's eyes narrowed. "It is the weapon I have," she said. "I would be a fool to relinquish it."

"I don't deny its efficacy," Kiriet said, "but you are Rhaioni. Doesn't the cost trouble you?"

Cost?

Kiriet said, "So no one told you." Her anger focused on the ghost.

"A weapon is a weapon," the ghost said. At Lisse's indrawn breath, it said, "The kites take their sustenance from the deaths they deal. It was necessary to strengthen ours by letting it feast on smaller targets first. This is the particular craft of my people, as ghostweight was the craft of yours, Lisse."

Sustenance. "So this is why you want to destroy the kite," Lisse said to Kiriet.

"Yes." The other woman's smile was bitter. "As you might imagine, the Imperium did not approve. It wanted to negotiate another hundred-year contract. I dissented."

"Were you in a position to dissent?" the ghost asked, in a way that made Lisse think that it was translating some idiom from its native language.

"I challenged my way up the chain of command and unseated the head of Wolf Command," Kiriet said. "It was not a popular move. I have been destroying kites ever since. If the Imperium is so keen on further conquest, let it dirty its own hands."

"Yet you wield a kite yourself," Lisse said.

"*Candle* is my home. But on the day that every kite is accounted for in words of ash and cinders, I will turn my own hand against it."

It appealed to Lisse's sense of irony. All the same, she did not trust Kiriet.

She heard a new voice. Kiriet's head turned. "Someone's followed you." She said a curt phrase in her own language, then: "You'll want my assistance—"

Lisse shook her head.

"It's a small flight, as these things go, but it represents a threat to you. Let me—"

"No," Lisse said, more abruptly than she had meant to. "I'll handle it myself."

"If you insist," Kiriet said, looking even more tired. "Don't say I didn't warn you." Then her face was replaced, for a flicker, with her emblem: a black candle crossed slantwise by an empty sheath.

"The *Candle* is headed for a vortex, probably for cover," the ghost said, very softly. "But it can return at any moment."

Lisse thought that she was all right, and then the reaction set in. She spent several irrecoverable breaths shaking, arms wrapped around herself, before she was able to concentrate on the tapestry data.

At one time, every war-kite displayed a calligraphy scroll in its command spindle. The words are, approximately:

> *I have only*
> *one candle*

Even by the mercenaries' standards, it is not much of a poem. But the woman who wrote it was a soldier, not a poet.

The mercenaries no longer have a homeland. Even so, they keep certain traditions, and one of them is the Night of Vigils. Each mercenary honors the year's dead by lighting a candle. They used to do this on the winter solstice of an ancient calendar. Now the Night of Vigils is on the anniversary of the day the first war-kites were launched; the day the mercenaries slaughtered their own people to feed the kites.

The kites fly, the mercenaries' commandant said. *But they do not know how to hunt.*

When he was done, they knew how to hunt. Few of the mercenaries forgave him, but it was too late by then.

The poem says: So many people have died, yet I have only one candle for them all.

It is worth noting that "have" is expressed by a particular construction for alienable possession: not only is the having subject to change, it is additionally under threat of being taken away.

Kiriet's warning had been correct. An Imperial flight in perfect formation had advanced toward them, inhibiting their avenues of escape. They outnumbered her forty-eight to one. The numbers did not concern her, but the Imperium's resources meant that if she dealt with this flight, there would be twenty more waiting for her, and the numbers would only grow worse. That they had not opened fire already meant they had some trickery in mind.

One of the flyers peeled away, describing an elegant curve and exposing its most vulnerable surface, painted with a rose.

"That one's not armed," Lisse said, puzzled.

The ghost's expression was unreadable. "How very wise of them," it said.

The forward tapestry flickered. "Accept the communication," Lisse said.

The emblem that appeared was a trefoil flanked by two roses, one stem-up, one stem-down. Not for the first time, Lisse wondered why people from a culture that lavished attention on miniatures and sculptures were so intent on masking themselves in emblems.

"Commander Fai Guen, this is Envoy Nhai Bara." A woman's voice, deep and resonant, with an accent Lisse didn't recognize.

So I've been promoted? Lisse thought sardonically, feeling herself tense up. The Imperium never gave you anything, even a meaningless rank, without expecting something in return.

Softly, she said to the ghost, "They were bound to catch up to us sooner or later." Then, to the kite: "Communications to Envoy Nhai: I am Lisse of Rhaion. What words between us could possibly be worth exchanging? Your people are not known for mercy."

"If you will not listen to me," Nhai said, "perhaps you will listen to the envoy after me, or the one after that. We are patient and we are many. But I am not interested in discussing mercy: that's something we have in common."

"I'm listening," Lisse said, despite the ghost's chilly stiffness. All her life she had honed herself against the Imperium. It was unbearable to consider that she might have been mistaken. But she had to know what Nhai's purpose was.

"Commander Lisse," the envoy said, and it hurt like a stab to hear her name spoken by a voice other than the ghost's, a voice that was not Rhaioni. Even if she knew, now, that the ghost was not Rhaioni, either. "I have a proposal for you. You have proven your military effectiveness—"

Military effectiveness. She had tallied all the deaths, she had marked each massacre on the walls of her heart, and this faceless envoy collapsed them into two words empty of number.

"—quite thoroughly. We are in need of a strong sword. What is your price for hire, Commander Lisse?"

"What is my—" She stared at the trefoil emblem, and then her face went ashen.

It is not true that the dead cannot be folded. Square becomes kite becomes swan; history becomes rumor becomes song. Even the act of remembrance creases the truth.

But the same can be said of the living.

HOW TO TALK TO GIRLS AT PARTIES

NEIL GAIMAN

Come on," said Vic. "It'll be great."

"No, it won't," I said, although I'd lost this fight hours ago, and I knew it.

"It'll be brilliant," said Vic, for the hundredth time. "Girls! Girls! Girls!" He grinned with white teeth.

We both attended an all-boys' school in south London. While it would be a lie to say that we had no experience with girls—Vic seemed to have had many girlfriends, while I had kissed three of my sister's friends—it would, I think, be perfectly true to say that we both chiefly spoke to, interacted with, and only truly understood, other boys. Well, I did, anyway. It's hard to speak for someone else, and I've not seen Vic for thirty years. I'm not sure that I would know what to say to him now if I did.

We were walking the backstreets that used to twine in a grimy maze behind East Croydon station—a friend had told Vic about a party, and Vic was determined to go whether I liked it or not, and I didn't. But my parents were away that week at a conference, and I was Vic's guest at his house, so I was trailing along beside him.

"It'll be the same as it always is," I said. "After an hour you'll be off somewhere snogging the prettiest girl at the party, and I'll be in the kitchen listening to somebody's mum going on about politics or poetry or something."

"You just have to talk to them," he said. "I think it's probably that road at the end here." He gestured cheerfully, swinging the bag with the bottle in it.

"Don't you know?"

"Alison gave me directions and I wrote them on a bit of paper, but I left it on the hall table. S'okay. I can find it."

"How?" Hope welled slowly up inside me.

"We walk down the road," he said, as if speaking to an idiot child. "And we look for the party. Easy."

I looked, but saw no party: just narrow houses with rusting cars or bikes in their concreted front gardens; and the dusty glass fronts of newsagents, which smelled of alien spices and sold everything from birthday cards and secondhand comics to the kind of magazines that were so pornographic that they were sold already sealed in plastic bags. I had been there when Vic had slipped one of those magazines beneath his sweater, but the owner caught him on the pavement outside and made him give it back.

We reached the end of the road and turned into a narrow street of terraced houses. Everything looked very still and empty in the Summer's evening. "It's all right for you," I said. "They fancy you. You don't actually have to talk to them." It was true: one urchin grin from Vic and he could have his pick of the room.

"Nah. S'not like that. You've just got to talk."

The times I had kissed my sister's friends I had not spoken to them. They had been around while my sister was off doing something elsewhere, and they had drifted into my orbit, and so I had kissed them. I do not remember any talking. I did not know what to say to girls, and I told him so.

"They're just girls," said Vic. "They don't come from another planet."

As we followed the curve of the road around, my hopes that the party would prove unfindable began to fade: a low pulsing noise, music muffled by walls and doors, could be heard from a house up ahead. It was eight in the evening, not that early if you aren't yet sixteen, and we weren't. Not quite.

I had parents who liked to know where I was, but I don't think Vic's parents cared that much. He was the youngest of five boys. That in itself seemed magical to me: I merely had two sisters, both younger than I was, and I felt both unique and lonely. I had wanted a brother as far back as I could remember. When I turned thirteen, I stopped wishing on falling stars or first stars, but back when I did, a brother was what I had wished for.

We went up the garden path, crazy paving leading us past a hedge and a solitary rosebush to a pebble-dashed facade. We rang the doorbell, and the door was opened by a girl. I could not have told you how old she was, which was one of the things about girls I had begun to hate: when you start out as kids you're just boys and girls, going through time at the same speed, and you're all five, or seven, or eleven, together. And then one day there's a lurch and the girls just sort of sprint off into the future ahead of you, and they know all about everything, and they have periods and breasts and makeup and God-only-knew-what-else—for I certainly didn't. The diagrams in biology textbooks were no substitute for being, in a very real sense, young adults. And the girls of our age were.

Vic and I weren't young adults, and I was beginning to suspect that even when I started needing to shave every day, instead of once every couple of weeks, I would still be way behind.

The girl said, "Hello?"

Vic said, "We're friends of Alison's." We had met Alison, all freckles and orange hair and a wicked smile, in Hamburg, on a German exchange. The exchange organizers had sent some girls with us, from a local girls' school, to balance the sexes. The girls, our age, more or less, were raucous and funny, and had more or less adult boyfriends with cars and jobs and motorbikes and—in the case of one girl with crooked teeth and a raccoon coat, who spoke to me about it sadly at the end of a party in Hamburg, in, of course, the kitchen—a wife and kids.

"She isn't here," said the girl at the door. "No Alison."

"Not to worry," said Vic, with an easy grin. "I'm Vic. This is Enn." A beat, and then the girl smiled back at him. Vic had a bottle of white wine in a plastic bag, removed from his parents' kitchen cabinet. "Where should I put this, then?"

She stood out of the way, letting us enter. "There's a kitchen in the back," she said. "Put it on the table there, with the other bottles." She had golden, wavy hair, and she was very beautiful. The hall was dim in the twilight, but I could see that she was beautiful.

"What's your name, then?" said Vic.

She told him it was Stella, and he grinned his crooked white grin and told her that that had to be the prettiest name he had ever heard. Smooth bastard. And what was worse was that he said it like he meant it.

Vic headed back to drop off the wine in the kitchen, and I looked into the front room, where the music was coming from. There were people dancing in there. Stella walked in, and she started to dance, swaying to the music all alone, and I watched her.

This was during the early days of punk. On our own record players we would play the Adverts and the Jam, the Stranglers and the Clash and the Sex Pistols. At other people's parties you'd hear ELO or 10cc or even Roxy Music. Maybe some Bowie, if you were lucky. During the German exchange, the only LP that we had all been able to agree on was Neil Young's *Harvest*, and his song "Heart of Gold" had threaded through the trip like a refrain: *I crossed the ocean for a heart of gold*. . . .

The music playing in that front room wasn't anything I recognized.

It sounded a bit like a German electronic pop group called Kraftwerk, and a bit like an LP I'd been given for my last birthday, of strange sounds made by the BBC Radiophonic Workshop. The music had a beat, though, and the half-dozen girls in that room were moving gently to it, although I only looked at Stella. She shone.

Vic pushed past me, into the room. He was holding a can of lager. "There's booze back in the kitchen," he told me. He wandered over to Stella and he began to talk to her. I couldn't hear what they were saying over the music, but I knew that there was no room for me in that conversation.

I didn't like beer, not back then. I went off to see if there was something I wanted to drink. On the kitchen table stood a large bottle of Coca-Cola, and I poured myself a plastic tumblerful, and I didn't dare say anything to the pair of girls who were talking in the underlit kitchen. They were animated and utterly lovely. Each of them had very black skin and glossy hair and movie star clothes, and their accents were foreign, and each of them was out of my league.

I wandered, Coke in hand.

The house was deeper than it looked, larger and more complex than the two-up two-down model I had imagined. The rooms were underlit—I doubt there was a bulb of more than 40 watts in the building—and each room I went into was inhabited: in my memory, inhabited only by girls. I did not go upstairs.

A girl was the only occupant of the conservatory. Her hair was so fair it was white, and long, and straight, and she sat at the glass-topped table, her hands clasped together, staring at the garden outside, and the gathering dusk. She seemed wistful.

"Do you mind if I sit here?" I asked, gesturing with my cup. She shook her head, and then followed it up with a shrug, to indicate that it was all the same to her. I sat down.

Vic walked past the conservatory door. He was talking to Stella, but he looked in at me, sitting at the table, wrapped in shyness and awkwardness, and he opened and closed his hand in a parody of a speaking mouth. Talk. Right.

"Are you from around here?" I asked the girl.

She shook her head. She wore a low-cut silvery top, and I tried not to stare at the swell of her breasts.

I said, "What's your name? I'm Enn."

"Wain's Wain," she said, or something that sounded like it. "I'm a second."

"That's uh. That's a different name."

She fixed me with huge, liquid eyes. "It indicates that my progenitor was also Wain, and that I am obliged to report back to her. I may not breed."

"Ah. Well. Bit early for that anyway, isn't it?"

She unclasped her hands, raised them above the table, spread her fingers. "You see?" The little finger on her left hand was crooked, and it bifurcated at the top, splitting into two smaller fingertips. A minor deformity. "When I was finished a decision was needed. Would I be retained, or eliminated? I was fortunate that the decision was with me. Now, I travel, while my more perfect sisters remain at home in stasis. They were firsts. I am a second.

Soon I must return to Wain, and tell her all I have seen. All my impressions of this place of yours."

"I don't actually live in Croydon," I said. "I don't come from here." I wondered if she was American. I had no idea what she was talking about.

"As you say," she agreed, "neither of us comes from here." She folded her six-fingered left hand beneath her right, as if tucking it out of sight. "I had expected it to be bigger, and cleaner, and more colorful. But still, it is a jewel."

She yawned, covered her mouth with her right hand, only for a moment, before it was back on the table again. "I grow weary of the journeying, and I wish sometimes that it would end. On a street in Rio at Carnival, I saw them on a bridge, golden and tall and insect-eyed and winged, and elated I almost ran to greet them, before I saw that they were only people in costumes. I said to Hola Colt, 'Why do they try so hard to look like us?' and Hola Colt replied, 'Because they hate themselves, all shades of pink and brown, and so small.' It is what I experience, even me, and I am not grown. It is like a world of children, or of elves." Then she smiled, and said, "It was a good thing they could not any of them see Hola Colt."

"Um," I said, "do you want to dance?"

She shook her head immediately. "It is not permitted," she said. "I can do nothing that might cause damage to property. I am Wain's."

"Would you like something to drink, then?"

"Water," she said.

I went back to the kitchen and poured myself another Coke, and filled a cup with water from the tap. From the kitchen back to the hall, and from there into the conservatory, but now it was quite empty.

I wondered if the girl had gone to the toilet, and if she might change her mind about dancing later. I walked back to the front room and stared in. The place was filling up. There were more girls dancing, and several lads I didn't know, who looked a few years older than me and Vic. The lads and the girls all kept their distance, but Vic was holding Stella's hand as they danced, and when the song ended he put an arm around her, casually, almost proprietorially, to make sure that nobody else cut in.

I wondered if the girl I had been talking to in the conservatory was now upstairs, as she did not appear to be on the ground floor.

I walked into the living room, which was across the hall from the room where the people were dancing, and I sat down on the sofa. There was a girl sitting there already. She had dark hair, cut short and spiky, and a nervous manner.

Talk, I thought. "Um, this mug of water's going spare," I told her, "if you want it?"

She nodded, and reached out her hand and took the mug, extremely carefully, as if she were unused to taking things, as if she could trust neither her vision nor her hands.

"I love being a tourist," she said, and smiled hesitantly. She had a gap between her two front teeth, and she sipped the tap water as if she were an adult sipping a fine wine. "The last tour, we went to sun, and we swam in sunfire pools with the whales. We heard their histories and we shivered in the chill of the outer places, then we swam deepward where the heat churned and comforted us.

"I wanted to go back. This time, I wanted it. There was so much I had not seen. Instead we came to world. Do you like it?"

"Like what?"

She gestured vaguely to the room—the sofa, the armchairs, the curtains, the unused gas fire.

"It's all right, I suppose."

"I told them I did not wish to visit world," she said. "My parent-teacher was unimpressed. 'You will have much to learn,' it told me. I said, 'I could learn more in sun, again. Or in the deeps. Jessa spun webs between galaxies. I want to do that.'

"But there was no reasoning with it, and I came to world. Parent-teacher engulfed me, and I was here, embodied in a decaying lump of meat hanging on a frame of calcium. As I incarnated I felt things deep inside me, fluttering and pumping and squishing. It was my first experience with pushing air through the mouth, vibrating the vocal cords on the way, and I used it to tell parent-teacher that I wished that I would die, which it acknowledged was the inevitable exit strategy from world."

There were black worry beads wrapped around her wrist, and she fiddled with them as she spoke. "But knowledge is there, in the meat," she said, "and I am resolved to learn from it."

We were sitting close at the center of the sofa now. I decided I should put an arm around her, but casually. I would extend my arm along the back of the sofa and eventually sort of creep it down, almost imperceptibly, until it was touching her. She said, "The thing with the liquid in the eyes, when the world blurs. Nobody told me, and I still do not understand. I have touched the folds of the Whisper and pulsed and flown with the tachyon swans, and I still do not understand."

She wasn't the prettiest girl there, but she seemed nice enough, and she was a girl, anyway. I let my arm slide down a little, tentatively, so that it made contact with her back, and she did not tell me to take it away.

Vic called to me then, from the doorway. He was standing with his arm around Stella, protectively, waving at me. I tried to let him know, by shaking my head, that I was onto something, but he called my name and, reluctantly, I got up from the sofa and walked over to the door. "What?"

"Er. Look. The party," said Vic, apologetically. "It's not the one I thought it was. I've been talking to Stella and I figured it out. Well, she sort of explained it to me. We're at a different party."

"Christ. Are we in trouble? Do we have to go?"

Stella shook her head. He leaned down and kissed her, gently, on the lips. "You're just happy to have me here, aren't you darlin'?"

"You know I am," she told him.

He looked from her back to me, and he smiled his white smile: roguish, lovable, a little bit Artful Dodger, a little bit wide-boy Prince Charming. "Don't worry. They're all tourists here anyway. It's a foreign exchange thing, innit? Like when we all went to Germany."

"It is?"

"Enn. You got to talk to them. And that means you got to listen to them, too. You understand?"

"I did. I already talked to a couple of them."

"You getting anywhere?"

"I was till you called me over."

"Sorry about that. Look, I just wanted to fill you in. Right?"

And he patted my arm and he walked away with Stella. Then, together, the two of them went up the stairs.

Understand me, all the girls at that party, in the twilight, were lovely; they all had perfect faces but, more important than that, they had whatever strangeness of proportion, of oddness or humanity it is that makes a beauty something more than a shop window dummy.

Stella was the most lovely of any of them, but she, of course, was Vic's, and they were going upstairs together, and that was just how things would always be.

There were several people now sitting on the sofa, talking to the gap-toothed girl. Someone told a joke, and they all laughed. I would have had to push my way in there to sit next to her again, and it didn't look like she was expecting me back, or cared that I had gone, so I wandered out into the hall. I glanced in at the dancers, and found myself wondering where the music was coming from. I couldn't see a record player or speakers.

From the hall I walked back to the kitchen.

Kitchens are good at parties. You never need an excuse to be there, and, on the good side, at this party I couldn't see any signs of someone's mum. I inspected the various bottles and cans on the kitchen table, then I poured a half an inch of Pernod into the bottom of my plastic cup, which I filled to the top with Coke. I dropped in a couple of ice cubes and took a sip, relishing the sweet-shop tang of the drink.

"What's that you're drinking?" A girl's voice.

"It's Pernod," I told her. "It tastes like aniseed balls, only it's alcoholic." I didn't say that I only tried it because I'd heard someone in the crowd ask for a Pernod on a live Velvet Underground LP.

"Can I have one?" I poured another Pernod, topped it off with Coke, passed it to her. Her hair was a coppery auburn, and it tumbled around her head in ringlets. It's not a hair style you see much now, but you saw it a lot back then.

"What's your name?" I asked.

"Triolet," she said.

"Pretty name," I told her, although I wasn't sure that it was. She was pretty, though.

"It's a verse form," she said, proudly. "Like me."

"You're a poem?"

She smiled, and looked down and away, perhaps bashfully. Her profile was almost flat—a perfect Grecian nose that came down from her forehead in a straight line. We did Antigone in the school theater the previous year. I was the messenger who brings Creon the news of Antigone's death. We wore half-masks that made us look like that. I thought of that play, looking at her face, in the kitchen, and I thought of Barry Smith's drawings of women in the Conan comics: five years later I would have thought of the Pre-Raphaelites, of Jane Morris and Lizzie Siddall. But I was only fifteen then.

"You're a poem?" I repeated.

She chewed her lower lip. "If you want. I am a poem, or I am a pattern, or a race of people whose world was swallowed by the sea."

"Isn't it hard to be three things at the same time?"

"What's your name?"

"Enn."

"So you are Enn," she said. "And you are a male. And you are a biped. Is it hard to be three things at the same time?"

"But they aren't different things. I mean, they aren't contradictory." It was a word I had read many times but never said aloud before that night, and I put the stresses in the wrong places. *Contradictory.*

She wore a thin dress made of a white, silky fabric. Her eyes were a pale green, a color that would now make me think of tinted contact lenses; but this was thirty years ago; things were different then. I remember wondering about Vic and Stella, upstairs. By now, I was sure that they were in one of the bedrooms, and I envied Vic so much it almost hurt.

Still, I was talking to this girl, even if we were talking nonsense, even if her name wasn't really Triolet (my generation had not been given hippie names: all the Rainbows and the Sunshines and the Moons, they were only six, seven, eight years old back then). She said, "We knew that it would soon be over, and so we put it all into a poem, to tell the universe who we were, and why we were here, and what we said and did and thought and dreamed and yearned for. We wrapped our dreams in words and patterned the words so that they would live forever, unforgettable. Then we sent the poem as a pattern of flux, to wait in the heart of a star, beaming out its message in pulses and bursts and fuzzes across the electromagnetic spectrum, until the time when, on worlds a thousand sun systems distant, the pattern would be decoded and read, and it would become a poem once again."

"And then what happened?"

She looked at me with her green eyes, and it was as if she stared out at me from her own Antigone half-mask; but as if her pale green eyes were just a different, deeper, part of the mask. "You cannot hear a poem without it changing you," she told me. "They heard it, and it colonized them. It inherited them and it inhabited them, its rhythms becoming part of the way that they thought; its images permanently transmuting their metaphors; its verses, its outlook, its aspirations becoming their lives. Within a generation their children would be born already knowing the poem, and, sooner rather than later, as these things go, there were no more children born. There was no need for them, not any longer. There was only a poem, which took flesh and walked and spread itself across the vastness of the known."

I edged closer to her, so I could feel my leg pressing against hers.

She seemed to welcome it: she put her hand on my arm, affectionately, and I felt a smile spreading across my face.

"There are places that we are welcomed," said Triolet, "and places where we are regarded as a noxious weed, or as a disease, something immediately to be quarantined and eliminated. But where does contagion end and art begin?"

"I don't know," I said, still smiling. I could hear the unfamiliar music as it pulsed and scattered and boomed in the front room.

She leaned into me then and—I suppose it was a kiss. . . . I suppose. She pressed her lips to my lips, anyway, and then, satisfied, she pulled back, as if she had now marked me as her own.

"Would you like to hear it?" she asked, and I nodded, unsure what she was offering me, but certain that I needed anything she was willing to give me.

She began to whisper something in my ear. It's the strangest thing about poetry—you can tell it's poetry, even if you don't speak the language. You can hear Homer's Greek without understanding a word, and you still know it's poetry. I've heard Polish poetry, and Inuit poetry, and I knew what it was without knowing. Her whisper was like that. I didn't know the language, but her words washed through me, perfect, and in my mind's eye I saw towers of glass and diamond; and people with eyes of the palest green; and, unstoppable, beneath every syllable, I could feel the relentless advance of the ocean.

Perhaps I kissed her properly. I don't remember. I know I wanted to.

And then Vic was shaking me violently. "Come on!" he was shouting. "Quickly. Come on!"

In my head I began to come back from a thousand miles away.

"Idiot. Come on. Just get a move on," he said, and he swore at me. There was fury in his voice.

For the first time that evening I recognized one of the songs being played in the front room. A sad saxophone wail followed by a cascade of liquid chords, a man's voice singing cut-up lyrics about the sons of the silent age. I wanted to stay and hear the song.

She said, "I am not finished. There is yet more of me."

"Sorry love," said Vic, but he wasn't smiling any longer. "There'll be another time," and he grabbed me by the elbow and he twisted and pulled, forcing me from the room. I did not resist. I knew from experience that Vic could beat the stuffing out me if he got it into his head to do so. He wouldn't do it unless he was upset or angry, but he was angry now.

Out into the front hall. As Vic pulled open the door, I looked back one last time, over my shoulder, hoping to see Triolet in the doorway to the kitchen, but she was not there. I saw Stella, though, at the top of the stairs. She was staring down at Vic, and I saw her face.

This all happened thirty years ago. I have forgotten much, and I will forget more, and in the end I will forget everything; yet, if I have any certainty of life beyond death, it is all wrapped up not in psalms or hymns, but in this one thing alone: I cannot believe that I will ever forget that moment, or forget the expression on Stella's face as she watched Vic hurrying away from her. Even in death I shall remember that.

Her clothes were in disarray, and there was makeup smudged across her face, and her eyes—

You wouldn't want to make a universe angry. I bet an angry universe would look at you with eyes like that.

We ran then, me and Vic, away from the party and the tourists and the twilight, ran as if a lightning storm was on our heels, a mad helter-skelter dash down the confusion of streets, threading through the maze, and we did not look back, and we did not stop until we could not breathe; and then we stopped and panted, unable to run any longer. We were in pain. I held on to a wall, and Vic threw up, hard and long, into the gutter.

He wiped his mouth.

"She wasn't a—" He stopped.

He shook his head.

Then he said, "You know . . . I think there's a thing. When you've gone as far as you dare. And if you go any further, you wouldn't be you anymore? You'd be the person who'd done that? The places you just can't go. . . . I think that happened to me tonight."

I thought I knew what he was saying. "Screw her, you mean?" I said.

He rammed a knuckle hard against my temple, and twisted it violently. I wondered if I was going to have to fight him—and lose—but after a moment he lowered his hand and moved away from me, making a low, gulping noise.

I looked at him curiously, and I realized that he was crying: his face was scarlet; snot and tears ran down his cheeks. Vic was sobbing in the street, as unselfconsciously and heartbreakingly as a little boy.

He walked away from me then, shoulders heaving, and he hurried down the road so he was in front of me and I could no longer see his face. I wondered what had occurred in that upstairs room to make him behave like that, to scare him so, and I could not even begin to guess.

The streetlights came on, one by one; Vic stumbled on ahead, while I trudged down the street behind him in the dusk, my feet treading out the measure of a poem that, try as I might, I could not properly remember and would never be able to repeat.

NIGHT THEY MISSED THE HORROR SHOW

JOE R. LANSDALE

If they'd gone to the drive-in like they'd planned, none of this would have happened. But Leonard didn't like drive-ins when he didn't have a date, and he'd heard about *Night Of the Living Dead*, and he knew a nigger starred in it. He didn't want to see no movie with a nigger star. Niggers chopped cotton, fixed flats, and pimped nigger girls, but he'd never heard of one that killed zombies. And he'd heard too that there was a white girl in the movie that let the nigger touch her, and that peeved him. Any white gal that would let a nigger touch her must be the lowest trash in the world. Probably from Hollywood, New York, or Waco, some god-forsaken place like that.

Now Steve McQueen would have been all right for zombie killing and girl handling. He would have been the ticket. But a nigger? No sir.

Boy, that Steve McQueen was one cool head. Way he said stuff in them pictures was so good you couldn't help but think someone had written it down for him. He could sure think fast on his feet to come up with the things he said, and he had that real cool, mean look.

Leonard wished he could be Steve McQueen, or Paul Newman even. Someone like that always knew what to say, and he figured they got plenty of bush too. Certainly they didn't get as bored as he did. He was so bored he felt as if he were going to die from it before the night was out. Bored, bored, bored. Just wasn't nothing exciting about being in the Dairy Queen parking lot leaning on the front of his '64 Impala looking out at the highway. He figured maybe old crazy Harry who janitored at the high school might be right about them flying saucers. Harry was always seeing something. Bigfoot, six-legged weasels, all manner of things. But maybe he was right about the saucers. He said he'd seen one a couple nights back hovering over Mud Creek and it was shooting down these rays that looked like wet peppermint sticks. Leonard figured if Harry really had seen the saucers and the rays, then those rays were boredom rays. It would be a way for space critters to get at Earth folks, boring them to death. Getting melted down by heat rays would have been better. That was at least quick, but being bored to death was sort of like being nibbled to death by ducks.

Leonard continued looking at the highway, trying to imagine flying saucers and boredom rays, but he couldn't keep his mind on it. He finally focused on something in the highway. A dead dog.

Not just a dead dog. But a DEAD DOG. The mutt had been hit by a semi at least, maybe several. It looked as if it had rained dog. There were pieces of that pooch all over the concrete and one leg was lying on the curbing on the opposite side, stuck up in such a way that it seemed to be waving hello. Doctor Frankenstein with a grant from Johns Hopkins and assistance from NASA couldn't have put that sucker together again.

Leonard leaned over to his faithful, drunk companion, Billy—known among the gang as Farto, because he was fart-lighting champion of Mud Creek—and said, "See that dog there?"

Farto looked where Leonard was pointing. He hadn't noticed the dog before, and he wasn't nearly as casual about it as Leonard. The puzzle-piece hound brought back memories. It reminded him of a dog he'd had when he was thirteen. A big, fine German shepherd that loved him better than his Mama.

Sonofabitch dog tangled its chain through and over a barbed wire fence somehow and hung itself. When Farto found the dog its tongue looked like a stuffed, black sock and he could see where its claws had just been able to scrape the ground, but not quite enough to get a toehold. It looked as if the dog had been scratching out some sort of coded message in the dirt. When Farto told his old man about it later, crying as he did, his old man laughed and said, "Probably a goddamn suicide note."

Now, as he looked out at the highway, and his whisky-laced Coke collected warmly in his gut, he felt a tear form in his eyes. Last time he'd felt that sappy was when he'd won the fart-lighting championship with a four-inch burner that singed the hairs of his ass and the gang awarded him with a pair of colored boxing shorts. Brown and yellow ones so he could wear them without having to change them too often.

So there they were. Leonard and Farto, parked outside the DQ, leaning on the hood of Leonard's Impala, sipping Coke and whisky, feeling bored and blue and horny, looking at a dead dog and having nothing to do but go to a show with a nigger starring in it. Which, to be up front, wouldn't have been so bad if they'd had dates. Dates could make up for a lot of sins, or help make a few good ones, depending on one's outlook.

But the night was criminal. Dates they didn't have. Worse yet, wasn't a girl in the entire high school would date them. Not even Marylou Flowers, and she had some kind of disease.

All this nagged Leonard something awful. He could see what the problem was with Farto. He was ugly. Had the kind of face that attracted flies. And though being fart-lighting champion of Mud Creek had a certain prestige among the gang, it lacked a certain something when it came to charming the gals.

But for the life of him, Leonard couldn't figure his own problem. He was handsome, had some good clothes, and his car ran good when he didn't buy that old cheap gas. He even had a few bucks in his jeans from breaking into washaterias. Yet his right arm had damn near grown to the size of his thigh from all the whacking off he did. Last time he'd been out with a girl had been a month ago, and as he'd been out with her along with nine other guys, he wasn't rightly sure he could call that a date. He wondered about it so much, he'd asked Farto if he thought it qualified as a date. Farto, who had been fifth in line, said he didn't think so, but if Leonard wanted to call it one, wasn't no skin off his dick.

But Leonard didn't want to call it a date. It just didn't have the feel of one, lacked that something special. There was no romance to it.

True, Big Red had called him Honey when he put the mule in the barn, but she called everyone Honey—except Stoney. Stoney was Possum Sweets, and he was the one who talked her into wearing the grocery bag with the mouth and eye holes. Stoney was like that. He could sweet talk the camel out from under a sand nigger. When he got through chatting Big Red down, she was plumb proud to wear that bag.

When finally it came his turn to do Big Red, Leonard had let her take the bag off as a gesture of goodwill. That was a mistake. He just hadn't known a good thing when he had it. Stoney had had the right idea. The bag coming off spoiled everything. With it on, it was sort of like balling the Lone Hippo or some such thing, but with the bag off, you were absolutely certain what you were getting, and it wasn't pretty.

Even closing his eyes hadn't helped. He found that the ugliness of that face had branded itself on the back of his eyeballs. He couldn't even imagine the sack back over her head. All he could think about was that puffy, too-painted face with the sort of bad complexion that began at the bone.

He'd gotten so disappointed, he'd had to fake an orgasm and get off before his hooter shriveled up and his Trojan fell off and was lost in the vacuum.

Thinking back on it, Leonard sighed. It would certainly be nice for a change to go with a girl that didn't pull the train or had a hole between her legs that looked like a manhole cover ought to be on it. Sometimes he wished he could be like Farto, who was as happy as if he had good sense. Anything thrilled him. Give him a can of Wolf Brand Chili, a big Moon Pie, Coke and whisky and he could spend the rest of his life fucking Big Red and lighting the gas out of his asshole.

God, but this was no way to live. No women and no fun. Bored, bored, bored. Leonard found himself looking overhead for spaceships and peppermint-colored boredom rays, but he saw only a few moths fluttering drunkenly through the beams of the DQ's lights.

Lowering his eyes back to the highway and the dog, Leonard had a sudden flash. "Why don't we get the chain out of the back and hook it up to Rex there? Take him for a ride."

"You mean drag his dead ass around?" Farto asked.

Leonard nodded.

"Beats stepping on a tack," Farto said.

They drove the Impala into the middle of the highway at a safe moment and got out for a look. Up close the mutt was a lot worse. Its innards had been mashed out of its mouth and asshole and it stunk something awful. The dog was wearing a thick, metal-studded collar and they fastened one end of their fifteen-foot chain to that and the other to the rear bumper.

Bob, the Dairy Queen manager, noticed them through the window, came outside and yelled, "What are you fucking morons doing?"

"Taking this doggie to the vet," Leonard said. "We think this sumbitch looks a might peeked. He may have been hit by a car."

"That's so fucking funny I'm about to piss myself," Bob said.

"Old folks have that problem," Leonard said.

Leonard got behind the wheel and Farto climbed in on the passenger side. They maneuvered the car and dog around and out of the path of a tractor-trailer truck just in time. As they drove off, Bob screamed after them, "I hope you two no-dicks wrap that Chevy piece of shit around a goddamn pole."

As they roared along, parts of the dog, like crumbs from a flakey loaf of bread, came off. A tooth here. Some hair there. A string of guts. A dew claw. And some unidentifiable pink stuff. The metal-studded collar and chain threw up sparks now and then like fiery crickets. Finally they hit seventy-five and the dog was swinging wider and wider on the chain, like it was looking for an opportunity to pass.

Farto poured him and Leonard up Coke and whiskys as they drove along. He handed Leonard his paper cup and Leonard knocked it back, a lot happier now than he had been a moment ago. Maybe this night wasn't going to turn out so bad after all.

They drove by a crowd at the side of the road, a tan station wagon and a wreck of a Ford up on a jack. At a glance they could see that there was a nigger in the middle of the crowd and he wasn't witnessing to the white boys. He was hopping around like a pig with a hotshot up his ass, trying to find a break in the white boys so he could make a run for it. But there wasn't any break to be found and there were too many to fight. Nine white boys were knocking him around like he was a pinball and they were a malicious machine.

"Ain't that one of our niggers?" Farto asked. "And ain't that some of the White Tree football players that's trying to kill him?"

"Scott," Leonard said, and the name was dogshit in his mouth. It had been Scott who had outdone him for the position of quarterback on the team. That damn jig could put together a play more tangled than a can of fishing worms, but it damn near always worked. And he could run like a spotted-ass ape.

As they passed, Farto said, "We'll read about him tomorrow in the papers."

But Leonard drove only a short way before slamming on the brakes and whipping the Impala around. Rex swung way out and clipped off some tall, dried sunflowers at the edge of the road like a scythe.

"We gonna go back and watch?" Farto asked. "I don't think them White Tree boys would bother us none if that's all we was gonna do, watch."

"He may be a nigger," Leonard said, not liking himself, "but he's our nigger and we can't let them do that. They kill him they'll beat us in football."

Farto saw the truth of this immediately. "Damn right. They can't do that to our nigger."

Leonard crossed the road again and went straight for the White

Tree boys, hit down hard on the horn. The White Tree boys abandoned beating their prey and jumped in all directions. Bullfrogs couldn't have done any better.

Scott stood startled and weak where he was, his knees bent in and touching one another, his eyes big as pizza pans. He had never noticed how big grillwork was. It looked like teeth there in the night and the headlights looked like eyes. He felt like a stupid fish about to be eaten by a shark.

Leonard braked hard, but off the highway in the dirt it wasn't enough to keep from bumping Scott, sending him flying over the hood and against the glass where his face mashed to it then rolled away, his shirt snagging one of the windshield wipers and pulling it off.

Leonard opened the car door and called to Scott, who lay on the ground, "It's now or never."

A White Tree boy made for the car, and Leonard pulled the taped hammer handle out from beneath the seat and stepped out of the car and hit him with it. The White Tree boy went down to his knees and said something that sounded like French but wasn't. Leonard grabbed Scott by the back of the shirt and pulled him up and guided him around and threw him into the open door. Scott scrambled over the front seat and into the back. Leonard threw the hammer handle at one of the White Tree boys and stepped back, whirled into the car behind the wheel. He put the car in gear again and stepped on the gas. The Impala lurched forward, and with one hand on the door Leonard flipped it wider and clipped a White Tree boy with it as if he were flexing a wing. The car bumped back on the highway and the chain swung out and Rex cut the feet out from under two White Tree boys as neatly as he had taken down the dried sunflowers.

Leonard looked in his rearview mirror and saw two White Tree boys carrying the one he had clubbed with the hammer handle to the station wagon. The others he and the dog had knocked down were getting up. One had kicked the jack out from under Scott's car and was using it to smash the headlights and windshield.

"Hope you got insurance on that thing," Leonard said.

"I borrowed it," Scott said, peeling the windshield wiper out of his T-shirt. "Here, you might want this." He dropped the wiper over the seat and between Leonard and Farto.

"That's a borrowed car?" Farto said. "That's worse."

"Nah," Scott said. "Owner don't know I borrowed it. I'd have had that flat changed if that sucker had had him a spare tire, but I got back there and wasn't nothing but the rim, man. Say, thanks for not letting me get killed, else we couldn't have run that ole pig together no more. Course, you almost run over me. My chest hurts."

Leonard checked the rearview again. The White Tree boys were coming fast. "You complaining?" Leonard said.

"Nah," Scott said, and turned to look through the back glass. He could see the dog swinging in short arcs and pieces of it going wide and far. "Hope you didn't go off and forget your dog tied to the bumper."

"Goddamn," said Farto, "and him registered too."

"This ain't so funny," Leonard said, "them White Tree boys are gaining."

"Well speed it up," Scott said.

Leonard gnashed his teeth. "I could always get rid of some excess baggage, you know."

"Throwing that windshield wiper out ain't gonna help," Scott said.

Leonard looked in his mirror and saw the grinning nigger in the backseat. Nothing worse than a comic coon. He didn't even look grateful. Leonard had a sudden horrid vision of being overtaken by the White Tree boys. What if he were killed with the nigger? Getting killed was bad enough, but what if tomorrow they found him in a ditch with Farto and the nigger? Or maybe them White Tree boys would make him do something awful with the nigger before they killed them. Like making him suck the nigger's dick or some such thing. Leonard held his foot all the way to the floor; as they passed the Dairy Queen he took a hard left and the car just made it and Rex swung out and slammed a light pole then popped back in line behind them.

The White Tree boys couldn't make the corner in the station wagon and they didn't even try. They screeched into a car lot down a piece, turned around and came back. By that time the taillights of the Impala were moving away from them rapidly, looking like two inflamed hemorrhoids in a dark asshole.

"Take the next right coming up," Scott said, "then you'll see a little road off to the left. Kill your lights and take that."

Leonard hated taking orders from Scott on the field, but this was worse. Insulting. Still, Scott called good plays on the field, and the habit of following instructions from the quarterback died hard. Leonard made the right and Rex made it with them after taking a dip in a water-filled bar ditch.

Leonard saw the little road and killed his lights and took it. It carried them down between several rows of large tin storage buildings, and Leonard pulled between two of them and drove down a little alley lined with more. He stopped the car and they waited and listened. After about five minutes, Farto said, "I think we skunked those father-rapers."

"Ain't we a team?" Scott said.

In spite of himself, Leonard felt good. It was like when the nigger called a play that worked and they were all patting each other on the ass and not minding what color the other was because they were just creatures in football suits.

"Let's have a drink," Leonard said.

Farto got a paper cup off the floorboard for Scott and poured him up some warm Coke and whisky. Last time they had gone to Longview, he had peed in that paper cup so they wouldn't have to stop, but that had long since been poured out, and besides, it was for a nigger. He poured Leonard and himself drinks in their same cups.

Scott took a sip and said, "Shit, man, that tastes kind of rank."

"Like piss," Farto said.

Leonard held up his cup. "To the Mud Creek Wildcats and fuck them White Tree boys."

"You fuck 'em," Scott said. They touched their cups, and at that moment the car filled with light.

Cups upraised, the Three Musketeers turned blinking toward it. The light was coming from an open storage building door and there was a fat man standing in the center of the glow like a bloated fly on a lemon wedge. Behind him was a big screen made of a sheet and there was some kind of movie playing on it. And though the light was bright and fading out the movie, Leonard, who was in the best position to see, got a look at it. What he could make out looked like a gal down on her knees sucking this fat guy's dick (the man was visible only from the belly down) and the guy had a short, black revolver pressed to her forehead. She pulled her mouth off of him for an instant and the man came in her face then fired the revolver. The woman's head snapped out of frame and the sheet seemed to drip blood, like dark condensation on a window pane. Then Leonard couldn't see anymore because another man had appeared in the doorway, and like the first he was fat. Both looked like huge bowling balls that had been set on top of shoes. More men appeared behind these two, but one of the fat men turned and held up his hand and the others moved out of sight. The two fat guys stepped outside and one pulled the door almost shut, except for a thin band of light that fell across the front seat of the Impala.

Fat Man Number One went over to the car and opened Farto's door and said, "You fucks and the nigger get out." It was the voice of doom. They had only thought the White Tree boys were dangerous. They realized now they had been kidding themselves. This was the real article. This guy would have eaten the hammer handle and shit a two-by-four.

They got out of the car and the fat man waved them around and lined them up on Farto's side and looked at them. The boys still had their drinks in their hands, and sparing that, they looked like cons in a lineup.

Fat Man Number Two came over and looked at the trio and smiled. It was obvious the fatties were twins. They had the same bad features in the same fat faces. They wore Hawaiian shirts that varied only in profiles and color of parrots and had on white socks and too-short black slacks and black, shiny Italian shoes with toes sharp enough to thread needles.

Fat Man Number One took the cup away from Scott and sniffed it. "A nigger with liquor," he said. "That's like a cunt with brains. It don't go together. Guess you was getting tanked up so you could put the old black snake to some chocolate pudding after a while. Or maybe you was wantin' some vanilla and these boys were gonna set it up."

"I'm not wanting anything but to go home," Scott said.

Fat Man Number Two looked at Fat Man Number One and said, "So he can fuck his mother."

The fatties looked at Scott to see what he'd say but he didn't say anything. They could say he screwed dogs and that was all right with him. Hell, bring one on and he'd fuck it now if they'd let him go afterwards.

Fat Man Number One said, "You boys running around with a jungle bunny makes me sick."

"He's just a nigger from school," Farto said. "We don't like him none. We just picked him up because some White Tree boys were beating on him and we didn't want him to get wrecked on account of he's our quarterback."

"Ah," Fat Man Number One said, "I see. Personally, me and Vinnie don't cotton to niggers in sports. They start taking showers with white boys the next thing they want is to take white girls to bed. It's just one step from one to the other."

"We don't have nothing to do with him playing," Leonard said. "We didn't integrate the schools."

"No," Fat Man Number One said, "that was ole Big Ears Johnson, but you're running around with him and drinking with him."

"His cup's been peed in," Farto said. "That was kind of a joke on him, you see. He ain't our friend, I swear it. He's just a nigger that plays football."

"Peed in his cup, huh?" said the one called Vinnie. "I like that, Pork, don't you? Peed in his fucking cup."

Pork dropped Scott's cup on the ground and smiled at him. "Come here, nigger. I got something to tell you."

Scott looked at Farto and Leonard. No help there. They had suddenly become interested in the toes of their shoes; they examined them as if they were true marvels of the world.

Scott moved toward Pork, and Pork, still smiling, put his arm around Scott's shoulders and walked him toward the big storage building. Scott said, "What are we doing?"

Pork turned Scott around so they were facing Leonard and Farto who still stood holding their drinks and contemplating their shoes. "I didn't want to get it on the new gravel drive," Pork said and pulled Scott's head in close to his own and with his free hand reached back and under his Hawaiian shirt and brought out a short black revolver and put it to Scott's temple and pulled the trigger. There was a snap like a bad knee going out and Scott's feet lifted in unison and went to the side and something dark squirted from his head and his feet swung back toward Pork and his shoes shuffled, snapped, and twisted on the concrete in front of the building.

"Ain't that somethin'," Pork said as Scott went limp and dangled from the thick crook of his arm, "the rhythm is the last thing to go."

Leonard couldn't make a sound. His guts were in his throat. He wanted to melt and run under the car. Scott was dead and the brains that had made plays twisted as fishing worms and commanded his feet on down the football field were scrambled like breakfast eggs.

Farto said, "Holy shit."

Pork let go of Scott and Scott's legs split and he sat down and his head went forward and clapped on the cement between his knees. A dark pool formed under his face.

"He's better off, boys," Vinnie said. "Nigger was begat by Cain and the ape and he ain't quite monkey and he ain't quite man. He's got no place in this world 'cept as a beast of burden. You start trying to train them to do things like drive cars and run with footballs it ain't nothing but grief to them and the whites too. Get any on your shirt, Pork?"

"Nary a drop."

Vinnie went inside the building and said something to the men there that could be heard but not understood, then he came back with some crumpled newspapers. He went over to Scott and wrapped them around the bloody head and let it drop back on the cement. "You try hosing down that shit when it's dried, Pork, and you wouldn't worry none about that gravel. The gravel ain't nothing."

Then Vinnie said to Farto, "Open the back door of that car." Farto nearly twisted an ankle doing it. Vinnie picked Scott up by the back of the neck and seat of his pants and threw him onto the floorboard of the Impala.

Pork used the short barrel of his revolver to scratch his nuts, then put the gun behind him, under his Hawaiian shirt. "You boys are gonna go to the river bottoms with us and help us get shed of this nigger."

"Yes, sir," Farto said. "We'll toss his ass in the Sabine for you."

"How about you?" Pork asked Leonard. "You trying to go weak sister?"

"No," Leonard croaked. "I'm with you."

"That's good," Pork said. "Vinnie, you take the truck and lead the way."

Vinnie took a key from his pocket and unlocked the building door next to the one with the light, went inside, and backed out a sharp-looking gold Dodge pickup. He backed it in front of the Impala and sat there with the motor running.

"You boys keep your place," Pork said. He went inside the lighted building for a moment. They heard him say to the men inside, "Go on and watch the movies. And save some of them beers for us. We'll be back." Then the light went out and Pork came out, shutting the door. He looked at Leonard and Farto and said, "Drink up, boys."

Leonard and Farto tossed off their warm Coke and whisky and dropped the cups on the ground.

"Now," Pork said, "you get in the back with the nigger, I'll ride with the driver."

Farto got in the back and put his feet on Scott's knees. He tried not to look at the head wrapped in newspaper, but he couldn't help it. When Pork opened the front door and the overhead light came on Farto saw there was a split in the paper and Scott's eye was visible behind it. Across the forehead the wrapping had turned dark. Down by the mouth and chin was an ad for a fish sale.

Leonard got behind the wheel and started the car. Pork reached over and honked the horn. Vinnie rolled the pickup forward and Leonard followed him to the river bottoms. No one spoke. Leonard found himself wishing with all his heart that he had gone to the outdoor picture show to see the movie with the nigger starring in it.

The river bottoms were steamy and hot from the closeness of the trees and the under and overgrowth. As Leonard wound the Impala down the narrow red clay roads amidst the dense foliage, he felt as if his car were a crab crawling about in a pubic thatch. He could feel from the way the steering wheel handled that the dog and the chain were catching brush and limbs here and there. He had forgotten all about the dog and now being reminded of it worried him. What if the dog got tangled and he had to stop? He didn't think Pork would take kindly to stopping, not with the dead burrhead in the floorboard and him wanting to get rid of the body.

Finally they came to where the woods cleared out a spell and they drove along the edge of the Sabine River. Leonard hated water and always had. In the moonlight the river looked like poisoned coffee flowing there. Leonard knew there were alligators and gars big as little alligators and water moccasins by the thousands swimming underneath the water, and just the thought of all those slick, darting bodies made him queasy.

They came to what was known as Broken Bridge. It was an old worn-out bridge that had fallen apart in the middle and it was connected to the land on this side only. People sometimes fished off of it. There was no one fishing tonight.

Vinnie stopped the pickup and Leonard pulled up beside him, the nose of the Chevy pointing at the mouth of the bridge. They all got out and Pork made Farto pull Scott out by the feet. Some of the newspaper came loose from Scott's head exposing an ear and part of the face. Farto patted the newspaper back into place.

"Fuck that," Vinnie said. "It don't hurt if he stains the fucking ground. You two idgits find some stuff to weigh this coon down so we can sink him."

Farto and Leonard started scurrying about like squirrels, looking for rocks or big, heavy logs. Suddenly they heard Vinnie cry out. "Godamighty, fucking A. Pork. Come look at this."

Leonard looked over and saw that Vinnie had discovered Rex. He was standing looking down with his hands on his hips. Pork went over to stand by him, then Pork turned around and looked at them. "Hey, you fucks, come here."

Leonard and Farto joined them in looking at the dog. There was mostly just a head now, with a little bit of meat and fur hanging off a spine and some broken ribs.

"That's the sickest fucking thing I've ever fucking seen," Pork said.

"Godamighty," Vinnie said.

"Doing a dog like that. Shit, don't you got no heart? A dog. Man's best fucking goddamn friend and you two killed him like this."

"We didn't kill him," Farto said.

"You trying to fucking tell me he done this to himself? Had a bad fucking day and done this."

"Godamighty," Vinnie said.

"No sir," Leonard said. "We chained him on there after he was dead."

"I believe that," Vinnie said. "That's some rich shit. You guys murdered this dog. Godamighty."

"Just thinking about him trying to keep up and you fucks driving faster and faster makes me mad as a wasp," Pork said.

"No," Farto said. "It wasn't like that. He was dead and we were drunk and we didn't have anything to do, so we—"

"Shut the fuck up," Pork said sticking a finger hard against Farto's forehead. "You just shut the fuck up. We can see what the fuck you fucks did. You drug this here dog around until all his goddamn hide came off. . . . What kind of mothers you boys got anyhow that they didn't tell you better about animals?"

"Godamighty," Vinnie said.

Everyone grew silent, stood looking at the dog. Finally Farto said, "You want us to go back to getting some stuff to hold the nigger down?"

Pork looked at Farto as if he had just grown up whole from the ground. "You fucks are worse than niggers, doing a dog like that. Get on back over to the car."

Leonard and Farto went over to the Impala and stood looking down at Scott's body in much the same way they had stared at the dog. There, in the dim moonlight shadowed by trees, the paper wrapped around Scott's head made him look like a giant papier-mâché doll. Pork came up and kicked Scott in the face with a swift motion that sent newspaper flying and sent a thonking sound across the water that made frogs jump.

"Forget the nigger," Pork said. "Give me your car keys, ball sweat." Leonard took out his keys and gave them to Pork and Pork went around to the trunk and opened it. "Drag the nigger over here."

Leonard took one of Scott's arms and Farto took the other and they pulled him over to the back of the car.

"Put him in the trunk," Pork said.

"What for?" Leonard asked.

"'Cause I fucking said so," Pork said.

Leonard and Farto heaved Scott into the trunk. He looked pathetic lying there next to the spare tire, his face partially covered with newspaper. Leonard thought, if only the nigger had stolen a car with a spare he might not be here tonight. He could have gotten that flat changed and driven on before the White Tree boys even came along.

"All right, you get in there with him," Pork said, gesturing to Farto.

"Me?" Farto said.

"Nah, not fucking you, the fucking elephant on your fucking shoulder. Yeah, you, get in the trunk. I ain't got all night."

"Jesus, we didn't do anything to that dog, mister. We told you that. I swear. Me and Leonard hooked him up after he was dead. . . . It was Leonard's idea."

Pork didn't say a word. He just stood there with one hand on the trunk lid looking at Farto. Farto looked at Pork, then the trunk, then back to Pork. Lastly he looked at Leonard, then climbed into the trunk, his back to Scott.

"Like spoons," Pork said, and closed the lid. "Now you, whatsit, Leonard? You come over here." But Pork didn't wait for Leonard to move. He scooped the back of Leonard's neck with a chubby hand and pushed him over to where Rex lay at the end of the chain with Vinnie still looking down at him.

"What you think, Vinnie?" Pork asked. "You got what I got in mind?"

Vinnie nodded. He bent down and took the collar off the dog. He fastened it on Leonard. Leonard could smell the odor of the dead dog in his nostrils. He bent his head and puked.

"There goes my shoeshine," Vinnie said, and he hit Leonard a short one in the stomach. Leonard went to his knees and puked some more of the hot Coke and whisky.

"You fucks are the lowest pieces of shit on this earth, doing a dog like that," Vinnie said. "A nigger ain't no lower."

Vinnie got some strong fishing line out of the back of the truck and they tied Leonard's hands behind his back. Leonard began to cry.

"Oh shut up," Pork said. "It ain't that bad. Ain't nothing that bad."

But Leonard couldn't shut up. He was caterwauling now and it was echoing through the trees. He closed his eyes and tried to pretend he had gone to the show with the nigger starring in it and had fallen asleep in his car and was having a bad dream, but he couldn't imagine that. He thought about Harry the janitor's flying saucers with the peppermint rays, and he knew if there were any saucers shooting rays down, they weren't boredom rays after all. He wasn't a bit bored.

Pork pulled off Leonard's shoes and pushed him back flat on the ground and pulled off the socks and stuck them in Leonard's mouth so tight he couldn't spit them out. It wasn't that Pork thought anyone was going to hear Leonard, he just didn't like the noise. It hurt his ears.

Leonard lay on the ground in the vomit next to the dog and cried silently. Pork and Vinnie went over to the Impala and opened the doors and stood so they could get a grip on the car to push. Vinnie reached in and moved the gear from park to neutral and he and Pork began to shove the car forward. It moved slowly at first, but as it made the slight incline that led down to the old bridge, it picked up speed. From inside the trunk, Farto hammered lightly at the lid as if he didn't really mean it. The chain took up slack and Leonard felt it jerk and pop his neck. He began to slide along the ground like a snake.

Vinnie and Pork jumped out of the way and watched the car make the bridge and go over the edge and disappear into the water with amazing quietness. Leonard, tugged by the weight of the car, rustled past them. When he hit the bridge, splinters tugged at his clothes so hard they ripped his pants and underwear down almost to his knees.

The chain swung out once toward the edge of the bridge and the rotten railing, and Leonard tried to hook a leg around an upright board there, but that proved wasted. The weight of the car just pulled his knee out of joint and jerked the board out of place with a screech of nails and lumber.

Leonard picked up speed and the chain rattled over the edge of the bridge, into the water and out of sight, pulling its connection after it like a pull toy. The last sight of Leonard was the soles of his bare feet, white as the bellies of fish.

"It's deep there," Vinnie said. "I caught an old channel cat there once, remember? Big sucker. I bet it's over fifty feet deep down there."

They got in the truck and Vinnie cranked it.

"I think we did them boys a favor," Pork said. "Them running around with niggers and what they did to that dog and all. They weren't worth a thing."

"I know it," Vinnie said. "We should have filmed this, Pork, it would have been good. Where the car and that nigger-lover went off in the water was choice."

"Nah, there wasn't any women."

"Point," Vinnie said, and he backed around and drove onto the trail that wound its way out of the bottoms.

IF YOU WERE A DINOSAUR, MY LOVE

RACHEL SWIRSKY

If you were a dinosaur, my love, then you would be a T-Rex. You'd be a small one, only five feet, ten inches, the same height as human-you. You'd be fragile-boned and you'd walk with as delicate and polite a gait as you could manage on massive talons. Your eyes would gaze gently from beneath your bony brow-ridge.

If you were a T-Rex, then I would become a zookeeper so that I could spend all my time with you. I'd bring you raw chickens and live goats. I'd watch the gore shining on your teeth. I'd make my bed on the floor of your cage, in the moist dirt, cushioned by leaves. When you couldn't sleep, I'd sing you lullabies.

If I sang you lullabies, I'd soon notice how quickly you picked up music. You'd harmonize with me, your rough, vibrating voice a strange counterpoint to mine. When you thought I was asleep, you'd cry unrequited love songs into the night.

If you sang unrequited love songs, I'd take you on tour. We'd go to Broadway. You'd stand onstage, talons digging into the floorboards. Audiences would weep at the melancholic beauty of your singing.

If audiences wept at the melancholic beauty of your singing, they'd rally to fund new research into reviving extinct species. Money would flood into scientific institutions. Biologists would reverse engineer chickens until they could discover how to give them jaws with teeth. Paleontologists would mine ancient fossils for traces of collagen. Geneticists would figure out how to build a dinosaur from nothing by discovering exactly what DNA sequences code everything about a creature, from the size of its pupils to what enables a brain to contemplate a sunset. They'd work until they'd built you a mate.

If they built you a mate, I'd stand as the best woman at your wedding.

IF YOU WERE A DINOSAUR, MY LOVE

I'd watch awkwardly in green chiffon that made me look sallow, as I listened to your vows. I'd be jealous, of course, and also sad, because I want to marry you. Still, I'd know that it was for the best that you marry another creature like yourself, one that shares your body and bone and genetic template. I'd stare at the two of you standing together by the altar and I'd love you even more than I do now. My soul would feel light because I'd know that you and I had made something new in the world and at the same time revived something very old. I would be borrowed, too, because I'd be borrowing your happiness. All I'd need would be something blue.

If all I needed was something blue, I'd run across the church, heels clicking on the marble, until I reached a vase by the front pew. I'd pull out a hydrangea the shade of the sky and press it against my heart and my heart would beat like a flower. I'd bloom. My happiness would become petals. Green chiffon would turn into leaves. My legs would be pale stems, my hair delicate pistils. From my throat, bees would drink exotic nectars. I would astonish everyone assembled, the biologists and the paleontologists and the geneticists, the reporters and the rubberneckers and the music aficionados, all those people who—deceived by the helix-and-fossil trappings of cloned dinosaurs—believed that they lived in a science fictional world when really they lived in a world of magic where anything was possible.

If we lived in a world of magic where anything was possible, then you would be a dinosaur, my love. You'd be a creature of courage and strength but also gentleness. Your claws and fangs would intimidate your foes effortlessly. Whereas you—fragile, lovely, human you—must rely on wits and charm.

A T-Rex, even a small one, would never have to stand against five blustering men soaked in gin and malice. A T-Rex would bare its fangs and they would cower. They'd hide beneath the tables instead of knocking them over. They'd grasp each other for comfort instead of seizing the pool cues with which they beat you, calling you a fag, a towel-head, a shemale, a sissy, a spic, every epithet they could think of, regardless of whether it had anything to do with you or not, shouting and shouting as you slid to the floor in the slick of your own blood.

If you were a dinosaur, my love, I'd teach you the scents of those men. I'd lead you to them quietly, oh so quietly. Still, they would see you. They'd run. Your nostrils would flare as you inhaled the night and then, with the suddenness of a predator, you'd strike. I'd watch as you decanted their lives—the flood of red; the spill of glistening, coiled things—and I'd laugh, laugh, laugh.

If I laughed, laughed, laughed, I'd eventually feel guilty. I'd promise never to do something like that again. I'd avert my eyes from the newspapers when they showed photographs of the men's tearful widows and fatherless children, just as they must avert their eyes from the newspapers that show my face. How reporters adore my face, the face of the paleontologist's fiancée with her half-planned wedding, bouquets of hydrangeas already ordered, green chiffon bridesmaid dresses already picked out. The paleontologist's fiancée who waits by the bedside of a man who will probably never wake.

If you were a dinosaur, my love, then nothing could break you, and if nothing could break you, then nothing could break me. I would bloom into the most beautiful flower. I would stretch joyfully toward the sun. I'd trust in your teeth and talons to keep you/me/us safe now and forever from the scratch of chalk on pool cues, and the scuff of the nurses' shoes in the hospital corridor, and the stuttering of my broken heart.

GIVE HER HONEY WHEN YOU HEAR HER SCREAM

MARIA DAHVANA HEADLEY

In the middle of the maze, there's always a monster.

If there were no monster, people would happily set up house where it's warm and windowless and comfortable. The monster is required. The monster is a real estate disclosure.

So. In the middle of the maze, there is a monster made of everything forgotten, everything flung aside, everything kept secret. That's one thing to know. The other thing to know is that it is always harder to get out than it is to get in. That should be obvious. It's true of love as well.

In the history of labyrinths and of monsters, no set of lovers has ever turned back because the path looked too dark, or because they knew that monsters are always worse than expected. Monsters are always angry. They are always scared. They are always kept on short rations. They always want honey.

Lovers, for their part, are always immortal. They forget about the monster.

The monster doesn't forget about them. Monsters remember everything. So, in the middle of the maze, there is a monster living on memory. Know that, if you know nothing else. Know that going in.

They meet at someone else's celebration, wedding upstate, Japanese paper lanterns, sparklers for each guest, gin plus tonic. They see each other across the dance floor. They each consider the marzipan flowers of the wedding cake and decide not to eat them.

Notes on an eclipse: Her blue cotton dress, transparent in the sunlight at the end of the dock, as she wonders about jumping into the water and swimming away. His button-down shirt, and the way the pocket is torn by his pen. Her shining hair, curled around her fingers. His arms and the veins in them, traceable from fifty feet.

They resist as long as it is possible to resist, but it is only half dark when the sparklers are lit, from possibly dry-cleaned matches he finds in his pocket. She looks up at him and the air bursts into flame between them.

They are each with someone else, but the other two people in this four-person equation are not at this wedding. They know nothing.

Yet.

In the shadow of a chestnut tree, confetti in her cleavage, party favors in his pockets, they find themselves falling madly, falling utterly, falling without the use of words, into one another's arms.

Run. There is always a monster—

No one runs. She puts her hand over her mouth and mumbles three words into her palm. She bites said hand, hard.

"What did you say?" he asks.

"I didn't," she answers.

So, this is what is meant when people say *love at first sight*. So this is what everyone has been talking about for seven thousand years.

He looks at her. He shakes his head, his brow furrowed.

They touch fingertips in the dark. Her fingerprints to his. Ridge against furrow. They fit together as though they are two parts of the same tree. He moves his hand from hers, and touches her breastbone. Her heart beats against his fingers.

"What are you?" he asks.

"What are *you*?" she replies, and her heart pounds so hard that the Japanese lanterns jostle and the moths sucking light there complain and reshuffle their wings.

They lean into each other, his hands moving first on her shoulders, and then on her waist, and then, rumpling the blue dress, shifting the hem upward, onto her thighs. Her mouth opens onto his mouth, and—

Then it's done. It doesn't take any work to make it magic. It doesn't even take any *magic* to make it magic.

Sometime soon after, he carries her to the bed in his hotel room. In the morning, though she does not notice it now, the hooks that fasten her bra will be bent over backward. The black lace of her underwear will be torn.

This is what falling in love looks like. It is birds and wings and voodoo dolls pricking their fingers as they sing of desire. It is blood bond and flooded street and champagne and O, holy night.

It is Happily Ever.

Give it a minute. Soon it will be After.

So, say her man's a magician. Say that when he enters a forest, trees stand up and run away from their leaves, jeering at their bonfired dead. Say that in his presence people drop over dead during the punchlines of the funniest jokes they've ever managed to get through without dying of laughing, except—

Like that.

So, say he knew it all along. This is one of a number of worst things itemized already from the beginning of time by magicians. This falls into the category of What To Do When Your Woman Falls In Love With Someone Who Is Something Which Is Not The Least Bit Like The Something You Are.

The magician shuffles a deck of cards, very pissed off. The cards have altered his fingerprints. Scars from papercuts, scars from paper birds and paper flowers, from candle-heated coins, and scars from the teeth of the girls from whose mouths he pulled the category Things They Were Not Expecting.

Turns out, no woman has ever wanted to find a surprise rabbit in her mouth.

He finds this to be one of many failings in his wife. Her crooked nose, her dominant left hand, her incipient crow's feet. He hates crows. But she is his, and so he tries to forgive her flaws.

His wife has woken sometimes, blinking and horrified, her mouth packed with fur. No one ever finds the rabbits. His wife looks at him suspiciously as she brushes her teeth.

Sometimes it hasn't been rabbits. When they first met, years and years ago, she found her mouth full of a dozen roses, just as she began to eat a tasting menu at a candlelit restaurant. She choked over her oyster, and then spat out an electric red hybrid tea known as *Love's Promise*. By the end of evening, she was sitting before a pile of regurgitated roses, her tuxedoed magician bowing, the rest of the room applauding.

She excused herself to the bathroom—golden faucets in the shape of swans—to pick the thorns from her tongue. And then sometime later, what did she do?

She married him.

The magician continues to shuffle his cards. He clubs his heart, buries said heart with his wife's many diamonds, and uses his spade to do it.

Some of those diamonds are made of glass. She never knew it.

In their hotel room, the lovers sleep an hour. He's looking at her as she opens her eyes.

"What?" she asks.

He puts his hand over his mouth and says three words into it. He bites down on his palm. She reaches out for him. It is morning, and they are meant to part.

They do not.

This is meant to be a one-night love story not involving love.

It is not.

They stay another day and night in bed. They've each accidentally brought half the ingredients of a spell, objects rare and rummaged, philters and distillations, words that don't exist until spoken.

They get halfway through a piece of room service toast before they're on the floor, tea dripping off the table from the upended pot, a smear of compote across her face, buttered crumbs in his chest hair.

They think, foolish as any true lovers have ever been, that this is so sweet that nothing awful would dare happen now.

They think, *what could go wrong?*

Right.

And so, say his wife is a witch. A cave full of moonlight and black goats and bats, housed in a linen closet in the city. Taxicabs that speak in tongues and have cracked blinking headlights and wings. An aquarium full of something bright as sunlight, hissing its way up and out into the apartment hallway, and a few chickens, which mate, on occasion, with the crocodiles that live in the bathtub.

Like that.

Say she knew about this too, from the moment she met her man, foretold the mess in a glass full of tea, the heart-shaped, crow-footed face of this woman who is nothing like the witch.

The night the two true-lovers meet, his wife is sitting in their shared apartment. Coffee grounds shift in the bottom of her cup. A yellow cat streaks up the fire escape, shrieking a song of love and lamentation. The witch's hair tangles in her hands, and she breaks the knot, tears the strands, throws them from the window and down into the neighbor's place, where he, wide-eyed, elderly, and stoned on criminal levels of pot, drops the witch's hair into the flame of his gas stove and leaves it be while it shoots fireworks over the range and sets off the smoke detector.

The witch looks for allies. There is one. He's a magician. Typically, she works alone, but she suspects her skills will be blurred by sorrow and fury.

She sees him in her coffee grounds, shuffling a deck of cards and crying. He pulls a coin from beneath his own eyelid. A white rabbit appears in his mouth and then climbs out, looking appalled, dragging with it a rainbow of silk scarves and a bouquet of dead roses. The magician lets the table rise beneath his fingers, propelled by the rattling ghosts of other magicians' wives.

The witch has no patience for any of this. She spills milk so that no one needs to cry over it anymore. There. It's done. It's happened. After a moment, though, the waste begins to irritate her, and so she unspills the milk and pours it into her coffee cup. She sweetens it with a drop of her own blood, and drinks it.

She's strong enough to kill him, but she doesn't want to kill him.

She is not, unfortunately, strong enough to make him fall out of love. Making someone fall out of love, particularly when it is the kind of love that is meant to be, is much harder than murder. There are thousands of notoriously unreliable spells meant to accomplish just this. Typically, they backfire and end up transforming eyebrows into tiny, roaring bears, or turning hearts inside out and leaving them that way.

Once, when attempting something similar, the witch found her own heart ticking like a timebomb. This was expensive to fix, and in truth, the fixing did not go well. Her heart is mostly made of starfish these days. At least it could regenerate when something went wrong.

When the witch first fell in love with her husband, she showed him all of her spells, a quick revue of revelations.

She crouched on the floor of the apartment, and opened her closet full of cave, let the bats and goats and ghosts come pouring out into the room, and he laughed and told her she might need an exterminator. She crumpled herbs from ancient hillsides, and in their dust she planted seeds shaken carefully from a tiny envelope. She watched him as the flowers bloomed up out of nothingness. Each flower had his face. She wasn't sure he'd noticed. She pointed it out, and he said, "Thank you."

She worried he was not impressed enough. They stayed together.

At night sometimes, she took down buildings brick by brick, all over the city, but left their bedchamber untouched.

The witch is busy too. She has things to accomplish. She has no time for fate. She doesn't wish to let her man go off into his own story, giving *fate* as his reason.

Fate is never fair. This is why there is such a thing as magic.

The witch picks up her phone and calls the magician. She monitors him in the coffee grounds as he answers. He's dressed in a full tuxedo and most of a sequined gown. He's sawed himself in half, and is carefully examining the parts. The witch could have told him that this'd yield nothing in the way of satisfaction. Years ago, just as she met this man and learned about the other woman in his future, she dismantled her own body, and shook it out like laundry, hoping to purge the urge to love. It hid, and when she replaced her skin with cocoa-colored silk, the urge to love got loose, and hid elsewhere.

She never told him about the woman he's meant to meet. Men were often blind. He might miss her.

Love was blind too, though, and this was the witch's mistake. Had he been blind and deaf and mute, he'd still have met the other woman, in the dark, in the silence.

This doesn't mean there isn't something to be done.

"Meet me," she says to the magician. "We have things to do together."

Together, the lovers walk through a cemetery holding hands, laughing over the fact that they are tempting fate by walking through a cemetery holding hands.

Together, they walk through a torrential storm, heads bent to look at each other's rain-streaming faces.

Together, they have faith in traffic.

Together, they fuck in the stairwell, on the floor, against the bookshelves, on the couch, in their sleep, while waking, while dreaming, while reading aloud, while talking, while eating takeout first with chopsticks and then with fingers and then from each other's fingers, and then?

Lover's arithmetic: test to see how many fingers can be fit into her mouth, how many fingers can be fit inside her body. Test to see how many times she can come. They chalk it up on an imaginary blackboard. She lays still, her hair spread across the pillow, and comes simply by looking at him.

Together they compare histories, secrets, treasures.

Together, they're reduced to cooing and whirring like nesting birds, junketing on joy.

Together, they try to doubt it.

It's no use. There are too many ways to break a heart. One of them is to tear that heart in half and part company. And so, they don't.

"Fate," he says. And it is.

"Magic," she says. And it is.

"*Meant to be together*," they say, together. And it is.

Careful. There need be no mention of star-crossing, not of Desdemona and Othello, nor of Romeo and Juliet. Not of any of those people who never existed, anyway. Someone made those people up. If any of them died for love, it's someone else's business.

Together, they compare fingerprints again, this time with ink. He rolls her thumb over his page, and looks at the mark, and they memorize each other's lines.

Together, they say, "Forever."

Look. Everyone knows that *forever* is, and has always been, a magic word. Forever isn't always something one would choose, given all the information.

And so, the magician and the witch hunch over a table in the neutral zone of a Greek diner, brutalized by a grumpy waitress and bitter coffee. Outside, the sky's pouring sleet. Inside, the ceiling's streaming fluorescent light. The witch's taxicabs patrol the streets, crowing miserably, wings folded. Too nasty out there to fly.

The magician is in formal dress, including top hat. The witch is wearing a fleece blanket that has sleeves and a pocket for Kleenex, and though she's managed lipstick, it's crooked. She's wearing fishnet stockings, which the magician suspects are an illusion.

Neither witch nor magician are in top form. Both have head colds, and are heartbroken. Each has a sack of disaster.

The witch coughs violently, and removes a tiny, red-smudged white rabbit from between her lipsticked lips. She holds the rabbit in her hand, weighing it.

The magician stares steadily at her, one eyebrow raised, and after a moment, the witch laughs, puts the rabbit back into her mouth, chews, and swallows it.

The magician blinks rapidly. A moment later, he chokes, and tugs at the neck of his tuxedo shirt, where his bowtie was, but is no longer.

He glances sideways at the witch, and then fishes a black bat from his own mouth. The bat is wild-eyed and frothing, its wings jerking with fury. It has a single black sequin attached to its forehead.

"Are you ready to stop fucking around?" asks the witch.

"Yes," says the magician, humbled, and the bat in his hand stops struggling and goes back to being a bowtie.

The waitress passes the table, her lip curled.

"No animals," she says, pointing at the sign. She sloshes boiled coffee into each of their cups.

"What do you have for me?" says the witch.

"What do you have for *me*?" says the magician. "I love my wife."

"We're past that. You're not getting her back, unless you want half a wife and I want half a husband. Look."

She pulls an x-ray from her bag. It's a bird's-eye skeletal of two people entwined in a bed, her back to his front. In the image, it's appallingly clear that their two hearts have merged, his leaning forward through his chest, her heart backbending out of her body, and into his.

"How did you get this?" the magician says, both fascinated and repulsed.

The witch shrugs.

She hands him another image, this one a dark and blurry shot of a heart. On the left ventricle, the magician reads his wife's name, in her own cramped handwriting. "Hospital records from forty years ago," she says. "None of this is our fault. He was born with a murmur. Now we know who was murmuring."

She passes him another photo. He doesn't even want to look. He does.

His wife's bare breasts, and this photo sees through them, and into the heart of the magician's own wife, tattooed with the name of the witch's own husband.

"What's the point, then? Revenge?" he asks, removing his tailcoat, unfastening his cufflinks, and rolling up his sleeves. There's a little bit of fluffy bunny tail stuck at the corner of the witch's mouth. He reaches out and plucks it from her lips.

"Revenge," she repeats. "Together forever. That's what they want."

She pulls out a notebook. When she opens the cover, there's a sound of wind and wings and stamping, and a low roar, growing louder. Something's caged in there, in those pages. Something's been feeding on *forever*.

The magician smiles weakly and pours out the saltshaker onto the page. He uses his pen to carve a complicated maze in salt. He feels like throwing up.

"Something like this?" he says, and the witch nods. She feels like throwing up too. No one ever wants things to turn out this way. But they do.

"Something like that. I'll do the blood."

"I could do it if you don't want to," the magician volunteers, not entirely sincerely. That kind of magic's never been his specialty.

"No, I owe you. I ate your rabbit."

He rummages in his sack of disaster and brings out a pair of torn black lace panties. A bra with bent hooks. A photograph of a woman in a blue dress, laughing, giddy, her eyes huge, her hair flying in the wind. He looks at the crow's feet around her eyes. Side effect of smiling. Crows walk on those who laugh in their sleep. He tried to tell her, but she did it anyway.

He pushes his items to the witch's side of the table. The witch rummages in her own sack and removes a razor, a t-shirt ripped and ink-stained, a used condom (the magician suppresses a shudder), a gleaming golden thread. She suppresses the urge to smash the t-shirt to her face and inhale. She suppresses the desire to run her wrist along the razor blade.

She signals to the waitress. "Steak," she says. "Bloody. I don't normally do meat, but I get anemic when I do this. And a martini."

"Two," says the magician.

"We don't serve steak," says the waitress. "You can get a gyro, if you want a gyro. That's probably chicken."

The magician flicks his fingers, and the waitress pirouettes like a ballerina.

A moment later she returns with a white damask tablecloth, and two lit candles. Two plates of prime float out of the kitchen, smoking and bleeding. The fluorescent lights flicker off. The witch and the magician raise their glasses in a toast.

They toast to "Forever."

And even when *they* say it, it is, as it always has been, a magic word.

The monster, newly uncaged, runs hands over new skin. The monster opens a new mouth and learns to roar.

She fell asleep holding his right hand in her left. She wakes up alone.

There's a playing card stuck to her left breast. It is not the Queen of Hearts. It's a two of spades.

She's in a hospital.

Her husband is a magician. Her lover's wife is a witch. She knew better than to do this, this forever. But here she is, and here's a nice nurse who asks her what she thinks she's doing when she asks for the return of her shoelaces and belt and purse strap.

"I don't belong here," she says, in a very calm voice.

"Then why do you think you *are* here?" asks the nurse, in a voice equally calm.

Her wedding ring is missing too, but she doesn't miss it. Her mouth tastes of rabbit and overhandled playing card. Where historically she has felt sympathetic to her husband, to his oddities, to his pain, she now begins to feel angry.

She looks down at her left hand and feels her lover still there. She looks at her ring finger, and sees something new there, a bright thing in her fingerprint.

A red mark. A movement, spinning through the whorls, slowly, tentatively. Someone is there, and the moment she thinks *someone*, she knows who it is.

She brings her fingertips closer to her face. She looks at them, hard. She concentrates. One does not spend years married to a magician without picking up some magic.

His eyes open. He's freezing. His blood's turned to slush and he remembers that time, when he did his girlfriend a significant wrong via text message. She salted him, limed him, and then drank him with a straw for seven hollow-cheeked minutes.

Last night, he held his lover in his arms, and kissed the back of her neck. She curled closer to him, pressing her spine into him.

He heard the crowing of taxicabs in his dreams.

There are looping, curving walls on either side of him. Above him, far above, the sky is dazzling, fluorescently white.

A flash across the heavens of rose-colored clouds. They press down upon him, soft and heavy. They depart. A rain of saltwater begins, and splashes through the narrow passage he inhabits. He hears his love's voice, whispering to him, but he can't find her. Her voice is everywhere, shaking the walls, shaking the sky.

"I have you," she says. "You're with me. Don't worry."

But he can't see her. He's frightened.

Something has started singing, somewhere, a horrible, beautiful, sugary roar. He's suddenly hit by a memory of fucking his wife, on the floor surrounded by flowers that had his face. They both failed to come, bewildered by lack. It was years after the beginning, back then, but still nowhere near the end.

"I have you," his beloved whispers. "You're safe with me. I know the way." He wonders if he's imagining her.

The walls shake around him. He can feel her heartbeat, moving the maze, and his own heart returns to beating a counterpoint, however tiny in comparison.

He opens his hand and finds a ball of string in it.

The witch and the magician fumble in the car on the way to her place. Her sleeved blanket is rumpled. His top hat and tuxedo have turned to ponytail and hoodie. He may or may not be wearing a nude-colored unitard beneath his clothes. Old habits.

"Unbelievable dick," she says, not crying yet. "He deserves this."

"Believable," he says. "Some people are idiots. *She* deserves this. I think maybe she never loved me."

He's looking at the witch's black curls, at the way her red lipstick is smeared out from the corner of her lip. He's thinking about his rabbit, working its way through her digestive tract. She's still wearing the fishnet stockings he'd thought she conjured.

"It's hard to make fishnets look right," she says, turning her face toward his. Her eyelashes are wet. "They're complicated geometry."

He pulls an ancient Roman coin from behind her ear, clacking awkwardly against her earrings. She looks at him, half-smiling, and then pulls a tiny white rabbit from out of his hoodie. He's stunned.

"It seemed wasteful to let it stay dead," she says.

He puts his shaking hand on her knee. She moves his hand to inside her blanket. He takes off his glasses. She takes off her bra.

There are still people in madhouses and mazes. There are still monsters. Love is still as stupid and delirious as it ever was.

The monster in the middle of the labyrinth opens its mouth. It starts to sing for someone to bring it what it wants, its claws trembling, its tail lashing, its eyes wide and mascaraed to look wider, its horns multiplying until the ceiling is scratched and its own face is bloody.

The monster screams for honey, for sugar, for love, and its world comes into existence around it. Bends and twists, dead ends, whorling curves and barricades and false walls, all leading, at last, to the tiny room at the center of the maze, where the monster lives alone.

The other thing that's always being forgotten, the other thing that no one remembers, is that monsters have hearts, just as everyone else does.

Here, in the middle of the maze, the monster sings for sweetness. As it does, it holds its own heart in its hands and breaks it, over and over and over.

And over.

THE HORSE LATITUDES

SUNNY MORAINE

"We need not wait for God
The animals do judge"
—Madeleine L'Engle

Once upon a time there were two worlds. There was the world of a quiet bedroom, love and sleep. And there was the world of the smoke and the flies on dead eyes, a foreman fucking a prostitute in a dirty bunkhouse.

Once upon a time there were two worlds. There was the world of open sea, fair winds, waves and joyful movement. And there was the world of stillness, thirst, the endless screams of drowning horses.

The two worlds were married. The marriage was not a happy one.

On deck men slump under the sun.

The sun pushes down and crushes, beams unbroken by a breeze. The sails hang limp like the men on the filthy deck, hanging heads and hands listlessly tossing dice, chewing their cracked lips and betting on nothing. No purpose in it. Ships get purpose from movement. Ships get life from purpose.

Now both are gone.

In the beginning there might have been hope, there might have been optimistic prayers offered to the still sky and only a slight tightening of rations. Then voices falling silent, prayers muttered as though they're shameful things. Everything begins to pull toward the center; the extraneous is sacrificed when it can no longer be supported.

The deck shakes, the men look up, and the horses begin to scream.

Across miles and centuries a woman is screaming in the street.

Her screams are alien things in a humid afternoon. They cause Sebastian to awaken, to swipe at his face with sticky fingers. In Buenaventura's summer afternoons the air is like an old towel soaked in sweat, smelling of mildew and garbage. Sometimes there's blood on the concrete, steaming. Has Sebastian been dreaming of blood? Behind his closed eyes everything is red. He presses his naked body against Jaime's; sweat is glue and they stick. He sinks back into the folds of the afternoon. The unbalanced ceiling fan thumps the rhythm of the slow, lazy fucking that they're too tired and too hot to do.

Nights are for working. Days are for this. He's dreaming again, plastered along Jaime's broad back.

Horses aren't foolish creatures. They can see their deaths coming. One of them—black and glossy in spite of the weeks of low rations—rears up, and her hoof barely misses the forehead of the man reaching for her bridle. Another man falls to his knees, lifts a copper medal in trembling fingers—beseeching the Saint, God, the Blessed Virgin and the horse all at once.

None of them listen. The mare hurls back her head and screams, her white eyes rolling. The still sea bears them up like a dead hand. The men would say this is the worst part, but for the fact that none of them have ever been here before, and none of them have ever spoken to anyone who was. Some ships return from the state of Becalmed but to speak of such things is to invite them in.

Many of the men have already turned away. Water must be saved and for this other things must be sacrificed. But it's easier to do such things when one does not have to watch them done.

In the receding tide of his sleep, Sebastian dreams the sun beating down on the coca plants, the smell of the burning forest mixing with the smell of damp soil, stinging his eyes and nose and making both run.

They did not always burn the trees—Sebastian is fairly sure of this. But his dreams are myopic, tightly focused on this one detail. He would like to dream of other things—of the foreman's boy who had been his first fumbling, salty kiss, of bathing in well-water that tasted of hard minerals and cold. He wakes up into the evening, Jaime stirring beside him. The coca fields were long-ago-and-far-away, south in the mountains, and now he lives by the sea. The burning wood, the smoke—these things are like bright threads that run across time's thick and fibrous cord, but Buenaventura is not the plantation.

He has to go to work. There are kilos to move. He turns, pushes Jaime gently aside, and rises, Jaime's sleep-heavy fingers trailing over his lower back as he gets to his feet. As he looks for a semi-clean shirt in the rumpled piles of their clothing, he thinks about the smoke, the coca, and he wonders about many things.

On the street, Jaime moves like a dancer. He turns elegantly in Sebastian's path and presses a tamale into Sebastian's hand—fiercely spiced, but Sebastian barely tastes it. His mind is on his work, picking at it like a troublesome knot. People surge around him in waves of colored cloth, faces precariously lit in the flicker of neon. They pass tin-roofed shops, goods displayed through sheets of plastic: tiny LED-flickering cell phones, racks of bootleg blu-ray with compressed jpeg covers, knock-off clothes with distressed hems, mounds of food. The street mercado—now all the streets are *mercados*, and this market touches all markets.

Even his market. And this is a problem. Because the rich *norteamericanos* are still buying *perica*—*la cocaina*, but there are fewer of the rich *norteamericanos* these days. Meth is domestically produced and cheap, and there's something from Russia called *cocodrilo*. It rots the flesh off your bones, but it's cheaper than perica or even the jagged white nuggets of *basuco*, so they say that it makes you feel disgusting but you shoot your veins full of it anyway. Addicts. Such is the way of things. But tonight one deal has already fallen through, and things are hard for a middle man caught in the middle. No one is willing to organize a push north and across the border for all that cash in slippery *norteamericano* fingers.

Women stand in doorways, hips swaying. They are beautiful in the way that shadows and neon make everyone beautiful. Sebastian pulls Jaime against him with fingers greasy from the tamale, frames his face with his hands and kisses him until Jaime laughs against his mouth. The women laugh too, cat-call. No one else notices them.

In his dream, Sebastian is small and running up to the bunkhouse with a toad in his hand, its eyes huge and gold and lovely. He runs with it held out in his hands like he means to make a gift of it, but when he bursts through the door of the women's dormitory, his mother is bent over her bed with her skirt hiked up and the foreman jerking his hips against her. The foreman is breathing in panting snorts like one of the old horses ridden hard. Sebastian can't see his mother's face.

He must have seen it before. But this is the first memory of it. The first fire, the first spill of blood in the dirt, the first crash of the charred fragments of a tree down through still-living branches while the horses rear and scream.

Sebastian drops the toad onto the floor.

When he has the foreman's boy up against the cinderblock, tongue slipping into his smoky mouth and hands making their crawling spider-way up under his shirt, it's years later, and he won't think that one thing has anything at all to do with the other. But in his dream they come one after the other, and there are things that are hard to miss, even when one tries.

There was no school on the plantation, but Sebastian paid close attention to everything. He learned about use. He learned about using.

"I'm sorry, my friend. It cannot be done."

Sebastian wants to throw the glass in his hand, watch the tequila run down the wall. He feels Jaime's arm on his elbow, restraining.

"Paolo, I have three sellers breathing down my neck, looking to move product. There's no one who can take this stuff north?"

Paolo is an Italian ex-pat, mountainous and solid, and in the cantina's dimness he looks even more so. His dark brows lower—he may be attempting apology but the effect is unsettling, as if he might drop his head and charge. "I can't move what I can't sell, and I can't sell what no one will buy. It's difficult everywhere. You know this."

"In difficult times we should help one another." Jaime's fingers roll his cigarette between them. "Favors for favors. We've always done it that way."

"Times change. The world is smaller now." Paolo shrugs, lifts a hand to summon the man behind the bar. "I can buy you a drink. More . . . not today. Try me again next week."

"Next week," Jaime murmurs when Paolo is gone. "Do we have until next week? We have to eat."

Sebastian is quiet, staring at the shifting lights. He is not worried about whether or not they will eat next week. Breathing seems like a more pressing issue.

No one ever explained it to Sebastian, but at ten years of age he could draw his own conclusions. A deal gone bad. The guerillas offended somehow. Or another drug lord, perhaps a rival, sending a message.

He heard the voices first, low and tense. Then he heard the buzz of flies, and then he smelled it. He was small; he could wriggle between the legs of the adults circled in the burned clearing and see.

A row of horses' heads on stakes, their decapitated bodies in a heap behind. The horses' eyes were open and staring at him, reproachful. Flies were landing on their glazed surfaces, crawling, taking off again in little clouds. Like smoke, he thought at the time. Like living smoke that ate where it descended.

His first big dead things. He had never seen a dead man.

That changed.

The first horse is at the edge of the deck now, faltering. She hasn't had a full ration of water in days. She hangs her head, panting as the sun presses a heavy hand down on her back. The air cracks. The men huddled against the rail think of lightning. Crossing themselves and crucifix-kissing, they watch as the first mate, a giant of a man with arms like tree branches, cracks the whip against the horse's flank.

The horse rears. A horrible shriek rises from her great throat. And she leaps out over the water in a graceful arc. Silence descends as she goes, her final scream echoing in the air, falling as she falls.

Here is another thing that Sebastian learned on the plantation: decisions are not made all at once. It's a process. So that last night, his legs dangling off the back of the truck as it bumped down the unpaved road, the lights of the gate receding in the distance, he did not wonder at his own choice. It had taken him a long time to make it. And it had been made for a long time.

Years later, a mule told him that everyone was murdered and it burned to the ground and the forest swallowed up the ashes and bones. He never bothered to verify the story. Perhaps it was better to leave all possibilities open. Perhaps Sebastian has never been very good at looking back.

"Word is that you're leaving town."

Sebastian whirls. He knows the man, though he's momentarily lost for the name—Argentinean, a small-time dealer who keeps his ear close to the ground. All details more important than a name in a tight place. But this place is not tight. They're standing in a wide square, the street mercado already beginning to unfurl itself like flowers at dusk. If there is safety, it might be here.

"Perhaps. Why do you care?"

He doesn't need to ask. The street trades in information, an invisible market as real and as powerful as any global high finance.

"Another word . . . some people are less than thrilled with this. People to whom you owe money."

Sebastian feels his stomach sink down into the cracked pavement. There are always debts. But some of them are old, and where will he get money to pay them if *narcotrafico* is no longer profitable?

His lips twist. "Thank you for your concern."

The man slides closer. Sebastian moves instinctively backward. "Go quickly, if you want to go. Someone will come for you soon, you and that pretty boy of yours. If you go sooner. . . . And I can forget I saw you at all."

Sebastian turns and pushes his way through the crowd. He should have seen this coming. The man's proposal of amnesia is probably a lie, but there's nothing to be done about that. If information is one trade, favors are another. One must diversify.

Things happen out on the still water that seem, later, like memories of a dream. There's a series of cracks, the sound of splintering wood, and a herd of horses breaks loose from their stalls and rushes across the deck. The first mate stands and watches mutely. There is the thunder of those hooves, and in the final moments of their lives—whether those moments come in a few days or decades—everyone there will hear that thunder again.

The air, like the sea, is still and hot, and now it is reeking with the smell of dung and rotting hay and death. Men clutch their talismans, their rosaries and their crucifixes, but they do so with less conviction, as though these last resorts of hope have lost their potency and cannot now be trusted. The horses are drowning.

They are not doing it quietly.

Dios te salve, María. Whispered on a breath of air, halted in place and looping in a refrain. *Dios te salve*.

They go at dawn.

It will be hot traveling on the bus with its utter lack of air conditioning and then on the train north to the coast. But in the heat Sebastian figures they're less likely to be followed. Jaime is casting glances like dice as he packs clothes into a duffel bag and hunts through the chaos of their apartment for their last usable credit cards.

Do you trust me?

Forever and always.

The bus terminal is less than a mile away. They are walking hand in hand like children in a fairytale, leaving no scatter of breadcrumbs to mark their passage. If they are lucky, they'll simply vanish into the woods of the world and be gone.

They are less than twenty yards from the bus terminal when the earth begins to shake.

At first Sebastian wonders if it might be only a hallucination born of his own fear. But Jaime grips his hand more tightly, looks around with eyes gone wide. In the buildings around them, hybrids of adobe and corrugated tin and aluminum, he feels a wave of shifting bodies and indrawn breath, people rising out of sleep in confusion. Buenaventura stirring in a dream.

The ground *jerks*.

Jaime stumbles; their hands slip apart. Sebastian sees things in a succession of still images, lit in the gold shimmer of the early morning. Jaime in midair as though he's dancing, only the terror on his lovely face an indication otherwise. A flowerpot frozen at the moment of shattering against the pavement, the withered twig of the pot's occupant suspended in a cloud of ruin. A shower of broken glass, a hundred thousand tiny mirrors. Then sun.

Then darkness.

There is a woman screaming in the street. Her voice is many voices, an uneven and fractured chorus, and Sebastian realizes, still trying to claw his way up from the darkness in his head, that it's many women. Many screams. His eyelids come painfully unstuck; he turns onto his back, lifts a hand to his face, and his fingers come away smeared with blood.

He drags his knees under him, levers himself off the broken ground. He looks up and sees the pale globe of the sun, high through billowing plumes of smoke.

Jaime.

Sebastian lurches forward. One arm swings loose at his side. Flames are licking the darkness. The running shapes twist into cavorting demons. The smoke stings his eyes; that must be why tears are running down his cheeks.

"Jaime!"

His hands settle on a figure hunched in the rubble. He knows the angle of these shoulder blades—they heave under his hands and Jaime turns, reaching for him, crying out something that extends itself past words.

Buenaventura is burning.

Buenaventura. Good fortune. A city named in a flush of hysterical hope. The naming of things is a very important matter. Adam named the animals before he slaughtered them.

In times of crisis the most fundamental instinct is to move. Movement is life, is purpose. Stillness and death are co-morbid. Sebastian and Jaime move without knowing why, without knowing where—leaning against each other, they stumble away from the collapsed bus terminal. Driven by instinct, they are heading away from the sea, winding up through the broken streets. Until they notice more shapes moving around them, letting out frightened cries. When they hear it, it comes to them like the terrified murmur of the city itself—not one voice but thousands, carried up on heated winds.

Tsunami.

Then they find their purpose and it carries them higher.

On the day the earth shakes, the horses come out of the sea.

They come with the sea. They come of the sea. At first people think that it is the sea, surging up over walls and beaches, cars and shacks, tin and adobe and concrete—buoying up the rubble, carrying it like a gift. Some of the older ones have seen this before.

But no. They have never seen this.

The horses are running when they come, hooves softened by centuries in the salty water. They shake their dripping manes, seaweed clinging. Their flesh is gray, uneven, bloated in some places and gone in others; there is a gleam of exposed bone in the light of the fires. Their eyes are milky and staring and dead.

People are driven before them, clinging together, hands in hands, babies held against chests, professions of love, of hate, the final instincts of lethal fear. In the seconds before the hooves pull them down and crush them they try to understand.

At the crest of a hill Sebastian stops again, Jaime stops with him and they turn.

It's a mourning process done at high speed and in the midst of utter confusion, because how can any sense be made of this? But there is sense. Sebastian feels it like the hidden shape in a picture puzzle as he watches the water surging into the city.

All at once Jaime is dragged away from him. There is the flash of a blade. Sebastian stares stupidly at it, at the wild-eyed man holding the machete to Jaime's throat. Jaime is staring back at him, hands limp at his sides—his surprise and the resulting lack of a struggle may be what, for the moment, has saved him.

"Heard you were running." The man presses the blade into Jaime's throat and there's a corresponding trickle of blood. Jaime does not cry out and Sebastian feels a strange flush of pride. "You can't just run. Not with that kind of *plata* tangled up with your ankles."

Sebastian holds out his hands. His gaze flicks from Jaime's face, abnormally pale in the red light, to the shattered road that continues up the hill. He hears thunder behind him. "Please . . ."

"Yes, say please. Plead with me. Make it so much sweeter when I cut this little *cacorro's* head off."

His eyes meet Jaime's again; there is nothing he can say because fear makes men crazy. And in the last minutes of both of their lives, with all their good fortune burning and drowning below them, he is not going to abase himself. He feels every muscle coiled, ready to spring.

He never does. A rearing horse, white-eyed, rotten hooves crashing into the side of the man's head in a spray of blood and pinkish brain matter. The man doesn't have time to scream. Jaime, as he drops to the ground, does not scream either.

But the horse does. And then there are more, surging around them, thundering, reeking. Sebastian has fallen to one knee. Jaime is motionless. The horse stands over him, nostrils flaring. Its eyes are white, but not without expression. Lost rage. Hatred. Sebastian has seen it before. At that flash of familiarity all the fear vanishes and he understands: it's about using. It's about being used. And cast aside when one is used up.

He reaches up in supplication, his head bowed. He is thinking of the flies on the eyes of the dead horses, how he had wished then that someone had closed their eyes while they were sticking their heads on the stakes, because it had seemed like such a final insult.

"Lo siento," he whispers. "Perdoname. Por favor. Forgive us all."

The horse stares at him for a long moment. White-eyed gaze, drowned in hate. More horses around them, more white eyes. Ring upon ring of them, staring, surging. Going still. Sebastian drops his arms.

And then, one by one, the horses go.

It doesn't feel like forgiveness. It feels like blood for blood.

Buenaventura lies burned and drowned, and the parts of it that have not perished in water continue to do so in fire. There is still screaming but it sounds weary and thin. The last of the dead down in the city, a chorus of silent eyes arrayed in the hills. *What now?*

There has never been an answer.

Sebastian pulls Jaime into his arms. One shallow breath. Another. Sebastian tilts his head back and looks up. The sun is gone. There is a tear in the clouds. Through it—for only a moment, for the first time in many years—he can see the stars.

BOYFRIEND AND SHARK

BERIT ELLINGSEN

Brandon didn't want to be boyfriend and boyfriend, yet when it suited him, friends with benefits was fine. Michael didn't take it personally. Brandon didn't have any other lovers. In that light, he and Michael were boyfriend and boyfriend.

Michael wondered if he was undermining his own dignity by servicing Brandon, but came to the conclusion that he probably wasn't. There weren't many good people in circulation and he didn't have the patience to search for another someone when he had one, even if occasionally and on whims.

Brandon slept next to him in bed. At least he didn't run off in postcoital panic like some of the others. He even stayed for breakfast. But then he was just Michael's friend, not his lover.

Michael wriggled over to Brandon and hugged him.

"Don't hug me when I'm sleeping," Brandon would have said had he been awake. "It feels like you're crushing me."

"How can you tell?" Michael would have replied. "You're asleep."

"I can still feel it and I can't get away because I'm paralyzed," Brandon would have said. "It hurts. Don't do it."

He did anyway.

Sometimes Michael wished Brandon would have an aneurism and become locked inside his own body. Then Brandon would be helpless in bed, able to move only his eyes. He'd take care of Brandon, every day, every night.

The sheets beneath Michael were cold and wet and smelled of ocean. What the hell? He jerked back and fumbled for the lamp on the nightstand.

There was a shark in his bed! A shark! With a dark back and white belly and black-tipped fins, just like on nature shows. Michael screamed. He was on his feet, up against the bedroom wall, hand over his mouth.

The shark had dark eyes and a sleek body. It opened and closed its maw. Michael didn't dare look at it; the teeth were probably enormous. The shark's eyes took in the room, the walls, the ceiling, him. Did it look hungry? Michael moved to get out of the fish's field of view. The gills fluttered, opened, and then sank back into the skin with a wet sound.

Okay, okay, stay calm. He had a shark in his bed. He had to call animal rescue or a vet or something. The shark moved like a released spring. It flailed and shattered the lamp on the nightstand. Michael watched, like an animal caught in headlights. The shark made another attempt at moving, then stopped. The dark eyes searched Michael's face.

Oh, water! The thing couldn't breathe air. Michael ran to the bathroom and filled the tub with medium-cold water. He heard the shark thrash, but when he returned to the bedroom, it just lay there.

He lifted the shark without thinking. It was as long as a man, and as heavy, yet he managed and put it front first into the tub. There wasn't room for the tail, but at least the fish got its head under water. The eyes rolled shut. The gills pumped hard.

The shark was breathing and Michael had survived getting it inside the tub. Time to call for help. Where was Brandon? Had he fled after all and left a shark in bed as a warning against more sleep-hugs? His suit and shirt hung over the chair. Michael looked at the shark. There was something familiar about the dark eyes and slender body.

The employees from the aquarium rolled the shark onto a blue net, carried it downstairs, out of the semi-detached house, and into a large truck containing a plastic tank. Michael stood in the doorway and watched them drive away.

Every day he visited the shark at the aquarium. He told friends and colleagues he was seeing a sick friend at the hospital.

"You're so giving," they said.

"Thank you," he said and smiled.

At first, the shark just lay on the other side of the floor-to-ceiling window and tracked Michael with its eyes, gills moving slowly. Michael pressed his hands against the cold glass. The shark ignored him.

After a week, the shark started swimming in circles, around and around. When Michael approached the tank, the shark came close and rolled its eyes at him, before it sped off into the gloomy water.

"How's the new blacktip doing?" Michael asked one of the aquarium employees, a man with too much body and not enough hair. "Looks like it has lost some weight."

"He's not eating," the employee said. "Just swimming and swimming."

"How are the other sharks treating him?" The tank held several white tip and tiger sharks, even some hammerheads, and many species of skate and eel.

"He's ignoring them," the man said.

Brandon was being fickle about his food, like always when he was unhappy.

Michael got a job at the aquarium. He bought fine meat without bones: farmed boar, forest moose, Argentinian ox, Arctic reindeer, and thoroughbred horse. He smuggled it inside in a large canvas bag and fed only the slender, blacktip shark.

Once, he nearly fell into the tank. He leaned too far forward on the catwalk above the water. The shark shot up and almost closed its jaws around his hand. He fell backwards on the sharp grating, sloshing liquid high. After that the shark refused to take his meat.

Michael wanted to write letters in thick black marker on white paper and press the sheets against the glass: I M S O R R Y. But what would be the point in that? He already knew the shark's reply.

The shark kept swimming, around and around, as if it wanted out. It grew thin and full of sores, its tail and fins ragged with nips and bites from the other predators. Michael tried to make eye contact with the shark. The slick body passed over him like a shadow.

There was just one thing to do. Michael bribed a colleague on the night shift with liquor and money. They lifted the shark out of the tank in the blue net it had arrived on. The shark bucked a few times, then lay still.

They drove to the bay and lowered the shark into the sleeping water. Michael looked over the edge of the net. The shark took him in, searched his face like it had in the bedroom.

"I'm not holding you any longer," Michael said. "Goodbye. Please be happy." The shark circled him twice, then cut the dark surface with its tail and disappeared.

NEVER THE SAME

POLENTH BLAKE

Everyone thinks my brother is nice. He set up a rescue centre for birds, after the terraforming accident poisoned the lake. That's always the image of him, holding a bird covered in sludge. The birds are never the same after they're cleaned, but the gossips never talk about that.

Cleaning birds is a safe way to make people notice you, and my brother likes safe. I jumped off a cliff once. He was all, "You'll die if you jump." I broke most of my bones, but I made it. It's worth trying for the feel of it. Not the bones part, but the rush of something new. It should have been something, falling and surviving. But the gossips only cared about how much it upset my brother.

When I was younger, people assumed I was nice. I knew when to smile and when to cry. They never believed it was me who stole the biscuits or set the cushions on fire. Until they ran the routine scans and I failed. Then every tear was viewed with suspicion. Every smile was cause to check for smoke. My sister was the only one who disagreed. "You can't fail a scan," she said. "We're all different."

That's why I choose the role of the supportive sibling. I turn up to her party wearing her favourite colour. There's fruit on the food table, because they've spared no expense. I load up a plate with cherries and mango slices.

An old man passes me, with hair glowing a subtle shade of peach. "Like the hair," I lie with a smile. He smiles back, but he won't look at me properly. He won't come near me again.

There are banners above the table. My sister is running for president of the world. It sounds grand, but the world is so tiny I recognise everyone in it. They've only seeded a few hundred square miles, and most of that is stunted grass. The only people out there are scientists, because the air's too thin to be comfortable. We huddle in our domes, making occasional wheezing trips outdoors just to prove we can.

I see my sister, but she's with her girlfriend. She has people to meet and greet. Sometimes the supportive sibling has to stand back.

"You must be proud of her," says a person I've only seen before at a distance. They're wearing a fashionable patchwork suit, but have avoided the ghastly hair glow trend.

"Yes. She always gets what she wants."

It's unusual to meet someone who wants to talk to me. Most gawk from a distance at the world's only psychopath. But this person doesn't have that look of hidden fear.

"It'll be a landslide, if the polls stay on track," they say.

I smile and ask, "I don't think we've talked before?"

"I'm on the terraforming crew."

"It must be a luxury, being back where there's air."

"You get used to it," they say.

That's not the whole truth. The wheezing might subside after some time, but it's never comfortable. I'm not the only one who lies.

The person looks past me and I glance back. My brother has arrived. There's something odd in the person's reaction. The sudden intent gaze on my brother. A hard edge that implies they know my brother is not as nice as people believe him to be.

I smile at the person. This time, it's genuine.

I dream of the cliff most nights. I landed in the sludge and it saved me. The poisons slowed down the internal bleeding. The thickened water held me up even when I couldn't swim.

The gossips think it made me worse, like the birds. That isn't true. I was the same person before and after. All it did was make me bolder about speaking my mind. I jumped from a cliff and survived. It's more than they'd ever done.

My brother likes to keep score with my sister. She invited me to a party, so he has to take me out to the park. It's a fancy park where people with credits go. It makes the gossips think he cares.

He walks over the grass towards a cart selling toffee apples. People act like I don't understand the idea of rules, but I understand better than they do. There's a sign saying to keep off the grass, yet everyone walks over it. The same people wouldn't steal a toffee apple from the cart. Why is the grass less important than the apple? It isn't, but they've made themselves believe that. They have to believe that, so they can break the rules and not feel guilty.

I take the long route around the grass. It's my own form of defiance. They all expect me to break the rules, but I keep them better than anyone else.

My brother waits for me to finish traversing the gravel paths, his arms folded in irritation. He buys me an apple anyway. It suits me. The more he buys, the less I have to work.

We take our apples to a bench, facing the clear dome wall. It's the best view of the lake and grasslands beyond the dome. The lake is brown from dead algae. It should be green, but the terraforming is not going as expected and no one knows why. My sister's going to solve that. It's part of her election promise, to assess the terraforming and ask the hard questions. Some politicians wouldn't mean it, but she keeps her promises.

He examines the bite marks he's left in the apple. "Have you thought, it'd be easier if she was gone?" Not even a glance my way. That's the trouble with guilt.

"Where would she go?" I say.

"Don't say you've never thought about hurting us."

I shrug. He wouldn't believe denial. My games don't need violence, but this isn't something my brother understands. His games with me involve his fists, because no one believes the psychopath.

"She loves me," I say.

That ends the conversation.

When we were young, my sister had a bird. It slept in a cage, but the rest of the time it travelled on her shoulder. She taught it to speak. She made sure it got to fly. I didn't see the point in the bird, but my sister liked it and I didn't have to look after it, so that was that.

I set fire to a lot of things. Cushions, boxes, and food I didn't want to eat. I didn't set fire to the cage that night. My brother did that.

My sister cried. I worked on stoic mourning, as I wasn't close to the bird. I hoped it was the right level of reaction, but it wasn't enough to avoid the blame.

"I know killing animals is wrong," I told my parents. I knew the lists. Harming animals was wrong. Hugging your sister when she's sad was right. Walking on the grass was wrong. Honesty was right. I'd forgotten to hug my sister when she was sad. It was too late now.

After that, I was careful about my fires, so I couldn't be blamed. I signed up to cremate bodies, because some things are acceptable to burn. I didn't pretend to understand that.

What my brother signed up to burn was a mystery.

My sister's kitchen has murals of blue birds on a green sky. She dreams of the day the terraforming succeeds, and we can run outside with the wild birds. I thought it was a random desire, until one day she admitted to missing her bird. So many years and she still mourns it.

We sit at the table, eating a protein cake she made herself. I compliment the cake and do the expected things, before I ask, "Do you think our brother is nice?"

"Don't you?"

He wants me to kill you, but you won't believe that. "Have you talked to the terraforming people?"

"Not yet. I've been busy on the campaign."

"It'd make a good visit," I say. "Show you're going to figure things out."

Talk to them. They know something.

"I'm glad you're taking an interest," she says, taking my hand.

I smile. "I try."

I want to say I've also been thinking about her bird. I want her to know I didn't care enough to kill it. Because all these years later, I finally understand my brother's game. He didn't hate the bird. He wanted to hurt her. Wanted her out of the game. This time he might be more direct and I've no idea what to do about it.

There was a murder a few years before I was born. The world didn't know what to do. Most crimes meant community service, but those were minor thefts and disturbances. They couldn't let a murderer walk freely, so they built a box for her.

When I failed my scan, they wanted to put me in the box with her. I cried and promised to be good. The act wasn't entirely false. I had no interest in being locked away. I wanted a life, like anyone else. Someday, maybe I'd have children, though my parents weren't happy about the prospect. Mentioning it'd be fine because I'd done animal husbandry at school was a mistake. I thought it made me sound responsible.

But still, I was curious. I visited her once, to see if she was like me. All I found was guilty silence.

I don't wait for my sister to take my advice. The terraforming station isn't far away, and the air seems a little thicker today. I reach it in good health.

The main building isn't much to look at. It's small, grey, and rectangular. The roof is covered with spheres and poles. Something to do with measurements or transmissions. I wasn't that interested in science at school.

The rest of the compound is far more interesting. Three large greenhouses contain plants and animals ready for release. Other round pods surround the area, with whatever supplies the terraformers need. At this stage, biodiversity is supposed to be the main aim. Not worrying about the atmosphere or why released things keep dying.

Much as I'd like to see inside the greenhouses, I head to the grey building and knock on the door.

A woman opens it. We'd been in the same year at school. That's probably why she immediately tries to close it. I jam my foot in the door. "I'm here for a brief inspection, for my sister."

She opens the door again, without leaving too many bruises on my foot. "Sorry, I thought . . . well, come in."

As though murderers turn up unarmed and knock on the door politely. If I did want to kill someone, they wouldn't see me coming.

The woman goes back to her work and I'm left to roam. It's a single room, with multiple work stations. Some are computers. Some are lab benches with samples. I offer random pleasantries, and the workers relax a little. I recognise some of what's going on. One rack of test tubes has sludge samples, tightly sealed and marked with hazard labels. Another has various grasses in pots. A worker is measuring each clump and recording its growth. They look far healthier than the grass outside, so I wonder if the atmosphere is different inside. It didn't feel different to me.

The person from the party has been looking my way, but I don't want to appear as though I'm here for them. I reach them when I do, after examining each workstation. "Hello again."

"An unexpected visit," they say.

"Just getting a feel for my sister's work. Though I confess, I don't know much about science."

"If there's anything you want to know, just ask."

They have to say it, as every citizen has a right to see what's being done on their behalf. Though if I did ask about the science side, I'm not sure I'd get an honest answer. That's not a problem. I'm here for another reason. I cast my gaze slowly around the room, as though deciding what to ask about. I settle on the plaque a short distance away. It commemorates the world's first murder victim.

I indicate the plaque. "I didn't know there was a plaque. He was a scientist, right?"

"Oh. Yes. I didn't know him."

"I expect he did a lot of," I pause, for comic effect, and wave a hand vaguely, "science."

The person grins. "Yes, lots of science."

"Hey, I'm trying." I return the grin. "I know some things. The green things are plants."

"That's something."

I go back to a sombre face and look towards the sludge samples. The good side of the gossips is everyone knows I've been a bird in the sludge. People want me to be traumatised, so sometimes I give them that. Lighten the mood then switch on the trauma. It makes people drop their guard and say things they shouldn't.

"Are you okay?"

"Sure. It just reminds me."

The person pauses and I find their expression hard to read. "How do you feel?"

It's an odd question. I've been asked it many times by therapists, but everyone else tiptoes around it. I go with, "Frustrated." I'd hope for something more enlightening than a question about my emotions, so it was true.

They held a hearing shortly after I reached adulthood. The director of medicine was an expert in manipulation. He knew how to dehumanise me. "The psychopath has no conscience. No remorse. No concept of right and wrong."

Getting two out of three right wasn't bad, but did he really think I couldn't memorise a list of rules? Or I had no incentive to keep them? It wasn't in my best interest to end up in a box or to upset my family to the point they wanted nothing more to do with me. Perhaps he didn't realise that. Directors often weren't the most intelligent of any department. They were simply the ones who were good at speeches and routine administration tasks.

"It has a poor sense of self. It views others as objects for entertainment, to be discarded on a whim."

And others liked to suggest I wasn't truly human. That made us even. But that wasn't the main point. Everyone is an object, including me. The idea of self is a delusion to keep fear at bay. I don't feel fear, so I don't need the delusion.

What's important is objects can be unique. They need care and they can be hard to replace. When I care about an object, I'll look after it. When I don't, I'm indifferent to it. People murder because they care too much, not because they don't.

"It's true, good upbringing can counter some of the worst excesses, but the psychopath can never be trusted."

My family's reaction to that was mixed. My parents were trying not to cry. My sister was tense, ready to fight if this didn't go the right way. My brother shifted guiltily. The rest of the family were loving, so it was his fault if I did anything bad. He was lucky I valued my freedom more than that.

"There's no future in our community for the psychopath."

No mention of the letter from my boss, who praised my aptitude as an apprentice funeral director.

"This is about the essence of humanity."

The founding principle of the world, keeping humans human. Hidden away from those nasty sub-humans who mixed with aliens. Who integrated into other worlds. Everyone a pure human, blah blah blah. I didn't care about ideology. Only about survival.

My turn came to speak. I kept my face calm and my eyes down. False displays would be noted, and too much eye contact was threatening. After a suitable pause, as though wrestling with what I'd heard, I locked my gaze on the medical director. "I'm not an it. I'm a they."

I visit the box, because there's one thing no one knows: her motive. The two of them had been working late one night, during a time when everything was going well with the terraforming. Then she killed him. The ecosystem collapsed after that. It's the world's biggest mystery. And also a little coincidental that my sister wants to poke around outside, and suddenly my brother is trying to persuade me it'd be easier if she wasn't around.

She's sitting on her bed when I enter the visitor's area. A mesh separates us, so that nothing can be passed into her cell.

I sit on the visitor's chair. "We have some things in common."

"I'm nothing like you," she says.

"That's true. You're a murderer. I'm a valued citizen with a future as a funeral director."

She flinches away, bringing her legs up in a ball. She feels guilty. I can use that guilt.

"Do you get many visitors?" I ask.

"Only the guards," she says.

"If it were my choice, I wouldn't put you in a box. People who damage things have to repair them. People who drop waste have to clean things. There must be things you could do to fix things."

"They won't let me out."

"I could fix things for you. If people knew why, maybe they'd visit you." She had children, though they never liked to mention the relationship. Family love is unconditional, except when it isn't. Another inconsistency.

"Why would you want to? You don't care."

"I want to prove I can." It's the ultimate way to show I'm better than them. Not murdering anyone is too easy. Finding out why other people murder each other is a challenge.

"I can't help you," she says.

"Suit yourself, but he was only the first."

I get up to leave. Not too quickly, in case she has a change of heart. I reach the door and open it before she calls after me, "You fell in the sludge, didn't you? How do you feel?"

I continue through the door without a word.

There were two groups of people who liked to ask how I felt. Therapists and my parents. "I'm not feeling anything," was never the right answer. Of course, when I did feel things, that was wrong too. I once made the mistake of telling a therapist I enjoyed eating mango.

"Empathy is like a mango," she said.

"Rounded and sweet?"

"Not that. Think about what it'd be like if someone took your mango. That's how it feels when you hurt people."

I didn't like it when someone took things from me, but I got over it quickly. It wasn't the same as when I told my sister it'd been a stupid bird anyway, and I didn't see why she was still crying over it. I just wanted her to stop so she would come out with me, but it made her cry more. Empathy wasn't as simple as a mango. That's why I needed my rules. I should have hugged her, not tried to reason with her. But the therapists wouldn't accept that I was never going to understand. It wasn't enough to follow the rules. They wouldn't be happy until I could feel the rules.

Another time, I told a therapist I wanted to set fire to my brother. That's when they threatened to put me in the box.

I stand on the cliff, looking down into the dead-algae water. I'm not going to jump again, though the temptation is there. I have a question to answer. Why have two people in a day wanted to know how I felt? Usually, people don't want to know.

I close my eyes and try to focus on my innermost feelings, as a therapist long ago failed to teach me.

The thought of jumping still has a thrill attached. I remember the first time, wheezing up the path. I rested on the rocks until I caught my breath. Since then, I'd spent enough time outside that I don't wheeze when I walk. But there is nothing else. How am I supposed to feel about it?

I open my eyes again. Now it's water below, so the landing wouldn't be as deadly. In that moment, I know how I feel.

My life turned around on the day my sister snuck into my room. I wasn't supposed to be alone in the room with anyone else, but she did what she wanted. She'd started a job at the food warehouse, and saved up credits for sweets. Little jelly hearts with gooey centres. She knew I liked them, so she came to share. By then, I'd learnt enough about empathy to know it when I saw it. I knew I should do something in return, so I told jokes, and made shadow animals on the wall. It was like we were children again, before scans and therapy.

At the same time, someone set fire to my brother's bed.

I was blamed. It was the final sign of my inherent violence. Except it wasn't, because I was with my sister and everyone trusted her. That's when my parents realised it was my brother. They put it down to sibling rivalry, but I knew he wanted me gone.

The rules changed that day. It was no longer wrong to go out on my own, to be alone with people, and to decide what I wanted. I wasn't going to let anyone take that away from me again.

I set fire to a poster for my sister's election. It's pasted on the side of a metal storage unit, so there's little to burn out here other than the poster. I don't want the crime to be too big. It needs to be personal, with just the right level of apparent impulsiveness. Everyone knows I act on impulse.

The emergency systems note the fire. Alarms sound and people arrive. I look at the fire and I get the tears started. I don't fight as they take me to see the head of law enforcement.

"What are we going to do with you?" they ask.

"I didn't mean it." I make sure a tear runs down my cheek. "It's just . . . there's so much going on. Please don't put me in the box."

Their eyes soften, even though they know they shouldn't believe me. "I don't think we're there yet. But we're going to have to monitor you for a bit."

"I know. But my family . . ." I say tearfully.

"You're an adult. It's up to you if you tell them."

I nod. I have what I want, so the rest is going through the motions. I promise to behave. I fill out forms. They attach the monitor. It doesn't take them long to process me, as the only other criminals are two people who got into a fight over nothing important.

The monitor isn't obtrusive. It's a wrist band, easily hidden under the baggy-sleeved top I happened to wear for the fire. It'll record my every move and alert them if it thinks I'm committing a crime. It'll sound an alarm if I take it off. I have a lot in common with the monitor. It also doesn't need empathy to know right from wrong.

I don't knock at the bird cleaning centre, because only my brother works there. The other volunteers are long gone, now most of the sludge is cleared away.

I haven't seen the inside before, but it's much as I expected. The birds are in several rooms with glass screens separating them from the corridor. Their behaviour is listless.

My brother comes through a door. "What are you doing?"

"I came to see the birds," I say.

"Well, you've seen them."

"That's it? You're not going to show me around?"

My brother glares, but there's always the guilt. It eats away at him, and eventually he breaks eye contact. "I guess it might be your sort of thing." He leaves the corridor through a door with a lock. I haven't seen many locks, outside of the box and secure supply areas. I follow.

The room beyond is not my sort of thing. It's filled with birds, though not in a way my sister would like either. Some of them are strapped down on benches, with their blood flowing out through tubes, through a machine, and back into the birds. One is in the process of being dissected. A few wait in a cage, healthy but huddled, as they can see the scene in front of them. I walk around, so the monitor can scan the area.

"What are you doing to them?" I ask.

"Cleaning their blood. The sludge gets inside."

It justifies keeping the centre open, long past the sludge disappearing. But there's a problem with this. The sick birds in the rooms outside are how the birds act when they're released. I walk to the cage. "Are these the treated ones?"

"No, they need to be processed."

"But they're so healthy," I say.

"Better to be sick and clean, than healthy and dirty."

My brother doesn't trust me, but he's given me a truth he wouldn't want spread. It occurs to me this is more dangerous than recording a conversation. I consider my words, because I don't want to die right now. "You're making them sick. Why did you tell me that?"

"I want you to understand. What happened to the birds, to you, it isn't natural. It shouldn't have happened. It has to stay secret."

"So you told a psychopath?"

"At worst, no one will believe you."

"At best?"

"You'll kill our sister, before she finds out. For the sake of the world."

The world isn't my problem, as long as it continues existing. The damaged birds say my brother's actions aren't helping that. "What have you done for me?"

"What have I done?" His brow furrows and his voice raises. "Do you know what I've put up with? The lies. The things you've destroyed. You made our parents think I did those things. You were the innocent one. The perfect baby. But you've never cared. It's all a game to you."

"That was years ago, before the scans," I say.

The blow hits me before I can react. I hit the wall by the cage, causing the birds to screech.

"Get out," he says.

I don't argue. My face hurts and I have bruises down one side where

I struck the wall. It's not as exciting as jumping off a cliff. I choose to jump, but never to be hit.

I return to the terraforming station and ask the person to show me the greenhouses. I expect to have to persuade, but the response is enthusiastic. Some things surprise me. It's almost as though they like talking to me. But I have other things to focus on when we reach the first greenhouse. It's filled with leafy plants and insects.

"How many of these live outside?" I ask.

"None. They used to, but we had to bring them back inside."

Some of the insects have large colourful wings. They perch on a tray with slices of fruit, drinking the juices. "What are these?"

"Butterflies." The person picks up a piece of fruit with a butterfly, bringing it closer so I can see. The butterfly moves its wings slowly, but is more concerned with the fruit than the people.

"I never learnt about them at school."

"They think it's easier that way. If you see even a sample of what we have waiting in storage, it's obvious how bad it is outside." They put the butterfly back with the others.

"Why can the birds survive and these can't?"

"The birds can't survive. We have hidden feeding stations for them, so it looks like they're wild."

I don't need my emotions soothed, but the logic of it is also concerning. The world should be further on than this. All of these things should be outside already, with new things coming up from storage. The birds should be feeding themselves.

"I know how I feel," I say. "I feel healthy. I should have died. I should wheeze out here, but I ran here."

"Why do you think that is?"

"Something in the sludge."

The person stays focused on the butterflies. They're deciding, so I don't rush them. "The planet was scorched before we landed. They thought something lived here. Nothing too advanced, but there were signs."

"They missed something," I say.

"Underground. It's not dangerous," they assure me unnecessarily. "It's a symbiont. It gets a home from you, with warmth and plenty of food. You get healed. Does that make sense to you?"

"I understand mutual benefits." My social life is constructed around deciding if a person is beneficial enough to treat well. The sludge is apparently more open about its choice of associate. "Aren't you worried I'll tell people?"

"You might, but you deserve to know. It's your body."

"Thank you."

The motives are obvious once I realise the sludge is alien. One terraformer conspires to release the sludge slowly, to strengthen the ecosystem. One wants to keep humans pure, so kills him and tries to clean up the sludge. The guilt is in the question of whether it was worth it. Whether the world really is better without the sludge, as the grass dies and the birds weaken. It's amazing how people destroy themselves when given so little rope.

I focus on the tour after that, noting unusual animals and plants. Forming a bond so I can ask a difficult question. I walk the person back to the terraforming station as I consider the wording.

"Did you release the sludge?" I ask.

"A storm damaged the pipeline. It's sealed now."

I note the direction they glance at the mention of the pipeline, though I have some idea already based on the patterns of the sludge. "Why seal it? Wouldn't it help?"

"The world isn't ready for it," they say.

I nod, face serious, as though I understand the dilemma. I say my farewells and walk away as though heading back to the domes. That's the trouble with emotion. Even when a choice is obvious, there's fear of the results, and guilt over the potential damage. These aren't weaknesses I share. It takes me a few hours to find the pipeline, but once I do, I turn the valve.

Shortly after my sister applied to run for office, one of my parents died. He'd been the one to give birth to me, so had been a prime target for the gossips.

"Do you miss him?" my sister asked.

"No," I said. "Your girlfriend is cheating on you."

She gave me that look, where she slightly raised her eyebrows. She didn't believe me. I didn't know if it was true or not. Her girlfriend stayed away from me, after I said my sister only wanted a partner to look good for the campaign.

"Why do you want us to break up?" she asked.

"If you leave, I'll only have our brother."

"Maybe she can be like another sister."

"No one would choose to be my sister."

"Drop the insults about how no one will ever love her, and she might."

I hadn't planned on family expansions. Children maybe, but I didn't think anyone would want children with me. It was something I'd do alone, the medical way. It hadn't bothered me much before, but now one of my parents was dead. My family weren't something I was guaranteed to keep. Expansion was a possible solution, though I wasn't comfortable with not controlling who got to be a part of that.

But my sister did her own thing, regardless of what I wanted. She wasn't easy to manipulate any more. Not in the bad ways. I could make her smile much more easily.

"Do you think she likes shadow animals?" I asked.

"It couldn't hurt to try."

I knock on the door, but my sister doesn't answer. I have all the answers now and I need to share them. I want everyone to know I figured it out. I want my sister to see the birds healthy again. I knock again, but I'm impatient, so I push the door open and enter.

Her main hall is similar shades of green to the kitchen. It's narrow, as its only purpose is to provide a route to the other rooms. The tiled floor has fresh mud on it. That's odd. Even if she'd visited the terraformers, she'd take her shoes off at the door. She hates cleaning, so she makes sure not to get things dirty if she can avoid it.

"Hello?" I listen and there's a faint sound of a chair scraping from the kitchen.

I rush to the kitchen door. She's inside, tied to a chair with tape over her mouth. Liquid covers her and the floor. She's trying to speak. I pull the tape free.

"Our brother—" is all she says before the world explodes, starting with the liquid around her feet. In the last moments as the heat surrounds us, I remove the monitor from my wrist.

My body recovers during the night, to the surprise of the hospital staff. They want to run tests. I humour them long enough to find out the monitor recordings survived, my brother is in custody and the sludge is back. After that, I wave off the staff and go looking for my sister.

She is in a room not far from mine. A machine gives her oxygen, to soothe her burnt lungs. Her skin is wrinkled and raw.

My sister's girlfriend is in a chair next to the bed. To go into the room, I'll have to acknowledge the girlfriend. If my sister dies, what I do won't matter. If she lives, I'll have to deal with whatever I say. My sister still hopes I'll end up with two sisters, which I've warmed to as an idea, if the girlfriend proves to be sufficiently interesting.

I move away from the room and search for the hospital's food area. I've seen the girlfriend's preferences, so get her favourite hot drink. I return to the room and enter. She looks at me with more horror than my previous manipulations warrant. I offer the drink silently.

She recovers from her reaction and takes it. "Thank you."

"How is she?" I ask.

"You were the same yesterday."

"I heal quickly," I say.

The girlfriend is tired. Her eyes are bloodshot and she's having trouble not yawning.

"You should sleep." I consider smiling, but decide it's the wrong reaction. "I can watch her for you."

"Your parents said they'd come."

"They'll be late. There's always one more thing at work. It's no problem." I'm good at reassuring. It's a tone of voice that's rarely assumed to be a lie, because everyone wants to believe it. They want to know the world will be fine in the end.

It takes some discussion, but the girlfriend finally leaves, and a nurse offers to find her a place to sleep. My parents aren't here yet, so I have time. I start work on detaching the wires.

I stand on the cliff, with my sister in my arms. She's gasping in the air, but still breathing, just about. Her eyes open a slit, as though she's aware.

"I'm sorry I killed your bird," I whisper.

Saying sorry to your sister when she's hurt is the right thing to do. I follow my lists. Better than the gossips. Better than my brother. They're worth less than a bird in a cage.

I jump and we fall towards the sludge. The birds are never the same.

MANTIS WIVES
KIJ JOHNSON

"As for the insects, their lives are sustained only by intricate processes of fantastic horror."
—John Wyndham

Eventually, the mantis women discovered that killing their husbands was not inseparable from the getting of young. Before this, a wife devoured her lover piece by piece during the act of coition: the head (and its shining eyes going dim as she ate); the long green prothorax; the forelegs crisp as straws; the bitter wings. She left for last the metathorax and its pumping legs, the abdomen, and finally the phallus. Mantis women needed nutrients for their pregnancies; their lovers offered this as well as their seed.

It was believed that mantis men would resist their deaths if permitted to choose the manner of their mating; but the women learned to turn elsewhere for nutrients after draining their husbands' members, and yet the men lingered. And so their ladies continued to kill them, but slowly, in the fashioning of difficult arts. What else could there be between them?

The Bitter Edge: A wife may cut through her husband's exoskeletal plates, each layer a different pattern, so that to look at a man is to see shining, hard brocade. At the deepest level are visible pieces of his core, the hint of internal parts bleeding out. He may suggest shapes.

The Eccentric Curve of His Thoughts: A wife may drill the tiniest hole into her lover's head and insert a fine hair. She presses carefully, striving for specific results: a seizure, a novel pheromone burst, a dance that ends in self-castration. If she replaces the hair with a wasp's narrow syringing stinger, she may blow air bubbles into his head and then he will react unpredictably. There is otherwise little he may do that will surprise her, or himself.

What is the art of the men, that they remain to die at the hands of their wives? What is the art of the wives, that they kill?

The Strength of Weight: Removing his wings, she leads him into the paths of ants.

Unready Jewels: A mantis wife may walk with her husband across the trunks of pines, until they come to a trail of sap and ascend to an insect-clustered wound. Staying to the side, she presses him down until his legs stick fast. He may grow restless as the sap sheathes his body and wings. His eyes may not dim for some time. Smaller insects may cluster upon his honeyed body like ornaments.

A mantis woman does not know why the men crave death, but she does not ask. Does she fear resistance? Does she hope for it? She has forgotten the ancient reasons for her acts, but in any case her art is more important.

The Oubliette: Or a wife may take not his life but his senses: plucking the antennae from his forehead; scouring with dust his clustered shining eyes; cracking apart his mandibles to scrape out the lining of his mouth and throat; plucking the sensing hairs from his foremost legs; excising the auditory thoracic organ; biting free the wings.

A mantis woman is not cruel. She gives her husband what he seeks. Who knows what poems he fashions in the darkness of a senseless life?

The Scent of Violets: They mate many times, until one dies.

Two Stones Grind Together: A wife collects with her forelegs small brightly colored poisonous insects, places them upon bitter green leaves, and encourages her husband to eat them. He is sometimes reluctant after the first taste but she speaks to him, or else he calms himself and eats.

He may foam at the mouth and anus, or grow paralyzed and fall from a branch. In extreme cases, he may stagger along the ground until he is seen by a bird and swallowed, and then even the bird may die.

MANTIS WIVES

A mantis has no veins; what passes for blood flows freely within its protective shell. It does have a heart.

The Desolate Junk-land: Or a mantis wife may lay her husband gently upon a soft bed and bring to him cool drinks and silver dishes filled with sweetmeats. She may offer him crossword puzzles and pornography; may kneel at his feet and tell him stories of mantis men who are heroes; may dance in veils before him.

He tears off his own legs before she begins. It is unclear whether The Desolate Junk-land is her art, or his.

Shame's Uniformity: A wife may return to the First Art and, in a variant, devour her husband, but from the abdomen forward. Of all the arts this is hardest. There is no hair, no ant's bite, no sap, no intervening instrument. He asks her questions until the end. He may doubt her motives, or she may.

The Paper-folder. Lichens' Dance. The Ambition of Aphids. Civil Wars. The Secret History of Cumulus. The Lost Eyes Found. Sedges. The Unbeaked Sparrow.

There are as many arts as there are husbands and wives.

The Cruel Web: Perhaps they wish to love each other, but they cannot see a way to exist that does not involve the barb, the sticking sap, the bitter taste of poison. The Cruel Web can be performed only in the brambles of woods, and only when there has been no recent rain and the spider's webs have grown thick. Wife and husband walk together. Webs catch and cling to their carapaces, their legs, their half-opened wings. They tear free, but the webs collect. Their glowing eyes grow veiled. Their curious antennae come to a tangled halt. Their pheromones become confused; their legs struggle against the gathering web. The spiders wait.

She is larger than he and stronger, but they often fall together.

How to Live: A mantis may dream of something else. This also may be a trap.

PROBOSCIS
LAIRD BARRON

1

After the debacle in British Columbia, we decided to crash the Bluegrass festival. Not we—Cruz. Everybody else just shrugged and said yeah, whatever you say, dude. Like always. Cruz was the alpha-alpha of our motley pack.

We followed the handmade signs onto a dirt road and ended up in a muddy pasture with maybe a thousand other cars and beat-to-hell tourist buses. It was a regular extravaganza—pavilions, a massive stage, floodlights. A bit farther out, they'd built a bonfire, and Dead-Heads were writhing with pagan exuberance among the cinder-streaked shadows. The brisk air swirled heavy scents of marijuana and clove, of electricity and sex.

The amplified ukulele music was giving me a migraine. Too many people smashed together, limbs flailing in paroxysms. Too much white light followed by too much darkness. I'd gone a couple beers over my limit because my face was Novocain-numb and I found myself dancing with some sloe-eyed coed who'd fixed her hair in corn rows. Her shirt said MILK.

She was perhaps a bit prettier than the starlet I'd ruined my marriage with way back in the days of yore, but resembled her in a few details. What were the odds? I didn't even attempt to calculate. A drunken man cheek to cheek with a strange woman under the harvest moon was a tricky proposition.

"Lookin' for somebody, or just rubberneckin'?" The girl had to shout over the hi-fi jug band. Her breath was peppermint and whiskey.

"I lost my friends," I shouted back. A sea of bobbing heads beneath a gulf of night sky and none of them belonged to anyone I knew. Six of us had piled out of two cars and now I was alone. Last of the Mohicans.

The girl grinned and patted my cheek. "You ain't got no friends, Ray-bo."

I tried to ask how she came up with that, but she was squirming and pointing over my shoulder.

"My gawd, look at all those stars, will ya?"

Sure enough the stars were on parade; cold, cruel radiation bleeding across improbable distances. I was more interested in the bikers lurking near the stage and the beer garden. Creepy and mean, spoiling for trouble. I guessed Cruz and Hart would be nearby, copping the vibe, as it were.

The girl asked me what I did and I said I was an actor between jobs. Anything she'd seen? No, probably not. Then I asked her and she said something I didn't quite catch. It was either etymologist or entomologist. There was another thing, impossible to hear. She looked so serious I asked her to repeat it.

"Right through your meninges. Sorta like a siphon."

"What?" I said.

"I guess it's a delicacy. They say it don't hurt much, but I say nuts to that."

"A delicacy?"

She made a face. "I'm goin' to the garden. Want a beer?"

"No, thanks." As it was, my legs were ready to fold. The girl smiled, a wistful imp, and kissed me briefly, chastely. She was swallowed into the masses and I didn't see her again.

After a while I staggered to the car and collapsed. I tried to call Sylvia, wanted to reassure her and Carly that I was okay, but my cell wouldn't cooperate. Couldn't raise my watchdog friend, Rob in LA. He'd be going bonkers too. I might as well have been marooned on a desert island. Modern technology, my ass. I watched the windows shift through a foggy spectrum of pink and yellow. Lulled by the monotone thrum, I slept.

Dreamt of wasp nests and wasps. And rare orchids, coronas tilted towards the awesome bulk of clouds. The flowers were a battery of organic radio telescopes receiving a sibilant communiqué just below my threshold of comprehension.

A mosquito pricked me and when I crushed it, blood ran down my finger, hung from my nail.

2

Cruz drove. He said, "I wanna see the Mima Mounds."

Hart said, "Who's Mima?" He rubbed the keloid on his beefy neck.

Bulletproof glass let in light from a blob of moon. I slumped in the tricked-out back seat, where our prisoner would've been if we'd managed to bring him home. I stared at the grille partition, the leg irons and the doors with no handles. A crusty vein traced black tributaries on the floorboard. Someone had scratched R+G and a fanciful depiction of Ronald Reagan's penis. This was an old car. It reeked of cigarette smoke, of stale beer, of a million exhalations.

Nobody asked my opinion. I'd melted into the background smear.

The brutes were smacked out of their gourds on junk they'd picked up on the Canadian side at the festival. Hart had tossed the bag of syringes and miscellaneous garbage off a bridge before we crossed the border. That was where we'd parted ways with the other guys—Leon, Rufus and Donnie. Donnie was the one who had gotten nicked by a stray bullet in Donkey Creek, earned himself bragging rights if nothing else. Jersey boys, the lot; they were going to take the high road home, maybe catch the rodeo in Montana.

Sunrise forged a pale seam above the distant mountains. We were rolling through certified boondocks, thumping across rickety wooden bridges that could've been thrown down around the Civil War. On either side of busted up two-lane blacktop were overgrown fields and hills dense with maples and poplar. Scotch broom reared on lean stalks, fire-yellow heads lolling hungrily. Scotch broom was Washington's rebuttal to kudzu. It was quietly everywhere, feeding in the cracks of the earth.

Road signs floated nearly extinct; letters faded, or bullet-raddled, dimmed by pollen and sap. Occasionally, dirt tracks cut through high grass to farmhouses. Cars passed us head-on, but not often, and usually local rigs—camouflage-green flatbeds with winches and trailers, two-tone pickups, decrepit jeeps. Nothing with out-of-state plates. I started thinking we'd missed a turn somewhere along the line. Not that I would've broached the subject. By then I'd learned to keep my mouth shut and let nature take its course.

"Do you even know where the hell they are?" Hart said. Hart was sour about the battle royale at the wharf. He figured it would give the bean counters an excuse to waffle about the payout for Piers's capture. I suspected he was correct.

"The Mima Mounds?"

"Yeah."

"Nope." Cruz rolled down the window, squirted beechnut over his shoulder, contributing another racing streak to the paint job. He twisted the radio dial and conjured Johnny Cash confessing that he'd "shot a man in Reno just to watch him die."

"Real man'd swallow," Hart said. "Like Josey Wales."

My cell beeped and I didn't catch Cruz's rejoinder. It was Carly. She'd seen the bust on the news and was worried, had been trying to reach me. The report mentioned shots-fired and a wounded person, and I said yeah, one of our guys got clipped in the ankle, but he was okay, I was okay and the whole thing was over. We'd bagged the bad guy and all was right with the world. I promised to be home in a couple of days and told her to say hi to her mom. A wave of static drowned the connection.

I hadn't mentioned that the Canadians contemplated jailing us for various legal infractions and inciting mayhem. Her mother's blood pressure was already sky-high over what Sylvia called my "midlife adventure." Hard to blame her—it was my youthful "adventures" that set the torch to our unhappy marriage.

What Sylvia didn't know, couldn't know, because I lacked the grit to bare my soul at this late stage of our separation, was during the fifteen-martini lunch meeting with Hart, he'd showed me a few pictures to seal the deal. A roster of smiling teenage girls that could've been Carly's schoolmates. Hart explained in graphic detail what the bad man liked to do to these kids. Right there it became less of an adventure and more of a mini-crusade. I'd been an absentee father for fifteen years. Here was my chance to play Lancelot.

Cruz said he was hungry enough to eat the ass-end of a rhino and Hart said stop and buy breakfast at the greasy spoon coming up on the left, materializing as if by sorcery, so they pulled in and parked alongside a rusted-out Pontiac on blocks. Hart remembered to open the door for me that time. One glimpse of the diner's filthy windows and the coils of dogshit sprinkled across the unpaved lot convinced me I wasn't exactly keen on going in for the special.

But I did.

The place was stamped 1950s from the long counter with a row of shiny black swivel stools and the too-small window booths, dingy Formica peeling at the edges of the tables, to the bubble-screen tv wedged high up in a corner alcove. The tv was flickering with grainy black and white images of a talk show I didn't recognize and couldn't hear because the volume was turned way down. Mercifully I didn't see myself during the commercials.

I slouched at the counter and waited for the waitress to notice me. Took a while—she was busy flirting with Hart and Cruz, who'd squeezed themselves into a booth, and of course they wasted no time in regaling her with their latest exploits as hardcase bounty hunters. By now it was purely mechanical; rote bravado. They were pale as sheets and running on fumes of adrenaline and junk. Oh, how I dreaded the next twenty-four to thirty-six hours.

Their story was edited for heroic effect. My private version played a little differently.

We finally caught the desperado and his best girl in the Maple Leaf Country. After a bit of "slap and tickle," as Hart put it, we handed the miscreants over to the Canadians, more or less intact. Well, the Canadians more or less took possession of the pair.

The bad man was named Russell Piers, a convicted rapist and kidnapper who'd cut a nasty swath across the great Pacific Northwest and British Columbia. The girl was Penny Aldon, a runaway, an orphan, the details varied, but she wasn't important, didn't even drive; was along for the thrill, according to the reports. They fled to a river town, were loitering wharf-side, munching on a fish basket from one of six jillion Vietnamese vendors when the team descended.

Piers proved something of a Boy Scout—always prepared. He yanked a pistol from his waistband and started blazing, but one of him versus six of us only works in the movies and he went down under a swarm of blackjacks, tasers and fists. I ran the hand-cam, got the whole jittering mess on film.

The film.

That was on my mind, sneaking around my subconscious like a night prowler. There was a moment during the scrum when a shiver of light distorted the scene, or I had a near-fainting spell, or who knows. The men on the sidewalk snapped and snarled, hyenas bringing down a wounded lion. Foam spattered the lens. I swayed, almost tumbled amid the violence. And Piers looked directly at me. Grinned at me. A big dude, even bigger than the troglodytes clinging to him, he had Cruz in a headlock, was ready to crush bones, to ravage flesh, to feast. A beast all right, with long, greasy hair, powerful hands scarred by prison tattoos, gold in his teeth. Inhuman, definitely. He wasn't a lion, though. I didn't know what kingdom he belonged to.

Somebody cold-cocked Piers behind the ear and he switched off, slumped like a manikin that'd been bowled over by the holiday stampede.

Flutter, flutter and all was right with the world, relatively speaking. Except my bones ached and I was experiencing a not-so-mild wave of paranoia that hung on for hours. Never completely dissipated, even here in the sticks at a godforsaken hole in the wall while my associates preened for an audience of one.

Cruz and Hart had starred on Cops and America's Most Wanted; they were celebrity experts. Too loud, the three of them honking and squawking, especially my ex brother-in-law. Hart resembled a hog that decided to put on a dirty shirt and steel toe boots and go on its hind legs. Him being high as a kite wasn't helping. Sylvia tried to warn me, she'd known what her brother was about since they were kids knocking around on the wrong side of Des Moines.

I didn't listen. *'C'mon, Sylvie, there's a book in this. Hell, a Movie of the Week!'* Hart was on the inside of a rather seamy yet wholly marketable industry. He had a friend who had a friend who had a general idea where Mad Dog Piers was running. Money in the bank. See you in a few weeks, hold my calls.

"Watcha want, hon?" The waitress, a strapping lady with a tag spelling Victoria, poured translucent coffee into a cup that suggested the dishwasher wasn't quite up to snuff. Like all pro waitresses she pulled off this trick without looking away from my face. "I know you?" And when I politely smiled and reached for the sugar, she kept coming, frowning now as her brain began to labor. "You somebody? An actor or somethin'?"

I shrugged in defeat. "Uh, yeah. I was in a couple tv movies. Small roles. Long time ago."

Her face animated, a craggy talking tree. "Hey! You were on that comedy, one with the blind guy and his seein' eye dog. Only the guy was a con man or somethin', wasn't really blind and his dog was an alien or somethin', a robot, don't recall. Yeah, I remember you. What happened to that show?"

"Cancelled." I glanced longingly through the screen door to our ugly Chevy.

"Ray does shampoo ads," Hart said. He said something to Cruz and they cracked up.

"Milk of magnesia!" Cruz said. "And 'If you suffer from erectile dysfunction, now there's an answer!'" He delivered the last in a passable radio announcer's voice, although I'd heard him do better. He was hoarse.

The sun went behind a cloud, but Victoria still wanted my autograph, just in case I made a comeback, or got killed in a sensational fashion and then my signature would be worth something. She even dragged Sven the cook out to shake my hand and he did it with the dedication of a zombie following its mistress's instructions before shambling back to whip up eggs and hash for my comrades.

The coffee tasted like bleach.

The talk show ended and the next program opened with a still shot of a field covered by mossy hummocks and blackberry thickets. The black and white imagery threw me. For a moment I didn't register the car parked between mounds was familiar. Our boxy Chevy with the driver-side door hanging ajar, mud-encrusted plates, taillights blinking SOS.

A grey hand reached from inside, slammed the door. A hand? Or something like a hand? A B-movie prosthesis? Too blurry, too fast to be certain.

Victoria changed the channel to All My Children.

3

Hart drove.

Cruz navigated. He tilted a road map, trying to follow the dots and dashes. Victoria had drawled a convoluted set of directions to the Mima Mounds, a one-star tourist attraction about thirty miles over. Cruise on through Poger Rock and head west. Real easy drive if you took the local shortcuts and suchlike.

Not an unreasonable detour; I-5 wasn't far from the site—we could do the tourist bit and still make the Portland night scene. That was Cruz's sales pitch. Kind of funny, really. I wondered at the man's sudden fixation on geological phenomena. He was a NASCAR and Soldier of Fortune Magazine type personality. Hart fit the profile too, for that matter. Damned world was turning upside down.

It was getting hot. Cracks in the windshield dazzled and danced.

The boys debated cattle mutilations and the inarguable complicity of the Federal government regarding the Grey Question and how the moon landing was fake and remember that flick from the 1970s, Capricorn One, goddamned if O.J. wasn't one of the astronauts. Freakin' hilarious.

I unpacked the camera, thumbed the playback button, and relived the

Donkey Creek fracas. Penny said to me, "Reduviidea—any of a species of large insects that feed on the blood of prey insects and some mammals. They are considered extremely beneficial by agricultural professionals." Her voice was made of tin and lagged behind her lip movements, like a badly dubbed foreign film. She stood on the periphery of the action, scrawny fingers pleating the wispy fabric of a blue sundress. She was smiling. "The indices of primate emotional thresholds indicate the [*click-click*] process is traumatic. However, point oh-two percent vertebrae harvest corresponds to non-[*click-click*] purposes. As an X haplotype you are a primary source of [*click-click*]. Lucky you!"

"Jesus!" I muttered and dropped the camera on the seat. *Are you talkin' to me?* I stared at too many trees while Robert Deniro did his mirror schtick as a low frequency monologue in the corner of my mind. Unlike Deniro, I'd never carried a gun. The guys wouldn't even loan me a taser.

"What?" Cruz said in a tone that suggested he'd almost jumped out of his skin. He glared through the partition, olive features drained to ash. Giant drops of sweat sparkled and dripped from his broad cheeks. The light wrapped his skull, halo of an angry saint. Withdrawals something fierce, I decided.

I shook my head, waited for the magnifying glass of his displeasure to swing back to the road map. When it was safe I hit the playback button. Same scene on the view panel. This time when Penny entered the frame she pointed at me and intoned in a robust, Slavic accent, "Supercalifragilisticexpialidocious is Latin for a death god of a primitive Mediterranean culture. Their civilization was buried in mudslides caused by unusual seismic activity. If you say it loud enough—" I hit the kill button. My stomach roiled with rancid coffee and incipient motion-sickness.

Third time's a charm, right? I played it back again. The entire sequence was erased. Nothing but deep-space black with jags of silvery light at the edges. In the middle, skimming by so swiftly I had to freeze things to get a clear image, was Piers with his lips nuzzling Cruz's ear, and Cruz's face was corpse-slack. And for an instant, a microsecond, the face was Hart's too; one of those three-dee poster illusions where the object changes depending on the angle. Then, more nothingness, and an odd feedback noise that faded in and out, like Gregorian monks chanting a litany in reverse.

Okay. ABC time.

I'd reviewed the footage shortly after the initial capture in Canada.

There was nothing unusual about it. We spent a few hours at the police station answering a series of polite yet penetrating questions. I assumed our cameras would be confiscated, but the inspector simply examined our equipment in the presence of a couple suits from a legal office. Eventually the inspector handed everything back with a stern admonishment to leave dangerous criminals to the authorities. Amen to that.

Had a cop tampered with the camera, doctored it in some way? I wasn't a film-maker, didn't know much more than point and shoot and change the batteries when the little red light started blinking. So, yeah, Horatio, it was possible someone had screwed with the recording. Was that likely? The answer was no—not unless they'd also managed to monkey with the television at the diner. More probable one of my associates had spiked the coffee with a miracle agent and I was hallucinating. Seemed out of character for those greedy bastards, even for the sake of a practical joke on their third wheel—dope was expensive and it wasn't like we were expecting a big payday.

The remaining options weren't very appealing.

My cell whined, a dentist's drill in my shirt pocket. It was Rob Fries from his patio office in Gardena. Rob was tall, bulky, pink on top and garbed according to his impression of what Miami vice cops might've worn in a bygone era, such as the '80s. Rob also had the notion he was my agent despite the fact I'd fired him ten years ago after he handed me one too-many scripts for laxative testimonials. I almost broke into tears when I heard his voice on the buzzing line. "Man, am I glad you called!" I said loudly enough to elicit another scowl from Cruz.

"Hola, compadre. What a splash y'all made on page 16. '*American Yahoos Run Amok!*' goes the headline, which is a quote of the Calgary rag. Too bad the stupid bastards let our birds fly the coop. Woulda been better press if they fried 'em. Well, they don't have the death penalty, but you get the point. Even so, I see a major motion picture deal in the works. Mucho dinero, Ray, buddy!"

"Fly the coop? What are you talking about?"

"Uh, you haven't heard? Piers and the broad walked. Hell, they probably beat you outta town."

"You better fill me in." Indigestion was eating the lining of my esophagus.

"Real weird story. Some schmuck from Central Casting accidentally turned 'em loose. The paperwork got misfiled or somesuch bullshit.

The muckety-mucks are po'd. Blows your mind, don't it?"

"Right," I said in my actor's tone. I fell back on this when my mind was in neutral but etiquette dictated a polite response. Up front, Cruz and Hart were bickering, hadn't caught my exclamation. No way was I going to illuminate them regarding this development—Christ, they'd almost certainly consider pulling a u-turn and speeding back to Canada. The home office would be calling any second now to relay the news; probably had been trying to get through for hours—Hart hated phones, usually kept his stashed in the glovebox.

There was a burst of chittery static. "—returning your call. Keep getting the answering service. You won't believe it—I was having lunch with this chick used to be one of Johnny Carson's secretaries, yeah? And she said her best friend is shacking with an exec who just frickin' adored you in *Clancy & Spot*. Frickin' adored you! I told my gal pal to pass the word you were riding along on this bounty hunter gig, see what shakes loose."

"Oh, thanks, Rob. Which exec?"

"Lemmesee—uh, Harry Buford. Remember him? He floated deals for the *Alpha Team*, some other stuff. Nice as hell. Frickin' adores you, buddy."

"Harry Buford? Looks like the Elephant Man's older, fatter brother, loves pastels and lives in Mexico half the year because he's fond of underage Chicano girls? Did an expose piece on the evils of Hollywood, got himself blackballed? That the guy?"

"Well, yeah. But he's still got an ear to the ground. And he frickin'—"

"Adores me. Got it. Tell your girlfriend we'll all do lunch, or whatever."

"Anywhoo, how you faring with the gorillas?"

"Um, great. We're on our way to see the Mima Mounds."

"What? You on a nature study?"

"Cruz's idea."

"The Mima Mounds. Wow. Never heard of them. Burial grounds, huh?"

"Earth heaves, I guess. They've got them all over the world—Norway, South America, Eastern Washington—I don't know where all. I lost the brochure."

"Cool." The silence hung for a long moment. "Your buddies wanna see some, whatchyacallem—?"

"Glacial deposits."

"They wanna look at some rocks instead of hitting a strip club? No bullshit?"

"Um, yeah."

It was easy to imagine Rob frowning at his flip-flops propped on the patio table while he stirred the ice in his rum and coke and tried to do the math. "Have a swell time, then."

"You do me a favor?"

"Yo, bro'. Hit me."

"Go on the Net and look up X haplotype. Do it right now, if you've got a minute."

"X-whatsis?"

I spelled it and said, "Call me back, okay? If I'm out of area, leave a message with the details."

"Be happy to." There was a pause as he scratched pen to pad. "Some kinda new meds, or what?"

"Or what, I think."

"Uh, huh. Well, I'm just happy the Canucks didn't make you an honorary citizen, eh. I'm dying to hear the scoop."

"I'm dying to dish it. I'm losing my signal, gotta sign off."

He said not to worry, bro', and we disconnected. I worried anyway.

4

Sure enough, Hart's phone rang a bit later and he exploded in a stream of repetitious profanity and dented the dash with his ham hock of a fist. He was still bubbling when we pulled into Poger Rock for gas and fresh directions. Cruz, on the other hand, accepted the news of Russell Piers's "early parole" with a Zen detachment demonstrably contrary to his nature.

"Screw it. Let's drink," was his official comment.

Poger Rock was sunk in a hollow about fifteen miles south of the state capitol in Olympia. It wasn't impressive—a dozen or so antiquated buildings moldering along the banks of a shallow creek posted with NO SHOOTING signs. Everything was peeling, rusting or collapsing toward the center of the earth. Only the elementary school loomed incongruously—a utopian brick and tile structure set back and slightly elevated, fresh paint glowing through the alders and dogwoods. Aliens might have landed and dedicated a monument.

Cruz filled up at a mom and pop gas station with the prehistoric pumps that took an eon to dribble forth their fuel. I bought some jerky and a carton of milk with a past-due expiration date to soothe my churning guts. The lady behind the counter had yellowish hair and wore a button with a fuzzy picture of a toddler in a bib. She smiled nervously as she punched keys and furiously smoked a Pall Mall. Didn't recognize me, thank God.

Cruz pushed through the door, setting off the ding-dong alarm. His gaze jumped all over the place and his chambray shirt was molded to his chest as if he'd been doused with a water hose. He crowded past me, trailing the odor of armpit funk and cheap cologne, grunted at the cashier and shoved his credit card across the counter.

I raised my hand to block the sun when I stepped outside. Hart was leaning on the hood. "We're gonna mosey over to the bar for a couple brewskis." He coughed his smoker's cough, spat in the gravel near a broken jar of marmalade. Bees darted among the wreckage.

"What about the Mima Mounds?"

"They ain't goin' anywhere. 'Sides, it ain't time, yet."

"Time?"

Hart's ferret-pink eyes narrowed and he smiled slightly. He finished his cigarette and lighted another from the smoldering butt. "Cruz says it ain't."

"Well, what does that mean? It 'ain't time'?"

"I dunno, Ray-bo. I dunno fuckall. Why'nchya ask Cruz?"

"Okay." I took a long pull of tepid milk while I considered the latest developments in what was becoming the most bizarre road trip of my life. "How are you feeling?"

"Groovy."

"You look like hell." I could still talk to him, after a fashion, when he was separated from Cruz. And I lied, "Sylvia's worried."

"What's she worried about?"

I shrugged, let it hang. Impossible to read his face, his swollen eyes. In truth, I wasn't sure I completely recognized him, this wasted hulk swaying against the car, features glazed into gargoyle contortions.

Hart nodded wisely, suddenly illuminated regarding a great and abiding mystery of the universe. His smile returned.

I glanced back, saw Cruz's murky shadow drifting in the station window.

"Man, what are we doing out here? We could be in Portland by three." What I wanted to say was, let's jump in the car and shag ass for California. Leave Cruz in the middle of the parking lot holding his pecker and swearing eternal vengeance for all I cared.

"Anxious to get going on your book, huh?"

"If there's a book. I'm not much of a writer. I don't even know if we'll get a movie out of this mess."

"Ain't much of an actor, either." He laughed and slapped my shoulder with an iron paw to show he was just kidding. "Hey, lemme tell'ya. Did'ya know Cruz studied geology at UCLA? He did. Real knowledgeable about glaciers an' rocks. All that good shit. Thought he was gonna work for the oil companies up in Alaska. Make some fat stacks. Ah, but you know how it goes, doncha, Ray-bo?"

"He graduated UCLA?" I tried not to sound astonished. It had been the University of Washington for me. The home of medicine, which wasn't my specialty, according to the proctors. Political science and drama were the last exits.

"Football scholarship. Hard hittin' safety with a nasty attitude. They fuckin' grow on trees in the ghetto."

That explained some things. I was inexplicably relieved.

Cruz emerged, cutting a plug of tobacco with his pocket knife. "C'mon, H. I'm parched." And precisely as a cowboy would unhitch his horse to ride across the street, he fired the engine and rumbled the one quarter block to Moony's Tavern and parked in a diagonal slot between a hay truck and a station wagon plastered with anti-Democrat, pro-gun bumper stickers.

Hart asked if I planned on joining them and I replied maybe in a while, I wanted to stretch my legs. The idea of entering that sweltering cavern and bellying up to the bar with the lowlife regulars and mine own dear chums made my stomach even more unhappy.

I grabbed my valise from the car and started walking. I walked along the street, past a row of dented mailboxes, rust-red flags erect; an outboard motor repair shop with a dusty police cruiser in front; the Poger Rock Grange, which appeared abandoned because its windows were boarded and where they weren't, kids had broken them with rocks and bottles, and maybe the same kids had drawn 666 and other satanic symbols on the whitewashed planks, or maybe real live Satanists did the deed; Bob's Liquor Mart, which was a corrugated shed with bars on the tiny windows; the Laundromat, full of tired women in oversized tee-shirts, and screeching, dirty-faced kids racing among the machinery while an A.M. radio broadcast a Rush Limbaugh rerun; and a trailer loaded with half-rotted firewood for 75 BUCKS! I finally sat on a rickety bench under some trees near the lone stoplight, close enough to hear it clunk through its cycle.

I drew a manila envelope from the valise, spread sloppy typed police reports and disjointed photographs beside me. The breeze stirred and I used a rock for a paper weight.

A whole slew of the pictures featured Russell Piers in various poses, mostly mug shots, although a few had been snapped during more pleasant times. There was even one of him and a younger brother standing in front of the Space Needle. The remaining photos were of Piers's latest girlfriend—Penny Aldon, the girl from Allen Town. Skinny, pimply, mouthful of braces. A flower child with a suitably vacuous smirk.

Something cold and nasty turned over in me as I studied the haphazard data, the disheveled photo collection. I felt the pattern, unwholesome as damp cobwebs against my skin. Felt it, yet couldn't put a name to it, couldn't put my finger on it and my heart began pumping dangerously and I looked away, thought of Carly instead, and how I'd forgotten to call her on her seventh birthday because I was in Spain with some friends at a Lipizzaner exhibition. Except, I hadn't forgotten, I was wired for sound from a snort of primo Colombian blow and the thought of dialing that long string of international numbers was too much for my circuits.

Ancient history, as they say. Those days of fast-living and superstar dreams belonged to another man, and he was welcome to them.

Waiting for cars to drive past so I could count them, I had an epiphany. I realized the shabby buildings were cardboard and the people milling here and there at opportune junctures were macaroni and glue. Dull blue construction paper sky and cotton ball clouds. And I wasn't really who I thought of myself as—I was an ant left over from a picnic raid, awaiting some petulant child god to put his boot down on my pathetic diorama existence.

My cell rang and an iceberg calved in my chest.

"Hey, Ray, you got any Indian in ya?" Rob asked.

I mulled that as a brand new Cadillac convertible paused at the light. A pair of yuppie tourists mildly argued about directions—a man behind the wheel in stylish wraparound shades and a polo shirt, and a woman wearing a floppy, wide-brimmed hat like the Queen Mum favored. They pretended not to notice me. The woman pointed right and they went right, leisurely, up the hill and beyond. "Comanche," I said. Next was a shiny green van loaded with Asian kids. Sign on the door said THE EVERGREEN STATE COLLEGE. It turned right and so did the one that came after. "About one thirty-second. Am I eligible for some reparation money? Did I inherit a casino?"

"Where the hell did the Comanche sneak in?"

"Great grandma. Tough old bird. Didn't like me much. Sent me a straight razor for Christmas. I was nine."

Rob laughed. "Cra-zee. I did a search and came up with a bunch of listings for genetic research. Lemme check this . . ." he shuffled paper close to the receiver, cleared his throat. "Turns out this X haplogroup has to do with mitochondrial DNA, genes passed down on the maternal side—and an X-haplogroup is a specific subdivision or cluster. The university wags are tryin' to use female lineage to trace tribal migrations and so forth. Something like three percent of Native Americans, Europeans and Basque belong to the X-group. Least, according to the stuff I thought looked reputable. Says here there's lots of controversy about its significance. Usual academic crap. Whatch you were after?"

"I don't know. Thanks, though."

"You okay, bud? You sound kinda odd."

"Shucks, Rob, I've been trapped in a car with two redneck psychos for weeks. Might be getting to me, I'll admit."

"Whoa, sorry. Sylvia called and started going on—"

"Everything's hunky-dory, All right?"

"Cool, bro." Rob's tone said nothing was truly cool, but he wasn't in any position to press the issue. There'd be a serious Q&A when I returned, no doubt about it.

Cruz's dad was Basque, wasn't he? Hart was definitely of good, solid German stock only a couple generations removed from the mother land.

Stop me if you've heard this one—a Spaniard, a German and a Comanche walk into a bar—

After we said goodbye, I dialed my ex and got her machine, caught myself and hung up as it was purring. It occurred to me then, what the pattern was, and I stared dumbly down at the fractured portraits of Penny and Piers as their faces were dappled by sunlight falling through a maze of leaves.

I laughed, bitter.

How in God's name had they ever fooled us into thinking they were people at all? The only things missing from this farce were strings and zippers, a boom mike.

I stuffed the photos and the reports into the valise, stood in the weeds at the edge of the asphalt. My blood still pulsed erratically. Shadows began to crawl deep and blue between the buildings and the trees and in the wake of low-gliding cumulus clouds. Moony's Tavern waited, back there in the golden dust, and Cruz's Chevy before it, stolid as a coffin on the altar.

Something was happening, wasn't it? This thing that was happening, had been happening, could it follow me home if I cut and ran? Would it follow me to Sylvia and Carly?

No way to be certain, no way to tell if I had simply fallen off my rocker—maybe the heat had cooked my brain, maybe I was having a long-overdue nervous breakdown. Maybe, shit. The sinister shape of the world contracted around me, gleamed like the curves of a great killing jar. I heard the lid screwing tight in the endless ultraviolet collisions, the white drone of insects.

I turned right and walked up the hill.

5

About two hours later, a guy in a vintage farm truck stopped. The truck had cruised by me twice, once going toward town, then on the way back. And here it was again. I hesitated; nobody braked for hitchhikers unless the hitcher was a babe in tight jeans.

I thought of Piers and Penny, their expressions in the video, drinking us with their smiling mouths, marking us. And if that was true, we'd been weighed, measured and marked, what was the implication? Piers and Penny were two from among a swarm. Was it open season?

The driver studied me with unsettling intensity, his beady eyes obscured by thick, black-rimmed glasses. He beckoned.

My legs were tired already and the back of my neck itched with sunburn. Also, what did it matter anyway? If I were doing anything besides playing out the hand, I would've gone into Olympia and caught a southbound Greyhound. I climbed aboard.

George was a retired civil engineer. Looked the part—crewcut, angular face like a piece of rock, wore a dress shirt with a row of clipped pens and a tie flung over his shoulder, and polyester slacks. He kept NPR on the radio at a mumble. Gripped the wheel with both gnarled hands.

He seemed familiar—a figure dredged from memories of scientists and engineers of my grandfather's generation. He could've *been* my grandfather.

George asked me where I was headed. I said Los Angeles and he gave me a glance that said LA was in the opposite direction. I told him

I wanted to visit the Mima Mounds—since I was in the neighborhood.

There was a heavy silence. A vast and unfathomable pressure built in the cab. At last George said, "Why, they're only a couple miles farther on. Do you know anything about them?"

I admitted that I didn't and he said he figured as much. He told me the Mounds were declared a national monument back in the '60s; the subject of scholarly debate and wildly inaccurate hypotheses. He hoped I wouldn't be disappointed—they weren't glamorous compared to real natural wonders such as Niagara Falls, the Grand Canyon or the California Redwoods. The preserve was on the order of five hundred acres, but that was nothing. The Mounds had stretched for miles and miles in the old days. The land grabs of the 1890s reduced the phenomenon to a pocket, surrounded it with rundown farms, pastures and cows. The ruins of America's agrarian era.

I said that it would be impossible to disappoint me.

George turned at a wooden marker with a faded white arrow. A nicely paved single lane wound through temperate rain forest for a mile and looped into a parking lot occupied by the Evergreen vans and a few other vehicles. There was a fence with a gate and beyond that, the vague border of a clearing. Official bulletins were posted every six feet, prohibiting dogs, alcohol and firearms.

"Sure you want me to leave you here?"

"I'll be fine."

George rustled, his clothes chitin sloughing. "X marks the spot."

I didn't regard him, my hand frozen on the door handle, more than slightly afraid the door wouldn't open. Time slowed, got stuck in molasses. "I know a secret, George."

"What kind of secret?" George said, too close, as if he'd leaned in tight.

The hairs stiffened on the nape of my neck. I swallowed and closed my eyes. "I saw a picture in a biology textbook. There was this bug, looked exactly like a piece of bark, and it was barely touching a beetle with its nose. The one that resembled bark was what entomologists call an assassin bug and it was draining the beetle dry. Know how? It poked the beetle with a razor sharp beak thingy—"

"A rostrum, you mean."

"Exactly. A rostrum, or a proboscis, depending on the species. Then the assassin bug injected digestive fluids, think hydrochloric acid, and sucked the beetle's insides out."

"How lovely," George said.

"No struggle, no fuss, just a couple bugs sitting on a branch. So I'm staring at this book and thinking the only reason the beetle got caught was because it fell for the old piece of bark trick, and then I realized that's how lots of predatory bugs operate. They camouflage themselves and sneak up on hapless critters to do their thing."

"Isn't that the way of the universe?"

"And I wondered if that theory only applied to insects."

"What do you suppose?"

"I suspect that theory applies to everything."

Zilch from George. Not even the rasp of his breath.

"Bye, George. Thanks for the ride." I pushed hard to open the door and jumped down; moved away without risking a backward glance. My knees were unsteady. After I passed through the gate and approached a bend in the path, I finally had the nerve to check the parking lot. George's truck was gone.

I kept going, almost falling forward.

The trees thinned to reveal the humpbacked plain from the tv picture. Nearby was a concrete bunker shaped like a squat mushroom—a park information kiosk and observation post. It was papered with articles and diagrams under plexiglass. Throngs of brightly-clad Asian kids buzzed around the kiosk, laughing over the wrinkled flyers, pointing cameras and chattering enthusiastically. A shaggy guy in a hemp sweater, presumably the professor, lectured a couple of wind-burned ladies who obviously ran marathons in their spare time. The ladies were enthralled.

I mounted the stairs to the observation platform and scanned the environs. As George predicted, the view wasn't inspiring. The mounds spread beneath my vantage, none greater than five or six feet in height and largely engulfed in blackberry brambles. Collectively, the hillocks formed a dewdrop hemmed by mixed forest, and toward the narrowing end, a dilapidated trailer court, its structures rendered toys by perspective. The paved footpath coiled unto obscurity.

A radio-controlled airplane whirred in the trailer court airspace. The plane's engine throbbed, a shrill metronome. I squinted against the glare, couldn't discern the operator. My skull ached. I slumped, hugged the valise to my chest, pressed my cheek against damp concrete, and drowsed. Shoes scraped along the platform. Voices occasionally floated by. Nobody challenged me, my derelict posture. I hadn't thought they would. Who'd dare disturb the wildlife in this remote enclave?

My sluggish daydreams were phantoms of the field, negatives of its buckled hide and stealthy plants, and the whispered words *Eastern Washington*, *South America*, *Norway*. Scientists might speculate about the geological method of the mounds' creation until doomsday. I knew this place and its sisters were unnatural as monoliths hacked from rude stone by primitive hands and stacked like so many dominos in the uninhabited spaces of the globe. What were they? Breeding grounds, feeding grounds, shrines? Or something utterly alien, something utterly incomprehensible to match the blighted fascination that dragged me ever closer and consumed my will to flee.

Hart's call yanked me from the doldrums. He was drunk. "You shoulda stuck around, Ray-bo. We been huntin' everywhere for you. Cruz ain't in a nice mood." The connection was weak, a transmission from the dark side of Pluto. Batteries were dying.

"Where are you?" I rubbed my gummy eyes and stood.

"We're at the goddamned Mounds. Where are *you*?"

I spied a tiny glint of moving metal. The Chevy rolled across the way where the road and the mobile homes intersected. I smiled—Cruz hadn't been looking for me; he'd been trolling around on the wrong side of the park, frustrated because he'd missed the entrance. As I watched, the car slowed and idled in the middle of the road. "I'm here."

The cell phone began to click like a Geiger counter that'd hit the mother lode. Bits of fiddle music pierced the garble.

The car jolted from a savage tromp on the gas and listed ditchward. It accelerated, jounced and bounded into the field, described a haphazard arc in my direction. I had a momentary terror that they'd seen me atop the tower, were coming for me, were planning some unhinged brand of retribution. But no, the distance was too great. I was no more than a speck, if I was anything. Soon, the car lurched behind the slope of intervening hillocks and didn't emerge.

"Hart, are you there?"

The clicking intensified and abruptly chopped off, replaced by smooth, bottomless static. Deep sea squeals and warbles began to filter through. Bees humming. A castrati choir on a gramophone. Giggling. Someone, perhaps Cruz, whispering a Latin prayer. I was grateful when the phone made an electronic protest and expired. I hurled it over the side.

The college crowd had disappeared. Gone too, the professor and his admirers. I might've joined the migration if I hadn't spotted the cab of George's truck mostly hidden by a tree. It was the only rig in the parking lot. I couldn't tell if anyone was behind the wheel.

The sun hung low and fat, reddening as it sank. The breeze had cooled. It plucked at my hair, dried my sweat, chilled me a little. I listened for the roar of the Chevy, buried to the axles in loose dirt, high-centered on a stump; or perhaps they'd abandoned the vehicle. Thus I strained to pick my companions from among the blackberry patches and softly undulating clumps of scotch broom which had invaded this place too.

Quiet.

I went down the stairs and let the path take me. I went as a man in a stupor, my muscles lethargic with dread. The lizard subprocessor in my brain urged me to sprint for the highway, to scuttle into a burrow. It possessed a hint of what waited over the hill, had possibly witnessed this melodrama many times before. I whistled a dirge through clenched teeth and the mounds closed ranks behind me.

Ahead, came the dull clank of a slamming door.

The car was stalled at the foot of a steep slope, its hood buried in a tangle of brush. The windows were dark as a muddy aquarium and festooned with fleshy creepers and algid scum.

I took root a few yards from the car, noting that the engine was dead, yet the vehicle rocked on its springs from some vigorous activity. A rhythmic motion that caused metal to complain. The brake lights stuttered.

Hart's doughy face materialized on the passenger side, bumped against the glass with the dispassion of a pale, exotic fish, and withdrew, descending into a marine trench. His forehead left a starry impact. Someone's palm smacked the rear window, hung there, fingers twitching.

I retreated. Ran, more like. I may have shrieked. Somewhere along the line the valise flew open and its contents spilled—a welter of files, the argyle socks Carly gave me for Father's Day, my toiletries. A handful of photographs pinwheeled in a gust. I dropped the bag. Ungainly, panicked, I didn't get far, tripped and collapsed as the sky blackened and a high-pitched keening erupted from several locations simultaneously. In moments all ambient light had been sucked away; I couldn't see the thorny bush gouging my neck as I wriggled for cover, couldn't make out my own hand before my eyes.

The keening ceased. Peculiar echoes bounced in its wake, gave me the absurd sensation of lying on a sound stage with the kliegs shut off. I received the impression of movement around my hunkered self, although I didn't hear footsteps. I shuddered, pressed my face deeper into musty soil. Ants investigated my pants cuffs.

Cruz called my name from the throat of a distant tunnel. I knew it wasn't him and kept silent. He cursed me and giggled the unpleasant giggle I'd heard on the phone. Hart tried to coax me out, but this imitation was even worse. They went down the entire list and despite everything I was tempted to answer when Carly began crying and hiccupping and begging me to help her, daddy please, in a baby girl voice she hadn't owned for several years. I stuffed my fist in my mouth, held on while the chorus drifted here and there and eventually receded into the buzz and chirr of field life.

The sun flickered on and the world was restored piecemeal—one root, one stump, one hill at a time. My head swam; reminded me of waking from anesthesia.

Dusk was blooming when I crept from the bushes and tasted the air, cocked an ear for predators. The Chevy was there, shimmering in the twilight. Motionless now.

I could've crouched in my blind forever, wild-eyed as a hare run to ground in a ruined shirt and piss-stained slacks. But it was getting cold and I was thirsty, so I slunk across the park at an angle that took me to the road near the trailer court. I went, casting glances over my shoulder for pursuit that never came.

6

I told a retiree sipping ice tea in a lawn chair that my car had broken down and he let me use his phone to call a taxi. If he witnessed Cruz crash the Chevy into the Mounds, he wasn't saying. The police didn't show while I waited and that said enough about the situation.

The taxi driver was a stolid Samoan who proved not the least bit interested in my frightful appearance or talking. He drove way too fast for comfort, if I'd been in a rational frame of mind, and dropped me at the Greyhound depot in downtown Olympia.

I wandered inside past the rag-tag gaggle of modern gypsies which inevitably haunted these terminals, studied the big board while the ticket agent pursed her lips in distaste. Her expression certified me as one of the unwashed mob.

I picked Seattle at random, bought a ticket. The ticket got me the key to the restroom, where I splashed my welted flesh, combed cat tails from my hair and looked almost human again. Almost. The fluorescent tube crackled and sizzled, threatened to plunge the crummy toilet into darkness, and in the discotheque flashes, my haggard face seemed strange.

The bus arrived an hour late and it was crammed. I shared a seat with a middle-aged woman wearing a shawl and scads of costume jewelry. Her ivory skin was hard and she smelled of chlorine. I didn't imagine she wanted to sit by me, judging from the flare of her nostrils, the crimp of her over-glossed mouth.

Soon the bus was chugging into the wasteland of night and the lights clicked off row by row as passengers succumbed to sleep. Except some guy near the front who left his overhead lamp on to read, and me. I was too exhausted to close my eyes.

I surprised myself by crying.

And the woman surprised me again by murmuring, "Hush, hush, dear. Hush, hush." She patted my trembling shoulder. Her hand lingered.

OUT THEY COME

ALEX DALLY MACFARLANE

She speaks so little, out they come: foxes. One after the other, falling like russet tears. They land on all fours and shake the saliva from their fur and bare their teeth, sharper than knives. She wants to say to the village, "I'm not sorry, I hate you all, you deserve this."

They are her strength, come to fight.

In the islands, foxes are food. Boiled with dandelions in a deep pot, flesh and marrow and bones all, they make many good meals for a woman living alone; and don't forget to keep the hide for winter, when the ice blows in. The tails make fine collars. Or put them at the edges of the door, to keep the drafts out. Keeps the sheep safe, too, especially in spring when the lambs are small on the damp grass.

At the edge of the village, any wild animal that sniffs at a stone wall goes into the pot.

Stey hides these foxes.

Her house is small and plain, stone walls and a grass roof for the goat, only one room inside. There she layers tapestries on the floor and walls to keep the cold out. Through winter nights there's precious little else to do but sit and work. In spring she starts trading her excess tapestries: the holy scenes with the church, the wild scenes with the other women. Though she works alone, she's fast, determined. If she stops being exceptional, there won't be any more chicks or fish or sheep-wool. In the scant weeks of summer, she opens the wooden door and the breeze blows in, full of sea salt. She scatters cushions on the floor, which is also her seat and her bed, and spins the wool, and the chickens run inside and out as freely as the air.

The foxes make her house crowded, but it is autumn when they fall from her mouth: their warmth is appreciated. She curls with them at night, like the chickens in their pen. There are only five, at first. The smell is not so bad.

She locks them inside the first time she goes into the village, and not just to keep them from pots. She doesn't trust them with the goat.

But it's not animals they're after.

When she's just eleven years old, Stey sneaks out of church to watch the foxes fight. Two vixens, barking, baring teeth, over someone's dead lamb. Stey tells stories about them: foxes that fight, foxes that fly, foxes that dive into the sea and bring back the rarest treasures. In church, she blocks her ears and thinks of the foxes. In school, she thinks of their teeth. How can you believe in what you've never seen?

Coughing up foxes makes sense: they are her comfort, they are her strength. She has believed in their teeth for years, from girl to woman. Only—the strength is in them, not her, and she doesn't think she can put them to their use.

They scratch at the door to get out.

At night they lie around her, content to sleep, but at day they interrupt her work. Stey sits by her stove, minding the mutton casserole—from her mother's flock, given for a cushion cover—and stretches out her recently woven nettle-cloth, pinning it to frames. She begins to sketch her winter's work on the cloth. Another selkie. Another warrior-lass, with brows hard as axes and thistles in her hair. Another Virgin, eyes on her golden son. In one design, new, a quintet of foxes gathers around a woman's feet, nipping at the ends of her long, dark hair—but she cannot decide the woman's expression: hidden behind her hair—or not. She spins more wool as she thinks.

The foxes put their jaws on her knees and stare at her. They scratch and bark. They circle her small house, like caged animals, which she guiltily supposes they are—of a sort. Animals that don't need to eat or defecate.

She goes walking to gather lichens and dulse for her dye-jars, leaving the foxes behind.

She meets the man whose name begins with J, whom she has tried to avoid for years, on his way to the beach to shoot gulls. Cringing deep inside, she smiles and hugs him and asks how he has been, in the years since they ate together in the school hall, all the village's children under one roof. He tells her that it's so good to see her again. She agrees.

Five more foxes fall from her throat that night, hurting her on the way out. They join the others as she gasps and cries into the cold air of her house. They gather around her, hot as anger. Lying on her tapestries, wrapped up in blankets as the wind whistles draft-songs around her door, she welcomes them, companions to her thoughts, which are too big to bear alone. The foxes surround her.

They scratch at the door, unrelenting.

There is never a moment when she decides to let the foxes out. Only that the following afternoon she looks up and the door is open and her house is strangely quiet, empty. Pungent.

Though she smiles, with a malice that would frighten even her mother, she doesn't join them.

It doesn't take a lot to teach silence. No. It takes: a boy whose jokes are putting his hands on her, ignoring her insistent "No!", and almost all of their friends laughing with him. It's just a joke! It's just hands on her thighs, just sticks poking her breasts, her crotch, day after day for two years. It's nothing serious, nothing bad, nothing, *nothing*.

It is far harder to teach herself not to be silent, not to put her anger behind smiles.

She sketches the woman with her face hidden by her hair.

She begins to stitch the woman with fox-teeth, gleaming with the last of her gold-thread, a church bequeathment.

The village doesn't react well.

The foxes run down every road, baring teeth sharper than knives, and they tear at ankles and legs. They leave blood on the cobblestones. In the afternoon, when the stoves are cold, they scramble down chimneys and stain the tapestries. They run into the village hall, into the school. On Sundays, when people gather in the church for the warmth of many throats speaking prayers, they run under the pews and wait by the prayer cushions for knees. No one notices that they eat air, not sheep. No one notices that they don't attack everyone.

Stey hears of the names: men—mostly men—and some women, who laughed, who didn't care. So many of them, in this small village.

A meeting is called, in a room floored with stone not earth, its doors locked tight, its corners lit too bright for foxes to hide.

They call it a plague of foxes and Stey laughs, silently.

She cannot laugh when she next walks through the village. Foxes: two strung up on fences, one hanging outside the pub like its name-sign, one curtaining the village hall, the others decorating the shoulders of the people with the most tattered legs. Those men limp, smiling. Stey flees from them. The foxes' eyes are dull. Russet-haired children hide indoors, their mothers cautious. A dog pup is flayed for looking too foxy.

She is practical, and the winters are long and cold: she has killed foxes before. Put their bodies into a pot in pieces, added the hides to a blanket.

This is not winter's need.

Better to spend the months of ice in her house, making her tapestries, good working woman, burning wood slowly, preciously in the stove, milking the goat, collecting eggs, sipping nettle tea.

She weeps for the foxes and imagines that they must be scared now, because her throat remains empty. The smell gradually leaves. She wants them back. No. She wants silence and forgetfulness and tapestries. The selkies need the sea around their ankles, the sky as grey as their sturdy seal-skins. The gold-toothed woman is not even half-finished. There is work to be done, year after year, and what good is remembering? Just pain and dead foxes.

No.

She wants the foxes' warm bodies against hers, she wants their teeth. She's tired, so tired, of silence and quiet, but she knows she can't end it alone.

The nights are long.

When she thinks of the man she loved when they were young, whose name begins with T—who taught her the word "over-reacting"—she coughs a green-eyed fox onto the warm stones in front of her stove.

"It won't stop, will it?" she whispers.

The fox gives what passes for a smile on such a pointy face.

"Well, now we can *make* it stop."

She keeps thinking of her memories and out the foxes keep coming, though it hurts her throat again, though it gets her dragged from her house—because eventually someone notices how the foxes go out of her door and never in, how her ankles are bare of bites, how she holds up her chin when she passes a strung-up fox in the street and smiles at any still living.

"Pray," they say, throwing her in the jail, where there are no tapestries to keep out the bitter winter cold, "that the punishment is light."

She believes in nothing but the foxes.

She makes enough of them to keep her warm. The men who watch the jail—who were once boys, laughing in the school hall—stare through the barred window in the top of her door, telling her how the foxes will die at the ends of their shotguns, but there is already fear in their voices.

Once a week, her mother visits with fish stew and nettle tea. "It's not right." She's not talking about the foxes. Her pale eyes remind Stey of the winter sky, which she cannot see from her cell, and she wants to be on the other side of the door, staring at the sky by her mother's side. She wants to be making tapestries of warriors and selkies, not thinking of hands, not fighting. "You shouldn't have to do this." Echoes of older words.

"I wish I'd listened to you," Stey says, because she has wanted to say it for years. "You were right. I don't know why I never told anyone."

"No. None of this is your fault."

Stey smiles, fox-like. "I know."

She's so tired of waiting for the village to change.

Now she has the foxes, whose teeth are sharper than her small voice, and they will do far more than tear at ankles.

The floor of the cell is russet fur, is upturned jaws with teeth bared. Stey stands among them, barely bending over as she coughs, multiplying what she starts to think of as her army.

The guards don't dare open the door.

"There are foxes in the wind," she says, in-between coughing them up. "Why do you think your cheeks are nipped pink? They're always hungry." She laughs, and the men outside the door shudder. "There are foxes in the sleet, landing on your fingers when you milk the goats. There are foxes in the drifts, collapsing your sheep pens. String up as many of them as you want, make a whole village out of foxes, but you won't stop them."

Better yet, she thinks, *run into the sea and drown. Let the rest of us live in peace.*

I hope they tear you apart before you can kill a single one.

The village waits, afraid.

The green-eyed fox nuzzles her hands and she thinks: *There are a lot of awful people. I need to make a lot more foxes to overcome them all.* It is easy to remember, over and over, and though it hurts, she gets used to it: the retch and cough, the slide of fur over her throat, the flick of a tail against her teeth. Her smile, broad as a sword.

Out they come.

AND LOVE SHALL HAVE NO DOMINION
LIVIA LLEWELLYN

*craigslist > hell > district unknown > personals > **missed connections** > d4hf*

Date Unknown

*h*uman star, are u my gate to the world?—(central park west, August 2003)

it was the night of the blackout—do u remember? time is as one to me time is nothing to me time is nothing, but in ur linear existence it was Then, it was the night the city closed her hundred million eyes. one hundred degrees and still rising as heat bled up from the buildings and streets, anxious to escape into the cool of space, never again to be bound. u were walking up the western edge of that man-made forest in the hard pitch of night, humans stumbling all around, flailing and quaking under an unfolding sky of stars they had never before seen, or simply forgotten existed. humans, brilliant with the Creator's life like star fire and u the brightest of all, but red and gold and white like my fallen Majesty, my sweet Prince, shining in the cesspools of earth he eternally spirals through, a necklace of diamonds crashing over shit-covered stone. and i? i was wandering to and fro upon and over the world, as our divine Prince taught us, and as i glanced down i caught the faint flash of a spark. that is what drew me down and in, the force and fuse of life that comprises ur soul. u felt it 2. do not deny: i know u saw the thick branches of the trees bend and toss in my wake, rippling and bowing before my unseen passage. i saw ur eyes widen, and the bright gold fuse of stargodfire coil in ur heart, darken and drop lower. u quickened ur pace, but u never stopped staring into the primal green mass, ur desire rising with the heat with the wind with every thunderous vibration of my coming. mystery power and the unseen currents of un-nature, revealed in the absence of confusion of un-light and machines—these things drew ur most inner self toward me even as u turned away walking up the long walled side of the forest, running ur hand against the ancient rock, fingers catching thick moss and small weeds, soft fingers scrabbling over hard cold granite sparkling-veined with the crushed bones of things long past. and the wall became my body my horns my mind and i lapped at ur creamy thoughts and the city shuddered in unease, and so did u.

all parts of u all fissures all hollows all voids will i fill until u open ur mouth and there is only my voice / open ur eyes only my sight / touch ur cunt only my cock / slice ur flesh bleed only my tears.

no need to respond. u will. u already have.

Date Unknown

a thousand times ill-met, yet not met once—(fifteenth floor, office building, midtown, 2005)

u were at a work machine, shaking a malformed manmade thing— fine sprays of obsidian liquid shot up, landing against white silk and skin. the last of the ink, spent against lonely flesh. do u remember this day? laughter, floating across the floor. and u dropped the object, put ur hands to ur throat as u fled to ur women's rooms, where u sat on cold porcelain and cried, wondering what to make of such a life, a life so open to wonderful wide pain, and yet so mean, so small. u wept, and i licked at the tears—u felt me. fear leapt and coursed through ur body like a hunted hart. but u did not flinch or scream or draw away. i have trained u well—contact such as this in the public arena of slithering man has taught u to suffer my touch in silence, feigning ignorance. my talons slithered up ur thighs, leaving beaded trails of red against ur skin, and while u shuddered in silent terror and pain, i thought of many things.

i thought of u.

i have traveled now, many times through time, threading back through ur life to childhood, to the very first breath. with each stitch i stole, with each nip of the needle and thread of my will and desire, a moment of joy, of hope, of love, of beauty, of wonder was snipped from ur life like cancer, working open the hole through which i will inevitably enter. age two, sitting in ur front yard under the spring's warm sun, watching ur father plant flowers that later burst into glorious blooms—/—that later withered into putrid stinking masses at the touch of my vomit and piss. ur first true memory, forever changed, because i made it so. ur dog ate those decaying flowers, and died. u wept in ur little bed, and i sifted down through starry night and raised u high in ur nightmares toward them, showing u the whorls of the milky way as i nibbled the tears away. working working working, i stitched myself into every moment of ur life—even at the start, when my clawed hands twisted u from ur mother's womb in a gyre of blood—until the pressing horror of my unseen presence was as familiar and constant as the rain, the hole as wide as the reach of the magellanic. i am everywhere and everywhen: there is no moment when i have not existed for u / prepared for u / planned for u / toiled for u. and now, there is no moment in ur life when u have not existed for me. do u love my work, love?—but u love nothing now, nothing u can see, nothing u can taste or touch with the meaty cage by which u are bound. this is my work, and all those unbidden moments of heart-cracking loneliness, covering ur years until u can barely take a breath, until u long for anything except where and what u are? u are welcome.

despair of everything, my love, even ur pretty blouse, but never despair of this:

we shall soon meet.

Sat Oct 23

of all the things I've made—(apartment, west chelsea, 2009)
u are the finest. our terror / our pain / our horror / our screams / our blood that pours from ur skin as i rake it with horns / talons / teeth. my flame-haired shooting star plummeting to earth and u know it is me u are falling into, and u cannot stop. i clear the path like a maelstrom—books and crockery dashed to ur floors, chairs swept aside, food rotted and flyblown with my single breath. un-lights explode, and in the darkness i expand like disease, driving friends / family / lovers / life from ur world. do u not understand? when we are as one, there will be no room for any of this in ur world. no room, no need. only our need. only mine.

u were sitting in that part of the building u have claimed as ur own, curled up in the corner of the largest room, on the largest cushions. images flickered in and out from a screen, and u watched them in silence as u drank yet again from the glass cup in ur steady hands. many times had the sun risen and set over ur city since i last touched and tasted u, laid waste to the possessions u think u love. the screen flickered. u swallowed ur wine and smiled. i watched the soft glint of hair at the back of ur neck, the fine lines around the corners of ur mouth, the curl of ur plump pink toes. untroubled breath, as even and smooth as the beat of ur heart. life, creamy placid and it washed over me, and and andand outside, afternoon sank and evening spread indigo feelers throughout the canyons of machines, and all over the world the swarming insect masses lit their candles and fires and devices, desperate pathetic futile in their attempts to hold night at bay, but firm in conviction. safety like their prayers, false and comforting. no different than u and i. and the little machines ticked the time away and the screen grew dark and u crept to bed. un-light washed in from the streets, dappling neon flashes from cars and signs, oranges yellows reds. and carefully, carefully: i hovered over ur sleeping flesh, sinking as slowly as the constant decay of space. ur heartbeat weakened, ur breath deepened—i tasted fear, felt the cold familiar terror envelope u. a dream i came to u as—a nightmare, and u frozen in my grip. but yes. yes. i descended, sliding my arms around u, the phantom lover of ur dreams, dark and dangerous, all-enveloping. and u unfroze, ur body pooling against mine. we lay together under the unfurling universe, my exhaling breath caught by ur inhalations. so soft and warm, so perfect a fit. as if this is what we were made to be.

do u remember Catala, on the beach, thirty-six years ago, before it sank into the sands? u were only twelve, and u fell through the rotting deck of the beached ship while looking for treasure. i stayed with u for a day and night, until they found u. i made the cold ocean waters warm and kept the crabs and gulls at bay, and i put my hand on ur heart and held u ever so tight, my horns and wings ur shelter, my body ur bed. i thought u saw me, through the veil of your tears. i thought u smiled. i thought i kissed ur lips. i may be wrong.

no, that memory is gone. it never happened. i ate it away; and then i broke ur legs.

human star, do u remember this night, this moment? remember it now, for tomorrow i shall wander to and fro again, back into the night into this pocket of time very pocket this NOW and i shall cut and fuck and burrow and rape my way into us and devour devour DEVOUR us until it has never happened until until we have never until until until FUCK FUCK FUCKING COCKSUCKING CUNTFUCK laksd WOEIFF

Δ; kd Σκι;φκΛΚΦΚΔσδφΣκδΛ ΛΚΔΦ ll;ΣΙΕ λδσσδ;

o

Sat Oct 23

iron fist in a pale-skinned human glove—(apartment, west chelsea, 2009)

star nursery of my desire, womb of my existence, do u remember this afternoon remember this afternoon and how it bled into the night like the child u had in windy ellensburg, the girl u left in long glistening strands of plasma redblack gouts of soft flesh blood on the floor of the bathroom as i stroked ur salt-wet hair, great rending sobs and the quaking pain splitting through ur curves ur tears lost like Catala in the fires of my touch

no.

NO NO NO

do u remember this afternoon, pale and grey in ur endless grey city, open-mouthed ziggurats gnawing at the sunless sky? u stood at the window, wine glass full and dribbling in ur hand, staring at scudding clouds tentacling their way over silent-screamed rooftops, that familiar buzz undrowned by the drink, that familiar whisper and soft thundered deja-vu that this day was happening again. yes. ur breath fogged the window, and u placed the glass on the sill, raised ur hand to wipe it away, and—within that sliver of a second as the tiny beads of moisture floated off the glass u saw me behind it, saw the glint and gleam of my eyes, the curve of my fanged smile, the heft of my fist and all the attendant power and glory of the universe, all the secret places the Creator has forever kept from u all the stretches of dark matter and the knowledge that blossoms under the light of a hundred billion alien suns. u saw all, and the blood rushed into the core of ur flesh surrounding the stargodfire and u staggered back from the glass, pissing urself as I burst into the room, slamming through u like an errant asteroid. U hit ur head on a table, small moans seeping from grimacing lips but no time to scream or shout because this isn't happening how could this happen this only happens in dreams. I grabbed ur ankles and swung u around, my footfalls like lightning strikes against the polished stone, and ur fingers grabbed at tables chairs fallen books the edges of doors, and I rose u high like a flag, ur hands sliding up the doorframe, little threads of blood left behind with ur nails, and I ripped ur garments like tissue like breath like clouds and thrust my wriggling claws up inside, and finally u screamed, and in the bedroom against the quilts and childhood blankets I threw u down, pressing pressing and still u screamed in a city that only ever screams, only ever the sound of our breath the low dark explosions of my heart and clap of wings and the endless thrum of traffic and the uncaring world outside. I punched ur face and blood sprayed benedictine against our mouths, broke ur wrists down against the cloth, forced ur legs wide open my talons biting ur flesh ur cunt dark red and raw like a setting sun and I sunk into u my barbed cock splitting working working the hole and o god the bright gold fuse, the Creator's spark so close and my tongue deep in ur throat and my fingers against it choking and ur breasts soft warm scratched a thousand times by scales and I rammed u rammed u rammed u and this world so close now so close to everything that had ever been torn away

small fingers against the curve of my tail, u smiled

what have i

there, there, and ur sobs so soft and low and u spoke a word, a single gold fused plea passed from ur lips to mine i drank it in a gossamer silken wisp of the Creator, of u: and i slowed, i slowed. o my love, i slowed.

Sat Oct 23

is this what Humans want?—(bedroom, west chelsea, 2009)

this day i have plunged into a hundred thousand times, and all about us the universe spins and reverses, spins once more, once more. do u remember this day, this afternoon, this evening, unfolding again and again and again, unfolding like the bruised cream white of ur thighs, the swollen purple dusk of ur sex, the blood-split lips of ur quivering mouth? i sliced into ur beach like the Catala, i thrust the sands part, and there was no resolution, no joining, and the golden red stargodfuse flickered and floated in the unreachable distance as i lay spent between ur wet dunes, rusting, sinking into entropy and decay. that moment, that slow delicious moment, i have yet to find again. u said nothing u say nothing, every troy-like day upon day, u flinch and grimace and turn away and i pin ur face like a wriggling insect crushing ur jaws with my nails until the bones grind and bend, roaring and biting obscenities into ur tongue, and still u do not speak. do u remember it, that single slow moment when our eyes met, when u truly saw me, when u touched and whispered to me as a lover? i think i no longer do. i think it was a human infection, a trick of the Creator, a cancerous dream.

shadows sifted through the room like ghosts, cast from the same clouds, the same sun, the same sky as ten thousand days before. they are as familiar now to me as ur body against the red-stained sheets, staring past the ceiling into a future i cannot fathom or divine. my hand pressed down on ur chest, feeling ur heart gallop under all the layers of bone and skin, and u grew quiet and ur breath stilled and daylight crept from the room. i thought many times of peeling u apart, burrowing clawing through the layers into ur dying center, gnawing the bones and piercing ur eyes with the shards, snapping each rib one by one by one until ur lungs grew still and the arteries drained and ur small firm heart nestled against my palm, until i bathed in all the molecules of ur meaningless life, draped myself in ur soul, and rose anew, as one with everything u ever were.

how everything changes with a single word

how do u live ur life like this, so apart from everything in this vast existence except ur distant Creator, so at peace with being alone, apart. we lay next to each other in blood and piss and tears, my horns tangled in ur matted hair, our breath winds in and out of the others lungs, and ur eyes see nothing, ur skin feels nothing, u do NOTHING to seek me out, to discover what terrible invisible glorious power binds u to this moment, compels u to relive this day again and again. all my work, all throughout time, to make u pliable / soften resolve / sweeten despair / sharpen fear, so long have i toiled and crashed against uFUCKING LOOK AT ME LOOK AT ME SEE ME. see me like u did that first day that one time please i beg of u SPEAK TO ME O human star o love. are u a test. have i failed.

do u remember the word u spoke to me. do u remember the smile. will u not give these again? must i bite and scratch and claw it out of ur face and cracked teeth clattering down as i pull apart the cartilage grind the tongue meat forked and shredded searching seeking destroying but u do not remember. i eat each day and vomit it up and gorge it down again, until everything u ever were in me resides, the fuse that drives u mine.

must i take everything. do i.

yes

Date Unknown

a Gnossienne of the Heart—(unknown)

do u remember when i left u? do i remember when u left me? Time is measureless to me, Time is as air is as the dark wounds and tears through which i travel unseen and endless horizonless alone. and the city spreads out below me glittering sequins of tiny human souls thrown down against a net of electric fire an inferno of falsity and lies encased in canyons of profane steel. and i but rancid garbage caught in the dervishes of machine-made wind, adrift and without purpose. o my Prince, is this what u see, u feel, as u wander to and fro amongst ur souls? and the forest below is still, and ur brown-stained bed sheets empty.

Time is weight. Time is measured calculable movements of human-forged horror, each as slow and meaningless as the one behind and before, Time a river, Time a great hooked chain dragging us to no place with no purpose, tethered bits of flesh. Time divides.

o empty star, each day i descended into the churning engines of Time, of un-nature and un-light, i descended amidst static and disruption, iron blades backwards, clocks unwinding, water in circles recoiling fast away. and the hospital shuddered at its granite foundation, patients vomited and bled, tongues spewed languages long dead, and all things foul and fair cried out as i worked worked worked against Time. before ur bed ur wasting flesh i stitched myself to the fetid air, commanding u to arise, to wake and fall into my arms, to say the Word as u had once said it before. walls cracked and mirrors shattered, and the Creator's minions scurried back and forth in their wine-dark robes, chanting His lies, evoking our brothers to save u. but my flies and shit kept all who thwarted me away, their eyes bled when they read His lies, and His book became as ash in their broken hands. again and again, i lowered myself upon u. u did not stir. milkglass eyes. parched lips. i placed my tight-sewn mouth ever so gently against urs, against ur nipples, ur cunt. everything u ever were is gone. everything i ever

no

in the indigo hour before dawn, in that fleeting sliver of light when i can catch my reflection in glass / silver / stone, i stare at the wide black gash of my mouth, now forever shut. cruel Prince, to give ur loved ones only half the knowledge, all the pain. beneath the thick iron stitches, swollen skin, bright gold stargodfire rests beneath my tongue, warm and alive. everything u ever were, everything u will ever be. everything i ever—

and the pain comes not blood or flesh or bone it rolls over me and the knowledge o sweet Prince the knowledge the burden of Time, the horrible skip of my heart. i have u have all of u possess u tight and neat and IT IS NOTHING. NOTHING. nothing. and ur hand, so small, at the small of my back. what i would give. what i would give. and i cannot swallow cannot breathe. it is all that is left.

and in the indigo hour before dawn, after the quakes have subsided, i slipped between the rough sheets, curled by ur side. my hand so large against ur belly. ur hip warmed my cock, and my breath dampened ur breasts. and when i left, when morning chased me away, they found u bruised and beaten, ribs cracked, acid teardrops festering in the hollows of ur neck, skin dissolving like sand in the hissing waves.

o my human star. one second. one moment. one word. i have all of you and nothing, except one moment one word. i would give anything. i would give everything, to bring it back.

everything.

so.

Date Unknown

the last lost day—(ocean shores, washington, 1975)

and ur little body lay crumpled in pools of water, cold ocean-old pools of salt and sand and rust. the groan and crack of decaying metal all around, hiss of the waves rolling in with winds and night, and above u, the jagged hole still weeping with ur blood. beyond: endless darkening skies, and nothing at all. pain at one shoulder and fear at the other, clarion-calling each other like long-lost lovers, and the waters rising ever so higher, hitching up ur broken bones, ur flowered dress, ur slender shivering thighs. screams pure and high as starlight shot through the air, never breaching the hold, falling back down all around the cavernous waste.

u closed ur eyes. and the waves rushed and thumped against the wreck like the beating of some great unseen heart, and the waters lapped and caressed ur waist, slid across ur small breasts, lifting u up and down. and the cold grew in power and nimble fingers of water pushed the hair from ur forehead and eyes and black winged summer night closed in, around, down, furnace-warm but not enough to keep away the cold. and hard uncaring, unloving ocean covered ur lips, slid forked rivulets of brine into ur mouth, down ur throat and u breathed it in, and the world and the waves and the wind grew to pinpoint, ur body a million years away, and all that was left of the universe was nothing—/

/—was a kiss: a bright gold fuse of stargodfire unfurling from a single unstitched whispered word coiling into ur heart, an explosion of wings unfurling and lifting up, hot breath against ur face, warmth thunderclapping through ur blood and bones, and the roar of the waves thrusting against the beach, the hand at the small of ur back, a lover's touch at ur face as u opened ur eyes, standing alive and whole on the beach before the Catala, rusting high and dry above the grassy dunes.

and u stood shivering hound-like, dripping wet hand at heart, under the white gulls' cries, under the scudding clouds and the lowering sun, stood before the Catala, the ship with the hidden treasure, the ship u had never set foot on—/—fallen on bled on died. Stood until the nerves bit and prickled in ur legs, and the shadows lengthened and reached u, brushing against ur toes / the small of ur back / the tender hollow of ur neck / the translucent flesh of ur ear, all set afire by unseen whispers warning u away, and: u flew, a girl-shaped human star shooting up the long flat dunes through the grass and over the naked driftwood piles, racing away the miles of stone cold coast until u seemed as small and unreachable as the far-off circling gulls, never stopping, never looking back through all the joyful goldenfused years of ur life at the broken wreck back on the beach, the broken black-hulled monster rusting away, un-stitching un-working un-working, repairing all the broken moments until Time endless Time spiraling Time swept it all away, scrubbed it down to clean pure sand upon which my love, my memory, had no reach or purchase, until all that remained of the moment was U, and the Glorious Word.

do u remember now?

you do not.

i do.

YOU GO WHERE IT TAKES YOU
NATHAN BALLINGRUD

He did not look like a man who would change her life. He was big, roped with muscles from working on offshore oil rigs, and tending to fat. His face was broad and inoffensively ugly, as though he had spent a lifetime taking blows and delivering them. He wore a brown raincoat against the light morning drizzle and against the threat of something more powerful held in abeyance. He breathed heavily, moved slowly, found a booth by the window overlooking the water, and collapsed into it. He picked up a syrup-smeared menu and studied it with his whole attention, like a student deciphering Middle English. He was like every man who ever walked into that diner. He did not look like a beginning or an end.

That day, the Gulf of Mexico and all the earth was blue and still. The little town of Port Fourchon clung like a barnacle to Louisiana's southern coast, and behind it the water stretched into the distance for as many miles as the eye could hold. Hidden by distance were the oil rigs and the workers who supplied the town with its economy. At night she could see their lights, ringing the horizon like candles in a vestibule. Toni's morning shift was nearing its end; the dining area was nearly empty. She liked to spend those slow hours out on the diner's balcony, overlooking the water.

Her thoughts were troubled by the phone call she had received that morning. Gwen, her three-year-old daughter, was offering increasing resistance to the male staffers at the Daylight Daycare, resorting lately to biting them or kicking them in the ribs when they knelt to calm her. Only days before, Toni had been waylaid there by a lurking social worker who talked to her in a gentle saccharine voice, who touched her hand maddeningly and said, "No one is judging you; we just want to help." The social worker had mentioned the word "psychologist" and asked about their home life. Toni had been embarrassed and enraged, and was only able to conclude the interview with a mumbled promise to schedule another one soon. That her daughter was already displaying such grievous signs of social ineptitude stunned Toni, left her feeling hopeless and betrayed.

It also made her think about Donny again, who had abandoned her years ago to move to New Orleans, leaving her a single mother at twenty-three. She wished death on him that morning, staring over the railing at the unrelenting progression of waves. She willed it along the miles and into his heart.

"You know what you want?" she asked.

"Um . . . just coffee." He looked at her breasts and then at her eyes.

"Cream and sugar?"

"No thanks. Just coffee."

"Suit yourself."

The only other customer in the diner was Crazy Claude by the door, speaking conversationally to a cooling plate of scrambled eggs and listening to his radio through his earphones. A tinny roar leaked out around his ears. Pedro, the short order cook, lounged behind the counter, his big round body encased in layers of soiled white clothing, enthralled by a guitar magazine which he had spread out by the cash register. The kitchen slumbered behind him, exuding a thick fug of onions and burnt frying oil. It would stay mostly dormant until the middle of the week, when the shifts would change on the rigs, and tides of men would ebb and flow through the small town.

So when she brought the coffee back to the man, she thought nothing of it when he asked her to join him. She fetched herself a cup of coffee as well and then sat across from him in the booth, grateful to transfer the weight from her feet.

"You ain't got no nametag," he said.

"Oh . . . I guess I lost it somewhere. My name's Toni."

"That's real pretty."

She gave a quick derisive laugh. "The hell it is. It's short for Antoinette."

He held out his hand and said, "I'm Alex."

She took it and they shook. "You work offshore, Alex?"

"Some. I ain't been out there for a while, though." He smiled and gazed into the murk of his coffee. "I've been doing a lot of driving around."

Toni shook loose a cigarette from her pack and lit it. She lied and said, "Sounds exciting."

"I don't guess it is, though. But I bet this place could be, sometimes. I bet you see all kinds of people come through here."

"Well . . . I guess so."

"How long you been here?"

"About three years."

"You like it?"

A flare of anger. "Yeah, Alex, I fucking love it. Who wouldn't?"

"Oh, hey, all right." He held up his hands. "I'm sorry."

She shook her head. "No. I'm sorry. I just got a lot on my mind today I guess. This place is fine."

He cocked a half smile. "So why don't you come out with me after work? Maybe I can help distract you." His thick hands were on the table between them. They looked like they could break rocks.

Toni smiled at him. "You known me for what. Five minutes?"

"What can I say. I'm an impulsive guy. Caution to the wind!" He drained his cup in two swallows, as though to illustrate his recklessness.

"Well, let me go get you some more coffee, Danger Man." She patted his hand as she rose.

It was reckless impulse that brought Donny back to her, briefly, just over a year ago. After a series of phone calls that progressed from petulant to playful to newly curious, he drove back down to Port Fourchon in his disintegrating blue Pinto one Friday afternoon to spend a weekend with them. It was nice at first, though there was no talk of what might happen after Sunday.

Gwen had just started going to daycare. Stunned by the vertiginous growth of the world, she was beset by huge emotions; varieties of rage passed through her little body like weather systems, and no amount of coddling from Toni would settle her.

Although he wouldn't admit it, Toni knew Donny was curious about the baby, that his vanity was satisfied by the knowledge that she would grow to reflect many of his own features and behaviors.

But Gwen refused to participate in generating any kind of mystique that might keep him landed here, revealing herself instead as what Toni knew her to be: a pink, pudgy little assemblage of flesh and ferocity that giggled or raved seemingly without discrimination, that walked without grace and appeared to lack any qualities of beauty or intelligence whatsoever.

But the sex with Donny was as good as it had ever been, and he didn't seem to mind the baby too much. When he talked about calling in sick to work on Monday, she began to hope for something lasting.

Early Sunday afternoon, they decided to put Gwen to bed early and free up the evening for themselves. First she had to have a bath, and Donny assumed that responsibility with the air of a man handling nitroglycerin. He filled the tub with eight inches of water and plunked her in, then sat back and stared as, with furrowed brow, she went about the serious business of dropping the shampoo bottles into the water with her. Toni sat on the toilet seat behind him, and it occurred to her that this was her family. She felt buoyant, sated.

Then Gwen rose abruptly from the water and clapped her hands joyously. "Two! Two poops! One, two!"

Aghast, Toni saw two little turds sitting on the bottom of the tub, rolling slightly in the currents generated by Gwen's capering feet. Donny's hand shot out and cuffed his daughter on the side of her head. She fell against the wall and bounced into the water with a terrific splash. And then she screamed: the most godawful sound Toni had ever heard in her life.

Toni stared at him, agape. She could not summon the will to move. The baby, sitting on her butt in the soiled water, filled the tiny bathroom with a sound like a bomb siren, and she just wanted her to shut up, shut up, just shut the fuck up.

"Shut up, goddamnit! Shut up!"

Donny looked at her, his face an unreadable mess of confused emotion; he got to his feet and pushed roughly past her. Soon she heard the sound of a door closing. His car started up, and he was gone. She stared at her stricken daughter and tried to quiet the sudden stampeding fury.

She refilled Alex's coffee and sat down with him, leaving the pot on the table. She retrieved her cigarette from the ashtray only to discover that it has expired in her absence. "Well, shit," she said.

Alex nodded agreeably. "I'm on the run," he said.

"What?"

"It's true. I'm on the run. I stole a car."

Alarmed, Toni looked out the window, but the parking lot was on the other side of the diner. All she could see from here was the Gulf.

"Why are you telling me this? I don't want to know this."

"It's a station wagon. I can't believe it even runs anymore. I was in Morgan City, and I had to get out fast. The car was right there. I took it."

He had a manic look in his eye, and although he was smiling, his movements seemed agitated; his fingers tapped the table, the cords in his hands standing out like pipe. She felt a growing disquiet coupled with a mounting excitement. He was dangerous, this man. He was a falling hammer.

"I don't think that guy over there likes me," he said.

"What?" She turned and saw Crazy Claude in stasis, staring at Alex. His jaw was cantilevered in mid-chew. "That's just Claude," she said. "He's all right."

Alex was still smiling, but it had taken on a different character, one she couldn't place and which set loose a strange, giddy feeling inside her. "No, I think it's me. He keeps looking over here."

"Really, Claude's okay. He's harmless as a kitten."

"I want to show you something." Alex reached inside his raincoat, and for a moment Toni thought he was going to pull out a gun and start shooting. She felt no inclination to move, though; she waited for what would come. Instead, he withdrew a crumpled Panama hat. It had been considerably crushed to fit into his pocket, and once freed it began to unfold itself, like something blooming.

She looked at it. "It's a hat," she said.

He stared at it like he expected it to lurch across the table with some hideous agenda. "That's an object of terrible power," he said.

"Alex—it's a hat. It's a thing you put on your head."

"It belongs to the man I stole the car from. Here," he said, pushing it across to her. "Put it on."

She did. She was growing tired of the serious turn he seemed to have taken and decided to be a little playful. She turned her chin to her shoulder and pouted her lips, looking at him out of the corner of her eye, like she thought a model might.

He smiled. "Who are you?"

"I'm a supermodel."

"What's your name? Where are you from?"

She affected a light, breathy voice. "My name is Violet, I'm from L.A., and I'm strutting down a catwalk wearing this hat and nothing else. Everybody loves me and is taking my picture."

They laughed, and he was leaning over the table at her. She could see the tip of his tongue between his teeth. He just watched her for a second. "See? It's powerful. You can be anybody."

She gave the hat back.

"You know," Alex said, "the guy I stole the car from was something of a thief himself, it turns out. You should see what he left in there."

"Why don't you show me?"

He smiled again, and glanced at the nearly empty diner. "Now?"

"No. In half an hour. When I get off work."

"But it's all packed up. I don't let that stuff just fly around loose."

"Then you can show me at my place."

And so it was decided. She got up and went about preparing for the next shift, which consisted of restocking a few ketchup packets and starting a fresh pot of coffee. She refilled Crazy Claude's cup and gave him another ten packets of sugar, all of which he methodically opened and dumped into his drink. When her relief arrived, Toni hung her apron by the waitress station and collected Alex on her way to the door.

"We have to stop by the daycare and pick up my kid," she said.

If this news fazed him, he didn't show it.

As they passed Claude's table they heard a distant, raucous sound coming from his earphones.

Alex curled his lip. "Idiot. How does he hear himself think?"

"He doesn't. That's the point. He hears voices in his head. He plays the radio loud so he can drown them out."

"You're kidding me."

"Nope."

Alex stopped and turned around, regarding the back of Claude's head with renewed interest. "How many people does he have in there?"

"I never asked."

"Well, holy shit."

Outside, the sun was setting, the day beginning to cool down. The rain had stopped at some point, and the world glowed with a bright, wet sheen. They decided that he would follow her in his car. It was a rusty old battle wagon from the Seventies; several boxes were piled in the back. She paid them no attention.

She knew, when they stepped into her little apartment, that they would wind up making love, and she found herself wondering what it would be like. She watched him move, noted the graceful articulation of his body, the careful restraint he displayed in her living room, which was filled with fragile things. She saw the skin beneath his clothing, watched it stretch and move.

"Don't worry," she said, touching the place between his shoulder blades. "You won't break nothing."

About Gwen there was more doubt. Unleashed like a darting fish into the apartment, she was gone with a bright squeal, away from the strange new man around whom she had been so quiet and doleful, into the dark grottoes of her home.

"It's real pretty," Alex said.

"A bunch a knickknacks mostly. Nothing special."

He shook his head like he did not believe it. Her apartment was decorated mostly with the inherited flotsam of her grandmother's life: bland wall hangings, beaten old furniture which had hosted too many bodies spreading gracelessly into old age, and a vast and silly collection of glass figurines: leaping dolphins and sleeping dragons and such. It was all meant to be homey and reassuring, but it just reminded her of how far away she was from the life she really wanted. It seemed like a desperate construct, and she hated it very much.

For now, Alex made no mention of the objects in his car or the hat in his pocket. He appeared to be more interested in Gwen, who was peering around the corner of the living room and regarding him with a suspicious and hungry eye, who seemed to intuit that from this large alien figure on her mama's couch would come mighty upheavals.

He was a man—that much Gwen knew immediately—and therefore a dangerous

creature. He would make her mama behave unnaturally; maybe even cry. He was too big, like the giant in her storybook. She wondered if he ate children. Or mamas.

Mama was sitting next to him.

"Come here, Mama." She slapped her thigh like Mama did when she wanted Gwen to pay attention to her. Maybe she could lure Mama away from the giant, and they could wait in the closet until he got bored and went away. "Come here, Mama, come here."

"Go on and play now, Gwen."

"No! Come here!"

"She don't do too well around men," said Mama.

"That's okay," said the giant. "These days I don't either." He patted the cushion next to him. "Come over here, baby. Let me say hi."

Gwen, alarmed at this turn of events, retreated a step behind a corner. They were in the living room, which had her bed in it, and her toys. Behind her, Mama's darkened room yawned like a throat. She sat between the two places, wrapped her arms around her knees, and waited.

"She's so afraid," Alex said after she retreated from view. "You know why?"

"Um, because you're big and scary?"

"Because she already knows about possibilities. Long as you know there are options in life, you get scared of choosing the wrong one."

Toni leaned away from him and gave him a mistrustful smile. "Okay, Einstein. Easy with the philosophy."

"No, really. She's like a thousand different people right now, all waiting to be, and every time she makes a choice, one of those peoples goes away forever. Until finally you run out of choices and you are whoever you are. She's afraid of what she'll lose by coming out to see me. Of who she'll never get to be."

Toni thought of her daughter and saw nothing but a series of shut doors. "Are you
drunk?"

"What? You know I ain't drunk."

"Stop talking like you are, then. I've had enough of that shit to last me my whole life."

"Jesus, I'm sorry."

"Forget it." Toni got up and rounded the corner to scoop up her daughter. "I got to bathe her and put her to bed. If you want to wait, it's up to you."

She carried Gwen into the bathroom and began the nightly ministrations. She felt Donny's presence too strongly tonight, and Alex's sophomoric philosophizing sounded just like him when he'd had too many beers. She found herself hoping that the prosaic obligations of motherhood would bore Alex, and that he would leave. She listened for the sound of the front door.

Instead, she heard footsteps behind her and felt his heavy hand on her shoulder. It squeezed her gently, and his big body settled down beside her. He said something kind to Gwen and brushed a strand of wet hair from her eyes. Toni felt something move slowly in her chest, subtly yet with powerful effect, like Atlas rolling a shoulder.

Gwen suddenly shrieked and collapsed into the water, sending a surge of water over them both. Alex reached in to stop her from knocking her head against the porcelain and received a kick in the mouth for his troubles. Toni shouldered him aside and jerked her out of the tub. She hugged her daughter tightly to her chest and whispered motherly incantations into her ear. After a brief struggle, Gwen finally settled into her mother's embrace and whimpered quietly, turning her whole focus onto the warm, familiar hand rubbing her back, up and down, up and down, until, finally, her energy flagged, and she drifted into a tentative sleep.

When Gwen was dressed and in her bed, Toni turned her attention to Alex. "Here, let's clean you up."

She steered him back into the bathroom. She opened the shower curtain and pointed to the soap and the shampoo and said, "It smells kind of flowery, but it gets the job done," and the whole time he was looking at her, and she thought: So this is it; this is how it happens.

"Help me," he said, lifting his arms over his head. She smiled wanly and began to undress him. She watched his body as she unwrapped it, and when he was naked she pressed herself against him and ran her fingers down his back.

Later, when they were in bed together, she said, "I'm sorry about tonight."

"She's just a kid."

"No, I mean about snapping at you. I don't know why I did."

"It's okay."

"I just don't like to think about what could have been. There's no point to it. Sometimes I think a person doesn't have much to say about what happens to them anyway."

"I really don't know."

She stared out the little window across from the bed and watched slate gray clouds skim across the sky. Behind them were the stars.

"Ain't you gonna tell me why you stole a car?"

"I had to."

"But why?"

He was silent for a little while. "It don't matter," he said.

"If you don't tell me, it makes me think you mighta killed somebody."

"Maybe I did."

She thought about that for a minute. It was too dark to see anything in the bedroom, but she scanned her eyes across it anyway, knowing the location of every piece of furniture, every worn tube of lipstick and leaning stack of lifestyle magazines. She could see through the walls and feel the sagging weight of the figurines on the shelves. She tried to envision each one in turn, as though searching for one that would act as a talisman against this subject and the weird celebration it raised in her.

"Did you hate him?"

"I don't hate anybody," he said. "I wish I did. I wish I had it in me."

"Come on, Alex. You're in my house. You got to tell me something."

After a long moment, he said, "The guy I stole the car from. I call him Mr. Gray. I never saw him, except in dreams. I don't know anything about him, really. But I don't think he's human. And I know he's after me."

"What do you mean?"

"I have to show you." Without another word, he got to his feet and pulled on his jeans. She could sense a mounting excitement in his demeanor, and it inspired a similar feeling in herself. She followed him out of her bedroom, pulling a long t-shirt over her head as she went. Gwen slept deeply in the living room; they stepped over her mattress on the way out.

The grass was wet under their bare feet, the air heavy with the salty smell of the sea. Alex's car was parked at the curb, hugging the ground like a great beetle. He opened the rear hatch and pulled the closest box toward them.

"Look," he said, and opened the box.

At first, Toni could not comprehend what she was seeing. She thought it was a cat lying on a stack of tan leather jackets, but that wasn't right, and only when Alex grabbed a handful of the cat and pulled it out did she realize that it was human hair. Alex lifted the whole object out of the box, and she found herself staring at the tanned and cured hide of a human being, dark empty holes in its face like some rubber Halloween mask.

"I call this one Willie, 'cause he's so well hung," said Alex, and offered an absurd laugh.

Toni fell back a step.

"But there's women in here too, all kinds of people. I counted ninety-six. All carefully folded." He offered the skin to Toni, but when she made no move to touch it he started to fold it up again. "I guess there ain't no reason to see them all. You get the idea."

"Alex, I want to go back inside."

"Okay, just hang on a second."

She waited while he closed the lid of the box and slid it back into place. With the hide tucked under one arm, he shut the hatch, locked it, and turned to face her. He was grinning, bouncing on the balls of his feet. "Okeydokey," he said, and they headed back indoors.

They returned quietly to the bedroom, stepping softly to avoid waking Gwen.

"Did you kill all those people?" Toni asked when the door was closed.

"What? Didn't you hear me? I stole a car. That's what was in it."

"Mr. Gray's car."

"That's right."

"Who is he? What are they for?" she asked; but she already knew what they were for.

"They're alternatives," he said. "They're so you can be somebody else."

She thought about that. "Have you worn any of them?"

"One. I haven't got up the balls to do it again yet." He reached into the front pocket of his jeans and withdrew a leather sheath. From it he pulled a small, ugly little knife that looked like an eagle's talon. "You got to take off the one you're wearing, first. It hurts."

Toni swallowed. The sound was thunderous in her ears. "Where's your first skin? The one you was born with?"

Alex shrugged. "I threw that one out. I ain't like Mr. Gray, I don't know how to preserve them. Besides, what do I want to keep it for? I must not have liked to too much in the first place, right?"

She felt a tear accumulate in the corner of her eye and willed it not to fall. She was afraid and exhilarated. "Are you going to take mine?"

Alex looked startled, then seemed to remember he was holding the knife. He put it back in its sheath. "I told you, baby, I'm not the one who killed those people. I don't need any more than what's already there." She nodded, and the tear streaked down her face. He touched it away with the back of his fingers. "Hey now," he said.

She grabbed his hand. "Where's mine?" She gestured at the skin folded beside him. "I want one, too. I want to come with you."

"Oh, Jesus, no, Toni. You can't."

"But why not? Why can't I go?"

"Come on now, you got a family here."

"It's just me and her. That ain't no family."

"You have a little girl, Toni. What's wrong with you? That's your life now." He stepped out of his pants and, naked, pulled the knife from its sheath. "I can't argue about this. I'm going now. I'm gonna change first, though, so you might not want to watch." She made no move to leave. He paused, considering something. "I got to ask you something," he said. "I been wondering about this lately. Do you think it's possible for something beautiful to come out of an awful thing? Do you think a good life can redeem a horrible act?"

"Of course I do," she said quickly, sensing some second chance here, if only she said the right words. "Yes."

Alex touched the blade to his scalp just above his right ear and drew it in an arc over the crown of his head until it reached his left ear. Bright red blood crept down from his hairline in a slow tide, sending rivulets and tributaries along his jaw and his throat, hanging from his eyelashes like raindrops from flower petals. "God, I really hope so," he said. He worked his fingers into the incision and began to tug violently.

Watching the skin fall away from him, she was reminded of nothing so much as a butterfly struggling into daylight.

She is driving west on I-10. The morning sun, which has just breached the horizon, flares in her rearview mirror. Port Fourchon is far behind her, and the Texas border looms. Beside her, Gwen is sitting on the floor of the passenger seat, playing with the Panama hat Alex left behind when he drove North. Toni has never seen the need for a car seat. Gwen is happier moving about on her own, and in times like this, when Toni feels a slow, crawling anger in her blood, the last thing she needs is a temper tantrum from her daughter.

After he left, she was faced with a few options. She could put on her stupid pink uniform, take Gwen to daycare, and go back to work. She could drive up to New Orleans and find Donny. Or she could say fuck it all and just get in the car and drive, aimlessly and free of expectation, which is what she is doing.

She cries for the first dozen miles or so, and it is such a luxury that she just lets it come, feeling no guilt.

Gwen, still feeling the dregs of sleep and as yet undecided whether to be cranky for being awakened early or excited by the trip, pats her on the leg. "You okay, Mama, you okay?"

"Yes, baby. Mama's okay."

Toni sees the sign she has been looking for coming up on the side of the road. Rest Stop, 2 miles.

When they get there, she pulls in, coming to a stop in an empty lot. Gwen climbs up in the seat and peers out the window. She sees the warm red glow of a Coke machine and decides that she will be happy today, that waking up early means excitement and the possibility of treats.

"Have the Coke, Mama? Have it, have the Coke?"

"Okay, sweetie."

They get out and walk up to the Coke machine. Gwen laughs happily and slaps it several times, listening to the distant dull echo inside. Toni puts in some coins and grabs the tumbling can. She cracks it open and gives it to her daughter, who takes it delightedly.

"Coke!"

"That's right." Toni kneels beside her as Gwen takes several ambitious swigs. "Gwen? Honey? Mama's got to go potty, okay? You stay right here, okay? Mama will be right back."

Gwen lowers the can, a little overwhelmed by the cold blast of carbonation, and nods her head. "Right back!"

"That's right, baby."

Toni starts away. Gwen watches her mama as she heads back to the car and climbs in. She shuts the door and starts the engine. Gwen takes another drink of Coke. The car pulls away from the curb, and she feels a bright stab of fear. But Mama said she was coming right back, so she will wait right here.

Toni turns the wheel and speeds back out onto the highway. There is no traffic in sight. The sign welcoming her to Texas flashes by and is gone. She presses the accelerator. Her heart is beating.

DREAM OF THE FISHERMAN'S WIFE

A.C. WISE

The fisherman's wife breathes out, and tendrils of smoke curl around her. She listens to the tide inside and out—salt sea and salt blood, eroding shores of sand and making a hollow space within her skin and bones. She listens, and the ebb and flow tells her what she does not want to hear.

She needs no doctor to know: When the moon swells to full, she will bleed again.

A sigh laced with more smoke. This time, for just an instant, the tendrils thicken, become solid. One brushes her cheek, chasing salt slipped from within to without, aching to join to sea. The fisherman's wife starts, but doesn't move, holding her body quivering-taut.

The touch does not withdraw. Cautious, she pulls on the pipe again, adding more smoke, more weight. The first tendril, more a tentacle now, is joined by a second and a third. One slips past parted lips; one traces the edge of her parted robe and curls around the swell of a breast that isn't as full as she wishes.

Dive. She feels the word against her flesh, then the smoke is gone. She shudders, hairs rising, skin puckering tight.

It was a dream. Was it?

She draws her robe close, tucks her legs up, and waits for her husband to come home.

Below the pier where their hut crouches—all one room and no place to hide—waves surge, bringing the scent of green weeds wrapped around wooden piles. The fisherman's wife raises her head from the drawn-up pillow of her knees. Through sleep-puffed eyes, she squints at the edge of the lowered shades. Still daylight. She didn't mean to doze. Outside, seabirds call, squabbling over fish guts baked dry by the sun.

She rises as her husband steps through the door. The fish-stink on him is laced with sweat. It is his scent, her scent, the scent of their life together, and for a moment it breaks her. Her eyes sting, but no more salt falls.

The boards creak, the light changes as her husband shifts, uncertain, as though afraid of and for her until she folds into him. Her hands go to the nape of his neck, the small of his back. His fingers meet and lace together between her shoulder blades, pulling her close. There is black blood under her nails and his fingers are calloused from tying knots, casting nets, hauling lines. They are the hands of a fisherman and a fisherman's wife. They fit together, two halves of a whole.

"No." She murmurs the word against his throat, breathing in the salt-sweat of him, answering his unspoken question. It is the same answer she gave last month, and the month before. He softens a moment, before tightening his grip, fingers stroking her spine to soothe.

She shivers, reminded of . . . what? Should she tell him of the dream that wasn't a dream, the word spoken into her jaw by a smoke-tentacle, caressing her tongue?

The fisherman draws back, concern in his eyes. "Wife? What is wrong?"

She shakes her head. "Only a chill wind from the sea."

The fisherman's wife rises. Is she sleeping still? If she glances back to the pool of moonlight holding her husband in their tangled sheets will she see herself lying beside him, chest moving steady with the in-out tide of breath? She steps outside, barefoot; from the pier to the sand, to the edge of the shore where the water traces a silver line against her toes.

She sheds her robe. The memory of poppy-smoke lies heavy on her tongue, slicks her throat, slows her blood. Could it be a vision? Must it be a dream? Salt-tinged breeze stirs her black hair, all loosed down her back. Cold slaps her skin as she steps into the waves. Deeper. Her hair spreads like an octopus' legs, spilled ink on the sea.

Dive.

Underwater, she opens her eyes. It is bright as the noon day sun. There is so much life, color everywhere. Above-wave, the world is grey and increasingly dull, whether with poppy-sheen or age, the fisherman's wife cannot say. She knows only that with each year that passes there is more emptiness. It is not just want of a child. She feels the changing of the world within her bones. It is drying up, falling silent. But underwater, armies march. Children play. A blind man sculpts coral into delicate figures with too many eyes. Women with shark skin and shark teeth tend kelp gardens. Buildings crumble and rise again. The world, drowned, is reborn.

A shape darts at the corner of her eye—smoke made solid. She reaches after it as it slips past. A tentacle coils around her wrist, strokes her palm.

This is and was and can be again. All you have to do is choose.

The fisherman's wife blinks, disoriented. The current has tugged her, turned her; the many-limbed creature is gone.

The blind old man takes her hand. "Mother," he says and kisses her cheek. Even below the waves, his lips are paper dry.

A little girl leaves the army march to press a bouquet of sea anemones into her hand. "Mother," she says, before swimming away.

Silver bright fish form an aura around her. Their mouths open and close. "Mother," they say.

Eels and sharks and starfish and whales join the chorus, repeating the word. It booms like thunder, a low, reverberating note rolling out from the epicenter of her being, stirring a tidal wave to wash away the land.

"I don't understand," she tries to say, but salt-water floods her mouth.

She kicks, chokes, her head breaks the waves, coughing up icy water and strands of seaweed that slick her skin until she claws them away. She thinks she sees her husband on the pier, waving. But when she wipes salt-heavy hair from her eyes, he is gone.

A tendril traces the arch of her foot, strokes her calf, beckoning.

"No." The fisherman's wife kicks free. "Not yet. It is too soon."

She wakes, or she swims, long, powerful strokes carrying her back to the shore, back to her husband's arms.

The fisherman's boat rocks gentle as a lullaby. He would catch more with the other fishers, working together instead of alone. There is a woman who sings her catch into the boat without ever casting a line. There is a man who knots the full moon into his nets and lowers it to lure a large, flat fish like a flounder, but bigger than anyone has ever seen. It is the same fish every time, the man says, and the whole village gathers to make a fire on the beach, bright enough to light the darkened sky. They roast the fish on long wooden poles, then burn their fingers pulling flesh from bone as fast as they can. As the fish cools, the bones poison the flesh. If they don't eat the fish fast enough it will kill them.

The fisherman has no patience for the company of others today. Last night, he thinks he woke in bed alone. He also thinks he woke with his heart thumping like the tide, his wife lying beside him, insubstantial limbs the hollow color of moonlight; his fingers would pass through if he tried to touch her. Both things are true. When he looked through the window, he saw his wife's head break the waves, hair like ink against her sea-chilled flesh, swimming toward the shore. When he turned, she breathed beside him, troubled in her dreams.

He has been restless ever since. Afraid. So, in his smallest boat, painted white like a pearl, he drifts alone. A jar balanced in the boat's prow brews salt-water tea with the heat of the sun. It tastes of squid ink and tears, but he has heard it is used for prophecy, and so he drains the last drop. It sears a word on his tongue.

Dive.

The word slams into him, sudden certainty. He must follow his wife down; he must find her under the waves. They must find each other. As the sun passes the apex of the sky, the fisherman strips and describes a perfect arc into the blue.

The water slices him open, steals his breath. Cutting knife-clean through the dark, he swims down and down. As a boy, he dove with his brothers for silver coins falling from rich men's fingers. He could always go the longest without coming up for air. The fisherman's chest is narrow, but his lungs are strong.

A tendril brushes his leg, an octopus' arm or only a weed. An electric thrill, which is also panic. He kicks away, streaming bubbles like pearls. The shadow slips past him, ahead of him, ink darting in a jet of bubbles all its own. It pauses, turns as if knowing the fisherman watches. Its limbs bloom like ribbons of hair. The fisherman stops, suspended, rocked by the current. In the center of that tangle of limbs he catches a glimpse of his wife's face, moon pale. Then the creature is gone.

Panic of a different kind—pulse beating a new rhythm of hope and desire, the fisherman gives chase. He dives deeper, fighting the aching cold in his legs, the pressure of breath in his lungs. He follows a smoke swirl here, an unfurling of ink there.

His chilled fingers grope. Fish nibble his callused skin. He is almost there, even though he doesn't know what he's reaching for. A moment longer and he will allow himself to breathe.

There. The tip of one finger brushes a smooth curve, a perfect round. But sharp, the razor edge of a shell meets his skin, draws blood. He kicks, instinct shooting him to the surface. *No!* he thinks. *I was almost there. It's too soon.*

His head breaks waves and he draws ragged, stinging air into wounded lungs. He shakes water-wet hair from his eyes. His little boat bobs beside him, patient and waiting. Stars prick the sky like a million eyes. Impossibly, the sun has set and the moon risen while the fisherman sought beneath the waves.

The hut is dark, but neither the fisherman's wife nor the fisherman sleep. The walls smell of smoke and fish and salt. They hold a space of emptiness between them, an absence sharp-edged. Then, between one heartbeat and the next, they both decide. The wife reaches out, fingers seeking like a starfish across the vast gulf of the bed. Her husband's hand is waiting.

"Wife," he says. "I have dreamed."

"Husband," she answers, "I, too, have dreamed."

Lips almost touching so the fearful words will not escape them, the fisherman and the fisherman's wife whisper of what they have seen.

"Limbs like ink."

"Smoke."

"A song."

"A pearl."

"It is a prophecy, not a dream," the fisherman's wife says.

"What do we do?" the fisherman asks.

Fear curls and uncurls; a tide within and without.

"I don't know," the fisherman's wife says. "Not yet. But I will soon."

Sun draws sweat from the back of her neck as the fisherman's wife bends to her work. Her legs cramp. Her hands are slick with blood, her little knife quick as she guts fish to hang on racks above the fire. The air around her stinks of offal. Below, the tide rushes in; she peers through the slats and she sees it, dizzying, fraught with secret glints of light.

Ropes of intestines fall through her hands, glittering green and black, slithering back into the sea. The scales and blood that catch on the wood and wink in the sun make a pattern, spelling the future. She half-closes her eyes, scrying, dreaming.

Her hands continue their steady rhythm of work. At the same time, she stands on the edge of what used to be a shore. The world is hollowed, the oceans and seas gone, all the secret places dried out and laid bare. The bones of vast creatures litter new-formed canyons. Wind stirs her hair, laden with the memory of salt. The sun, red-gold and low, peeks between withered pillars of stone, drags her shadow away from her heels, and tatters it across the sand.

There are cities in the skeletons of the drowned-in-air creatures—arching Temples of Whale, intricate Labyrinths of Squid, strong Fortresses of Turtle, and perfect, recursive Gardens of Nautilus and Conch. This is the world that might be.

There are buildings she recognizes, too—the Temple, the Market Square, her neighbors' homes—all empty. This is the world that was.

Two futures fork away from her. It is for her and her husband to choose. Embracing one world forsakes another. The land or the sea. If one rises, the other must fall.

What is there for them here? The hope of a child that never comes? Poppy smoke and a village growing emptier every day. One day, the woman will not sing her catch from the sea; one day, the man will not net the moon so they can burn their fingers on flesh hot from the fire. Then it will be only her—the fisherman's wife—and her husband. The world is moving on without them, drying up, blowing away like dust on the wind. But there is color and life below the sea, and if they will it, it will rise to meet them.

The fisherman's wife glances down. A bundle lies cradled in her arms—delicate, moonlight-translucent bones, wrapped in a fine-woven net of silk; a fleshless, milk-tooth mouth held to her breast. With a shout, she opens arms. The bones tumble toward the sea floor and she shouts again, reaching too late to catch them.

She opens eyes never fully closed. Not yet, but soon, it will be time to choose.

The fisherman rises from the bed he shares with his wife. Is he dreaming? He dares not look back to see. Naked, he climbs the ladder at the end of the pier, down to his little boat, tied and bobbing on the waves. He rows, muscles bunching, following the path of moonlight laid across the sea.

The sky's pearl is full tonight, swollen. Its twin lies beneath the waves. Here.

The fisherman jumps, a needle threading the waves. He is blind, no sun tracing his descent. He gropes, hands outstretched, chasing the elusive thing that slipped from his grasp last time.

Shapes move around him, shadow-soft in the dark. A questing tentacle wraps around his leg, brushes belly, chest, and thigh. He shivers on the edge of ecstasy.

No, he thinks. *Not yet*. His wife must be with him. And he pulls away.

Stars burst behind the fisherman's eyes. How long has he been underwater? Surely by now he must have drowned.

There, again, a tentacle brushes his leg, not a question this time, but a directive: *Follow. Dive.*

Touch, soft, strokes his cheeks, his back. The fisherman nearly weeps, already surrounded by the salt sea. It is still too soon. He pictures his wife crouched on the pier, her back aching, her hands bloody. He can't leave without her.

The tentacles tap, lighter this time, relenting but still directing—*here, here*. The fisherman's breath is running out. His hands sweep, frantic, and *there, there*, his fingers close.

They snatch. They pry. The sharp-edged shell draws blood again, but this time he doesn't let go. Not until he has his prize.

Stars trail from his lips and blaze behind his eyes as he shoots upward. He breaks the surface as the sun climbs over the horizon, weeping, a pearl clutched in his hand.

"We could leave," the fisherman's wife says, but she doesn't mean it. "Leave rather than choose."

"The sea is our life," the fisherman says.

He is here, but he is swimming through the dark at the edge of a vast continental shelf. She is here, but she is standing on a shore, willing the water to return and restore flesh to a city of squid carcass and whale bone. If he goes further, everything will drop from beneath him. He'll be weightless, surrounded by water made of night, lit by drowned stars. If she opens her arms, she will no longer feel the dust-dry breeze and cradle wind-stripped bones. The world will call her mother, and she won't be afraid.

They are choosing. They have already chosen.

"There is life in the sea," the fisherman's wife says.

"Yes," the fisherman says. "But how . . ."

The fisherman's wife closes her eyes. The memory of a tendril of smoke grown solid, a tentacle of ink and flesh chases across her skin.

She opens her mouth, parts lips, breathes out a sound that is not quite a sigh.

"There is a song," she murmurs, and lays moon-cool fingers against the fisherman's skin. Thrum, from the point of contact—a note, shivering through both of them. The fisherman's teeth clench tight a moment, the reverberation in his jaw, then he lets go.

"A song."

The walls of the hut drop away, leaving them exposed to the wind and crashing waves.

Gentle, with net-abraded hands, the fisherman unties his wife's robes. Beside the bed stands a bucket of fresh water drawn from the rain barrel outside. He dips a cloth and passes it over her skin, washing the sweat of the day's work away.

Water beads, droplets catching the light. The fisherman's wife trembles with the strength of her desire. As her husband moves the cloth, she snatches a moment here to unlace his shirt, there to undo his trousers. His clothes are salt-stiff and smell of fish; they resist when she pushes them to the floor.

The fisherman removes the pins from his wife's hair. It spills around her, dark as limbs unfurling beneath the waves. She takes the washcloth and touches him as gently as he touched her. His chest and shoulders are beaten bronze from the sun, but from the waist-down he is fish-belly pale. She is the same. Only the nape of her neck is tan where the sun beats all day, and the tops of her feet where they peek from beneath her robes.

She drops the cloth into the bucket and watches it sink. It is a living thing, spreading limbs, darting away, then only cloth again.

The fisherman holds up the pearl, cupped in his palms—an unspoken question. By way of unspoken answer, the fisherman's wife plucks the pearl from his hands and places it against his mouth. He accepts it with a curl of his tongue, and holds it cradled there. His skin glows.

The fisherman's wife traces the light in her husband's veins. It pulses in his belly, his groin, and the hollow of his throat. She chases the light with her fingertips—an underwater sea creature, a pilot fish leading her to delight and doom.

The fisherman groans, a soft sound. She follows her fingers with her lips. Her tongue. The fisherman tastes of brine—rainwater-washed—of sunlight and wind. Her fingers catch in the fisherman's salt-stiff hair, the one place she did not wash. She pulls him close, urgent but not rough. Full of need.

Her lips press to his, drinking, crushing. His tongue passes the pearl into her mouth; its taste is nothing she can describe.

The fisherman's hands are on her back, her buttocks, holding her close.

They drift in untold seas.

Their cheeks are wet with not-unhappy tears. She wants to swallow the pearl, but she's afraid. She traps it between soft palate and tongue, pressing it against the roof of her mouth until it hurts. She is drowning on dry land.

The fisherman and the fisherman's wife tumble into their narrow bed. The wind gusts over them, snapping the linens like sails. Crashing waves shake the pier and the entire house trembles, a ship spun upon the sea.

The pearl passes back and forth between them. It is in her mouth. It rests in his navel. She catches it between her fingers. He steals it with his tongue. Through shared motion, they press it between her legs.

Close, she thinks, *so close*. But not there. Not yet.

"Dive." She sears the word against his lips with a kiss, and hears it echoed back to her from him.

She closes her eyes, opens her throat, and tries to replicate a song from her dreams.

They are here and they are now, but they are elsewhere and elsewhen, too. Smoke pours from the fisherman's wife's mouth and becomes a creature with many limbs. It unfurls down her body. She rises to meet it, mouth open, legs open.

It winds around her, singing of oceans rising to devour the world— birth of a different kind. Together they can call it, the water, the dark-limbed creature, to reclaim dry canyons, nautilus cities, temples of whale bone. A tendril, a tentacle, wraps round her tongue. Its motion teaches her a song.

She is already singing it. Has always been singing it. She will sing it until the end of time.

There is life in the ocean's pulse and swell. Her hands cradle her belly. She lets the music pull her down.

The fisherman clings to his wife. Beyond the horizon of her shoulder, it is midnight, or the sun is just now rising. The sun is sinking; it shines high overhead. Beneath them, wooden floorboards thrum with the surge of waves. Stars wheel overhead. He remembers the touch of ink-dark limbs guiding him through water only a shade lighter than themselves.

He chases them down.

"We have to go farther," the fisherman's wife says.

"Are you afraid?" the fisherman asks.

"Yes." She takes his hand. Their fingers fit together as they always have—two parts of a whole. But they are not complete yet.

"So am I," the fisherman says. "But not too afraid."

The fisherman and the fisherman's wife rise and walk together out onto the pier.

The waters will rise if they call them, but it is better than a slow-emptying village—the Market, the Temple, their neighbors' houses abandoned one by one. There is so much color beneath the waves, so much life, and it will call them mother and father if they choose. It is not the child they once wanted; it is greater—the destruction of a dying village and the birthing of a whole new world.

Together, they sing.

Salt water washes around them, but they do not drown. Called by the notes thrumming from their bodies, the creature rises to meet them. Ink dark, everything they have ever dreamed. It is as small as their hopes and big as the world—a tangle of limbs the color of midnight, blue-black and glimmering with light. It lays the fisherman and the fisherman's wife down on the wooden pier. Below them, the pulse of the waves matches the tide of their blood and their desire.

The fisherman's wife turns toward her husband, their fingers still entwined.

"Are you afraid?" she asks.

"Not anymore."

Legs part, hips rise. The creature knots between them, stroking hip, breast, thigh. It binds them. Swell of belly, swell of tide. Smoke made solid slips inside the fisherman's wife. Her husband joins it. She sings.

Touch traces the fisherman's spine, his legs. His body opens, responds. Ink fills him and he shudders in answer.

The fisherman kisses his wife's lips, and kisses her lips. He savors her pearl, and savors their pearl.

The many-limbed creature flows between them. It twines and re-twines, a creation myth in reverse, stirring sea from the land.

On the pier, with the waves crashing beneath them, their bodies move to the rhythm of salt and blood. Their children swim around them, waiting to be born. Children with human faces and skin and teeth like sharks. Their smiles glow like moonlight among a tangle of hair like a multitude of limbs.

Yes, the fisherman thinks, rising to meet them.

Yes, the fisherman's wife thinks, her body thrumming with song.

Together, they choose—a strange apocalypse of rising tide over the barren canyons of desolate buildings. They re-enflesh the drowned world of squid rot and whale bone, bringing back a new world, an old world, with a surge of the tide.

Together, the fisherman, the fisherman's wife, and the creature of ink and smoke, sing.

THEORIES OF PAIN

ROSE LEMBERG

If pains are representations, then what do they represent?" (Maund, "Tyne on Pain and Representational Content," *Pain*, 2006: 145)

There are two large apples inside his head. He's sure, yes—he can feel their waxed red skins rubbing against each other. Red delicious, the most commonly cultivated apple in the known universe. Janet insisted on buying those, even though he begged her no, you won't eat them— they're treacherous, they'll turn mushy on the way home, you'll take one biteful of elderly brown bruises and leave the rest inside the fridge to sit, and then in secret they will ooze yellowish fluid out their sagging butts. She said he was vulgar. Inside the fridge, the apples withered to blackness, their tops furry with mold; then collapsed.

But the seeds, the seeds, his fingers are full of them, black shiny pain-seeds with a tender whitish core. If you bite into them they are bitter, the kind of sweet shallow bitterness that chases away nausea. But he cannot bite hard enough, and all he can taste is skin, unwashed and smoky. Janet is late again.

She doesn't understand why it's oranges when she yells.

"My color experience represents colors, or color-like properties. According to me, there is no obvious candidate for an objectively assessable property that bears to pain experience the same relation that color bears to color experience." (Block, "Bodily Sensations," *Pain*, 2006: 138)

She likes the shape of fruit, the way it looks at the supermarket, washed and polished with the promise of real 100% flavor not from concentrate. Buying it is the real thing. Eating is not, she says. Waxy, lifeless doll-taste, not real like the advertisements. And so she leaves the fruit to rot, unless it's boiled into cookies.

"The sense of disruption to expectations, life plans, and the 'seductive predictability' of everyday life is a recurring theme in the life narratives of people who have experienced unexpected life events." (Hammell, *Perspectives on Disability*, 2006: 114)

She cannot find the flavor within the wax effigies of the fruit. He has it all, inside. She yelled at him last night. The pain in his ears was oranges bursting full of juice needles like summer into his head.

How did it begin, the doctor asked. He remembers the screeching of the car, and for the first time, hot tar pomegranates. Mashed into the earth like summer's betrayal. We don't notice summer deaths, the unclaimed crushed ripe bursting into granulated red. Just a little concussion, they said, lucky bastard. The car was totaled.

His pain is trite like the supermarket aisle. Headache apples, green soapy bananas in his stiff neck. Strawberries, full and slightly moldy and nibbled in little bitter seeds, for the abdomen. Every day she goes away to work, and every night she is late in the car, and there are never, ever grapes for anything.

"But first, let us ask a prior question: what in the domain of pain corresponds to the tomato, namely, the thing that is red?" (Block, "Bodily Sensations," *Pain*, 2006: 138)

There are no pomegranates at the supermarket. Perhaps they are seasonal, a once in a lifetime purchase on an interstate, red and rotten like a crushed underworld.

"Living with socially de-skilled people who have undergone major personality change can be a considerable burden, straining marriages and relationships." (Wood and McMillan, *Neurobehavioral Disability and Social Handicap Following Traumatic Brain Injury*, 2004: 83)

She came home drunk one night, smelling of someone's cheap cologne and cigarettes. She fell asleep on the edge of the bed, folded into herself, her back to him. He discovered blackberries, dark and full like the night, bursting on his tongue with the memory of that first date, when they had ridden out on their bikes, and bushes grew thick on the paths, and her polka-dot dress. Despair was blackberries and the forever sunshined cigarette smoke of someone else's body between them.

He went to the supermarket today, searched the aisles for something unexpected, but it was all the same, waxy and beautiful and harboring mold like a marriage.

ROSE LEMBERG

"The primary needs . . . a need to have hope" (Wood and McMillan, *Neurobehavioral Disability and Social Handicap*, 2004: 55)

They say that durian is the king of fruits. It is huge and thorn-covered, and its pulp is yellow like the sun. Durian is not found in supermarkets. Its taste, they say, is an obscene explosion of flavor, brandy and cream cheese and onion dip. The smell of durian is revolting like paradise. To taste it is to hate and love and to forget and never stop.

He presses the elevator button for the fifty-second floor.

TERRIBLE LIZARDS

MEGHAN MCCARRON

You are on a desert island. The sand, stirred by the hot wind, pricks your tender, waxed calves. A duffle of makeup sits at your feet; you wish it held water, or guns. The producers tell you to strike a pose. You perch your foot on your duffle, lengthen your neck. The producers are flanked by contractors armed with automatic weapons. Something big stomps through the forest. It roars.

On his first night of college, a shy boy sneaks up onto the dorm's roof with his hallmates. They sit in a circle, a false tribe that will quickly fracture. A hippie kid in bare feet lights a blunt and passes it to a girl wearing a lacy slip and a necklace of plastic pearls. The hippie picks out "Like a Rolling Stone." They smile like they're practicing to be famous. The shy boy is a southern kid in ill-fitting jeans. He actually will be famous. It starts when he dresses up as Lou Reed for Halloween.

On her first day at work, a girl sits in a cubicle looking up two hundred and forty-eight direct-to-video horror movies on IMDb. Her company acquired the rights to these movies, but they came with no information besides their titles, *Blood Bathz 6* and *Death Cruise*. She edits summaries by users like BigBob777 and LadieVampyre. Triplets separated at birth discover they are all werewolves. Passive-aggressive Satanists encourage suicides to jump off the Golden Gate Bridge. Vampires are actually aliens. They live at the center of the earth.

A vampire lives in the tunnels underneath the dorms. The tunnels once housed a small acid factory; the vampire stumbles across blotters, still, mixed in with the rest of the kipple. The school locked up the tunnels in the eighties. All the graffiti is archeology, Bokonon quotes and naked rainbow women and tags from a graffiti artist featured in *Style Wars*. The vampire hungers for company.

My nine A.M. Chinese class releases us into a bright Tuesday morning. A kid I've known for three weeks stops me on the green to say a plane flew into a building. I laugh out loud.

The office worker hides her spreadsheet and pulls up video of a new reality show. She watches a girl she knew in college arrive on a desert island. The model holds a triumphant pose, like a conquistador. Behind her, a T. Rex lumbers onscreen.

A girl takes off her clothes in the bedroom and returns to the party naked. Everyone is naked. The paint ran out because people splattered it on the walls, and now there's only markers. She never realized how strongly a room full of naked people would smell. Some girl scrawls her name across her back, like when people signed each others' shirts the last day of high school. *KIT!* A boy draws a pot leaf on her arm, ha ha. A stranger draws a picture of a wolf and bites her on the shoulder. He draws blood. Ha ha.

At fall break, every house on my cul-de-sac is flying an American flag, like it's the angry Fourth of July. Plastic wrap and duct tape sit in neat stacks on my mother's dining room table. My stepfather bought a BMW to do his part for the economy. I get drunk in the backyard on dusty liquor cabinet leavings, high school style. Before bed, I drink one of the hoarded bottles of water in the basement so I won't be hungover. Ha ha.

The office worker has finished editing the summaries, but she has to look busy. On Facebook, someone tagged pictures of the boy who dressed up as Lou Reed. He's on the cover of a magazine, licking maple syrup off a hunting knife. The office worker opens her screenplay. She's writing a high school comedy. High school seems far away and imaginary, but not like a movie. She clicks back to IMDb. There is a sequel to the vampires-at-the-center-of-the-earth movie. It is set on their spaceship, which looks like a castle. On the movie poster, they all look like Nosferatu, including the teeth.

The werewolf wakes up naked. She is alone at dawn in a graveyard dating back to 1650. Brownstone grave markers list towards her, their messages washed away by the rain. *Here lies . . . Anno Domini . . . Betsey . . . Lord.* A dead dog lies next to her. A black lab she's seen around campus. Her name was Derrida, ha ha. Derri for short. Derri's throat has been ripped out, and the werewolf's mouth is caked in blood.

I jump the police barricades to join the protestors swarming down Madison Avenue. The crowd is a spectacular sea. There are signs and hats and puppets and bugles and girls in suits, toting pies. This will be on the front page of *The New York Times.* The avenue will flood CNN. No way. No way will they start this war.

On the next episode, the models tie a goat to a stake *a la* Jurassic Park and finish hair and makeup in the trees. When the T. Rex emerges, one of the models rushes out to greet the dinosaur first. The scene ends abruptly. The group is reprimanded by the judging panel, but there seem to be fewer contestants than before. The office worker looks closer. The girl she knew from college is missing.

The next full moon, the werewolf unlocks the tunnels with a stolen key. The corridors are lined with doorless rooms filled with discarded children's desks, rusting campus-issue bedframes, piles of flammable trash. The werewolf picks a room occupied by a lone orange armchair and undresses in the last wash of sunlight. When the change starts, her nose twitches with a new smell. Nosferatu leaps out of the darkness, and her mouth fills with teeth.

We play a State of the Union drinking game with arak, because it rhymes. *Iraq!* We cry, throwing back shots. *Arak!* I wake up outside my room, number 303, in my underwear. The door is covered in runny, never-drying paint from when my roommate shot it up with paintballs. People are smoking hash down the hall, and the carpet smells like stale cupcakes. Someone has covered me with a little tent of cardboard, like my torso is homeless.

The office worker finds a YouTube video, a single shot of a goat tied to a stake. The quality is terrible, but she recognizes the goat. The T. Rex massive head shoots down into the frame and gobbles the goat whole. Then it shoots down again and snatches up the model. The office worker's college friend charges by with an elephant gun. Shots are fired. There is a flash of pumping legs, and the smoking barrel of the elephant gun, disappearing into the trees.

The werewolf wakes underground naked and bruised. The vampire is curled up next to her on a pile of blankets like a loyal dog. It has a bite on its leg. Does this make her a vampire now? But no, pale light leaks through the tiny window and she does not burn. Her body feels electric and exhausted, like she's just taken a vigorous swim. She thinks she has found a solution to the problem of being a monster.

The secret dance party is in a white mansion in a room covered with graffiti. A giant's chair, red and decaying, looms in the center. People dance, people thrash. A friend slaps his chest and roars. The crowd sings along, *lies lies*. It's toxic, it's high voltage, it's like a Polaroid picture. But we can't shake forever, pictures do emerge, and they're of naked bodies and hooded men, thumbs up.

When the office worker calls Model Reality's production company, they claim to be a biotech firm. They financed most of the movies she's looking up on IMDb. One movie's title suggested zombies, but it's actually about terrorists who hijack a rock star's party plane. The rock star drives them out of the cockpit with disco. The go-go dancers put their panties on the terrorists' heads. The drummer dunks them in the hot tub. They land somewhere in the California desert, laughing and screaming like old friends. Ha ha.

The next month, the vampire greets the werewolf with submissive, fangy smiles. She bares her teeth; she has been looking forward to this. He hovers around her as she undresses, and she wonders if they fuck. But when the fur springs from her skin, the vampire snatches the keys and throws the tunnel door open. She shouldn't follow, but the world has never smelled so good.

For my final in Dystopian Literature, I make an 8mm movie. I shave my actors' heads and cover them in fried eggs. I steal skinned deerheads from the taxidermist's dumpster. I paste headlines about nuclear war onto *The New York Times*. I feed everyone Dunkin' Donuts. But I loaded the film wrong, and the entire reel comes back blank, except for a shot of the paper, falsely declaring the end is nigh.

The office worker meets her fellow alums at a bar with deer antler chandeliers. A hurricane is about to hit New Orleans. Everyone watches the televisions as if their careful attention can avert disaster. The model walks in. There's something different about her eyes, or maybe the way she walks. The office worker rushes up to her and asks if she's okay. "I'm good," the model laughs, in a voice that's not quite right. Something metallic glints in her eye, but her skin is warm as they embrace. "So, what's your story?"

The werewolf wakes up naked, lying in a parking lot. Next to her, a human foot is dangling out of a car door. The foot is marble-white, lined with tufts of dark hair. Another foot lies on the ground, bloody and lonesome. The vampire is nowhere to be found. It's just her, on the other side of a big, fat, yellow line.

The boy who dressed as Lou Reed gives an interview to the alumni magazine. The interviewer asks why he doesn't make protest music. He points out that Bob Dylan and Dick Cheney were born in the same year. He'd be better off joining the Pentagon and playing the long game.

You are the only one left on the island. The production crew fled weeks ago after they were beset by animal attacks. You hate them, but sometimes you pretend they are still here, judging you, dangling a prize. Your ammo stayed dry, and you think you can pull the trigger with your claws. Tomorrow is the full moon. Something stomps in the forest. It roars.

The last week of school I spend in my room drinking whiskey and reading science fiction. The sun is too bright, and everyone's acting like there's nothing wrong. One afternoon, a boom in the distance announces that the first bombs have started to fall. Then I see lightning. Rain.

I call my mother and start to cry. She tells me when I was a baby she thought Reagan would kill us all. "I used to rock you and plan on how I'd keep you alive. It's okay, baby. Here you are."

ACKNOWLEDGEMENTS

This book has been a long time in the making. It's been coming together in bits and pieces since about 2011, actually. So not as long as some books, longer than others. But that incubation period has meant that a lot of things moved around, some things worked and others didn't, and a great deal of advice and aid was given by various parties.

Given that, it's only fair to start in reasonably chronological order, which means first thanking Mike Kelly, who provided a hell of a lot of the foundational aid on this project, and with whom I bounced back and forth a lot of story selection ideas early on. For which I'm deeply grateful since some of these discussions took place while Mike was getting his own *Year's Best Weird* anthology series up and running.

A similar thank you is owed to Leah Bobet for ongoing conversations, advice, and story selection once things got further underway. Advice given while Leah was also negotiating some fairly large projects.

(It's an ongoing reality of the publishing industry that everyone in it, content creator or content shepherds, has a lot of different balls in the air at any given time. Mostly in aid of just trying to have a life in addition to everything else.)

Following which, I owe a well-deserved thank you to Sandra Kasturi for several things. First, for taking on the book at ChiZine. Second, for coming up with the title. And third, for additional advice on writers to approach.

Some anthologies are put together in editorial isolation. This, thankfully, was not one of the latter. Oh, there was a fair amount of work done holed up alone working on this book, especially early on, but much of what happened here was done in consultation and collaboration with friends and colleagues.

That said, I'm going to forget some of the names I should be listing here, given that it's been four years spent on this project. Some of the conversations around it fleeting. Others drawn out over months, sometimes years. And still more just so ongoing that this book came up I don't know how many times in the course of other conversations, had longer still.

But additional thanks are owed to Paula Guran for prior conversations about more general anthology concerns that aided very much putting this one together. Rose Lemberg and Sonya Taaffe for additional story recommendations. All of the authors for their enthusiasm and patience. Dominik Parisien for proofreading the final manuscript. Natasha Bozorgi for her work on the layout. And Erik Mohr for his work on the cover.

And to anyone else I've forgotten, consider yourself thanked in absentia; it is not my intention to overlook anyone's aid. All of which has been much appreciated and *very* welcome.

ABOUT THE AUTHORS

Nathan Ballingrud is the author of *North American Lake Monsters: Stories*, from Small Beer Press; and *The Visible Filth*, a novella from This Is Horror. His work has appeared in numerous Year's Best anthologies, and he has twice won the Shirley Jackson Award. He lives with his daughter in Asheville, NC.

Laird Barron is the author of several books, including *The Croning*, *Occultation*, and *The Beautiful Thing That Awaits Us All*. His work has also appeared in many magazines and anthologies. An expatriate Alaskan, Barron currently resides in upstate New York.

Polenth Blake lives with cockroaches and likes photographing tiny things. Polenth's work has appeared in *Nature*, *Strange Horizons*, and *Unlikely Story*. More can be found at http://www.polenthblake.com.

Leah Bobet's first novel, *Above*, was nominated for the 2012 Andre Norton Award and the 2013 Aurora Award, and her short fiction has appeared in several Year's Best anthologies and as part of the online serial *Shadow Unit*. She lives in Toronto, Ontario, where she edits *Ideomancer Speculative Fiction*, picks urban apple trees, does civic engagement activism, and works as a bookseller at Bakka-Phoenix Books, Canada's oldest science fiction bookstore. Leah's second novel, *An Inheritance of Ashes*—a dustbowl-style epic fantasy with a touch of the weird—will appear from Clarion Books in the US and Scholastic in Canada in October 2015.

Indrapramit Das is a writer from Kolkata. His debut novel *The Devourers* (written as Indra Das) is out from Penguin Books India. His short fiction has appeared in various publications and anthologies including *Asimov's Science Fiction*, *Tor.com*, *Strange Horizons*, and *The Year's Best Science Fiction* (St. Martin's Griffin). He has an MFA in Creative Writing from the University of British Columbia, Vancouver, and is a grateful graduate of the 2012 Clarion West Writers' Workshop and a recipient of the Octavia E. Butler Scholarship Award.

Berit Ellingsen is the author of one short story collection, *Beneath the Liquid Skin* (firthFORTH Books 2012), and two novels, *Une Ville Vide* (PublieMonde 2013), and *Landscapes, Fragments* (Two Dollar Radio 2015). Berit's work has appeared in *W.W. Norton's Flash Fiction International Anthology*, the Litro Blog, *SmokeLong Quarterly*, *Unstuck*, and other places, and been nominated for the Pushcart Prize and the British Science Fiction Award. Find out more at http://beritellingsen.com.

Film critic and teacher turned award-winning horror author **Gemma Files** is best known for her Weird Western Hexslinger series (*A Book of Tongues*, *A Rope of Thorns*, and *A Tree of Bones*, all from ChiZine Publications). Her short fiction has been collected in two volumes (*Kissing Carrion* and *The Worm in Every Heart*), as well as a story cycle, *We Will All Go Down Together: Stories of the Five-Family Coven* (CZP), and her poetry has been collected in two chapbooks (*Bent Under Night* and *Dust Radio*). Her next novel, *Experimental Film*, will also be published by CZP. Why mess with success?

Neil Gaiman is the bestselling author of books for adults and children. The recipient of numerous awards, his works have been adapted for film, television, stage, and radio. Some of Neil's most notable titles include the novels *The Graveyard Book* (the first book to ever win both the Newbery and Carnegie medals), *American Gods*, and the UK's National Book Award 2013 Book of the Year, *The Ocean at the End of the Lane*. His enchantingly reimagined fairy tale, *The Sleeper and the Spindle* (illustrated by Chris Riddell) was published in September. Born in England, Neil now lives in the US with his wife, the musician and author, Amanda Palmer.

Maria Dahvana Headley is the author of the young adult fantasy novel *Magonia* (HarperCollins), the dark fantasy/alt-history novel *Queen of Kings* (Dutton), and the internationally bestselling memoir *The Year of Yes* (Hyperion). With Neil Gaiman, she is the New York Times-bestselling co-editor of the anthology *Unnatural Creatures* (HarperChildrens), benefitting 826DC. With Kat Howard, she is the author of the novella *The End of the Sentence* (Subterranean Press)—recently named one of NPR's Best Books of 2014. Her Nebula and Shirley Jackson Award-nominated short fiction has recently appeared in *Lightspeed*, *Uncanny*, *Nightmare*, *Tor.com*, *Apex*, *The Journal of Unlikely Entomology*, *Subterranean Online*, and many more, as well as in many Year's Bests.

She lives in Brooklyn in an apartment shared with a seven-foot-long stuffed crocodile, and a heap of French anatomical charts from the 1950s.

Kij Johnson is the author of several novels, including *The Fox Woman* and *Fudoki*; a short story collection, *At the Mouth of the River of Bees*; and about fifty short stories. She is a three-time winner of the Nebula Award, and has also won the Hugo, World Fantasy, Sturgeon, and Crawford Awards. She teaches at the University of Kansas, where she is associate director for the Center for the Study of Science Fiction.

Joe R. Lansdale is the author of over 40 novels and three hundred short works of fiction and non-fiction. He has received The Edgar Award and 9 Bram Stokers, including Lifetime Achievement. He has written for animation, film, and comics. His story *Bubba Ho-Tep* has been filmed, as has his novel *Cold In July*. His newest novel is *Paradise Sky*.

Yoon Ha Lee's work has appeared in *Tor.com*, *Clarkesworld*, *Lightspeed*, *Beneath Ceaseless Skies*, *The Magazine of Fantasy and Science Fiction*, and other venues. Their collection *Conservation of Shadows* came out from Prime Books in 2013. They live in Louisiana with family and have not yet been eaten by gators.

Rose Lemberg is a queer immigrant from Eastern Europe. Her work has appeared in *Apex*, *Strange Horizons*, *Beneath Ceaseless Skies*, *Interfictions*, and other venues. Rose edits *Stone Telling*, a magazine of boundary-crossing poetry, with Shweta Narayan. She has edited *Here, We Cross*, an anthology of queer and genderfluid speculative poetry from *Stone Telling* (Stone Bird Press), and *The Moment of Change*, an anthology of feminist speculative poetry (Aqueduct Press), and is currently editing a new fiction anthology, *An Alphabet of Embers*. You can find rose Rose at http://roselemberg.net and @roselemberg, and support her on Patreon at patreon.com/roselemberg.

Livia Llewellyn is a writer of horror, dark fantasy, and erotica, whose fiction has appeared in *ChiZine*, *Subterranean*, *Apex Magazine*, *Postscripts*, *Nightmare Magazine*, as well as numerous anthologies. Her first collection, *Engines of Desire: Tales of Love & Other Horrors*, was published in 2011 by Lethe Press, and received two Shirley Jackson Award nominations, for Best Collection, and Best Novelette (for "Omphalos"). Her story "Furnace" received a 2013 SJA nomination for Best Short Fiction. You can find her online at liviallewellyn.com.

Alex Dally MacFarlane is a writer, editor and historian. When not researching narrative maps in the legendary traditions of Alexander III of Macedon, she writes stories, found in *Clarkesworld*, *Interfictions Online*, *Strange Horizons*, *Beneath Ceaseless Skies*, and the anthologies *Phantasm Japan*, *Solaris Rising 3*, and *The Year's Best Science Fiction & Fantasy: 2014*. She is the editor of *Aliens: Recent Encounters* (2013) and *The Mammoth Book of SF Stories by Women* (2014). In 2015, she joined Sofia Samatar as co-editor of non-fiction and poetry for *Interfictions Online*. For *Tor.com*, she runs the Post-Binary Gender in SF column. Find her on Twitter: @foxvertebrae.

Michael Matheson is a genderfluid writer, editor, poet, book reviewer, and sometime anthologist. They're a graduate of the 2014 Clarion West Writers' Workshop, and their fiction and poetry has appeared in *Ideomancer*, *Stone Telling*, and a handful of anthologies. They live in Toronto. *The Humanity of Monsters* is their first anthology as editor. Find them online at http://michaelmatheson.wordpress.com, or on Twitter @sekisetsu.

Meghan McCarron's fiction and essays have recently appeared in *The Toast*, *The Collagist*, *Electric Literature*, and *Gigantic Worlds*. She has been a finalist for the Nebula and World Fantasy Awards.

Sunny Moraine's short fiction has appeared in *Clarkesworld*, *Strange Horizons*, *Lightspeed*, *Uncanny*, and *Long Hidden: Speculative Fiction from the Margins of History*, among other places. They are also responsible for the novels *Line and Orbit* (co-written with Lisa Soem) and the *Casting the Bones* trilogy, as well as *Labyrinthian*, and *A Brief History of the Future:*

collected essays. In addition to authoring, Sunny is a doctoral candidate in sociology and a sometimes college instructor; that last may or may not have been a good move on the part of their department. They unfortunately live just outside Washington DC in a creepy house with two cats and a very long-suffering husband.

Mexican by birth, Canadian by inclination, **Silvia Moreno-Garcia** is the author of *Signal to Noise*, a novel about music, magic, and Mexico City. Her first collection, *This Strange Way of Dying*, was a finalist for The Sunburst Award for Excellence in Canadian Literature of the Fantastic. Her stories have also been collected in *Love & Other Poisons*. She can be found at http://www.silviamoreno-garcia.com.

Chinelo Onwualu is a writer, editor, journalist, and dog person living in Abuja, Nigeria. She is a graduate of the 2014 Clarion West Writers' Workshop which she attended as the recipient of the Octavia E. Butler Scholarship. Her writing has appeared in several places, including the *Kalahari Review*, *Saraba Magazine*, *Sentinel Nigeria Magazine*, *Jungle Jim Magazine*, and the anthologies *AfroSF: African Science Fiction by African Writers* and *Mothership: Tales of Afrofuturism and Beyond*. She runs Sylvia Fairchild Editorial Services, a consultancy providing writing, research, and editing services to individuals and organisations. Follow her on Twitter @chineloonwualu.

Sofia Samatar is the author of the novel *A Stranger in Olondria*, the Hugo and Nebula nominated short story "Selkie Stories Are for Losers," and other works. She is the winner of the John W. Campbell Award, the Crawford Award, the British Fantasy Award, and the World Fantasy Award for Best Novel. She is a co-editor for *Interfictions: A Journal of Interstitial Arts*, and teaches literature and writing at California State University Channel Islands.

Rachel Swirsky holds an MFA from the Iowa Writers Workshop. Her short fiction has been nominated for the Hugo Award, the World Fantasy Award, and the Locus Award, and received the Nebula Award twice. She is not a dinosaur, but if she were, she'd want to be a feathered one.

Sonya Taaffe's short fiction and poetry can be found in the collections *Ghost Signs* (Aqueduct Press), *A Mayse-Bikhl* (Papaveria Press), *Postcards* *from the Province of Hyphens* (Prime Books), and *Singing Innocence and Experience* (Prime Books), and in anthologies including *Aliens: Recent Encounters*, *Beyond Binary: Genderqueer and Sexually Fluid Speculative Fiction*, *The Moment of Change: An Anthology of Feminist Speculative Poetry*, *People of the Book: A Decade of Jewish Science Fiction & Fantasy*, *The Year's Best Fantasy and Horror*, *The Alchemy of Stars: Rhysling Award Winners Showcase*, and *The Best of Not One of Us*. She is currently senior poetry editor at *Strange Horizons*; she holds master's degrees in Classics from Brandeis and Yale and once named a Kuiper belt object. She lives in Somerville with her husband and two cats.

Catherynne M. Valente is the New York Times bestselling author of over a dozen works of fiction and poetry, including *Palimpsest*, the *Orphan's Tales* series, *Deathless*, and the crowdfunded phenomenon *The Girl Who Circumnavigated Fairyland in a Ship of Her Own Making*. She is the winner of the Andre Norton, Tiptree, Mythopoeic, Rhysling, Lambda, Locus, and Hugo awards. She has been a finalist for the Nebula and World Fantasy Awards. She lives on an island off the coast of Maine with a small but growing menagerie of beasts, some of which are human.

Bram Stoker Nominee and Shirley Jackson Award winner **Kaaron Warren** has lived in Melbourne, Sydney, Canberra and Fiji. Kaaron has written about monsters in many of her short stories and novels, including serial killers (*Slights*), vampires who steal the will to survive ("All You Can Do is Breathe") and magicians (*Mistification*). Her most recent short story collections are *The Gate Theory*, from Cohesion Press, and *Cemetery Dance Select: Kaaron Warren* from the *Cemetery Dance* series of that name.

Peter Watts is a multi-award-winning SF author, marine biologist, flesh-eating-disease survivor and convicted felon whose novels— despite an unhealthy focus on Space Vampires—are required texts for undergraduate courses ranging from Philosophy to Neuropsychology. His work is available in 18 languages. He also likes cats.

A.C. Wise is the author of numerous short stories appearing in publications such as *Clarkesworld*, *Shimmer*, *Uncanny*, and the *Year's Best Weird Fiction Vol. 1*, among others. In addition to her writing, she co-edits *Unlikely Story*. Her first collection, *The Ultra Fabulous Glitter Squadron Saves the World Again*, is available from Lethe Press. Visit her online at www.acwise.net.

COPYRIGHT ACKNOWLEDGEMENTS